# The
# Seven
# Last
# Years

# The Seven Last Years

CAROL BALIZET

Published by
√chosen books
Lincoln, Virginia 22078
Distributed by Word Books • Waco, Texas 76703

**Library of Congress Cataloging in Publication Data**

Balizet, Carol.
  The seven last years.

  I.  Title.
  PZ4.B1836Se   [PS3552.A4536]      813'.5'4      78–27012

ISBN 0-912376-47-3

First Printing, February 1979
Second Printing, August 1979
First Paperback Printing, August 1979

**To**

my precious sister
KATHARINE
who hears our Lord more clearly
than anyone I know

# Contents

# Acknowledgments

There are so many people to thank.
There's Father Pollard, who said, "You ought to write a book";
And my Papa, who did not try to talk me out of it;
And my Mother, who thinks everything I do is wonderful;
And my dear children, who were patient and loving;
And Katharine, Elizabeth, Teresa, Greg and Cynthia, who had
    faith in me;
And my Aunt Kitty, who knows a lot about English;
And Jim Westcot, who knows a lot about Latin;
And my Uncle Buddy, who knows a lot about everything;
And Katharine, Elizabeth, Dorothy and Shirley, who typed and
    typed;
And Hal Lindsey, whose book started it all;
And all the Chosen people, Len, Catherine, John, Tib, Dick,
    Ruth, Jeanne, who have not only great gifts, but also
    much fruit, who put up with me.

Thank you. Now all of you join me in giving God the glory.

# To The Reader

The question that fascinates or disturbs almost everyone in the world today is—are we inhabitants of the planet earth facing a cataclysmic end to life as we know it? Some claim we are already in what is being called the "end times." One group of thinkers sees the end coming through pollution and nuclear war. Many Christians believe that the second coming of Jesus Christ is at hand. There is intense study of the Bible, particularly the Book of Revelation, to find out what the prophecies are for the years just ahead.

This story is the result of a revelation to a woman who is not only a Bible teacher but a registered nurse working night duty in a Tampa hospital, a mother of four daughters, a person passionately involved in Christian causes. Aware of the intense differences of opinion by historians and theologians over such subjects as the Rapture, the coming of the Antichrist, the battle of Armageddon, the return of Jesus, and the Millennium period, Chosen Books presents in novel form one individual's vision of what awaits us in the years ahead. Whether you agree or not with the author's viewpoint, everyone loves a suspenseful tale.

THE PUBLISHER

# Book One

# The Prodromal Period

*May 23, 1988*
*to*
*June 4, 1988*

# News Bulletins

*Tallahassee.* Florida State University today granted its first degrees in witchcraft. The University has great hopes for this department. "There is a growing interest in all branches of the occult," stated Dr. Anthony Parnell, department head. "Within the next few years, I expect to see the study spread into high schools and even grammar schools."

*New York City.* The Advertising Council of America has published its code of practice for 1988 and surprised no one by accepting advertising for television of the newly refined marijuana cigarettes. This was brought about by the legalization of marijuana in Iowa, the last state in the Union to take this step. Cigarette manufacturers hailed this action as a forward step to strengthen the economy, pointing to millions of dollars spent on research over the past five years to remove impurities from marijuana.

*Washington.* Desertions from all branches of the armed forces exceeded the number of enlistments last month, and new legislation has been requested by the Secretary of Defense to try to stem the rising tide of desertions. In a test case in Federal Court in Baltimore the Navy is suing a deserter for breach of contract in the civil courts. Since the amnesty laws of the early '80s, the military has lacked legal recourse against service people who desert, and it is hoped that by establishing its rights in a civil court, the service can regain some control over enlistees.

*Washington.* The Bureau of Vital Statistics reported today that for the first time in history, the number of divorces exceeds the number of marriages—and by almost eleven percent.

*Washington.* Secretary of Agriculture Seymour Thompson announced today that fertilizer allotments for farmers will be cut by as much as one-third this year due to increasing shortages. This action, plus the continuing freakish weather, caused a slump in the commodities market unequalled in history.

*Geneva.* The World Council of Churches announced today the merger of their group with the International Confederation of Para-Religious Bodies. The latter organization includes in its membership such diverse groups as the Elementalists, who worship fire and water; the Agricolas, who worship plants; and the Olympians, who venerate the ancient gods of Greek and Roman mythology. The W.C.C. and the I.C.P.R.B. issued a joint statement hailing this move toward universal tolerance and inviting other such groups to join them.

*Minneapolis.* Members of the Welfare Recipients' Union rioted last night at the food stamp office here and did an estimated $600,000 worth of damage. Spokesmen for the group stated that they were protesting the current spiraling food prices and advocating an increase in the guaranteed annual income of $9,600.00 as well as other government subsidies and benefits.

*Miami Beach.* Rabbi Abram Kanowitz of Hialeah, speaking at the monthly meeting of the Miami Beach Sons and Daughters of Sion, described his recent trip to Jerusalem where he attended the newly instituted school of instruction for Jewish priests. This school teaches the orthodox methods of preparing and offering blood sacrifices to God. This form of worship has been abandoned since A.D. 70 when the Temple in Jerusalem was destroyed by the Romans, but in recent years the Jewish priesthood has been preparing for the time when their temple is rebuilt. Rabbi Kanowitz told his audience, "The stones for the temple have been bought, numbered, stored and are ready to assemble when the Lord clears the holy site for the temple."

# I

Craig McKenzie stood before the bathroom mirror on a sweltering May morning and stared at his angular face with a frown. Two more bumps had appeared on his forehead. For an eighteen-year-old high school senior, acne was a disaster.

The tall thin youth took some medicated powder out of the cabinet and carefully rubbed it on each sore. The result did not satisfy him, but he decided he had upgraded his facial appearance from horrible to merely bad.

Craig finished dressing and joined his sixteen-year-old sister, Susie, and his parents in the kitchen for breakfast. His father, Hank McKenzie, face already flushed in the unseasonable heat, was lecturing his family once again on the need for economy. Martha, Hank's wife, was tight-lipped and tense. Susie watched her parents as she ate, her pretty face marred by a petulant mouth and bored eyes.

Although they were husband and wife, Hank and Martha McKenzie looked enough alike to be brother and sister. It was not so much their features as a general air of fatigue and discouragement. Hank at fifty-one was balding, his once athletic frame stooped, his eyes peering uncertainly behind thick, rimless glasses. He often imagined he could see his younger self reflected in his son, Craig, tall, dark-haired, slender.

Martha had never been as sensuously attractive as her daughter. She was a conscientious mother and homemaker, but long ago her personal grooming had begun to slip. Her thin blonde hair had not had professional care for months; she seldom wore makeup. Martha dressed carelessly, and at forty-five her only concession to vanity was her refusal to wear shorts even in the hottest weather.

Hank glanced at his watch, pushed his chair back and surveyed his family angrily. "Do you know what rats do when you put them in a maze with no way out? They sit down and chew their feet, that's what they do." He stood up and walked to the door. "Don't be surprised if I come home with bloody feet."

"Well, now," Susie said as she watched her father stride out the door and head for his insurance office, "that's better than his average exit line. What turned him on this time?"

"Money, what else?" Craig answered. "It's always money."

"It's more than that and as usual you weren't much help." Martha looked at her son with annoyance. "I know having the family eat together is old-fashioned, but you could at least make an effort to get to breakfast on time. And this vigilante group you want to join. You know how he feels about that."

"Look, I'll be nineteen next month," Craig said, his thin, angular face suddenly weary. "I get tired of asking for money like a little kid. I could make good money with the Protective Agency if you all weren't so prejudiced."

"Vigilantes get their houses bombed," Susie warned.

"And that's only half of it," Martha said. "Some of those men in the Agency are as bad as the criminals. They shoot first and ask questions later." She watched Craig as she spoke. His need for money was a problem, but no more than most teen-agers faced with the prolonged depression and the unemployment rate at over thirty percent. Grocery store bag boys, newspaper carriers and gas station attendants were now older family men, willing to take almost any job—but that of vigilante. Vigilantes were in constant danger of reprisals from lawless elements.

"I have tried to earn money, you know," Craig said. "The garden and the bees and all. And I've applied for part-time jobs everywhere in Tampa."

Martha nodded. Her son had never been lazy. The problem was the times. "I can remember when somebody like your father would be considered successful," she said wistfully. "When $25,000 a year was good money. Really! Now we can barely manage to eat."

"I know how Dad feels," Craig said quietly. "He's frustrated and I want to help. Maybe my honey project isn't completely hopeless. I hear old Judge Redmond's bees are still producing. I think I'll drop by his house after school—if I can borrow the car?"

Martha nodded in agreement and stared at her son somberly. He was almost a stranger to her, this tall, quiet boy-man who so seldom revealed how he felt about things. It was disappointing that she was not close to either of her children. Where was the bright promise, she sometimes wondered, she had felt when she and Hank married in 1968? The twenty years of their marriage had seen mind-numbing changes.

"Here's five dollars, Craig," Martha said. "That leaves me just a bit over $250 in the bank to try and buy groceries for the whole week. Why, I can remember when the four of us could eat for a hundred dollars a week. Really!"

"We've got to go, Craig," Susie stood and smoothed her jeans over her curvaceous hips. "It's almost time for the bus." She pecked her mother's cheek dutifully and picked up her school books.

Craig carried his dishes to the sink, pocketed the money from his mother and picked at his face as he followed his sister out the door. He envied her clear skin and her popularity. He hadn't had a date in over a year.

Martha followed her children to the door, watched as they walked by the Krafts' house next door toward the school bus stop. Craig's thin form trailed behind Susie's shorter, softer silhouette. They were not talking to each other, and this disturbed her. She turned away and began clearing the table. "Don't people talk to each other any more?" she asked herself.


The school bus was crowded and Craig was forced to stand but one of the boys made room for Susie to sit. Craig was aware of the aromatic fumes of marijuana wafting toward him from the rear of the bus but his mind was elsewhere. The garden was my best hope, he mused. But the weather this year's been impossible—first too cold, then too wet and now too hot. My bees are sick and aren't making honey at all. Suddenly, he was resolute. I'll call today and tell the Agency I'm ready to start.

Unknown to his parents, Craig had already applied for a position with the Tampa Protective Agency, the largest of the vigilante groups, and despite his youth had been accepted. Dad will be furious, he thought with foreboding.

The bus turned into the school grounds, and the gates of the high cyclone fence were unlocked by the guards. Craig walked slowly off the bus, showing his student card to the policeman who checked him in. No more of that ever, he thought. A few weeks before graduation seemed a dismal time to quit school, but it was all part of the childhood he was leaving behind. Today he would become a man.

Susie moved easily into the bus seat, the pout gone from her face. She ate and slept at home, but her real life was among her friends. With a sigh of relief, she unconsciously shed the protective coloration she wore at home, dropped the guard she kept on her language. Now, among these people, she could be herself. She spoke to the boy on her left, then turned with a conspiratorial air to her girl friend on the right.

"Are we still going?" she asked eagerly. "Did Brad get the money?"

Her friend Peggy passed the ragged end of a marijuana cigarette to her. "It's all set. We're leaving right after home room. We have some good stuff and some mushrooms. But we won't be back by any four o'clock, so you can forget that."

"Mama will get all bent out of shape if I don't show up on the school bus," Susie said doubtfully. "She might call the police or something dumb like that."

Peggy shrugged. "Nobody else has to get right home to Mama."

Susie's indecision was brief. "Well, okay. Count me in. They can't kill me, can they? They even skipped school back in the old days. Mama has admitted it."

"Yeah," Peggy agreed. "They smoked pot then, too, and went to the beach, but I bet they wore bathing suits."

The two girls entered the fenced school grounds giggling.

The parking lot at Food-A-Rama was sparsely occupied with a few cars and several bicycles. Before the drought and the depression, it had been lovely with palm trees and plantings, but most of these were dead now, the remainder dry and brown. One small pepper tree, still valiantly striving for life, afforded a bit of shade, and Martha steered her eight-year-old green Plymouth into its protection. As she walked toward the store the sun struck the top of her head like a physical blow. Martha could never recall heat like this for the month of May, well over 100 degrees each day for the past week, and not cooling off much at night. The print blouse she wore stuck to her body like moist hands. Gratefully she stepped through the automatic entrance door and gulped the dry, cool air.

There were very few shoppers. Even with the shorter business hours there was never a crowd here and Martha wondered vaguely when and where people did buy their groceries now. She took a cart from the rack and began her rounds. There was very little produce available, most of it unappetizing. A few hydroponic tomatoes made a bright red contrast to the otherwise pitiful display of vegetables. A big salad would be good in this weather, but $2.95 for a small, brownish head of lettuce cancelled that plan.

She wandered up and down the aisles, referring to her list. There were many staples on it: sugar, salt, flour, potatoes, all expensive if available. She felt a small delight at seeing paper products in supply: toilet paper, napkins, even facial tissue. There must have been a recent truck from some wholesaler. She piled the cart lavishly to the full extent of the allowance proclaimed on a sign above the counter. The shelves of canned goods were surprisingly full and she was pleased to have a choice. She bought large sacks of rice, dried beans and macaroni. She had learned to prepare a variety of casseroles and soups flavored with a little meat or bouillon. Not much like the old days of charcoaled steaks, baked potatoes and salad, but the McKenzies usually had enough to eat.

The soothing cool had improved Martha's disposition, and she faced the challenge of the meat counter bravely. There was some beef, but the cost was unthinkable. From a small selection of scrawny stewing hens, she selected two and was thrilled to discover real, commercially packed bacon. "I'll get fresh eggs, no matter what they cost, and we'll have a real breakfast Sunday," she said aloud. "I wonder if we could possibly afford butter."

She passed by items she hardly recognized, had never eaten and felt were far beneath her—brains, pigs' feet, sweetbreads. Americans were overcoming their habits of waste, but Martha McKenzie had not yet reached the point of eating foods like these. She was surprised to find beautiful meaty ribs and not what her son had dubbed "bare ribs." She smiled, thinking how thrilled he would be at the sight of real barbecued ribs. Craig was too thin, and Hank needed something tasty for a change. Feeling deliciously extravagant, she bought spareribs as in the old days, figuring what she wanted, not what she could afford.

There were fresh eggs and she bought two dozen, a pound wheel of cheese, and a sack of pecans. She was usually bored by shopping, and frustrated by the restrictions placed on her by prices, shortages, and Hank's budgeting, but today had been different. She felt she had done well. If Hank were not too tired tonight, maybe they could sit out on the porch after dinner, eat the pecans, and have a real family evening.

She pushed her cart through the checkout stand, undaunted by the surliness of the cashier. Martha had underestimated slightly and found when she presented her bank card that the cashier deducted only $230 from her account. "That was really good shopping," she said to herself. She wheeled the cart out the double doors, taking in one last breath of the cool air, and walked toward her car. She stopped by the sedan and fumbled in her purse for her keys, thinking that the steering wheel would be too hot to touch and the car like an oven.

"Don't bother, lady." A deep, rather pleasant voice spoke in her ear, and she whirled in surprise. Two middle-aged men, the taller in a faded blue shirt and the other of medium size in old army fatigues, stood behind her.

"I don't need help," she began. "I haven't got any change for a tip and I. . . ." She trailed off helplessly as she watched the two men calmly lift her grocery sacks out of the cart and place them in the bed of a dusty maroon pickup truck parked next to her car.

"You don't have to tip us, lady. This is free of charge," said the shorter man.

"You can't do that. I have a family, children. Please, that's stealing!" Martha found it impossible to believe this was happening in broad daylight. "Please don't," she repeated.

"I'm sorry, Ma'am." It was the tall man who spoke. "I'm not a bad man, if that matters to you. But I have some hungry kids and a wife who's sick. I need this food. It's just your bad luck you happened along when you did."

"But what will I do?" Martha felt close to tears. Something inside her was standing back, watching the scene and wondering why she wasn't outraged. But she felt no real anger, just a helpless defeat.

The shorter man spoke again. He had the door of the truck open, ready to climb in. She thought now they were probably brothers; there was a certain resemblance. "Look, lady. Be glad we aren't taking your car, or you yourself for that matter. We're giving you a break some people wouldn't. You just hop in your car and go home. Don't make any trouble, or we'll cut your tires. Come on, Jim." He got under the wheel and slammed the door.

Martha turned to the tall man. "Please don't, really. My husband will be so mad."

A look of exasperation crossed the man's face. Almost angrily he gestured for her purse. She handed it to him numbly. He opened the clasp, took out her wallet, then scowled again at finding only two dollars along with the usual collection of thumbprint and voice-print credit cards. Finally, he removed her car keys and gave her back the purse. He bounced the keys in his hand for a minute, watching her.

"Now I could just keep these keys, you know. We could drive off with them, and that'd make things a lot harder on you. But I'm not going to 'cause I'm a decent man when I can be. So I'm just going to delay you a little." The truck engine had started and the man turned toward it. Martha chewed her lip in an effort not to cry. As he opened the door, he threw the keys as far as he could. They twinkled brightly in the sun as they arced, and Martha spotted where they landed a hundred feet away. The door slammed and the truck roared away.

Martha watched it as it entered the highway, blue smoke pouring from the exhaust. "They need a tuneup," she said numbly. "They're polluting." She turned and walked slowly toward the keys, closing her ears resolutely against the baying voices which hounded her: anger, defeat, depression and hopelessness.

# II

It was shortly after 10 o'clock when Lawrence Royal walked through the wide glass doors of New York's 78-story Fidelity Trust Building. An armed guard nodded politely to the handsome, smartly tailored executive who strode briskly to the express elevator marked "Floors 70–78." In a matter of seconds Royal was entering the New York offices of Royal Enterprises, Incorporated.

The offices occupied eight floors at the top of this Manhattan skyscraper, barely space enough to house Royal's conglomerate of television and radio stations, newspapers and related industries. Royal, called "Lucky" by all who knew him, had recently been listed as one of the ten wealthiest men in the world, with assets estimated between two and three billion dollars. At forty-five, Lawrence Royal wore his wealth gracefully. On the surface he appeared charming, affable and gracious. In reality, he was cold, ruthless and calculating, perfectly adapted for a life of wealth and power. Called "the most eligible bachelor in the world," he was often seen in the company of show business personalities. His interest in mass communications, however, was merely the visible tip of the iceberg; underneath this showy part of his wealth, there rested a solid base of real estate, bank and utility stocks, oil, grain and commodity futures, and sweeping acres of farm and timberland.

Royal's private office was impressive by any standard. A large oval-shaped desk stood in front of tall windows, and expensive area rugs dotted the rich parquet floors. Along one wall were shelves of leather-bound books, a built-in bar and an eight-foot television screen. Overstuffed chairs flanked a functional fireplace. The most eye-catching feature of the room was an enormous glass aquarium which nearly filled the opposite wall. In it whole schools of tropical fish darted and banked above a multicolored collection of shells and water plants. Original oil paintings were softly spotlighted on the remaining wall space. There was a powerful and vital feel to the office which matched the personality of Lawrence Royal.

As he sat down at his desk, Royal checked the date on the combination clock-calendar—Monday, May 23, 1988—then he opened the maroon folder placed there by his secretary. The first item was a news clipping from the morning paper. Royal read it and burst out laughing. The headline said: LAWRENCE ROYAL WINS PROTESTANT AWARD. Underneath was a subheading: "Communications industrialist given special recognition at Stuyvesant Presbyterian Church." The award, he discovered reading further, was a plaque given each year by an organization called Protestants for a United World to the man or woman who had been the most active in "furthering the goals of peace, brotherhood and service to others."

Royal was still chuckling when there was a soft knock on his door. He grunted and a pale, pudgy man in his early thirties entered. Francis Chapman greeted his employer with the proper blending of familiarity and deference, then settled in an armchair next to Royal's desk and shuffled busily through the notes he had brought with him.

Royal thrust the clipping at his aide. "This is a master stroke. How much did it cost me?"

Chapman shrugged. "A hundred thousand, more or less."

"It's beautiful," Royal continued with a chuckle. "I haven't been near a church in years. How did you work it?"

"A contribution and a statement of your principles. I offered them $50,000 at first, but there was another businessman who was willing to go higher. We settled at $95,000. I slipped the PR man at Protestants for a United World seven thou. I explained that you were in the Sudan and couldn't accept the plaque personally. The award will help you a lot with Bishop Leonard."

Chapman's soft, manicured hands deftly selected a sheet of paper from the stack in his lap. "Now, Lucky, you've got this Zurich meeting next month. According to Bishop Leonard, you'll speak about fifteen minutes to the FML board. I think you should approach it from the business point of view. All the Christers will be playing the humanitarian angle, so a change to the practical should get attention. Right?"

Royal was pacing the width of the French Aubusson carpet,

nodding. He usually accepted his aide's ideas for speeches. It was an area of expertise in which Francis was almost infallible.

The project, entitled rather too cutely in Royal's opinion, "Feed My Lambs," was the brain child of Roman Catholic Bishop Uriah Leonard. It was a recently formed worldwide organization for the collection and distribution of food, clothing, tools, medicines, and other essentials for the poor of all nations. Massive in scope, it was widely endorsed by churches, labor unions, political parties, governments, and the general public. It was to put charity on a new and practical basis. The distribution of the world's goods was to be organized, efficient, equitable, and painless.

The chairman of the project, Bishop Leonard, had stated that he could wipe out starvation within a year after the inauguration of his project. Boldly he asked that a free-will gift of ten percent of every person's assets and income be donated to the world-encompassing Feed My Lambs. The most remarkable aspect of the plan was that so many people actually made such a donation. In the few months since its rather timid beginnings, the project had grown beyond anyone's wildest expectations. In trying to explain its grasp on the imagination of all peoples, social psychologists talked learnedly of collective guilt, of fears of worsening revolution, of the charisma and magnetism of Bishop Leonard. But in the final analysis, it was still inexplicable.

The popular theory, of course, was that given enough know-how man could perfect his society and that the time of this perfecting was near at hand. Royal didn't believe this for one moment. Man, he felt, was basically self-serving, and the billions of dollars donated to Feed My Lambs made him uneasy because it was so out of character. Yet he was delighted to be chosen to serve on its board.

A gentle cough from Francis reminded Royal of the question. "Oh, yes. The speech. Whatever you think, but don't make it cold. People feel warm about this project."

Francis daintily drew out a sheet of figures. He approached decisions about really large sums of money with a bravado he donned like a garment. Although he was now fairly wealthy in his own right, he was of a middle class background and felt out of his element in dealing with high finance.

"Lucky, that TV station down in Florida is ours. Seventy-three million was a steal, but they were desperate. TV is sagging now, with energy so expensive—to say nothing of unpredictable."

"Good. You know, I liked those people down there in Tampa. It's refreshing to deal with men who react to money alone. Simple men with simple responses. We've been involved too much with people who want power or political consideration."

Francis smiled with secret condescension. Although fourteen years older, Royal's quick intellect and eager curiosity often made him appear boyish to his amused assistant. Francis Chapman had found an ideal outlet for his considerable talents in his position as special aide to Lawrence Royal. In childhood, Francis had discovered that he was different from other boys he knew. He was raised by a protective mother after his father disappeared when Francis was two, and he had shown no aptitude for the sports around which the pecking order of the schoolyard revolved. To survive the taunts of other boys, he convinced himself that his type was more intelligent, more artistic, more successful. He graduated *summa cum laude* from the City College of New York and won a master's degree in business from the University of Chicago. At twenty-three he felt equipped to challenge the world. His education was his weapon; his command of language and his instincts about people were his ammunition. He spent several years with a public relations firm sharpening his skills, then moved into greener pastures with Royal Enterprises. Very quickly Francis had risen to his present position as special aide to the president. The two men had a close working relationship, based on mutual need, total understanding, and not one shred of affection.

"You're not worried about the viewing audience, then?" Francis asked.

"No," replied Royal. "I think TV will be the last thing people give up. Power may be rationed or cost an arm and a leg, but the public will insist on TV. What else can people do with their time? They don't talk any more or read books."

For two hours they discussed various business matters, then Royal left for a session of handball. Francis walked with him to the elevator before returning to his own office. In the center of his desk lay the file on a young man who was arriving from Tampa, Florida, the next day for an interview. This potential employee was Douglas Rymer whom Francis had met briefly in Tampa the week before. The impact of this handsome, blond young man on Francis had been considerable. It was only by a firm will that he kept his mind on business.


Judge Lucius Redmond took two ties off the hook behind his closet door and held them up to the light. Not satisfied, he walked over to the window before choosing one and placing it around his neck. Not even the current heat wave afflicting Tampa could induce this stately old gentleman to appear at the breakfast table without a tie.

He gave his bushy white hair a final stroke with the brush, then walked slowly down the wide staircase to the dining room. Judge Redmond had built his home forty years before, shortly after World War II and well in advance of the boom in one-story sprawling ranch houses. The twelve rooms were spacious and high ceilinged, and this plus large shade trees helped keep the house cool in this unprecedented heat. There was a gracious Old South atmosphere in the Redmond home; the view overlooking Hillsborough Bay was magnificent and the judge loved every inch of his house, the two-story garage and apartment behind, the well-kept shrubs and grounds. A part of the backyard was set aside for his favorite hobby, the care and cultivation of several hives of bees. Until recent months, they had produced marvelous honey that the judge bottled for household use and as gifts to friends.

In the dining room his two grandchildren were already eating. Howard Scott Redmond at twenty-eight was a newscaster, a "personality" at a local television station, and a well-known bachelor-about-town. Undersized at five-foot eight inches, his small stature did not diminish his charm and animal attractiveness, nor his success with women. Small pouches around his eyes and a slightly sallow complexion were the only signs of the high life which the judge deplored.

Mildred Redmond, called Molly, had just turned twenty. She was a striking redhead who dominated her grandfather through alternating displays of affection and temper. Molly was slender and athletic; her shapely legs never failed to catch men's eyes. Her large brown eyes and a pert, slightly upturned nose gave

Molly's face a piquant beauty, despite an expression of discontent.

Judge Redmond and his late wife had adopted these grand-children soon after their parents had drowned in a tragic boat accident. Scott (as he had always been called) was then fourteen, Molly six. Grief-stricken over the loss of their son, and sorrowing for their orphaned grandchildren, the Redmonds had tried to compensate by giving Scott and Molly whatever they wanted.

"What is this mess, Carrie Lee? Are you trying to poison us?" Scott poked suspiciously at the food on his plate.

"It's supposed to be sausage, Mister Scott." Carrie Lee, the black cook, set breakfast in front of the judge. "You're right, though. It don't look like any sausage I ever seen."

Judge Redmond took a bite and chewed cautiously. "It's not too bad," he reported. "It's not meat though."

"That's a point in its favor," Molly said. Her own breakfast consisted of a glass of high protein liquid. Molly's independence extended to her eating habits.

"Well, you can eat it if you want to, Grandpa," Scott said. "I think I'll settle for another cup of coffee."

Carrie Lee poured it for him from a silver urn on the side-board. "This is a hard family to cook for," she pointed out with the familiarity of years. "Miss Molly, she practically got to see it grow before she trusts it. And Mister Scott thinks I can still go to the store and pick out whatever I want."

"What about you, Carrie Lee?" Scott grinned. "You and your sowbelly and grits."

Molly drained her glass and looked at her older brother with contempt. "You know, Scott, I don't know how Douglas will stand it, being with you in New York. It'll probably contaminate him."

"You're just scared I'll give him the low-down on you. Like how charming you are at breakfast," Scott retorted.

"That's enough." Judge Redmond spoke wearily. The constant bickering of his grandchildren exhausted him. "When do you leave for New York?" he asked Scott.

"Douglas and I are flying up there early Tuesday. I'll be gone before you're up."

"I hope your interview with Lawrence Royal goes well." The judge still considered Scott's success as a television personality a surprising and probably temporary bit of luck.

"Do you think Douglas will get the job?" Molly asked. She was not sure she wanted her man to work with Royal Enterprises. She wanted him to succeed, certainly, but she had no desire to move from Tampa where she had status and friends.

Scott shrugged and drained his coffee. "I think so," he said. "They wouldn't pay his way up there if they weren't interested."

"It's a very high salary they're talking about," the judge said. "For a man with so little experience, $40,000 a year is remarkable."

"Douglas *is* remarkable, Grandpa," Molly said proudly. Golden-haired, Adonis-handsome, Douglas was considered quite a catch, even for the rich Molly Redmond.

"Actually, he's very ordinary except for his pretty face." Scott was being infuriating, but Molly decided to ignore the remark.

"I have a tennis lesson," she said, rising from the table. Scott took a last sip of coffee and pushed back his chair.

"You children have a nice day," Judge Redmond said, smiling affectionately at them as they left.

Carrie Lee set the stack of plates down on the table, obviously balancing her years of service against the comment she wanted to make. At last she spoke. "You know I love them two, Judge. I have from the time I held Miss Molly on my lap and talked to her about Jesus. I love them like I do my own."

"Yes, Carrie Lee. I know that."

"Well, they worry me, Judge. They worry me like my own Jason does." Carrie Lee looked straight into his eyes. "This world is evil, Judge, and getting worse. And they fit right into it. Mister Scott, he laughs when I tell him that. What if Mister Douglas gets that job in New York and Miss Molly goes with him? I heard a preacher say that if the Lord don't bury Los Angeles and New York, He's gonna have to dig up Sodom and Gomorrah and apologize to them."

"Well, Carrie Lee, maybe old folks like you and me exaggerate the perils of modern life."

"I'm praying," Carrie Lee said stoutly. "I'm praying the Lord will keep Miss Molly away from that sinful city."

"You do that, Carrie Lee." The judge smiled. "Those two are all I have left, and I'd like to have them right here with me."

Craig McKenzie walked straight from the school bus to the dean's office. Everything about the school building depressed him. Constructed of concrete block, square and almost windowless, it resembled a prison. He quickly discovered that the process of withdrawing from high school was surprisingly simple, despite the innumerable forms to be signed. No one made an effort to change his mind. He collected a few belongings from his locker. By ten o'clock he stood outside the locked gates, determined not even to look back. "No more pencils, no more books, no more teachers' dirty looks," his mind chanted as he strolled toward the city bus stop.

Craig felt an enormous relief that his mother was napping when he arrived home and he was not forced to explain his presence at this early hour. He drove off in the old Plymouth gratefully. Craig knew where Judge Redmond lived. He had driven past the southern-mansion style house many times, but had felt hesitant about introducing himself to such a distinguished man, even though they did have a common interest in bees. As he sighted the house and slowed the old Plymouth a small white sports car shot around him and zoomed into the Redmond driveway ahead of him. Craig followed and pulled up beside the mansion behind the white convertible.

A girl in white tennis shorts and bright blue shirt slid out from behind the wheel. There were spots of color in each cheek. Red curls framed a narrow face.

"Why are you following me?"

Craig stepped out of the car and stared at Molly Redmond, hardly hearing her question, so dazzled was he by her loveliness. Even the frown on her face did not detract from the large brown eyes and the copper-colored hair.

"I wasn't following you. I was about to turn into the driveway when you came around me."

She looked disdainfully from the old car with the crack in its windshield to the thin awkward boy standing before her. "If you're trying to sell us something," she said, "we're not interested."

"I'm not here to sell anything. I'm here to see Judge Redmond." Craig held his ground.

"My grandfather is busy," she snapped.

Craig's awe at her beauty was being swiftly replaced by irritation.

"Look, Miss. Your grandfather raises bees. I raise bees. I need to see him because bees everywhere are dying off."

For the first time she looked a bit uncertain. "I wouldn't know anything about that," she said.

"Is there something wrong?"

Both turned to the porch where Judge Redmond stood with a questioning look on his face.

"This *boy* wants to talk to you about bees." Molly told him.

The judge looked at Craig with sudden interest. With a disdainful toss of her head, Molly removed two tennis racquets from her car and went up the steps into the house. Craig forced himself to take his eyes off her and turn to the judge.

"The subject of bees is very painful to me," the old man said

"To me, too, sir," said Craig. "I thought maybe you'd have some answers."

"I wish I did. But come inside anyhow and let's talk." The judge opened the screen door and Craig followed him into the house.

It took a moment for his eyes to adjust to the cool dim interior. Craig had never been in a house with rooms so large, ceilings so far above him, such tall, scroll-framed windows, damask drapes drawn against the afternoon glare. Shyly he sat in the high-backed armchair the judge offered, then forgot everything in their mutual absorption with bees.

Later they went outside to inspect Lucius Redmond's row of hives, but despite the finest equipment and meticulous care, it was obvious that the judge's bees too were inexorably dying off. When Craig said good-bye, the judge put a friendly arm on his shoulder.

"If you learn anything, let me hear from you."

As Craig drove home, the glow he had felt at the judge's warm reception drained slowly away. His bee project apparently was doomed and he was still smarting over the put-down by the beautiful girl who lived in that fabulous house. Any lingering doubts about his next step disappeared. He would begin work at the Protective Agency the following night.

Craig's sister Susie also had no trouble leaving school. She stopped at the Student Health office where a few lies to the Abortion Consultant resulted in a pass to visit the Community Health Department. Susie's school did not yet employ individual Sex Counselors but the students had won rights to take pregnancy tests and seek abortion information without parental consent.

She and her friend Peggy left separately, then met at a deserted weed-grown shopping mall nearby. Most of the expected crowd was already there and Susie was soon paired with Brad.

Theirs was an acknowledged relationship, and Susie liked the sense of security it gave her, but she did not especially like Brad. This morning his eyes were already bloodshot from marijuana, and he smelled of old sweat and stale beer. He greeted Susie with a rough possessiveness that annoyed her. She wondered how high he was.

Brad climbed behind the wheel of his car. Susie opened her door and sat down gingerly. The seat was scorching hot where the sun had hit it, and her thighs burned against the sticky plastic. Peggy and her date were quickly locked together in the back seat.

"Gimme a beer, Peg," Brad demanded, reaching his hand toward the back seat.

"Here," Peggy said, placing a can in his hand. "Want a beer, Susie?"

"I guess so," Susie accepted a dripping can. It was warm and tasted bitter and she forced herself to swallow.

Brad finished his beer and tossed the can casually on the floor at her feet. "Drink up, Susie," he said cheerfully. "We have plenty." He patted her thigh with a moist hand and she moved closer. Peggy passed another beer forward without comment.

The car raced over the long causeway to Clearwater. Susie sat in silence, watching the brassy sunlight play across the dark, slimy-looking water. She sipped determinedly on the beer and by the time Brad shouted for another replacement she was ready too.

"Atta girl, Susie. You're way behind. Gotta play catch-up for a while."

At the prearranged meeting place, Brad swerved the car off the highway and parked on the broad expanse of littered sand.

Other cars with squealing tires soon veered off the road, and young people spilled out. Quickly blankets were spread, radios blared and clothes were stripped off to enjoy the nude bathing permitted here by ordinance. Susie lay beside Brad in a cozy stupor, smoking a "homemade" cigarette which blended legalized marijuana with stuff that had more kick to it. This was the life, she thought. Good fun with good friends. The day passed in a blur of noise, heat and confusion.

It was almost four o'clock before she felt the naggings of obligation. The school bus would be arriving home, Craig would walk in alone, and Mama would come apart at the seams.

"Brad, I have to get home," she said. She was coming down from her high, seeing things again with sharp edges. Brad was sprawled on his stomach, an unbroken snore his only response. Susie shook him roughly, but he was beyond reacting.

She began dressing, brushing the dirty sand from her body in anger. She was sunburned, her head throbbed and her long hair was damp and sandy. Peggy walked up and stood, blinking and swaying gently. "Don't go, Sue. Stick around."

"No, I'm going to hitch home." Susie picked up her shoes and purse and started walking toward the highway. "When Brad wakes up, if he ever does, tell him I said thanks a lot." Peggy watched her as she turned toward Tampa, miles to the east.

Susie was trying very hard not to face what a bad bargain she had made. For five hot scratchy hours of fun, she might be punished for weeks. A weary depression settled upon her, and her head beat a tom-tom in rhythm with her steps.

# III

Lawrence Royal had first met Madame Celeste at a cocktail party given by her publisher. Royal seldom read her nationally syndicated column which was followed by millions. "Celeste Sees," written in obscure and wordy style and captioned with zodiacal signs, struck him as ridiculous, although he admitted to himself that she had gotten off some surprising predictions. Her "Words to the Wise" with which she closed each column contained thinly veiled warnings to highly placed persons and many had hit their mark.

Royal had attended the party reluctantly—and to his surprise had found Madame Celeste fascinating. Blond and slender, slightly taller than average, her most striking feature was her startlingly white skin. She was not beautiful, but Royal soon forgot that in the electricity of her presence. She dressed expensively in a bizarre fashion which suited the exotic aura surrounding her. But what chiefly intrigued him, he acknowledged to himself as his chauffeur cautiously navigated the danger-ridden streets of New York after the party, was her complete indifference to Royal's position and influence.

He had dropped several unsubtle hints about a radio series, even a prime-time TV special, which he might be in a position to arrange, and she had received them with smiling condescension. The smile said that when she was ready she would have all the TV and radio time she desired and by her own doing, not his— and Royal was captivated. He was usually pursued, flattered and fawned over for the favors he could grant. And on the rare occasions when, like now, he allowed himself a moment for introspection, he realized that this was where the excitement of his work lay. Sex, travel, art collecting, big game hunting—all had long since ceased to entertain him. He had more money than he would ever be able to spend. But power—power over people's lives—that was endlessly exhilarating.

And yet . . . here was a woman who was only amused. If Royal's influence seemed so negligible to her, then this Madame Celeste must have sources of power he had never dreamed of.

And so, when several weeks after the cocktail party an invitation came to attend a seance at her apartment, he accepted with a sense of excitement. Several other guests were already there when he arrived, and Madame Celeste was describing to them the meditations, exercises and other disciplines she used to perfect her telepathic and sensitive abilities. As she spoke, Royal observed his surroundings. Contrary to the common impression about spiritualists, her apartment contained no red-flocked wallpaper; no glass ball and fringe-shaded bridge lamps. It was large, well lighted and furnished with great expense and modern taste.

At the far end of the living room was a marble-topped round table with an ornate hand-carved chair. It was not the usual size or shape for a desk, but it was obviously used by Celeste as one. Two low modern couches and several mustard-colored chairs comprised the main seating area, which was centered by a low coffee table. At the other corner of the room was an alcove area which was fitted out as a bar. Against the wall was a long table piled with popular magazines on the occult, miscellaneous books, overflowing ash trays and a collection of ivory figurines of oriental gods. Royal walked toward the bar pausing at a tall, narrow bookcase. Most of her books were old, many with illegible titles in old English script, but interspersed among them were several modern volumes. He moved on.

There was an exquisitely done statue of Venus, spotlighted and pedestaled within a niche in the wall. Royal admired her marble curves as he passed her. He walked behind the bar and, as others had done, mixed a drink, observing as he did the curious collection of masks which Celeste had displayed beside the bar. There were African ceremonial masks, the twin masks of comedy and tragedy, even a black cowl of the type worn by executioners of Tudor England. The bar itself was black, with disorderly piles of chunky, heavy-bottomed glasses here and there. A large green frog chiseled of some shiny stone squatted in regal formality at the end of the bar: his beady eyes watched Royal with a malevolent gleam.

Royal carried his drink back to the couch, noticing for the first time that the opposite wall was decorated as a gallery, with over a dozen pictures hung in confusing array. There was an enormous replica of the DeMedici tomb and several pastel temple rubbings, framed in silver. Some modern art prints, a pen and ink sketch of a nude boy and the star chart of Celeste's astrological reading were all on display. Royal viewed them casually, then sat down to drink and listen.

Royal was surprised by the lack of paraphernalia, the uncluttered setting and especially the ordinary-seeming people comprising the group. He found the seance itself uncomfortable and a bit dull. At times he had to suppress an urge to laugh.

There were some unusual happenings, however, either real or contrived. Celeste went into a trance and spoke in a low, accented voice, giving answers and instructions to various members of the group. There were requests for information which this guttural voice supplied. He was glad when the session was over and surprised to hear himself say he would come again. The curious attraction was still there, even though this first experience was disappointing.

The second session proved more lively. Celeste demonstrated a new ability. She spoke in two different voices and engaged in a roaring argument with herself over the fate of some village in Scotland. There was a rather whining request by one of the men present for help in obtaining an appointment at the State Department. At the close of the seance, in response to a signal from Celeste, Royal stayed behind after the others had departed. Afterwards he was never able to recall just how she had communicated her desire to him, but he was electrified to discover that she could transfer her enormous spiritual vitality into a variety of sex acts.

Several days later Royal read in the paper of an appointment to the State Department for the man at the seance. He felt a stirring of something just beyond his reach and he made it a point to visit Celeste that very day. A maid ushered him into the apartment. Celeste was sitting on the long modern sofa. "Hilda, get tea. Sit here." She patted the cushion next to her.

He began. "I saw that item in the paper about the man getting that State Department job. How did you manage that?"

She leaned forward, took both his hands in hers and stared directly into his eyes. He was embarrassed by this, especially since Hilda was now arranging the tea tray.

"You may leave, Hilda," she said, without looking away from Royal.

"I want to know the truth," Royal said forcefully. "There's something going on here besides strange voices telling people that Uncle Jack wants them to sell the Cape place. That State Department man couldn't be appointed dog catcher on his own."

Celeste released his hands and poured tea from the elaborate silver service. "You're quite right, but he has done his service. He had earned a reward."

"How? And for whom? You?"

"No. For my . . . Authority. The one I serve."

Royal set his cup untouched on the tray. "What do you mean?" he said.

Madame Celeste looked down at her hands. Royal found he had to lean closer to understand her. "I was chosen. I was called to be a channel. It has been difficult, but it is worth it. I have power and privileges and regions of experiences undreamed of by men like you."

They were very close. She looked up into his eyes, and he felt a visceral twist of fear and wild excitement. A flicker deep inside warned him to resist, that his life would never again be his own. Royal deliberately squelched it.

"Explain what you mean."

Celeste laughed. "Men are always so much happier when I speak in scientific language and talk about alpha waves or the like. Or if I speak metaphysical jargon about an inner reality of the eternal life forces, they can accept that. But the truth is much simpler."

"Okay. Come out with it," he said. "Is it voodoo? Hypnotism? What is it?"

She was quiet for a long time, looking at him searchingly. "It's prayer."

"Prayer? You mean like 'Now I lay me down to sleep'?" He was surprised and disappointed.

"Prayer," she repeated. "And prayer works. Have you never heard that 'more things are wrought by prayer than this world dreams of'?"

"But—who are you praying to?"

"Well, it's a personality. An intelligence capable of emotions."

She seemed suddenly hesitant, almost shy. Royal felt an increase in his heartbeat, as though he were on the verge of an important discovery. Without warning, Celeste slid from the couch and sank to a kneeling position on the floor, muttering in what sounded like Latin. Her hands were clasped together, her eyes closed. Then she raised her head, tilting it toward the ceiling. She opened her eyes, and Royal was dismayed to see that nothing showed but the whites. Her voice grew louder and more distinct, and he was aware now that it was not her own voice. The skin on the back of his neck moved in atavistic fear and he found he was suddenly cold.

*Amen. Malo a nos libera sed . . .* It sounded vaguely familiar to him, but made no sense. None of this did. Royal could see Celeste's breath in the sudden chill and it smelled sour. *. . . coelis en es qui Noster Pater.*

All at once Celeste shuddered, sank into a huddle and began to moan. Royal helped her back to the couch and rubbed her hands. She was still moaning, but it was her own voice again.

"Will you please tell me what that was all about?" he said.

Celeste looked haggard and exhausted, and suddenly ten years older. "He was here, Lucky. He came, even without being called. He wants you badly."

"Well, he sure has a weird way of recruiting. All I wanted to do was get out of here."

"He knows exactly what he's doing. He does nothing without a purpose." Celeste leaned back wearily, her eyes closed. With a shudder, Royal remembered those eyes during the chanting.

"Well, I don't know." He struggled to bring things back to normalcy. "If it weren't for that State Department man I'd walk out of here right now. But that proves it works."

"Oh yes. It works. Our lord works miracles." Celeste opened her eyes and smiled. "In fact he will grant you one small gift. What would you like? Ask and you shall receive."

Royal stared at her. "You mean, ask for a miracle?"

"I told you, he works wonders."

This thing was turning into a farce, Royal decided. And then suddenly, out of nowhere, a scene popped into his head. It had happened more than twenty years ago, back in the mid-sixties when he was the boy wonder of the television world, working on one of the series that made his reputation. It was called "Faith Across America" and one of its incidental effects had been to kill forever whatever faint interest Lawrence Royal might have felt in religion. The groups he filmed struck the brilliant young producer as either self-seeking or deluded.

However, one group had made an impression on his cynicism. It was an obscure sect of snake-handlers in the mountains of east Tennessee, thrown in to provide color in what might otherwise have been a routine series. The details of their faith eluded him at this distance, but he had never forgotten the snakes.

Snakes had always exerted a strange fascination on Royal; archetypical symbols of virility and power, he both feared and was excited by them. And these snakes were poisonous all right. He had brought along a herpetologist to make sure. One of his own cameramen, moving in for a close-up, had been bitten on the back of his hand; only a week of intensive treatment at a Knoxville hospital had saved his life.

And yet the sect members, in their religious ecstasy, had permitted themselves to be bitten again and again, without showing the slightest ill effect. Royal was faced with something his analytical mind could not fathom.

"Snakes," he said aloud. "I want to be able to pick up a deadly snake and not be hurt."

Celeste looked at him sharply, as though trying to decide if he was making fun of her. Apparently satisfied, her smile returned. "They shall take up serpents," she recited softly, "and if they drink any deadly thing it shall not hurt them."

She was quoting something, Royal suspected, but he did not ask her source.

"Your request is granted," she continued. "The snake will destroy many, but it will do no harm to you."

Safe enough to say, he told himself a few minutes later, as he signaled his waiting limousine from the portico of her apartment building. There were precious few snakes on East 54th Street. For a moment he wished he had asked for something more practical, then he was glad he had not. It was all nonsense, of course, but strangely exhilarating nonsense. Except for that one moment of sheer animal fear—or maybe because of it—he did not know when he had spent a more entertaining afternoon.


Susie McKenzie arrived home from the beach an hour and a half after the school bus, but her mother said nothing. Martha was still too upset by the morning's robbery to notice the time or the smell of beer on her daughter's breath.

Family life in the late 1980s was fractured and fragmented. Few families routinely had meals together as did the McKenzies.

Hank, however, clung to memories from his childhood of mealtime togetherness, even though dinner table conversation was often negative and destructive. Dinner this Monday night was even worse than usual. Martha glared balefully at the two dishes she had prepared. There was a bowlful of noodles over which she had poured thinned tomato soup in lieu of a sauce, and a skimpy offering of lima beans. "That's the worst meal I've ever fixed," she said mournfully. Her pale eyes were reddened from an afternoon of weeping.

She looked at her son's untouched plate. "You have to eat something, Craig." She thought of the lovely ribs and sniffled.

Craig stabbed some lima beans with his fork. "I may be able to help you out some in a week or so, Dad," he said, trying to appear casual.

"Oh, really?" Hank looked at him suspiciously. "How so?"

"I'm starting tomorrow with the Protective Agency," Craig said. "I quit school today. I'll be working from eight at night till six in the morning." He paused a moment. "There's no use getting all worked up about it."

"Craig, how could you?" Martha wailed. Her tears flowed again. "You'll never amount to anything if you don't finish school. And you'd make money in college. They pay students pretty well now."

Craig ignored her and spoke earnestly to his father. "Dad, I have to try and make some real money. You know what happened when I tried gardening. And now there's something wrong with the bees. I checked it out with old Judge Redmond over on Bayshore Boulevard today. I thought it might be pesticide poisoning or something, but the judge said bees are dying all over the world and nobody knows why. If they can't find a cure pretty soon, bees will be extinct."

Martha looked up, her tears temporarily halted. "There must be some reason," she said.

"A lot of scientists are working on it," Craig responded, pleased that his mother was distracted from his announcement.

"What have they discovered?" Hank asked. He ran a nervous hand over his bald head.

"The bees' tongues are drying up. Flaking around the edges. On the dead ones they find the tongues completely atrophied."

He turned to his sister. "That means 'shrivelled up,' " he explained.

"I know, Craig. I'm not stupid." She made a face at him.

"Well, anyhow. They can't eat or gather nectar. It started with bumblebees," Craig continued. "Now it's honeybees. They think it may be radiation." Craig shook his head. His bees had become far more than a hobby or a source of income. They were companions, a fascinating and absorbing world he could enter whenever his own grew unbearable.

"Well, surely the government's doing something," Hank said. "I mean, what will happen to crops, to vegetation, without bees? Bees pollinate everything."

"Yeah, Dad. The government's having conferences. I'm going to send for forms to help their investigation. They'll tell me things I'm supposed to keep notes on, dates when they die and all."

Hank stroked his head again. "So now it's bees. It's always something. It's going to be interesting to see what gets us first, radiation or starvation," he said grimly.

"Scientists will come up with something," Susie said blithely. "They always do." Actually, she voiced more confidence than she felt. The public's faith in science as the answer to the earth's problems had been severely shaken in recent years.

"Scientists hope that the bees will mutate, adapt to the new conditions." Craig spoke without conviction.

"I saw on television last week how changes are taking place faster every year," Martha put in. "But they said the government people are working it all out."

"That's pretty stupid," Hank snapped. Martha's unthinking acceptance of everything she heard on TV was one of his chief annoyances.

"What's stupid?" Martha bristled.

"The idea that the government can work it out. It's not that simple. There are probably hundreds of reasons for the decay of our civilization, and they're all intertwined."

Susie's good mood could not be dampened despite her parents' upset. It had been a fantastic stroke of luck that the family was too preoccupied with personal concerns to be aware of her. She spoke now, "Some kids at school say the end of the world is near. They're Jesus people, but sometimes they make you think."

"Yeah, I know some of them," Craig agreed. "This guy in my Spanish class says that all the Christians are going to be taken to heaven before the world ends. You ever hear that, Dad?"

"I know the theory," Hank said indifferently. "God is supposed to remove us from the mess on earth to some kind of utopia. But I think we're still stuck with this life, dying bees, heat wave, lousy food and all."

Alone in her room, Susie lay on the bed and stared at the ceiling. Bothered by her sunburn, she moved about restlessly to find a comfortable position. Despite her escape from parental anger, she was dissatisfied. She had bathed and taken one of the new retroactive birth control capsules, but she still felt sticky and unclean. For a moment she considered taking another bath, then rejected the thought.

The party had been disappointing. They all seemed to run together, all the parties. Nudity was exciting at first, then boring. The dirt, the sand, the polluted, brackish water were anything but romantic. Seeing bodies locked together on the beach right out in the open had reminded her of animals. She tossed and turned, wondering, "Why am I so depressed?" She had everything a girl could want: looks, popularity, freedom. She even had her own two original parents, a real rarity.

She rose from the bed in frustration and crossed the room to her dresser. Hidden beneath her underwear was a small cache of drugs —a few quaaludes would help her sleep. She stood clasping them in her hand and looked at her nude reflection in the mirror with bewilderment. Why was she so down? She was such a lucky, lucky girl.

She swallowed her pills without water and returned to bed.


Douglas Rymer was sitting on the edge of his bed, watching Molly apply mascara in front of the mirror. "I don't see why you object," he said. "What do you have against marriage?" In spite of his love for Molly Redmond, Douglas often found her aggravating.

"You're afraid if we just live together it will offend Grandpa," she teased him. "You think he might cut me out of his will or something." Molly began to brush her tangled copper-bright hair.

"You know it's not that. I just can't see why you object." He was trying hard to stifle his irritation. He wanted to remember the hours of love and closeness they had just shared and not get into still another argument about marriage. "If a ceremony doesn't mean anything one way or the other, then why object to it?"

"You are so old-fashioned, you really amaze me. How did I ever get mixed up with a Mr. Clean like you?" Molly smiled at her strikingly handsome lover with amusement. "But you're a muffin, and I love you. If it means that much to you, I'll go through a ceremony. We can always dissolve it later if it doesn't work out."

As Molly turned away from the mirror, Douglas eyed her approvingly. He felt a warm possessiveness as she sat down next to him and ran her fingers through his tousled blond hair.

"It'll work out, honey," he said. "You'll like being married." He recalled the first time he had seen Scott Redmond's little sister. She was playing tennis at the Tampa Country Club and her lithe grace had fascinated him. Douglas was also a tennis player. And he enjoyed diving and swimming, which showed off his co-ordinated body and blond good looks. It seemed natural that two people so attractive physically should be drawn together.

Douglas, at twenty-four, had yet to discover anything beyond sports—and Molly—which excited him very much. Almost unthinkingly he had drifted through school. Even the divorce of his parents soon after his graduation from the University of South Florida hadn't affected him a great deal. The only change in his life-style brought about by the divorce was that he had stopped going to Mass. His parents had given him a structured Roman Catholic upbringing; their divorce indicated to Douglas that the faith was no longer important. He had moved casually into a sales position at WTBA, the Tampa television station where Scott Redmond worked. He found even the job fairly boring—until last week.

That was when the most dynamic individual Douglas had ever met, the New York TV magnate Lawrence Royal, had come all the way to Tampa with an assistant (what was his name? Chapman. Francis Chapman) to make an offer for the station. Before their whirlwind visit was over, Royal had agreed, as part of the purchase agreement, to appear in a documentary Scott Redmond was preparing on the activities of the Feed My Lambs organization in the Tampa area, and Chapman had all but guaranteed Douglas a job with Royal Enterprises in New York City. Strange little guy, Chapman, openly flaunting his polished nails and subtle makeup, but apparently he had an inside track with Lawrence Royal.

"Maybe you'll know something about the job by this time tomorrow," Molly broke into his thoughts.

"I doubt it. I'll probably fly back with Scott when he's finished filming Mr. Royal and sit on my thumbs while they make up their minds." Just thinking about the job interview made Douglas tense; the salary Chapman had mentioned was more than double what he was now making. He arose and began to pace the floor. "I'd have to come back anyhow to get my stuff."

"Am I part of your 'stuff?' " Molly asked.

"You're part of my life," he assured her, proud of his quick answer. He was always somehow a little off-balance with Molly.

"You be careful up there, hear? New York's mighty dangerous and their weather is even worse than Tampa's. They haven't had rain in months."

Douglas nodded wearily. "I know all that. And there's a food shortage and the rats are taking over and I can be killed in the streets. So what else is new? I could stay here and have all that. Up there, at least, I'd be making a good living."

Molly had finished dressing now. It was 7 A.M. "I want to get home for breakfast. Grandpa comes down at 8 o'clock every morning of the year. You could set your watch by him."

"I'm going to miss you, Molly," Douglas said.

Molly gave him a light kiss on the cheek. "Scott has never been known as a good influence, so don't feel that you have to keep up with him."

"Don't worry. You're the only one for me."

Douglas walked with Molly to her car. He was ready now for her to leave, eager to pack and catch his 8:30 flight to New York, his mind focusing on the interview and the future he hoped to achieve. He was also tired and vaguely resentful of his night of lost sleep. He watched her drive away with a sudden sense of relief that surprised him.


Scott Redmond had never liked Douglas Rymer. He resented the younger man's tall blond good looks. At six feet two Douglas towered above him, and the thought of having this golden Greek god as a brother-in-law irritated him. Then too it seemed to Scott that everything came to Douglas without effort. After all, it had been Scott's brainstorm to include the documentary on Feed My Lambs as part of the bargaining for the sale of WTBA. He was the one who had pulled strings and won the right to film Lawrence Royal in his New York office. And then at the last minute the little gay crusader who worked as Royal's assistant had come up and dangled a posh job at Royal Enterprises right in front of Rymer's nose.

So here they were now, Douglas and he, getting their bags from the carousel at New York's sparsely filled Kennedy Airport. Riding the helicopter into town Scott was surprised to find an armed guard "riding shotgun." Scott knew something about vigilante groups, having done a show on them in Tampa. Things must be really bad in New York if guards were necessary on public transportation. Usually those in danger were people alone, old folks, housewives by themselves during the day. The wife of a cameraman at WTBA had been surprised by a gang of young hoodlums —teen-age boys and girls—who had found her kitchen door unlocked. The girls had held her down while the boys took turns raping her.

The vigilante groups had been started in upper and middleclass neighborhoods, manned by the men and older boys who operated with the tacit approval of the police. They wore arm bands and Scott decided that they enjoyed strutting around acting in a primitive and protective way. As crime increased, enterprising men put the vigilantes on a businesslike basis, selling the service. There had been abuses. As in the old gangster days in Chicago, people who did not buy protection often found they needed it. In most cases, however, the vigilantes helped the overworked police whether officials admitted it or not.

After checking into a hotel and viewing their cramped room, far from lavish at $150.00 a night, Scott and Douglas had a quick lunch, then took a cab to the Fidelity Trust Building. There they separated, Douglas going to the personnel department, Scott to the floor above, where Lawrence Royal's office was.

Royal's suite was the plushest Scott had ever seen. The anteroom was as large as the lobby at WTBA. After he had waited forty-five minutes Francis Chapman entered and offered him a soft, manicured hand.

"Mr. Royal can see you now." They walked along a carpeted hallway, then Chapman opened a massive door into an immense office. The president of Royal Enterprises had made a strong impact on Scott when they met briefly in Tampa. Tanned and relaxed, Royal had long ago learned how to use eye contact, casual good humor and calculated moments of silence to convey one central message: here was a rich and powerful man. Now he rose from his desk to greet his visitor.

With difficulty Scott tore his eyes from the amazing aquarium which filled one wall. Chapman had moved behind the bar and was setting out glasses. "What would you like, Mr. Redmond? Mr. Royal prides himself on being able to offer you any drink you can name."

"Just bourbon on the rocks, please." Scott wanted a double but refrained from asking. Royal accepted a small Scotch and soda. Chapman made himself something very pink. Scott was aghast. How could a grown man take a pink drink?

"I can offer any drink but pure water," Royal said. "You've heard about New York's water problems, I'm sure."

Scott nodded. "Typhoid cases are a problem in Florida too. But our rationing isn't too bad yet. We have plenty for baths, and you can always drink bourbon." He raised his glass.

"Tell me what you have planned for the documentary." Royal half sat on the edge of his desk.

"We've already filmed the local Tampa segment. I thought we'd show the rest through a montage of shots with voice-over explanation. I can get some good stuff on mass starvation in North Africa and Ireland and some of the bread riots out west. ABC has some footage they'll let us use. Then you come on, Mr. Royal, and describe Feed My Lambs."

"Do you have a script?" Royal asked.

"A series of questions. How it all started, the goals and results so far. I mailed it to Mr. Chapman last week. If you can give me fourteen minutes, Mr. Royal, I'll set it up so other stations can use all of it or part of it according to their programming needs."

"Sounds good. Tomorrow morning okay?"

"Any time you say, sir."

"Francis will arrange about equipment and crew. We'll film it right here in the office." Royal stood up. "We'll expect you at ten, Mr. Redmond."

The meeting was over and Scott hadn't even finished his drink. That was efficiency.


Francis Chapman met Douglas in the personnel office.

"Well, hello at last. I'm sorry I wasn't here to welcome you." Chapman was all chuckles and effusive warmth. "We've just arranged with your friend Redmond about the filming."

Douglas was ill at ease. Something about this small, pudgy, overly-friendly man disturbed him. Not so much that he was a homosexual. Douglas knew a lot of gays and had been propositioned by them many times. Over the years he had developed a relaxed attitude and looked tolerantly upon their life-style. Chapman, however, had an intent, possessive quality about him that was unsettling.

"Let's go up to my office where we can have privacy," said Chapman. "I've gone over your application but I have a few personal questions. We're a close-knit bunch here. I like to think of us as a family. The Royal family."

Douglas found this somewhat inconsistent with what he had already seen of the staff, but he followed Chapman docilely into an elevator and down a long corridor. In Chapman's office he took a chair opposite the desk.

"First, tell me more about yourself." Chapman did not sit at his desk but pulled a chair next to Douglas's.

"Well . . ." Douglas was at a loss where to begin. "I graduated from the University of South Florida two years ago and . . ."

"I know all that, old boy," Chapman interrupted. "I want to know the real you. What makes you tick? What do you do in your spare time, for instance?"

Douglas could answer that quickly. "I spend most of my free time with my girl. We plan to get married as soon as possible."

Chapman's eyebrows elevated slightly; he looked like a man who had just smelled something unpleasant. "Oh, really? I just somehow assumed you were unencumbered. Wouldn't marriage mean that you couldn't put all of yourself into your work?"

Douglas felt a flush of anger. "Not necessarily. It could mean I'd try harder."

"How important is this, uh, relationship?" Chapman asked.

Douglas deliberately pushed down his annoyance. After all, this man was obviously a power at Royal Enterprises. "Well, pretty important."

Chapman's eyebrows rose even higher. "So your ambition is to be a family man and the job would be just a means of attaining that lofty goal?"

Douglas's hands began to perspire. He did not want to blow his chances for the job. "I always thought family men make the most satisfactory employees."

"We have many married employees, of course, Mr. Rymer. The fact that both Mr. Royal and I are unmarried does not imply any prejudice against the married state on our part. But we have found that few family men have the time or dedication to rise very high in our organization."

Chapman suddenly smiled suggestively. "You have an attractive personality and a lot of ability, Mr. Rymer. I believe you could go far in this organization."

"Thank you," Douglas said. He hoped he was not blushing.

"Why don't you postpone your wedding plans just a teeny while and try it out here? I personally will help you all I can."

Douglas hoped his distress didn't show. Carefully he chose his words. "Okay, Mr. Chapman. The marriage can wait for a while. The job is of primary importance to me right now."

"That's smart," Chapman's voice purred again. "I don't want to discourage young love, but a job of power and influence can be the most stimulating thing in the world."

Douglas cleared his throat and employed his most engaging smile. "All this talk may be premature, anyhow. I may not be qualified for the position we talked about."

Chapman smiled back. "I doubt that. I fancy myself a fairly good judge of character, and I think you have tremendous potential. I expect you to become a valuable employee and I also want to be your friend."

Chapman rose from his chair. Douglas followed him into the hall, pushing to the back of his mind the feeling that he had betrayed himself. He knew quite well what a friendship with Chapman would involve.


Craig McKenzie reported for work nervous but full of anticipation. The headquarters for the Tampa Protective Agency was located in what had formerly been a large gas station. The pumps had been stripped away from the concrete area in front, which was now filled with the blue and yellow sedans used by the agency.

Inside, the L-shaped one-story building was jammed with tables, telephones, assorted radios, and desks piled with papers. A tall, beefy man was seated in a swivel chair at one desk, drinking coffee and writing notes on a clipboard. He was sweating profusely and this had darkened his uniform with stains. He looked up as Craig entered.

"Something I can do for you?"

"I'm Craig McKenzie. I'm supposed to start work here tonight." When nervous Craig was always conscious of his appearance and hoped his acne did not make him look younger than he was.

The man looked him over carefully. "You ever done anything like this before?"

"No, but I learn quickly." That sounded too much the eager-beaver. Craig consciously lowered his voice. "They said I'd pick up a uniform and an assignment."

The man nodded. "Okay, the uniforms are in the back room. Get dressed, and we'll get you a gun and your ID. You got proof you're eighteen?"

"Driver's license," said Craig.

"Okay. Fine."

In the back room Craig found two sagging iron racks full of clean uniforms: navy blue pants, light blue, short-sleeved shirts. He found pants that were only slightly too short and a shirt exactly his size. There was no braid or insignia of any kind, but Craig felt older the minute he donned the uniform. He folded his own clothes neatly and left them on a bench.

The official smiled as he reappeared. "Funny how a man just walks different in a uniform. I was in the Marines. Haven't felt natural in civilian clothes since then."

"Yeah," Craig answered. "It really gives you a feeling. What about my gun?"

The officer unlocked the wooden doors of a cabinet running under the counter. "What do you want?" he asked, crouching on one knee, turning over the cardboard tag on one of the guns.

"Thirty-eight calibre double-action revolver. Smith & Wesson if you've got it."

The man glanced up. "Know guns, do you?"

"That's the gun I learned on. I can handle it pretty good."

"Fine," the man said, rummaging through the weapons. "I don't have a Smith & Wesson, but I got a Colt. Sweet little gun and clean as a whistle. Formerly owned by a little old lady in Pasadena and only fired on Sundays." He laughed heartily as he handed it to Craig. "How about a holster?"

Craig selected a smart-looking, dull black leather holster and put it on proudly. Other uniformed men were crowding into the room, most of them large and rough-looking. Craig was taller than average but thin, and he felt frail and juvenile among them. Several of the men looked at him curiously, then picked up their assignments and began to leave in pairs, roughhousing and boisterous.

"Craig, this is Roger Hastings. You'll go with him tonight." Craig stared at a huge man, six three or four, who had just entered. Hastings was around forty, he guessed, overweight with sagging folds along his jaw line and thinning ginger-colored hair. He had probably been a good athlete at one time, and still looked ruggedly strong if somewhat out of shape. His eyes were sleepy, and he moved quietly for such a large man.

"Kid, we'll get along fine together." He smiled lazily at Craig. "We get good assignments 'cause me and Jacks here understand each other."

"I'm ready when you are," Craig said. He turned to the man he now knew as Jacks. "Thank you very much, sir."

"Sir?" Hastings echoed. "Boy, you got manners. A real gentleman." Jacks grinned, and Craig felt like a fool. It would take time, but he would learn to fit into this totally male environment.

Hastings crawled in behind the wheel of a 1984 Ford. The car groaned and sagged under his weight. Craig climbed into the passenger's side and soon they were driving south on the interstate highway. As they began a conversation, the radio squawked some barely intelligible instructions.

"We got to roll, kid. Distress call. Some dame got herself knifed."

As they squealed around a corner, Craig felt his senses quicken. "Why didn't they call the regular police?" he asked.

"Folks sometimes call us even when the police are around. We're quicker and we get the job done."

The car pulled to an abrupt stop before an aging frame house, fronted by a sagging porch. Hastings trotted up the steps and banged on the door.

"Protective Agency," he bellowed.

The door was opened immediately by a thin, pale child of about twelve. "Mama's in the kitchen," she said and led them down an unlit hall.

The kitchen was lighted by a Coleman lantern, the bright white glare throwing the dingy kitchen into blazing relief. A plump blonde woman was slumped over the kitchen table, resting her head on one arm. The other arm hung down at her side, and Craig saw to his horror that blood was streaming from her fingertips in a steady flow. The floor was covered with it.

"What happened?" Hastings demanded.

"Somebody stabbed her in the arm," the child said quietly. "She was walking home."

Hastings crossed to the woman and rolled her head back. Her face was a ghastly white. "We need a tourniquet."

Craig turned to the little girl. "Can you get me a—maybe a necktie, or a sash to a dress or something?"

The girl ran from the room.

But Hastings was shaking his head. "Afraid we're too late." Hastings manipulated the arm, and Craig could see a white flash of bone. The injured woman moaned.

"Apply pressure right there," Hastings pointed to the ragged cut through which the blood was flowing.

Craig moved closer and placed the heel of his hand in the wound. The blood was surprisingly warm, and he felt his stomach heave. The flow was slowing, thinning to a trickle around the edge of his hand. They stood for what seemed a long time, watching the pale woman in silence.

"It's stopping," Craig said finally. "Shouldn't we get her out to the car?"

Hastings stared at him silently. The little girl had returned and stood in the doorway holding a long blue scarf in her hands.

"Shouldn't we?" Craig asked again.

"Boy, she's dead." Hastings squatted in front of the little girl. "That your Mommie, sugar?"

"Yes, sir." Two tears fell unheeded down her thin cheeks, glistening in the harsh light.

"You got a daddy? Any kin folks?"

She stood quite still, her fingers rolling and unrolling the scarf. "My aunt will be back tomorrow. You can call our church," she said.

She showed Hastings the number and he made a brief telephone call.

"We'll stay till they get here," he told the child. "This is a mighty bad neighborhood for little girls to be alone."

"Jesus will look after me," the girl told him. "Mama said He would."

Hastings and Craig exchanged looks.

"That's right, honey," Hastings said. "You keep on being a good girl, and Jesus will take care of you."

"You're all mixed up," the little girl smiled briefly. "He doesn't love me because *I'm* good, but because *He's* good."

Again Craig and Hastings looked at each other. "Don't that beat all?" Hastings whispered.

In a few minutes there was a knock at the door and a middle-aged couple were hugging the child to them. Swiftly they hurried her from the horror in the kitchen, down the rickety front steps toward their automobile.

Hastings followed. At the front door, he muttered to Craig, "I hope Jesus takes better care of the kid than He did her mother."

But the little girl had heard. From the sidewalk she turned around. "He did take good care of Mama. He took her to heaven."

Back at headquarters Craig sat hunched over a mug of black,

bitter coffee. His right hand and arm were sore from the scrubbing he'd given them, but he still felt unclean. He wondered why he had looked forward to this job. In the background he could hear Hastings phoning the county coroner.

He drained his coffee, poured more. Hastings was talking now to Jacks. "Yeah, a rough way to start. He took it pretty good, though."

Jacks walked over to where Craig was sitting. "Okay, McKenzie, finish the coffee. You gotta get back on patrol. The night's still young." Jacks was watching him carefully.

Craig glanced at the wall clock. It seemed impossible, but he'd been working less than two hours. It was twenty minutes to ten. The whole night still to go. He rose and joined Hastings at the desk.

"I'm ready. Sorry I didn't help you with the paper work. That sort of got to me. I never saw anybody die before."

"That's okay, kid." Hastings grinned at him affectionately. "I puked my guts out the first time I saw anybody croak. I think you did fine. If you want one, you got a permanent partner."

Craig felt a warm glow of pride. To have been tried and not found wanting was a new feeling. "Okay, partner," he smiled. "Let's go."


Scott Redmond arrived at Royal's office at ten o'clock Wednesday morning, head pounding, mouth dry and sour. Last night's porno party had lasted until 2:00 A.M. Francis Chapman greeted him with a sharp look. "The crew's all here. Would you like some coffee? Or maybe a little hair of the dog?" He smiled knowingly.

"Coffee, please," said Scott. "I may have a touch of a virus. But it won't bother me. I'm used to it. To filming, I mean, not to being sick."

He laughed, feeling utterly foolish. Chapman said nothing but led him into Royal's office. A tray of pastries, coffee pot and cups were sitting on a table. Several men were moving about setting up the camera and lights.

"That aquarium is really something." Scott remarked, trying again for casual conversation. "How large is it?"

"Holds nearly two thousand gallons. They said at first it couldn't be done. Said glass couldn't stand that much pressure." The two men were silent, watching the flow of fish. "Lucky doesn't always follow the rules," Chapman said. "He has a way of doing things nobody else can do, even with fish tanks."

"Good morning, gentlemen. Are we ready?" Lawrence Royal entered and quickly dominated the room. As the camera crew did some final checking of the equipment, Royal took Scott's arm and led him to a pair of wing-backed chairs near the fireplace. In his hand was a sheet of paper. "Here are the questions Francis okayed. Shall we have a run-through first?"

Scott watched the men dollying the camera into place. "If you don't mind, sir. One rehearsal just to check the timing."

The make-up man was patting his face with powder before moving to Royal. Lights flooded on and Scott relaxed a bit. This was what he knew best. He accepted the list of questions from Royal and glanced at them. They were impeccably retyped on heavy paper.

"Ready any time, Mr. Royal," the crew chief said.

The practice interview began, the questions and answers flowing smoothly. Soon Royal was talking about Bishop Leonard. "He's not one of those in-the-cloister, on-his-knees ministers. He really cares about people. The hunger in the world sickens him and he's doing something about it. He started collecting money for the poor right in his own diocese. Then he went to other churches, to philanthropists, businessmen and legislators. In less than three months he's collected over two billion dollars in this country alone, and Feed My Lambs hasn't even been officially launched yet."

The interview wound to a close and Scott concluded it: ". . . so we wish all of you good luck and great success."

He and Royal exchanged smiles. "That was fine, Mr. Royal," he said.

They went through it again, this time with the camera rolling. The result, Scott felt, was even better with less verbiage and more crispness. When it was over he was elated. They both rose; the crew began dismantling the equipment.

"It's been a pleasure working with you, Mr. Royal," Scott said, grasping the executive's outstretched hand.

Chapman accompanied him down in the elevator to the front entrance of the building. "We'll have a tape of this flown to you in Tampa by the first of the week, Mr. Redmond."

Lawrence Royal meanwhile fidgeted in the anteroom, impatient for the men to clear the television equipment from his office. He was approaching the limits of his patience, when there was a crash, a sound of breaking glass, then a scream.

Secretaries erupted from rooms up and down the hall. Royal raced with them to the door of his office, then froze. A tableau of horror met his eyes. There was an overturned camera, its severed cord tangled in the legs of the tripod. The toppled camera had sideswiped the fish tank making a gaping wound in its glass wall. Cascades of water were erupting from the jagged hole, fish flopping on the floor. Four men stood ankle deep in the rising flood, staring in terror toward where the other end of the cord snaked from the wall socket across the parquet floor.

"My God!" somebody shouted. "It's connected!"

Even as he spoke the water reached the cord. There was a brilliant flash. Two of the men collapsed as though struck by lightning. The two others stumbled for the door, then they too convulsed and fell. Another bright flash, now sparks were crackling wildly.

Royal strode forward. Splashing into the water he thought only of disconnecting that cord. Grab it, pull it out, he thought.

The make-up man was among those crowding the doorway. "Don't, Mr. Royal!" he cried. He reached out to pull his employer back, went rigid as his feet encountered the charged water. Royal turned to see him writhing on the flooded floor. Just beneath the water Royal could see the long black cable, its severed snout twisting and darting like a living thing. He stooped and groped for it. His hand closed around something long and slippery: With a tremendous jerk he pulled it from the wall.

Panting, he surveyed the disaster. Broken glass, a smashed camera, hundreds of dead and dying fish. And five dead men. The office girls were still huddled in the doorway.

"Get Mr. Chapman," Royal said brusquely.

But Francis was already racing down the hall from the elevator bank. "What happened, Lucky?" he gasped.

"These dummies hit the fish tank with their camera. The water hit a live wire and they were electrocuted."

Francis stared from the men on the floor to the cord still dangling from Royal's hand. "Good thing for you the generator blew out," he said.

Royal didn't answer.

"You better lie down, Lucky. You're white as a ghost. I'll handle it with the police, keep it out of the papers and all. Go on, get some rest. Use the couch in my office."

Royal nodded mutely. He started down the hall, his shoes squishing soggily. He needed a rest all right, but not for the reason Francis thought. He had heard what his aide said with only half an ear. With the other half he was hearing his own voice, far away, it seemed, in another world:

"I want to be able to pick up a deadly snake. . . ."

# IV

"Well, how has it gone today? Are you liking your new job?" Francis Chapman asked. It was late afternoon and the last policeman had gone.

"Okay, I guess," Douglas said cautiously. "Only I still don't know what I'm supposed to be doing."

"All in good time, dear boy." Chapman opened a file drawer and thumbed through a folder. "Ever done any charity work?"

"Sure," Douglas lied.

"How would you like to handle press releases for this FML thing? Line up appearances for Mr. Royal, handle correspondence. You do know about Feed My Lambs, don't you?"

"I know Mr. Royal is going to be a director, and I know it's supposed to start next month. But I don't know anything about the organization."

"Well, here's the file. You'll get the memos from Bishop Leonard's headquarters as they come out, screen them for anything you think I need to see. Mr. Royal and I will be going to Switzerland next month for the big inaugural meeting. Maybe take you along." Chapman smiled like a sleepy toad.

Douglas felt a surge of excitement. "That would be great! I've never been to Europe." Travel, like everything else, had become increasingly expensive.

"What are you doing tonight?" Chapman asked suddenly.

"I'm meeting Scott at the hotel, but we don't have any plans."

"How about having dinner with me then? There's a great little place near my apartment where they do a wonderful stroganoff. I know it's ridiculously early, but I missed lunch and I'm just ravenous."

Douglas was reluctant, but apparently the invitation amounted to an order, so he accepted as graciously as possible.

The restaurant was small but exquisitely decorated. Douglas suspected he might be the only straight person among employees or clientele. The maitre d' and the waiters hovered over Chapman, greeting him by name. He ordered without consulting either the menu or Douglas, and the maitre d' nodded in delight and approval. The meal took almost two hours, served in many courses. There was a French wine, which Douglas found himself drinking like water. Either Chapman or the ubiquitous waiters kept his glass refilled. As they dined, they watched the colorful nude holograms which constituted the entertainment. The figures were almost lovely enough to distract from the obscene and degrading acts they performed. Douglas felt embarrassed, but Chapman's pale eyes gleamed and a thin sheen of perspiration moistened his plump face.

Conversation was effortless. Chapman seemed eager to hear all about Douglas, his family, Molly, his college days, even his dog. Douglas felt he was talking too much, but each time he fell silent Chapman would draw him out again.

After the meal, Chapman ordered thimblefuls of a potent aromatic liqueur. Douglas found himself growing warm and expansive. Chapman was really amazingly knowledgeable. The original dislike had faded in the wine and food and the genuine interest Chapman had shown in that most interesting of subjects, Douglas Rymer.

"Well, this has been fun, but we really ought to go over that FML file together." Chapman signaled the waiter. "I won't have much time to give you tomorrow. I'm behind because of an accident in Lucky's office today. Let's go ahead and get it done tonight at my apartment."

"I told Scott I'd meet him at the hotel," Douglas said doubtfully.

"We did leave the office early, you know." Chapman was just a shade less friendly. "If I wanted to get technical, you still owe us an hour or more."

"Sure, let's go," Douglas agreed. It was certainly easy to offend Chapman.

They walked two blocks to Chapman's apartment building. There was a door man, a desk man, and an elevator man. All were armed. They rode in silence to Chapman's floor.

The large apartment was done in deep vibrant tones of burgundy and rose, with pop art along the walls. Chapman escorted him through the rooms, describing the paintings, pointing out special *objets d'art* like a tour guide. Douglas was increasingly impressed. Although the apartment was not at all homey, everything was obviously expensive and of top quality.

He had hoped they could finish the file quickly, but Chapman insisted on more drinks. Wanting to decline, Douglas found himself faced again with Chapman's disapproval, and accepted a highball to keep peace. They sat on a couch in the den and went over in painstaking detail every scrap of paper in the file; a job that could have been done in one hour took almost three. Douglas found himself glassy-eyed, irritated, bored and more than a little drunk when Chapman at last brought the session to a close.

"Well, Doug, I think you have the background now. You'll be ready to take over. How about one more drink? Sort of a nightcap?" Chapman rose and started still another trip to the bar.

"I really can't, Mr. Chapman. I'm seeing double now. I have to get back. Scott will think I've been mugged on your famous streets."

"Surely you're not thinking of going back to the hotel! I simply won't permit you out in New York at this hour. Take the guest room." Chapman poured two more drinks.

Douglas stood up groggily. His head swam, his blond hair was tousled. He desperately wanted to fall into bed and sleep. Chapman had been restrained all evening; no hints, no passes. Why make a production of it? "Well, okay, if you're sure it won't be any trouble." He accepted the drink and took a sip.

Chapman placed a friendly arm around Douglas' shoulder. "Great. I get lonely here sometimes. Maybe we ought to talk about your moving in. I have plenty of room as you can see, and it would save you money. We seem to hit it off together, don't you think?"

Douglas had to force himself not to shrug off the affectionate arm. "That's generous of you, Mr. Chapman, but I don't know." He fished in his pocket for the phone number of the hotel, but Chapman had to dial it for him. Scott was not in the room and Douglas left a message.

At the door to the guest room he turned around. "Thanks again, Mr. Chapman."

"Now that we've become friends," said his host, "why don't you call me Francis?"


Hank and Martha McKenzie sat over glasses of iceless tea, the heat of the kitchen a palpable weight on their bodies. In the late spring of 1988 Tampa's unprecedented heat wave and drought were continuing. The river was down to a small stream, crops had dried up, people moved listlessly about their daily activities.

Except for essential businesses, medical facilities and government offices, air-conditioning was denied. The use of power was strictly rationed; electricity was available in homes only at specified hours. Many companies producing electrical supplies had gone out of business because of the power restrictions.

Like many Americans, the McKenzies viewed their world with distress. Martha in particular was alarmed by trends she could see but felt powerless to combat. To her, every area of life was changing for the worse and there seemed no way to reverse the process.

When she needed medical care, she resented being the "client" of an anonymous "health care team" which seemed to be drowning in paper work. She wanted to be the patient of an old-fashioned doctor, preferably grey-haired and kindly who knew her name, and asked about her family.

The entertainment industry had also changed sharply in the past fifteen years. It was not just the increase of nudity and obscenity. The fact was, drama in films and on the stage no longer merely represented life; now it often reenacted life. With steadily diminishing opposition, there was genuine sex, real violence and actual perversions in movies and on television, not merely portrayals of these things. People had even been killed at the climaxes of violent movies to increase the emotional response of the audience. American theatre now reflected the days of the Circus Maximus and the Roman Colosseum. Nudity, free love and mind-bending experimentation were hailed as healthy outlets. Wearying of the futility of mere opposition, religious groups more and more banded together in their own communities, providing their own recreation.

In her younger days, Martha had spent many idle hours in magazines, absorbed in light fiction, clothing ads, recipes. Now magazines assaulted her bewildered mind with sex, the psychic and humanistic answers to world problems. In the business world, greed and special interest continued to override basic pride in workmanship. With the military now unionized, retired admirals and generals shouted warnings that America could no longer defend herself. The law courts were a public scandal, with delays and inequities the rule. Bizarre clothing fashions and hair styles horrified Martha, who deplored their glorification of the ugly. But it made it easier to accept the fact that she did not have enough money to dress stylishly. The government and its agencies were increasingly dishonest and inefficient, with red tape strangling purposeless activity.

In addition to these disturbing changes all around her, Martha was upset by ever-growing voices of doom which recounted the planet's endangered resources. No longer did they warn merely of a loss of fossil fuels. Now they predicted a terminal point for such basics as fresh air, clean water, food. Martha dreaded each day's newspaper, but she could not stop reading it. Subconsciously, she was hoping for some answer, some absolute upon which she could rely in this unreliable world. Surely there must be some firm foundation, some part of life which was not being shaken.

In frustration, she would turn to Hank. He was, after all, her husband. They were alone this particular evening, as they were so many. Craig was at work, a man now with a man's responsibility. Susie had dashed outdoors to join her friends at the honk of a car horn. Funny, Martha thought. Many adults rode bicycles now, but teen-agers always seemed to have money for gasoline.

"I had another argument with Susie," she said. Hank seldom had helpful suggestions, but she still shared family problems with him.

"What was it this time?" he asked wearily.

"She wouldn't wear a bra; she didn't even want to wear a blouse, just a thin halter. You know how big she is." Martha's attitude toward her daughter's shapeliness included both jealousy and bewilderment.

Hank shrugged. "That's your department," he said. "Who's she out with tonight? Anybody we know?"

"They never come to the door. Just honk. It's like whistling for a dog or something." Martha had considered forbidding Susie to leave unless her date called at the door, but she could think of no way to enforce her dictates. Now that schools had Children's Rights Counselors there was always the specter of an official investigation if Susie were angered.

"Maybe we ought to get back into a church," Hank said hesitantly. "Those people are the only ones I know who seem to have any kind of grip on their kids. What do you think?"

"Churches are always after your money," Martha protested. "Anyhow Craig and Susie would never go. It was a fight to keep them in Sunday School as long as we did. I don't see the point anyway. People who go to church aren't any better than we are."

Hank said nothing. He sipped his lukewarm tea, his face drawn. Martha noticed with surprise how grey his thinning hair had become. His glasses were bent and she felt a sudden tenderness for him.

The silence stretched out in the darkening kitchen. Hank sighed and shifted in his chair. "I feel bad for the kids," he said.

"There's a lot I'd like to do for them I can't. As a matter of fact, I can't even talk to them."

The kitchen grew darker.


Royal was agitated when he rang the bell at Celeste's apartment. She opened the door herself and he strode in without waiting for an invitation.

"I got my miracle. I've never been so shaken up in my life."

"Sit down. Tell me about it." Celeste was dressed in black, her favorite. She wore no make-up. Around her neck she wore the cluster of charms and talismen she was never without—the small black fist, the crooked Italian horn, and the double twined fish of Pisces.

"You remember I said something about snakes? Picking them up in my hands?" Royal asked. "I didn't really mean it. I was just saying the first thing that came to my mind." She was nodding, amused. "Well, this morning it happened. Not a literal snake, but something a lot more deadly." He shuddered at the thought of the five bodies on his office floor.

"It happened in my office. . . . we'd finished taping a spot for television . . ." Royal told the story rapidly.

"So, I was standing there, holding this thing, and the others were all dead. I should have been dead too. Do you see?"

"Of course I see," Celeste replied, her eyes glowing. "How do you feel? Does it give you a sense of power?"

"I'm too stunned to know how I feel. It needs to sink in, I guess. I'm sorry I'll have to replace my tank and all those fish, of course." The dead men meant little to Royal; the fish would be missed every day.

"Would you like to thank our lord for his gift?" Celeste pursued.

"You mean all that kneeling and mumbling?" Royal sidestepped. "That's your style, not mine."

"You mustn't show yourself ungrateful. It would be most unwise." Celeste rose and started from the room. "I will make some tea. Hilda is out."

Royal felt let down. Celeste had taken it all for granted, and now she was going to bring tea and probably begin her mumbo-jumbo again. He would have preferred a wild time of sexual passion, especially with Hilda gone. Yet, he reminded himself, Celeste was the doorway to this new power which so fascinated him.

Celeste was back again, and he was relieved to see she carried no tray. Then Royal noticed her appearance and forgot all about tea. Her movements were jerky, awkward, her face mask-like. Her eyes looked stonily at him and he felt his skin crawl. She stood before him, her mouth moving strangely.

"Man, know me. I am here." The voice was male. Whoever spoke, it was not Celeste. He sat breathlessly and watched her.

"You shall serve me," the voice came again. Royal moved his head from side to side in an unconscious gesture of negation.

"Worship!" the voice thundered out, and Royal found himself propelled to the floor, kneeling. His head was bent forward, his eyes shut; he listened to strange words tumbling from his lips. His very being felt violated, and he slipped, screaming silently into unconsciousness.


There was no visible line of demarcation between the McKenzies' backyard and that of the Krafts. The dying grass recognized no difference, and the giant oak had been there long before either house. But the lives lived within those two similar concrete block homes were very different. The McKenzies were nominal Protestants; the Krafts were Jewish.

Saul Kraft had spent most of his life battling prejudice. Although better educated and more successful than his neighbors, he had never really been accepted. And though his son Saul Junior, known as Stubby, was bright and well behaved, he was seldom invited to join in neighborhood activities. The Krafts accepted this as normal—unfortunate perhaps, but normal. They found strength and approval within their own family unit and avoided painful contacts with outsiders. Illness within the family had been a genuine terror and they were only now recovering their equilibrium after such a calamity.

The visiting nurse moved back from the bed and replaced her stethoscope in her traveling case. This follow-up care was paid for by the national health program, and she had come regularly since Saul Kraft's discharge from the hospital.

"He's doing just fine, Mrs. Kraft. His blood pressure is normal and his chest is clear."

The wife and son moved toward the patient, and the three smiled at each other, a small family, close-knit. Stubby patted his father on the shoulder. "I'm glad you're better, Papa." The illness had distressed the fifteen-year-old boy. He had no comfort or security outside his parents, or outside this home.

"You've been so wonderful," Mrs. Kraft said to the nurse. "I can't thank you enough."

"Don't mention it," the nurse smiled. "I'll look in again soon." She checked her appointment book. "How about Saturday evening, June 4? Between eight-thirty and nine?"

"That will be just fine." Mrs. Kraft escorted the nurse toward the door.

Left alone, father and son hugged each other with unabashed sentimentality. "I love you, Papa," Stubby said. His voice was deep and rich, too large for his spindly body, and in it dwelt the tradition of cantors and psalmists. He had strong Jewish features —black curly hair, melting dark eyes, sallow skin and a large nose. His head appeared too large for his thin shoulders, and in his face was the racial heritage of pain and character.

Mrs. Kraft returned, bustling with good spirits. "She's a nice lady, that nurse. She really cares about people. Now, how shall we celebrate? A little wine, maybe?"

"Yes, Mama," Stubby said eagerly. "And the good cheese. I'll get it." He hurried to the kitchen, his heart brimming with happiness. The bad time was almost over.


Douglas awakened in Chapman's flowered guest room with a pounding headache. As he staggered down the hall in his shorts toward the bathroom, he passed the kitchen where Francis Chapman was cooking something on the stove.

Chapman gestured with a spatula, "Morning, Doug. I have coffee, aspirin and an omelette, in that order." His voice was cheery and Douglas winced. The bathroom smelled of violets.

Breakfast was an ordeal. Chapman was bright and chatty, obviously taking it for granted that Douglas was moving in. Douglas was quietly miserable. On the ride to work it was the same. Chapman assuming everything was decided, Douglas too depressed and ill to resist.

"You'd better give Personnel your new address," Chapman said as they reached the office.

That night there was another interminable meal, with cocktails and wine and too much food. Douglas began to get bored talking about himself, yet Chapman never lost interest. Back in the apartment the drinks came endlessly as Douglas described his Boy Scout camp, his paper route, the trip they had taken to the Smokies when he was nine. He finally escaped to the guest room at one A.M. The next morning he awoke with another throbbing head and a determination to go back to Florida that afternoon. "I will not go to dinner, or for a drink, or anything. I will go home," Douglas told himself sternly as he entered Chapman's office at noon on Friday.

"Well, Doug, ready for some lunch?"

"I told you, Francis, I have to go back to Florida today. I need clothes and I have to wind up some things in Tampa. Scott and I are booked on the two o'clock flight."

As confident as he tried to sound, Douglas knew that Francis would somehow talk him out of going. He felt at a loss to explain the control the other man seemed to have over him.

Chapman was staring at him cooly, his pale face set. "It's foolish to go all the way to Tampa for clothes when I'm more than willing to buy you a new wardrobe. It would be my pleasure."

"I couldn't let you do anything like that," Douglas protested, conscious that his will to resist was already dying.

"Of course you can! What's the use of money if I can't use it to help a friend?"

"How would I explain it to Scott?" To his surprise, Douglas found himself suddenly hoping that Chapman would take over that problem, face Scott and his accusations and handle the situation.

"Don't worry about that. I will attend to Mr. Redmond. And you and I will plan a shopping spree this afternoon. I have a fantastic tailor."

Douglas shook his head in wonder. He was really going to stay; he was going to forget Molly and Tampa and everything else. It was incredible but it was happening. Douglas Rymer, God's gift to women, was selling himself to Francis for a plush job, a fancy apartment and a new wardrobe. He could not understand this control Chapman exerted, but neither could he resist it. He nodded his head in submission.


The spacious home owned by Judge Redmond sat on two acres of land, palms and live oak trees separating it from the traffic of Bayshore Boulevard and other homes on each side. The mansion was like a white jewel, its sweeping lawns sloping down to the double lanes of the boulevard which followed the shoreline of Hillsborough Bay. Even now with its trees and shrubbery withered and parched, it seemed a stable symbol of affluence and permanence.

On Friday afternoon Molly Redmond gazed at all this without seeing it. There had been total silence from New York. Douglas had failed to telephone even once and only an iron will had prevented her from calling him. She sat on the front porch now as the sun sank in a metallic sky, bringing no breeze, waiting nervously as the time approached for his and Scott's return.

When Scott's car appeared, she saw with a thud of disappointment that he was alone. As he parked and walked up the steps she saw that his dark narrow face was tight with anger. He spoke more gently than usual.

"Before you ask, I'll tell you. He isn't here, and he's not coming back. You're well rid of him, Moll."

"What happened? What's going on?" Her voice was shrill as she searched Scott's face for clues to a disaster her mind could not imagine.

"Let me get a drink, and I'll tell you about it. You better have one, too." He went inside and soon reappeared with a tray containing two glasses, a bottle and soda water. "There's no ice. The darn refrigerator's like an oven." He sat on a wicker chair beside her.

"Did Douglas get the job? Does he like it?" Molly ran nervous fingers through her red curls.

"Yes, he got the job. I have no idea how he likes it. I haven't seen or heard from him since Tuesday. He never came back to the hotel after the first night." Scott sipped his drink.

"Where did he stay? Was there a woman?"

"No, Moll. It wasn't a woman."

"What do you mean it wasn't a woman? What was it? A horse?" Molly drank mechanically, her eyes intent on her brother's face.

"It was a man, Molly. Douglas is now the lap dog of Royal's right hand man. Or right hand *person,* I should say."

Molly sat in absolute silence. This was the ultimate insult, the final rejection. He had spurned not just her, but her very nature. For years Molly had been an outspoken advocate of total sexual liberty for everyone. Now her contempt over Douglas taking a male lover was like bile in her mouth.

"You're better off without him," Scott said again.

"Sure, Scott. A year from now maybe I'll be glad it happened and all that. Right now I just want to go off somewhere and die."

Unable to think of any consoling words, Scott finished his drink and left Molly staring angrily toward the bay, her lovely face hard and her eyes dry.


Jason Brown stepped delicately over a clump of sandspurs in the evening twilight and approached the building where his mother lived. He was a slim, well-built black in his early thirties dressed unobtrusively in expensively cut slacks. His mother, Carrie Lee Brown, would be home soon, and he wanted to see her. It was one-half of the double life he lived. But he would make the visit short for Jason was a drug dealer, and he had an appointment.

He unlocked the door of his mother's second floor room and surveyed it sadly. He still found it hard to accept that his mother cooked and cleaned for a white family. He wished he could do something to make her life easier. Jason had more than enough money to allow her to quit her job with the Redmonds, but he was confronted by the problem of explaining to her where it came from.

He opened his mother's small refrigerator. "Looks like Mother Hubbard's," he muttered. He hoped she ate a big lunch at the

Redmonds'. He heard her laboring steps on the stairway and went to the door to meet her.

"Hi, Momma. Prodigal son's home again."

Her face beamed and she moved as quickly as possible up the last few steps to embrace him warmly. "How long you here for, son?" she asked, sinking gratefully into the battered rocking chair.

"Just a little while, Momma. I have to meet a man later. You okay?"

"I'm doing fine, son. It's a real blessing to see you looking so fit. New pants, aren't they?"

"I got them cheap," he answered defensively.

"You don't need to make excuses, son. I'm proud to see you doing so well." She paused, considered. "You going to church regular? I know we haven't seen you at our church."

"Don't hassle me, Momma." He moved abruptly away and sat by the window. "I do all right like I'm doing."

Some of the warm joy left her face. "Nothing's right unless you're right with the Lord," she said.

He stared stonily out the window and she shook her head. "You eaten supper?"

"Yeah, I ate. You don't have anything to eat here anyhow. How do you manage, Momma? Are you getting enough?"

"I guess I could live on my hump for awhile, like a camel crossing the desert." Carrie Lee patted her ample body with good humor.

Jason smiled. "Yeah, I guess so. Well, tell me the news. What's been going on with you?" For twenty minutes he listened as she told him all the little things that made up her life. He was amazed at the narrowness of her horizons, yet she seemed completely happy. As dark fell, he rose to leave.

"I got some money for you, Momma. A business deal worked out for me." He pulled out his wallet and extracted three twenty-dollar bills.

"That's good of you, Jason. It'll come in mighty handy." She reached a hand toward him. "I got one other thing to say before you go. I don't want to mess into your life, but I got to say this one thing."

He looked at her in discomfort, standing by the door.

"Son, I know you better than you know yourself. I know there's something wrong in your life. You don't look me in the eye any more, and you smile like it tastes bad. You don't go to church or read your Bible or see decent folks; so maybe the only way the Lord has of talking to you is through me. So I'm going to say my say, and you listen whether you like it or not. Because the time is running out. You don't have another forty or fifty years to make your peace with the Lord. He's moving on this earth now, and He's coming soon. I mean *soon*, Jason! And you're going to be winnowed out with the chaff if you don't change."

She heaved herself from her chair and placed both hands on her son's shoulders. "You're young, Jason, and you want money and excitement and all the things young folks have always wanted. But you're going to lose your immortal soul and burn in hell for all eternity if you don't change. And change quick!" She sank back into the rocker. "Now you don't have to answer me, but God's going to try to talk to you, Jason. You be listening."

Jason trotted down the stairs, his face burning. I just won't come back here again; I don't have to take that kind of religious stuff, even from Momma, he thought furiously.


Saturday morning, June 4, Lawrence Royal and Francis Chapman sat in Royal's office awaiting the arrival of Bishop Uriah Leonard, whom neither man had met. The visit was a surprise, announced by telegram the previous evening. As they waited, Royal eyed the expanse of wall previously filled by the huge aquarium. "How are they coming with the new fish tank?" he asked.

"I've done everything I can to expedite things, Lucky. Try to relax."

The intercom buzzed and Francis leaned forward to flip the switch. The secretary's voice came through, excited. "It's Bishop Leonard."

The man who entered seemed to fill the doorway. A Roman collar was the one spot of white in the unrelieved black of his clothing. Large as he was he padded across the parquet floor as lithely as a cat. He moved across the room toward Royal, towering over the pudgy little aide. Two burning eyes dominated a ruggedly handsome face. His nose was long and slightly bent and his firm thin lips smiled as he shook hands with Lawrence Royal.

"Lawrence, how delightful to meet you. And how grateful I am that you are serving with me in bringing relief to this suffering world. There is no higher calling than that of service to our brothers."

The bishop spoke to Francis, sank regally into a chair and surveyed the room. "A magnificent room, truly magnificent." As he turned back, Royal saw with astonishment that his eyes were a clear, bright green. Royal found himself strangely awed by the bishop's magnetism; he felt an overwhelming desire to please.

"I'm honored by your visit, Bishop."

"I wanted to thank you personally for your help. I'm flying to the Middle East this noon, before our official launching in Switzerland." The bishop's voice was low and melodious, an instrument trained over the years and used with skill.

Royal reviewed in his mind what he knew of this man. Uriah Leonard had been born in a small Pennsylvania town; rumor had it that he was an illegitimate child. Gifted with incredible drive, he had used it unsparingly to rise above his humble beginnings. His mind had been disciplined in Catholic schools and his record was one of continuous achievement. After being ordained a Roman Catholic priest at the age of thirty, he quickly gained a reputation as a leader of the radicals in the church. His writings were widely read and the source of many difficulties with his superiors. His weighty book, *The Myths of the Messiah,* had almost succeeded in having him removed from his Order. Yet despite his conflicts with the established hierarchy, he had gathered a loyal and intense following and had become one of the most influential Roman Catholics of his time.

He was discoursing now, eloquently and movingly, on the initial inspiration for Feed My Lambs. When he had finished, Francis Chapman cleared his throat and spoke hesitantly. "And you really think you'll be officially underway by the end of the month? That seems incredible."

"We're going to be ready," the bishop purred. "We have warehouses full of food and an organization whose efficiency will surprise a lot of people. It *is* incredible, but hungry people will be eating our food and using our tools before the month is out. It is truly a miracle. We could never have done it without supernatural help."

"I'm gratified to be a part of it," Royal said.

"I must go now." The bishop rose. "I am delighted to have met you both. Please keep our project in your prayers."

He strode majestically from the room, with Royal and Francis trailing after him as far as the elevator, as though eager to remain in the glow of his presence till the last possible minute. They walked in silence back to the office. "A powerful personality," Royal murmured.

Francis nodded. "I feel like I've been hypnotized. I was hanging on his every word. No wonder he can do what he does."

Royal agreed. "There's something mystical about him, but not a churchy mysticism. And that's good. This kind of work needs practical men in the leadership."

To himself he reflected that it had been years since his own personality had been so dominated by another. Surprisingly, he had liked it.

# V

Francis and Douglas were eating lunch together at a restaurant near the office. "I met a remarkable man this morning," Francis began. "Bishop Leonard."

"I've heard he's impressive," Douglas replied.

"Impressive isn't a strong enough word. He's incredible—and not a bit pious, either. I usually can't stand clergymen with their holier-than-thou attitude."

"Seems to me that a bishop ought to be kind of holy," Douglas said mildly, but Francis talked on without hearing.

"I've never been fond of Catholics either. They seem so exclusive. Like they're the only ones. If I were a good Protestant, I'd resent their attitude."

"Some Protestants do," Douglas interposed, but again he was ignored. He found it significant that the subject of their conversations was no longer Douglas Rymer. Now it was the life and times of Francis Chapman they discussed in great and wearying detail.

A waitress appeared who glanced at Francis indifferently but warmed quickly to Douglas. "Have you decided?" she asked.

Francis rattled off his order, impatient to have her gone. "Small steak, rare, green salad, asparagus and tea. Hot tea." He looked irritably at Douglas who was perusing the menu. The price of Francis' meal almost exactly matched Douglas' salary for one day.

"Fish sandwich," Douglas said, "and do you have draft beer?"

"Certainly, sir. Glass or pitcher?"

"Oh, for heaven's sake, bring a pitcher," Francis snapped. The girl left, swaying her hips provocatively.

"I was an Episcopalian as a child. That's close to being a Catholic," Francis said.

Douglas felt a weary indifference to Francis' childhood religion, but since Francis was paying for the lunch he replied, "Most Catholics would disagree with you on that."

"You're a Catholic, aren't you? I'd forgotten." Francis smiled as though he had caught Douglas in a naughty but endearing act.

"Not much of one, I guess," Douglas answered ruefully. "How'd we get on this subject, anyhow?"

"I was telling you about Bishop Leonard," Francis reminded him. "Does religion make you uncomfortable?"

Douglas shrugged his shoulders and then for the first time in days said exactly what he felt. "It just strikes me that a discussion of religion between you and me is almost obscene."

Neither spoke as their food arrived. Francis began to eat in silence, delicately cutting the rare steak into tiny bites. "Are you regretting your decision?" he asked at last. "Nobody is forcing you, you know."

"I know. I'm just feeling, well . . ." Douglas didn't complete the sentence but sat staring at his beer.

"Guilty? Does that describe it?" Francis' voice was cold.

When Douglas remained silent, Francis leaned forward. "Don't you see your future is assured, the whole world opening up to you? Are you going to be a fool?"

"I just said I didn't want to talk about religion. Is that so strange? Neither one of us are religious, so why do we have to talk about it?"

" 'Neither one of us *is* religious,' Douglas. Not 'are.' Your grammar is atrocious."

"Sorry," Douglas muttered and drained his beer.

"What would you say if I told you that we are going to talk about religion whether you want to or not?"

"So let's discuss religion then."

"Good!" Francis said. "I am paying for your lodgings, your meals, your liquor and your clothes. I'm elevating you in your job beyond all reason. Therefore I don't think I have to tailor my conversation to accommodate your sensitivities."

Douglas started to reply, instead poured another glass of beer.

"You'd better tell me exactly where you stand, Mr. Rymer, before I waste any more time or money on you."

"I'm sorry for my bad manners. I also apologize for my rotten grammar. Okay?" Douglas raised his eyes and was astonished by the look of glee he saw on Francis' face. The look vanished quickly, and Francis resumed his usual smile.

"I accept your apology fully. And I'm sorry, too. I don't usually lose my temper. Let's forget the whole thing, shall we?"

Douglas returned the smile wanly. He was finding it necessary to tell himself over and over what a smart move he had made. And it was getting harder and harder to believe it.


While the people in New York and Tampa were eating their dinner on Saturday the fourth of June, it was already Sunday. morning in the Middle East. Shortly before 1:00 A.M., Sunday, June 5, 1988, two men met in secrecy in a hotel room in Tel Aviv.

The hotel was one of those in a strip along the Mediterranean shore, a sort of miniature Miami Beach. All were modern, luxurious, equipped to cater to American and European tastes. The particular room used for this meeting was the sitting area of a large suite with a picture window facing the sea. Heavy drapes of deep blue were pulled across the window to preserve privacy, and in spite of the late-night hour the most elaborate security was maintained. Both men were world-renowned figures, and few such rendezvous are truly secret.

They sat now, facing each other across a small table, small cups of bitter coffee pushed aside. It was the first meeting between Bishop Uriah Leonard and Israel's new prime minister, Naphtali Seth Ben Daniel.

Ben Daniel sat erect, his dark hooded eyes alert, his long, tanned fingers beating a subconscious tattoo on the table. He was a tall, slender man, quiet and self-contained. He spoke in flawless English. "I do not wish to appear brusque, Your Grace, but my time is limited. I would appreciate as much candor and brevity as your ecclesiastical role will permit."

Bishop Leonard was relaxed, graceful and comfortable as a big cat, his green eyes bright with hidden amusement. "Your Excellency, the sons of the church can be as direct and honest as politicians." He laughed softly. "I understand you bring a considerable knowledge of history to your new role as leader of your people."

Ben Daniel waved a hand, deprecatingly. "A Jew is always a student of history."

"I would like to talk with you about both the past and the future."

"Continue."

The bishop's voice was a soft purr. "In spite of your phenomenal growth in the past forty years, your nation could have progressed even further had you had reasonable security. You need strong friends in high places. What percentage of your national income is spent on defense? What untold time, resources and people have you lost to your hostile neighbors?"

"All too true. But war is a fact of life between Arab and Jew," Ben Daniel said. "And frankly, Your Grace, I cannot understand the church's interest." Ben Daniel smiled. "We are not among her sons."

"I am not here as a representative of the church."

"So you have a personal interest in our country?"

"I do. I also have a personal interest in you. I have studied you at some length, and if I may say so, I have an enormous admiration for you."

Ben Daniel nodded his head in acknowledgment. "Then please tell me why my country's security and my career interest you so much."

Bishop Leonard leaned forward and spoke more intensely than before. "You realize, of course, there is a great similarity between the church and any other political body? Our careers have more in common than might be apparent to the casual observer."

"I realize that, Your Grace. I am not one who assumes the princes of the church are more lofty in their motives than is the common man."

Bishop Leonard nodded and brushed back his mane of dark hair. "So it will not surprise or disappoint you if I state quite boldly that I am politicking for the Throne of Peter."

"No, Your Grace, I am not surprised."

"Can you see the benefits to your country and to you personally to have in your corner a firm friend in Rome? And, more especially, one who controls the distribution of most of the world's food?" The bishop's smile was confidential.

Ben Daniel nodded slowly. "I am not unaware of the influence of the Vatican. Over 600 million Roman Catholics are not without weight in this world, although I believe that they listen to the voice of the church with less docility than they did in the past. But, on your side of the bargain, what do you expect of us?"

"I will expect your personal backing and the backing of your country in my try for the papacy. In return, I will exert all of my influence in your behalf, in opposition to Arab territorial claims."

Bishop Leonard sat back and watched his companion carefully. The smooth, tanned face opposite him was expressionless.

"You are aware that I haven't the authority to make concessions. I am not a monarch."

The bishop nodded. "Neither of us has achieved the extent of power we desire. You will, without doubt, extend the constitutional prerogatives you possess at this moment. I seek now only a meeting of minds."

The prime minister frowned. "Of course, the only way such an agreement could weather the passage of time would be for each of us to feel he was getting the better part of the bargain. Without intending a personal affront, I do not consider a man's word sufficient insurance against capricious change, if such change were to benefit him."

Bishop Leonard laughed heartily. "Oh, I agree. In spite of my priesthood, I find the gift of faith a most tenuous possession. All I am asking for is your friendship."

"And in return you would give the very nebulous benefits of the church's influence, assuming of course that it becomes yours to give." Ben Daniel's eyes were half closed.

"I understand your doubts, Your Excellency. Consider these facts though. The present pope cannot survive long. The collapse of the Italian government has greatly lessened the stranglehold by the Italians on the Sacred College. The time is ripe for an American pope after centuries of European pontiffs."

"You are not yet even a cardinal. Is that not a prerequisite for the papacy?"

"No. I am a Roman Catholic male, over the age of twelve. The actual canonical requirements are not nearly so stringent as is commonly thought."

"Your Grace," Ben Daniel said, "I am not a fool. While it is doubtless true that politics makes strange bedfellows, I am impressed with the most extraordinary strangeness of an alliance between the two of us. Of all nations on earth, mine is probably the least susceptible to the multiple appeals of your faith. Surely you make no plans to proselytize? To attempt conversions? With all its perils, we enjoy our Judaism."

"My dear Ben Daniel, I am not so narrow-minded as to think that all men must worship as I do. Each man sees his god with his own eyes. I respect your beliefs as I trust you do mine. I promise you I will do all I can to protect your faith."

Ben Daniel relaxed. "Then I think we are basically in agreement."

Leonard's eyes gleamed. "I congratulate us both. And now I must be off. I will need all of the backing I can muster to assure my election as pope. I must see others, and swiftly. I am convinced things are moving to a climax."

Ben Daniel stood and extended his hand to Bishop Leonard. "Your Grace, I have not trusted another man in over thirty years. I can see without your mentioning them the alternatives you have at your disposal; the prospect, for example, of your turning to the Arabs instead of us. I want to point out to you that I too have my alternatives. Do not disappoint me or betray me. Remember me when you come into your power."

Bishop Leonard's eyes hardened for an instant. "We are both pragmatic men. I can assure you we will serve our individual interests much better as friends than enemies."

They shook hands again, and with the agreement between Leonard and the nation of Israel, the prodromal period ended. At that moment the appalling devastation which was to alter the globe and change human life began. A mountainous meteor struck the earth and the period of tribulation began.

*Book Two*

# Onset

*June 4, 1988*
*to*
*August 5, 1988*

# I

The first news report came on the air in Tampa shortly after 7:00 P.M. on June fourth.

We have a report of an explosion of tremendous force on the island of Cyprus. All communications from that island have been cut off.

A half hour later other bulletins were coming on the air:

Ladies and gentlemen, we interrupt this broadcast . . . the explosion on Cyprus has triggered a massive eruption of the volcano, Sanatorin, to the north. There are reports of widespread damage and loss of life . . .

Earthquakes are developing along a line extending eastward from the Arabian Sea to the Indian Ocean, and westward below South Africa into the South Atlantic. Shocks from these earthquakes have reached the Indian Ocean rift at a point south of the Bay of Bengal . . .

A Paris news source reports huge earthquake destruction moving along the mid-Atlantic Ridge. Severe damage has occurred in the British Isles and most of the Scandinavian countries . . .

When Craig arrived for work Saturday night at the Protective Agency, continued announcements about earthquakes were coming over the air. As he and Hastings left in their patrol car, they listened in wonder to the reports on earthquakes filtering through their car radio. Shortly before nine they pulled into a diner for coffee and rolls.

Silently Craig drained his cup. "Let's go see that little girl whose mother was stabbed," he said.

Hastings wiped his mouth with the back of a beefy hand. "You worried about her?"

Craig's angular face was thoughtful. "I don't know. I guess I feel . . . responsible for her. You don't mind, do you?"

"No, I don't mind. Most guys your age would spend their time chasing after a slightly older girl, that's all," Hastings grinned. The two were developing a real affection for each other.

"I met a girl a while back," Craig said slowly. "A redhead and a real beauty. It was a disaster."

"What happened?"

Craig fingered his acne, reliving the painful memory. "She couldn't see me for dirt. She nearly ran into me with her sports car as I was driving into their driveway."

"She sounds like someone to stay away from."

"Yeah," Craig sighed. "Do you know what it's like to meet a girl who knocks you dead on sight?"

Hastings laughed. "Not recently. I stay away from redheads in sports cars."

The last light of the long June day was fading from the sky when they arrived at the ramshackle house again. As they approached, they saw the young girl sitting on the porch in the glow of the Coleman lantern which she had placed on the railing.

"Are you all by yourself?" Craig sat on the bottom step and smiled up at her.

"Until my aunt gets home," she replied.

The sound of the car's radio got Hastings' attention and he moved toward it. He opened the door and listened to the tinny sound of the dispatcher. Then he waved for Craig who trotted back to the car. "Listen to this," he said, turning up the radio. The voice of a tense and excited news reporter crackled over the night air.

> We interrupt this broadcast to report further details on the destruction of Cyprus and the earthquakes which are occurring throughout the world. It now seems probable that it was not an atomic explosion but a giant meteorite which hit the island of Cyprus less than three hours ago . . .
>
> A seismologist from the Department of the Interior said moments ago that shock waves from the impact of a meteorite on Cyprus are causing the earthquakes which are being felt throughout the world. Communities around the Black Sea and the Caspian Sea report serious flooding in coastal areas . . .
>
> The tremors apparently traveled a line extending eastward to the

Indian Ocean. Earthquakes reaching maximum limits on the Richter Scale have been registered from the southern part of India to Burma, Indonesia and Australia . . .

We are getting no reports from broadcasting stations in Japan, Korea, or parts of Vietnam. Ham radio operators from California are reported as falling silent. Aerial surveillance is under way, and we will report any news as it comes in . . .

New earthquakes are reported in the Caribbean, as the tremors which crossed Africa united with those in the Atlantic. Within the hour these are expected to reach the Peruvian fault, which intersects the Caribbean fault south of Guatemala . . .

At this point the voice of the announcer broke from tension and excitement. "Excuse me, ladies and gentlemen. New reports are coming in of tremors heading this way through the Caribbean Sea. An alert is now going out to all residents of Florida and the Bahamas to prepare for severe earthquakes and tidal waves. I repeat: Florida residents prepare for earthquakes and flooding."

The voice cut off suddenly. Craig turned to Hastings. "What do they mean, prepare? What do they want us to do?"

"I don't know—but we sure ain't supposed to be just sitting here."

"Let's get that kid." Craig trotted back to the house and up the sagging steps. "Come with us, honey."

She smiled serenely. "I'll be okay."

Craig felt the porch move under his feet. He caught the lantern as it slid from the railing. The house swayed; he heard boards snapping.

"Come on!" he shouted at the child.

The little girl shook her head.

"Let's get out of here!" Hastings bellowed from the car.

For some reason Hastings' fright calmed Craig and he laughed. "What's the big rush? We're as safe here as we are anywhere. There's no place to hide from an earthquake."

A second shock struck with bone-shattering force. The house shuddered and groaned. Craig clung to the porch railing, his complacency gone.

Still clutching the lantern he turned to drag the little girl from the tilting porch. She was standing now staring at him, eyes enormous. No, he realized—not at him. Through him. Beyond him. Her face glowed like sunlight in the lantern beam. Craig swallowed hard. No lantern in the world could make the kind of light streaming from her face . . .

"Let's go!" Hastings shouted. "Hurry up!"

Craig turned toward the car. "I'm coming!" He swung back to the child, then felt his throat go dry.

She wasn't there.

An instant before, she was standing there. Now she was simply gone. Craig rushed into the house, but the lantern showed only an empty hallway. There was an earsplitting sound of wrenching wood as the floor rose under him. Craig reached the front lawn as the house collapsed.

Hastings roared from the car, fury and fright in his voice. "If you're coming with me, get your rear end in here!"

In a daze Craig climbed into the passenger seat. The car was moving before he had the door shut. Already cracks had appeared in the asphalt surface: Hastings swerved around them, swearing. "Interstate 4's gonna be impossible," he muttered between expletives. "We'll cross the river and head south. Maybe we can hit Route 60—get east that way."

Craig wasn't listening. "She disappeared, Hastings! Just disappeared in thin air!"

"Poor little kid," Hastings sympathized. "Buried under the house."

"But she wasn't in the house! Anyhow, it was before the place fell down. One minute she was as close to me as I am to you; the next minute she simply . . ." Craig's voice trailed away. How could he explain it to Hastings?

The streets were filled with milling crowds of people, scurrying in all directions. Through the car windows came the sound of shouts, honking horns and a distant siren. Craig roused himself to observe the chaos around them, eerie in the light of a fire somewhere off to their left.

"Where's everybody going?" he asked. "Looks like somebody kicked over an ant hill."

"Trying to get away from the bay, I guess. Watch out!" Hastings jerked the wheel to avoid hitting a man who suddenly loomed in the headlights.

They drove on, Craig looking in bewilderment at the mad scene unfolding along the streets. The radio squawked out a news bulletin: "The Tampa area has been hit by an earthquake. The extent of the damage is not yet known. Citizens are urged to stay in their homes and remain calm and . . ." Suddenly the radio went dead.

"If we can just get across the river—" Hastings began, "whoops, hang on!" A gaping fissure appeared in the roadbed ahead; Hastings swerved up onto the sidewalk, drove a few yards, then jerked back into the street, bumping violently off the curb.

"If we can get across the river," he repeated, "we ought to be okay." There were bridges spanning the river's width every mile or so and one loomed before them now. On it was a solidly packed mass of cars, all headed east.

"At least it's still standing," Hastings said, as he slowed to join the creeping line of traffic. Hastings had conquered his original panic and was bright-eyed with excitement.

Craig saw that pedestrians crowded the bridge as well, moving considerably faster than the cars.

"God help us if another quake comes now," Hastings said. Craig shuddered at the thought of bridge, cars and people falling in a confused mass into the river. He looked at the water below them and was astonished to see waves along its surface. Instead of its normal gentle flow, the river was contorted with whirlpools and eddies, rushing toward the bay.

"Can you see the river, Hastings?" he asked excitedly. "It's gone wild."

"So's everything else!" Hastings lurched the car forward as traffic speeded up on the far side of the bridge. "Now for those wide open spaces!"

Craig turned to him. "Let me out here."

"What do you mean? What for?"

"I want to get out. I'm going home."

"You'll never make it. It's ten miles at least, and the city's a mess."

"I don't care how bad it is. I'm going home."

Hastings pulled off the road. "Okay. I think you're crazy, but that's up to you."

Craig laid a hand on his partner's arm. "Good luck, Hastings."

"Keep your chin up, kid."

Craig watched as the car roared off, then started walking swiftly north, comforted by the loaded gun on his hip. The streets were littered with glass and rubble from fallen buildings. Trees were uprooted and broken; in places the ground slanted crazily. It might take all night, but he would get home. His mind turned back to the experience on the porch. His eyes hadn't played tricks on him: he was absolutely certain of what he had seen. One minute that little girl had been there, the next she was . . . where?

The first quake hit Tampa at twenty minutes after nine o'clock. Hank, Martha and Susie McKenzie were in the kitchen when the whole room seemed to vibrate. The three exchanged looks, and Martha moved from the sink to the table as though instinctively seeking protection from the others. "What was that?" she asked.

"It was weird," Susie whispered.

Hank rose and went to the back door. "Turn on the radio, Susie." The radio warmed into life, and the tense words of the announcer filled the kitchen.

> . . . Windward Islands. There have been tremors and volcanic activity throughout the mid-Atlantic and Indian Oceans. Others are predicted for the Caribbean, Central America and Mexico. Observers on the scene report casualties in the millions in Europe and the Middle East, property damage unmeasurable . . .

They exchanged awed looks, and Martha and Susie joined Hank at the back door. The backyard stretched toward the immense oak which stood just inside the Krafts' property line. In the deepening twilight they watched its spreading branches begin to sway as though stirred by a strong wind, although no breeze blew.

"Look at that!" Susie said softly.

"What makes—" began Martha. The house gave a convulsive heave and she was thrown to her knees. Hank, still standing in the doorway, saw the earth rise up in a grotesque imitation of the sea. The house groaned and shrieked as the wave passed beneath it.

When the earth stopped heaving, the three McKenzies picked themselves up off the floor and looked about in a daze. Their one-story Florida house was still standing but tilted and twisted. The kitchen was a shambles of broken dishes and glass. One corner of the living room had broken off; pictures, furniture and pieces of wallboard were in jumbled disarray. There were cracks in every wall and the ceilings were sagging.

"Let's get outside before the whole thing caves in," Hank ordered.

They stumbled into the yard, then stopped, staring. The giant oak tree was uprooted from the earth, its immense roots dimly outlined against the darkened sky. But it was the Krafts' house they were gaping at. The tree had fallen directly across it. All they could see of their neighbors' home was the roof, grotesquely flattened against the ground.

Jason Brown leaned back on his mother's couch, his thin brown fingers stroking the frayed fabric of the armrest. The tattered upholstery felt smooth against his head and he turned his cheek to rub against it as a cat does.

Jason seldom visited his mother when he was high. He was afraid of her sharp eyes and her intimate knowledge of him. But this evening he had felt an almost childlike longing to be with her.

He heard her heavy steps on the stairway; there was a ponderous rhythm to them. Jason blinked in alarm. He must be higher than he thought: for a moment it seemed to him that the whole room was moving. Carrie Lee entered the apartment and Jason rose to greet her.

"I love you, Momma," he said.

She smiled at him. The room moved again, the floor tilting upward. Be careful, Jason warned himself, don't let Momma see how dizzy you are.

Carrie Lee's face shone with love and tenderness. Almost literally, Jason thought; it was like a great light had turned on inside her. He stumbled in the reeling room and fell heavily at her feet. His mother did not look down, and now Jason saw that the adoring look was not directed at him at all. What was she looking at that he could not see?

The light was growing brighter and the floor kept rising beneath him. How many pills had he swallowed, Jason wondered. He had never been on a high like this. His mother was shining like the searchlight at the airport. Her head seemed to be going through the ceiling. And then suddenly she was not there.

"Momma?" he cried out.

He was sliding down a hill. The couch was sliding too, and Momma's rocking chair. The lamp crashed to the floor and the room went dark. Jason was a little boy at the top of a long dark slide and he was afraid.

"Momma, come find me!" he called.

But she did not come and he sobbed like a child as he fell into the terrifying darkness below him.


Later, Lawrence Royal could not remember why it had suddenly seemed so imperative to fly to his lodge in Canada for a few days' fishing. About four o'clock on Saturday June 4, he phoned Chapman: "If there's anything pending, cancel it. Tell them I was called out of town, and get the jet cleared for nine tonight."

By nine-ten that evening, Royal was sitting in the copilot's seat of his small swift jet, the *Lucky Seven.* His private pilot was running down the pre-flight checklist, whistling tunelessly through his teeth.

"It was tough this time, Boss. I had real trouble getting gas and a clearance. They're tightening up on these priority regulations."

"Don't take that from them. I was told explicitly that these things wouldn't affect me." Royal had been touched by few of the shortages and inconveniences that plagued his fellow men; he simply paid more for what he wanted. As a businessman Royal had long ago learned to make profits from bad times as well as good.

The pilot had begun his taxi toward the runway when he stiffened and pressed one hand to the earphones of his headset. He turned toward Royal with a stunned look. "There's an earthquake!"

"Where?"

"Everywhere," came the astonished answer. Royal watched the pilot's face suspiciously.

"Fix that receiver so I can hear it," Royal snapped.

The pilot fumbled with a switch, and a radio announcer's voice, relayed from the control tower, flooded the cabin.

. . . from seismologists monitoring the quakes. A chain of earthquakes is travelling in this direction and poses a definite threat to the eastern seaboard. This station will continue to bring you bulletins as they come in. All members of the National Guard, please . . .

"Get this plane in the air," Royal commanded and the pilot's head jerked around.

"They haven't cleared us for takeoff."

"Never mind that. Move."

Within minutes they were airborne. The pilot steadied the plane in an easterly course and turned to Royal. "You realize, don't you, that we're up here without being cleared. There are dozens of airports around here and probably every plane that can fly is in the air." The pilot's voice had a touch of hysteria in it.

"We're safe as in a mother's arms. Calm down! You're with Lucky Royal." It seemed so utterly right that he should be far above the danger below.

The pilot spoke urgently to the control tower, shouting back angrily at their reprimands. Then he glanced at Royal who was pointing to the ground.

In the dimming twilight, the tearing thrusts of the earthquake were clearly visible. They were low enough to see the ground in convulsion, high enough to get a panoramic view of the disaster. As the earth heaved and moved, a jagged fissure appeared beneath them, running an oblique course eastward across Long Island. They saw trees and buildings fall, fires break out. There was a large burst of flame on the Connecticut side of the Sound. "Gas," the pilot said briefly.

"I bet you the city is wild," Royal said. His eyes were shining with excitement. He had expensive real estate holdings in New York City; for a moment he wondered if he should go back. But the city would be a horror story, impassable streets, crowds of terrified people. "Canada here we come!" he exulted.

Fleetingly he wondered why the pilot seemed not to share his jubilation at their providential escape. The possibility that the man might have a family below never once occurred to Lawrence Royal.

Dinner Saturday at the Redmonds was not a cheerful meal. Carrie Lee served it, stacked the plates and silver from the main course, and left for her own apartment shortly after eight-thirty.

The Redmonds dawdled over dessert and coffee, Molly was lost in her private misery and not really listening to Scott's glowing account of the documentary on Feed My Lambs which he had completed during the past week.

The table suddenly lurched. Coffee spilled onto the tablecloth. They exchanged puzzled looks.

"What was that?" Scott asked.

Judge Redmond left the table and strode to the long windows. "Do you suppose they're blasting anywhere?" he asked.

"After nine at night?" Scott asked.

"Maybe it's an earthquake," Molly said. "It felt like the whole house moved."

"We don't have earthquakes in Florida," Scott explained patronizingly. "Florida's built on sand."

"Well, they have them under the ocean, and that's got sand, doesn't it?" Molly asked.

Scott ignored his sister and turned to the judge. "See anything, Grandpa?"

"Not a thing. Must have been a wreck or explosion up toward town. Traffic's really piling up out there."

Scott had started back to the table when a shout from his grandfather stopped him short.

"My stars! Look at that!"

Brother and sister hurried to the tall windows facing the bay. In the dimming light, they could see the incredible happening. The water in the bay was sinking—dropping at an unbelievable rate—rushing away from the seawall as though caught in some gigantic riptide.

"What's happening, Grandpa? What's making it do that?" Molly's voice formed the words, but her mind was crying, "Make it stop!"

"Oh, man. What a sight!" Scott breathed. "I'd give my soul for a camera now. I'd have my reputation made for all time."

Judge Redmond turned from the window. "Let's get some news. There's bound to be something on this." As he headed toward the living room, the house shuddered, then lurched.

Molly screamed and staggered against the wall. It was quivering as though alive and she moved away as if she had been burned. The lights went off suddenly, and the darkness lent an additional terror to the continuous trembling. Somewhere a window shattered and Molly screamed again.

"Lie down! Cover your head!" Scott crawled under the table and the judge quickly joined him.

Molly dropped to her knees, crawling clumsily toward the others. Abruptly the shaking ceased. "Let's get outside," said the judge. "Another tremor and the house could collapse."

At the foot of the ruined porch the three Redmonds looked about in amazement. A jagged fissure cleaved the lawn along one side of the house. Two palm trees had fallen across the driveway; beyond the trees the boulevard was clogged with honking, blaring automobiles. They could see one man standing on the roof of his car shouting. The bay had gone mad, with the water now swirling about in violent and aimless ferocity. Steam began rising from the bay, a new phenomenon.

"Well, it's obvious we can't drive out," said Scott. "Even if we got out on Bayshore Boulevard, that traffic's impossible."

The judge was looking back toward their house. "Except for the porch and that crack along there, the house seems all right. I think we should stay right here. If the water comes back in a flood, we can go to the roof."

"Keep looters away, too," Scott agreed. "A situation like this is made to order for thieves. They'll be breaking into stores downtown right this minute."

Molly looked from one to the other, trying to stifle her terror, yearning for some of her brother's insouciance.

Scott patted his sister on the shoulder. "I think the worst is over. If only I had a TV camera and crew."

The nurse smiled as she wrapped the blood pressure cuff around Saul Kraft's upper arm. "How have you been feeling?" she asked. "Any problems during the last week?"

Saul shook his head. "I'm just glad to be up and around." The nurse completed her examination and gave a small grunt of satisfaction as she removed her stethoscope. "Sounds just fine."

Mrs. Kraft leaned down and kissed her husband. Stubby seized his father's hand and pumped it in wordless rejoicing. Papa was out of danger!

As the nurse packed her equipment in her traveling case her eyes fell on a line of small olive-wood camels, marching irregularly across the bedside table. "I've been to Israel, too," she said. "I brought back some camels just like those."

"It's a beautiful land," Mr. Kraft responded with feeling. "We'll go back, soon maybe, and take our son with us."

"I think everybody always wants to go back," the nurse said. "I went with a group from our church, and we all want to go back."

Stubby shrugged. He was an American, as were his parents and grandparents. He felt no ties to Israel, no urge to go there. He picked up the nurse's case to carry it for her out to the car.

At that moment the house moved beneath their feet.

"My word! What was that?" The nurse looked startled. Stubby's parents without thought reached out for each other in frightened stillness as the house began to tremble.

Although terrified himself, Stubby found himself unable to take his eyes off the nurse. He saw the fear go out of her eyes, replaced by a look of speechless joy. Even as he watched, she began to change. Her face grew gloriously bright, her clothing too seemed to glisten. The lighting in the room dimmed as plaster dust drifted down from the ceiling, but the luminescence about the nurse's body remained.

"Mama, look!" Stubby breathed. "Look at her!"

He turned to his parents, huddled together on the bed. "Papa, can you see her?"

The walls buckled and with a noise of thunder the roof fell in. People and furniture vanished in a tangle of rubble and massive tree limbs.

Stubby, unhurt, saw a large figure, tall and powerful in appearance, standing nearby. To Stubby's dazed mind he appeared to be warding off roof boards and chunks of debris, undismayed by the ruin and turmoil all about him.

"Your parents' life on earth is finished, Stubby. But there is work for you if you will take it."

Tears started from the boy's large brown eyes at the certainty that his mother and father were dead. But the deep voice speaking his own name seemed to lend him courage. Silently he followed the tall figure from the ruins of his home. It was only when the man seemed to move through the wall and not through the door that Stubby's teeth began to chatter.

# II

Craig's walk home through the devastation of Tampa involved a thirteen-hour journey, much of it in darkness, his senses continually assaulted and his emotions torn.

His path was erratic, and he frequently stopped to help others or to watch some incredible, never-to-be-repeated sight. He pulled a bleeding man from a shattered trailer then watched him crawl to the downed power lines which had destroyed his home and die against the slanting pole. He saw the dead body of a woman, half hidden under a fallen building, and he watched with a surprising lack of horror as two large rats began to feast on her still warm flesh.

He held and comforted a young mother who told him repeatedly that the children had been "right there in the room" with her when the wall fell in. At one point, he waded hip-deep through a swiftly flowing stream of water, dodging masses of debris that swirled around him. Several blocks later, he came upon a circular sink hole approximately ten feet deep, its bottom covered with a greasy scum of mud that quivered and moved like some hideous gelatin. As he watched, the sides continued to crumble as the hole enlarged itself, slowly and thoroughly digesting everything that fell in.

Dawn came, an unnoticed splendor in the east. Craig walked through one section of town several blocks long where there was no apparent damage; young boys were languidly tossing a ball against a wall. He saw a large pack of dogs, all intently hurrying south. They swarmed around him like a living river, ignoring him as they ran past.

As he approached Interstate 75, only a mile from his home, he saw a blue and yellow sedan of his own agency go slowly by. It was followed by a large panel truck, the gilded crest of Feed My Lambs emblazoned on its side. The vehicles parked beside an unused service station and the driver of the truck and two vigilantes began erecting a large white canopy. Craig walked over.

"Need any help with that?" he offered.

"Thanks, but my crew is coming." A fussy little man climbed down from the passenger seat of the truck. "We're setting up a rescue station for this area. My crew will be putting up the first-aid tent."

"I was on patrol duty last night. Now I'm trying to get home and see how my folks are." Craig rested against the truck, weakened by his exertion.

"You do look all in. How long since you ate?" The little man's bird-like head tilted to one side. "Want a doughnut or some coffee? No, no coffee yet, but I have some cold drinks." He slid open the side door of the truck and hopped spryly in. "Here." He handed Craig a small waxed bag of doughnuts and a carton of milk.

Craig ate ravenously, watching the men at work. As they opened a folding aluminum table, several people approached. The little man moved among them, doling out food. A large flatbed truck rolled up. Three men jumped down and began stacking boxes in neat rows behind the table. Craig watched the activity a while longer, then resumed his journey.

From the end of his own street, he could see his house, damaged but still standing. He found himself bracing inwardly to prepare for what he might find. He entered the kitchen through the back door and called out. His mother answered, and he felt fear draining away. Some normalcy remained.


Francis and Douglas were at the office Saturday afternoon, catching up on a backlog of work. It was almost seven when Francis rose slowly, massaging the back of his neck with a pudgy hand. "Let's get a drink and some dinner," he said.

Douglas had found the long day rewarding. One of his major disappointments in his new job was the lack of challenging work.

"You know, Francis," he said. "I learned more about the business today than in all the rest of the time combined."

"You were a big help too." Francis eyed Douglas appraisingly. "Pretty sharp, aren't you?"

"Sure. I keep telling you that, but you don't believe me." They strolled companionably toward Royal's office, passing deserted offices, rows of typewriters covered for the weekend.

"We're the only ones here, aren't we?" Douglas asked. The rooms seemed larger, somehow, devoid of life and sound.

"I like it quiet like this," Francis said. "I can get twice as much done with everybody gone."

Douglas eyed him skeptically.

"Don't look at me like that. I know I've been slack lately, but ordinarily I work long hours. I didn't get my position on my looks, you know, and I never take it for granted. There are too many people ready to take over if I start slipping."

This had never occurred to Douglas; it made Francis seem more vulnerable, more human.

Francis placed some papers on Royal's desk and walked to the bar. "We might as well let the boss treat us to a drink. Have a seat. I'll do the honors."

Douglas sank willingly into an armchair. The increase in his alcohol intake bothered him. He felt he was getting soft with no exercise, too much food and drink. After all his handsome face and body were his best assets. As Francis handed him the glass, the private line rang and Francis picked up the receiver.

"Mr. Royal is not in the office. May I help you?"

Douglas heard the other voice again, indistinct and garbled, a woman's voice.

"No, he has left the city," he heard Francis answer. "Who is this?" He paused to listen. "Yes, I've heard him mention you." Francis looked at Douglas and shrugged his shoulders. He listened again.

"But—that's incredible! How do you know?" Francis was tensed and alert now.

"I don't know what to say . . . I—I'll certainly consider it. And thank you for the offer." Francis hung up the receiver slowly and stood for a moment, thinking.

"What is it, Francis? Who was that?" Douglas asked.

"Madame Celeste. You know—the astrologer. She's a friend of the boss's. She called to warn him of an earthquake that's coming, but he's not at his apartment. He must be on his way to the airport."

"An earthquake?" Douglas echoed. "That's crazy. Where'd she get that idea?"

"She said her contacts told her. I guess she means spirits. It should have been funny except it wasn't somehow. She invited us over to her place. She said it would be safe."

"Why safer than right here?"

"I don't know," Francis answered. "Talking to her, it was hard not to believe her. You know who she is? Ever read her column?"

"Yeah, sometimes. But I don't believe in it."

"I don't either," Francis agreed. "Only—well, suppose she's right? We don't have anything to lose, at any rate."

Douglas smiled. "It would be interesting to see her setup."

They turned off the lights and locked up. The streets were quiet, with nothing unusual that they could see. Francis flagged a taxi and a folded twenty-dollar bill quieted the driver's protests against taking only two passengers as opposed to the regulation four. As he pulled into traffic he asked, conversationally, "You guys see the animals?"

"What animals?" Douglas asked.

"All kinds, running around in circles. I seen rats, dogs, cats, streaking around like they was in a fit. It's crazy."

Douglas and Francis looked at each other, startled. The driver talked on. "I seen some pretty weird things in my day, but this topped them all. Them animals was running like they was trying to get away from something horrible."

Madame Celeste herself opened the door of her ground-floor apartment and Douglas's first thought was that if she were a witch, he must reappraise his ideas. Tall, slender and chic, she had pale blonde hair which framed a complexion smooth as alabaster.

"Please come in. Many people would have scoffed at my warning. You were wise to trust me."

She led the way into the ultramodern living room and indicated seats with a sweep of her arm. There was a lighted kerosene lamp on one table which Douglas thought at first must be part of the atmosphere for her well-known seances. Then he noticed beneath the table some large jars of bottled water and cartons of the kind of emergency food usually stored in fallout shelters.

Madame Celeste followed his gaze. "It wasn't easy to lay my hands on those things after five today, with all the stores shut."

"I'm sure it wasn't." Whatever else she might be, Douglas thought, she was not a charlatan: it was obvious that she believed in her mysterious voice of prophecy.

"I have wanted to meet you for some time," she was saying to Francis. "Lucky has had complimentary things to say about you."

"Thank you. But honestly, what's all this about an earthquake?"

"Later. When my prophecy has been fulfilled you will be open to what I have to say."

She left the room for a moment, soon returned with a tray of tea and some small tasteless cookies. There was something strange about her, Douglas decided, but he couldn't put his finger on exactly what. Her intensity, perhaps. She seemed to have little to say to him, reserving most of her attention for Francis, and after a while Douglas got up and began to drift idly about the room, peering at the pictures which lined the walls. As his interest in the pictures waned, Douglas wished he could switch on the TV or at least a radio to see if anyone else had yet detected this supposed earthquake, but he sensed that this would be interpreted as a lack of faith in Celeste's spiritual powers.

The evening wore on and Douglas became increasingly restless. What were they doing here wasting an evening because of the zany prediction of this crystal-ball gazer? Besides, he was starving. They had been here over two hours and all he had eaten since lunch were those lousy cookies and—

He clutched at a table to steady himself as the whole room swayed. The lights dimmed. There was a distant rumble and then the electricity went off. In the light of the kerosene lamp Douglas saw Francis grip the arm of his chair. Madame Celeste's face was exultant.

"Do you believe me now?" her voice fairly crowed with pride.

"I sure do." Francis's face in the yellow glow was ashen.

Madame Celeste closed her eyes. "There will be more. There must be silence for a time and the seas must be still and there must be no wind. Then the forces will be loosed, and the earth will shake like a reed in the hands of the elements. Then the power will be of this world, here among us as never before. Oh, praise the power. The time has come."

Douglas watched her in revulsion. How had he ever thought her attractive? Her face was twisted into a masklike parody of ecstasy. She made his skin crawl.

She knelt on the carpet when the second tremor hit, more powerful than the first, rocking the building and throwing Douglas to the floor. Madame Celeste seemed not to notice. "They will come now upon the earth," she chanted. "The scorpions, the serpents, the dragon and the beasts. Now is the time of the end. Now will the war be fought upon the earth among men and the powers. Oh, let the power come into me! Let me be filled! I offer myself to the power of the strong one."

The trembling of the building ceased. Just as abruptly Madame Celeste rose from her knees. She spoke normally, the religious transport past. "It is over. Now we can talk."


The McKenzies slept fitfully and uncomfortably that night on the floor of the living room. They awoke often as aftershocks moved the floor under them and debris continued to spill down from the ceiling. The noises of people and vehicles came in through the broken windows. Sore and disoriented, they rose early to face the new day.

Martha retrieved some clothes from the wreckage of their bedroom, then went into the bathroom where she found to her dismay that the water was not working. Hank came back from another visit to the ruins of the Krafts' house next door. "Stubby still won't come over here. Poor kid, he's in a state of shock I guess. Sat all night right where I left him, in front of where the bedroom used to be. I told him when Craig gets home we'd find out about getting his parents' bodies out and getting them buried. Apparently there was a visiting nurse at the house too. Her car's out front."

Martha began to weep. "We don't know if Craig will get home. He should have come by now."

Hank placed a hand on his wife's shoulder. "He's been busy, Martha. Craig will make it okay."

"I'm going out to see the neighborhood," Susie said, appearing from her bedroom. She wore tight blue shorts and a thin halter. Despite all the confusion, she had applied eye make-up.

Hank set out with her, Martha refusing to leave in case Craig arrived. Within an hour they were back. "It's just unbelievable, Martha. Everything's . . . changed." Hank blinked at his wife solemnly behind his thick glasses.

"There's a big crowd stealing food at the Snappy Shop," Susie added. "The windows are all broken and nobody's there to stop them."

"Maybe—" Martha paused only momentarily. "If everybody is helping themselves, maybe we should too. I mean, just until things get back to normal."

Hank and Susie started out again, and Martha felt a wave of guilt. Not so much at the idea of theft—that seemed forgivable under the circumstances—but at sending others to do the deed.

They were still gone when Craig returned. Martha heard him in the kitchen and called to him joyfully. Not until he was safe at home did she realize how greatly she had feared for him. She clung to him, sobbing. He seemed big and strong and very comforting to her. He pushed her gently to a seat on the dusty couch and sat beside her as she poured out the story of the night.

"Tell me about you," she finished.

He relayed his experiences, omitting the child's disappearance. "They're setting up a disaster center over on Florida Avenue with food and a first-aid tent. A guy was saying the Feed My Lambs people are taking charge in the emergency, and I told them I'd come back after I'd seen about you all. Dad and I can go get some bottled water and things like that."

"You can't go, Craig. Look at you. Did you get any sleep at all last night?"

"No, but who did really?" He rose and stretched.

"What about something to eat?" she asked.

"I had some doughnuts and milk at the disaster center. I'm okay." Craig looked at his mother hesitantly. "I keep thinking about what those Jesus people said about the end of the world.

They said there would be earthquakes and . . . people disappearing. I mean, if the world was to end, it might happen just like this."

Martha jumped up, irritated. "There's enough to worry about here and now," she said crossly, "without you starting to imagine things."

The morning after the earthquake in Tampa was hot, humid and hazy, the people numb and incredulous. Tampa and nearby communities were without power, running water or working sewers. Most radio and television stations were shut down. No newspapers could publish. Teletype and telegraph cables had been destroyed. A sense of unreality hung over the area.

Few of the bridges were left standing. The double bridge connecting the mainland to Davis Island had collapsed, and the bridges spanning the Hillsborough River at Buffalo and Hillsborough Avenues were both down. The overpasses on both Interstate highways had been damaged, further choking and delaying traffic.

The First Financial Tower, one of the tallest buildings in the state, had collapsed. It carried with it the Kennedy Street Bridge and several adjacent buildings. The enormous hulk of the fallen giant was visible over the entire downtown section, and one of the most frequently repeated news items that first day was, "The Tower has fallen."

Many sections of town sank as the limestone substrata which undergirded this portion of the state collapsed on itself. The result was a drop in the level of the ground and the creation of new lakes. The river's course was changed, the topography no longer recognizable.

Tampa had been blessed with many ancient and lovely oak trees, festooned with Spanish moss, trees that had witnessed the silent stalking of Indian feet. Now they fell, shudderingly ripping up roots which bore deeply into the soil. As they crashed, they carried with them power lines, telephone cables and water mains, uprooting and destroying the matrixes of a society which fed on communication and on lifelines of electricity and potable water.

Damage to Busch Gardens was fairly light, but thousands of

fun-seekers and employees at this amusement center spent a night of terror when fences about the wild animal preserve were demolished. Fear-crazed lions, tigers, leopards and elephants went charging off in all directions. Some had to be shot. Others escaped to add to the panic and confusion in northeast Tampa.

Across the bay, in Clearwater and St. Petersburg, the damage was even worse. The causeways which connected the beach communities to Tampa disintegrated and many areas were stranded without truck routes for food and medical supplies. Because both communities catered to older people, unprecedented numbers of heart attacks, strokes and hypertensive crises occurred.

Smoke hung like a pall over Tampa, dimming the sun. Without artificial light to counteract it, the city was in continual twilight and this was somehow as enervating as the widespread damage.

There was one exception to the general mood of bewilderment and apathy. The officials of Feed My Lambs had moved into action immediately after the quake. They had supplies, organization, workers and most importantly, the will to work. Without opposition, they took over control of the city, supervising the activities of the police, highway patrol, rescue squads, fire departments, vigilante groups, medical personnel, and that most important of all functions, the keeping of records.

An almost unbelievable number of people were unaccounted for, even allowing for the difficulty in communication, and for the hundreds who must still be buried under fallen buildings. Many others were injured, dying or displaced. The FML organization moved swiftly to fill the vacuum and quickly spread in both scope and power. Volunteers were added to the ranks as more and more control passed from decimated governmental agencies to this new, untested but most efficient organization. By Wednesday night, FML people were involved in almost every vital function in the city.

The average citizen was unaware of this shift in power. He was too concerned about his own family, too stunned by the violent upheaval that had rocked his world to think about how his city was being run. He merely looked at the damage, mourned his loss and viewed the busy new relief operations with gratitude. Soon he would begin to rebuild and repair. Today, he sat in misery and licked his wounds.

Hank was trying hard to control his irritation with Martha, who fretted over her missed comforts and who was annoyed that he and Susie had not helped themselves at the unpoliced Snappy Shop. "Hank, what are we going to do about water? When will they get it fixed?"

"No time soon. The pipes are probably broken underground in a hundred places. What else do we have to drink?"

"Well, there's a little water left in the pitcher, and we have a couple of cans of juice. Hank, the bath I can do without for a while, but we can't flush the toilet. What are we going to do about that?"

"There's always the yard."

"That's fine for you men," she retorted, "but hardly for Susie and me."

Craig emerged sleepily from the bedroom and Hank turned to him. "I saw some men from your protective agency. They're working for FML now."

"What's that?" Martha asked.

"Feed My Lambs, Mama. They're supervising things. They were asking for volunteers down on Florida Avenue, Dad, if you want to go too."

Martha began shaking her head but Hank spoke first. "That's a good idea. We can't just stay home and wait for somebody else to set things right."

In the end, Hank, Craig and Susie climbed into the old green Plymouth. Hank eased the car carefully over torn streets, headlights making reddish tunnels into the smoky air.

"It's getting darker," Susie said. "There are fires all over town and they can't put them out because there's no water." Her eyes were reddened from the smoke.

The activity at the disaster center had spread greatly since morning. Rows of tables stretched along Florida Avenue and a vacant lot nearby blossomed with tents and shelters. People stood placidly in several lines awaiting food or medicine, while trucks unloaded additional supplies.

Craig saw a blue and yellow car speeding toward them. It squealed to a halt within a foot of him and a large, heavyset man in uniform burst from the driver's seat. Their shouts of joy met in midair.

"Hastings!"

"Craig, boy!"

Craig found himself hugged tightly, the hamlike hand of his partner pounding his back painfully. "I thought sure you was dead, kid. I kept telling myself all night I should have knocked you out, kept you with me." Hastings' dirt-streaked face was split with a wide grin.

"I got by okay. How did you manage?" Craig was surprised at the rush of affection he had for the older man.

"I managed fine. It'll take more than an earthquake to flatten me. Where's your uniform, kid? You can't get no respect in that get-up." Hastings viewed Craig's shorts and T-shirt in distaste.

"We just came down to see what was going on. I didn't come to work. I only slept three hours."

"That's three hours more than I did," Hastings grinned.

Hank and Susie approached, and Craig made introductions. Hastings viewed Susie with appreciation; despite her smoke-dulled hair, she was attracting glances from all sides.

"Do you have any news? Anything reliable?" Hank asked.

"Only an estimate," said Hastings. "They're saying 75,000 dead in Tampa alone."

"Seventy-five thousand!" Hank repeated. "I had no idea there was that much destruction!"

"There wasn't," Hastings said, his sooty brow creased in perplexity. "Not actual buildings destroyed. That figure includes the missing too, of course, and maybe some of them will turn up."

"Missing?" asked Hank.

Hastings shrugged. "I got my own theory. I think there were probably some big cracks—you know, crevasses—that opened up, and people fell into them before they closed. That happens in earthquakes, you know. One guy I talked to, he thinks a lot of people might have been washed out to sea when the water was so rough. Well, we got work to do, Craig. We're operating out of this station now. Our old headquarters is gone, burned to the ground. I'll tell Jacks you're here."

Hastings lumbered toward the building, and Hank looked at his son in surprise. "Are you going to work now, Craig? With no more sleep?"

"I might as well, Dad."

"I got our assignment," said Hastings as Craig climbed into their patrol car.

"What is it?"

"We've got an area . . . Bayshore Boulevard. We're to check out the homes, see about casualties, damage, beds available for people whose homes have been destroyed, that sort of thing." Hastings patted a pile of forms beside him.

Craig's face lit up at the mention of Bayshore Boulevard. "I wish I'd worn my uniform," he said. He remembered Molly Redmond's copper-bright hair, her defiant chin. "Suppose people refuse to cooperate?"

"We just put that on the form."

Craig digested this news silently for a few minutes. "Well," he said at last, "I guess some group has to take charge."


The earthquake had done only minor damage to the Redmond home, but for the rest of Saturday night the three members of the family remained in the living room. About midnight the judge fell asleep in his chair, snoring gently, his white hair gleaming in the candlelight.

Scott hovered over the small battery-operated radio, switching continually between two stations which came in very faintly, feeling left out of the biggest story of the century—possibly the biggest of all time. Molly slept fitfully on the couch, uncomfortable but not willing to be alone. The first rays of the morning sun, seen hazily through drifting smoke clouds, found them all awake but unrested.

The dessert dishes from the previous night remained on the dining room table and no one moved to clear them away. There was no electricity for coffee. By midmorning Carrie Lee had still not arrived, and the judge set out boxes of cereal and the one remaining carton of milk.

That afternoon Scott learned that the WTBA transmitting tower had been only slightly damaged—something of a minor miracle—and that efforts were being made to get the station back on the air. Now his frustration at being trapped miles from the action became monumental. There was no way to get his car out of the driveway until the fallen trees were moved, no telephone service to summon help. He was in the driveway struggling to repair the chain on an ancient bicycle he had found in the garage when he saw the vigilante car stop on Bayshore Boulevard.

A heavy, muscular man with red hair got out from behind the wheel and his companion, a thin young man about Molly's age, followed, picking their way around the downed trees.

"You the Redmonds?"

"Who are you?" Scott had an interviewer's reluctance to being on the receiving end of questions.

"Protective Agency. That is, we were yesterday. I guess we're with the FML now," the big man replied. "Just making a survey."

Molly and the judge appeared. Both seemed to recognize Craig. The judge greeted him warmly; Molly looked irritated.

"What do you need to know?" asked Scott.

"Anyone dead or missing . . . injuries among survivors . . . damage to home . . . need for shelter—guess not." A quick look at the Redmond home convinced Hastings that it was still very livable.

"We're all in good shape here," said the judge thankfully. "Only minor damage to the house."

Craig was filling out the form. "Can you house some of the homeless?" he asked.

"No!" The answer came from Molly.

The judge looked at her reproachfully. "Why, child, of course we'll be glad to help in any way we can."

"I think you should know that the FML has authority from the governor to take over any home it needs." Hastings looked at Molly as he spoke.

"How can they do that?" asked Scott.

"Emergency grant of powers," Hastings shrugged.

As Hastings and Craig headed back to the car, Scott couldn't resist a dig at his sister. "Who's your skinny friend? Apparently you two know each other."

A flush of annoyance crept up Molly's cheeks. "He's just a pushy kid with pimples." With an angry twist of her head, Molly strode into the house. She still can't get Douglas out of her thoughts, Scott mused.

It was early evening when Hastings dropped Craig off at his street. Walking home, he saw Stubby Kraft sitting on a broken branch of the tree that had destroyed his home and killed his parents.

A wave of guilt passed over Craig. He had never really been friends with Stubby. Of course Stubby was only fifteen, nearly four years younger than Craig, but he was a nice kid and a next-door neighbor and Craig had pretty much ignored him. He crossed the lawn and offered embarrassed condolences.

"No sweat, Craig. Don't worry, I'm fine."

Incredibly, Stubby did seem fine; no sign of the dreadful trauma he had been through. He was pale but his dark eyes were bright. He moved over to make room on the tree limb and Craig had no choice but to sit down. Stubby looked off across the yard, his homely face eager.

"Craig, are you a Christian?"

It was an odd question. Embarrassing, in fact.

"Sure. I mean, I was baptized when I was ten, and I went to Sunday School and all that. Why?"

"Something happened to me last night, Craig. During the earth-quake. I'd like to tell you about it, but I don't want you to laugh at me."

"Okay. I won't laugh."

Stubby took a deep breath, almost a sigh. "It was the sort of thing where you know it's real, but you want to pretend it's a dream. I knew my parents were dead, after the roof fell in, and I was expecting to die, too. Then all of a sudden there was this man there. Don't ask me where he came from. But he was right there and he talked to me. He said I had been chosen and that he had some things to tell me."

He stopped and looked hesitantly at Craig. "Do you believe in angels?"

"I don't know, Stubby. I guess I never thought about it."

"Well anyhow, he said we had been wrong all along. We Jews, I mean. That Jesus had been the Messiah, and we should have known it. Then he told me how we were in a very difficult period —the last seven years before Jesus comes again. It seems that a long time ago—before Christ—God gave the Jews four hundred and ninety years to show the world what God is like, and we have seven of those years left. I don't understand that, do you?"

Craig shook his head.

"Well, it's all supposed to be in the Bible, the Book of Daniel. And he said something else, too, that's really heavy. He said all the truly committed Christians went to heaven during the earthquake."

Craig found himself nodding with mixed emotions. "It's what they call the Rapture. A kid at school told me about it."

"That explains something," Stubby went on. "When they came this afternoon to take Papa and Mama away, they never found the nurse who was right there with us. They dug through about a ton of stuff but she just wasn't there. I saw her face, Craig, just when the whole place was crashing down." Stubby looked at the older boy to see how he was taking all this. "It was like—like a light was on her."

Craig swallowed hard. "I saw exactly the same thing," he said. "I didn't know how to tell anyone. It was a little girl. She began shining like—just shining. And the next minute, Stubby, she was gone. Vanished."

They sat in silence, grappling with impossible thoughts.

"There's more, Craig." Stubby drew a deep breath. "This angel said that the Jews were God's chosen people until Christ was born. Then the Christians were. Now that the Christians have gone to heaven, the Jews are again. Does that make sense?"

"I don't know. My parents are Christians, sort of. They're still here. Why did some go and not others? Who decides?" Craig shook his head in bewilderment, then turned back to Stubby. "What did the angel ask you to do? Go preach?"

"I'm not sure. Study, I guess. Who's going to listen to a fifteen-year-old Jewish kid? He did say things are going to get pretty hairy before it's over." Stubby's liquid brown eyes were somber.

Craig stared into the dusty twilight, his mind in a turmoil.

"He put a mark on my forehead," Stubby added. "Can you see it?"

Craig looked at him, then shook his head. "I can't see anything."

"Maybe it comes and goes. Craig, can you help me learn about Jesus?"

"You've got to be kidding. You're the one who talks to angels. I'm just a fallen-away Baptist."

"Maybe we can learn together?" suggested Stubby. "I never read one word of the New Testament."

Craig looked at him again. Was it his imagination, or in the dying daylight had he seen on his friend's forehead, just below the dark widow's peak, a tiny glowing cross?

# III

It was two days after the earthquake before the Redmonds were able to learn anything about Carrie Lee. A crew from FML had cleared the driveway and Scott had driven to work. He returned shortly after five to pick up his grandfather and Molly.

Although he had spent his working day exposed to stories of death and destruction throughout the world, Scott had felt somehow that Tampa had gotten off lightly. Having a job during the day and a home to go to at night, his life had a semblance of normalcy and he knew that Tampa's disaster had been labeled "mild." But as they drove through the south section of the city, they were appalled at the demolished buildings and homes. In the lingering pall, everything had a sepia tone, like an old photograph, and the few people they passed appeared in shock.

"This makes me wonder what things are like in other places," the judge said. "We're supposed to be in fairly good shape."

"The reports are still fragmentary," Scott told him. "But what we are getting is scary. South America is devastated, the Pacific Islands have disappeared and a big section of southern California is gone, sunk, I guess. Mexico is a complete disaster area. About one third of the planet has been clobbered."

"What about Washington?"

"Not too bad," said Scott. "The big problem seems to be missing people. President Livingstone is okay, but no one can locate the vice president. He and his wife just vanished, although their home wasn't damaged at all. Quite a few members of the Cabinet and Congress are unaccounted for so far."

"How do they explain it?"

"No one's trying to explain anything at this point. There's too much cleanup to do. You've got to hand it to FML. They're doing the job. The government seems to be paralyzed, but these people are everywhere."

"Grandpa, look!" Molly cried from the back seat, and both men whirled around to look behind them, following her trembling finger.

At first Scott thought it was water, as a low, swirling gray mass poured into the street behind them. Then he realized in horror that it was alive. "Good God in heaven!" he said in a strangled voice. "It's rats!" He felt bile rising in his throat.

"Scott, get out of here!" Molly screamed. Her brother drove as fast as he could along the torn and broken street.

"What were they doing? Where'd they all come from?" asked the judge. The others didn't answer and he turned to Scott. "Perhaps we should stop on the way home and get a gun. What do you think?"

"You can't buy weapons any more. FML order. It's a peace-keeping move, to cut down on looting and rioting."

They drove in shaken silence until they reached Carrie Lee's tiny apartment. Scott parked the car in front of the old building, but a glance told them no one could be living there. The entire back half of the house had collapsed. The other three walls were inclined inward, a knock-kneed effect as though to hide the shambles inside.

"We better check with the neighbors," Scott said, though the lump in his throat told him their long-time cook had died in the wreckage of her home. They got out of the car and stood uncertainly on the sidewalk. Scott was wondering how far off the rats were, when suddenly the front door of the ruined building opened and a slim, well-built young black stood looking out. He was bruised and filthy and none of them recognized him until he spoke. "Momma's gone, Mr. Redmond. Jesus came and took her." His eyes were wild, his voice hoarse.

"Jason, is that you?" the judge asked. This disheveled fellow bore slight resemblance to the neat, mild-mannered young man they had met many times before.

"Yes, sir. It's me. If you've come for Momma, she's gone. Jesus came for her first."

The Redmonds exchanged looks. "Jason, are you all right?" the judge asked. "Do you have any food?"

"I don't need food. 'Man shall not live by bread alone.' "

"But he needs bread, just the same," the judge remonstrated mildly. "You can get free food at the disaster centers."

"I want to be here if Jesus comes back." Jason looked over his shoulder. "Momma met the Lord in the air, right at the top of those stairs, and that's where I'm waiting for Him."

The judge turned to the others. "We can't leave him here. He'll die of starvation."

"Grandpa, he's on drugs," said Molly disgustedly. "And he's dirty."

But the contempt in her voice was lost on Judge Redmond. "If anything had happened to me, Carrie Lee would have looked after you and Scott. I've never cared for Jason; he's caused his mother a lot of heartaches. But for her sake we can't just drive off and leave him."

He turned back to the wild-eyed black man. "Jason, please come with us. Don't you suppose God can locate you at our house just as fast as here?"

Jason looked at the judge thoughtfully. "You may be right."

"Get your things together, then."

Jason disappeared inside the house and returned a minute later with Carrie Lee's big frayed-edged Bible. The Redmonds had seen it in her hands a thousand times.

"This is all I need," he said.

This is all *we* need, Scott thought as he crawled grumpily behind the wheel. The guy was an acid-head, obviously went screwy when he saw his mother die, and on top of everything else, now he'd become a religious fanatic.


As soon as he could, Hank changed his status with FML from unpaid volunteer to full-time employee. His insurance office had closed down, along with most others, helpless even to sort through the avalanche of claims that began arriving as soon as mail service was even partially restored. It was a comfort no longer to be concerned with responsibilities or decision making; he could put in his time, collect his pay and avoid thought.

The second week in his new job, Hank was called into the tiny cubicle which served as an office for the small bird-like man who headed the local branch. The man sat behind his plain cluttered desk as Hank relaxed gingerly on a rickety folding chair. He peered at Hank. "Can you write?"

Hank ran a nervous hand over his bald head and blinked uncertainly at his new employer. Surely the man had no doubts as to Hank's literacy?

"You went to college, didn't you?" the man said accusingly.

"Yes. Business administration."

"Well, you're the only man I have with a degree. I need your help in writing up some reports." The man leaned forward, confidentially. "Headquarters is asking all local branches to send them in. If we get ours in early, it will be a real feather in our caps." Ambition gave an edge to his voice.

"Reports about what?" Hank asked, still confused.

"Well, about the disappearances for one thing." The little man gestured awkwardly. "People are still talking, and they need to be calmed down. Once they understand what happened, the rumors will die down."

"What did happen?" Hank asked, leaning forward eagerly on his unsteady chair.

"How should I know?" the man snapped. "People disappeared. I'm not a scientist. Or a mystic."

"Oh," Hank nodded. Evidently what the public was told did not have to be true. "I've heard all sorts of theories," he said, "but they don't make much sense."

"Like what?" the small man queried.

"Well, flying saucers. Some think that the missing people have been taken as hostages on flying saucers to some foreign planet."

The FML director snorted. "What else have you heard?"

"Well, some scientists believe that there was an interreaction between cosmic radiation and volcanic ash right after the earthquake which caused a spontaneous disintegration of bodies."

"That's not too bad. I believe we could build that one into something credible. Go on."

"Well, there's the theory about—what do they call it? The Rapture. That God took all the Christians to heaven. It's supposed to be in the Bible somewhere."

"That one has already been disproved. There are dozens of Christian clergymen here in Tampa who didn't disappear and who report large numbers of their congregations present and accounted for. Any more theories?"

"Something about astral travel. A neighbor of ours was talking about this. Through yoga and transcendental meditation, people disappear and travel to far-off places. It doesn't make sense to me, but some people believe it."

The bird-like head cocked reflectively. "Interesting possibility. Worth some study. Go on."

"That's all I can think of."

"Well, write me up a report on these possibilities. Leave out the Rapture. FML is squelching talk about that one. How soon can you get on it?"

Hank squirmed in his flimsy chair. "I never was very good at writing. FML must have psychologists who can do this sort of thing."

"There's nobody here like that." His superior's voice cracked with authority. "I want that report here in this office by next Monday morning at the latest."


Damage to their apartment building was not severe, but it was bad enough that Francis and Douglas accepted Madame Celeste's invitation to use her guest bedroom until repairs were made. It was a bad time for Douglas. He was scorned by Celeste and largely ignored by Francis who seemed absorbed in learning about the world of spirits. Celeste reveled in her role of priestess, the two of them huddling for hours as she instructed him in the details of her occult power.

At one time, his relationship with Francis had brought guilt and a sense of self-loathing. Now it seemed mild to Douglas compared to the evil he felt surrounding this woman. He spent most of his time wandering about the apartment drinking bourbon from Celeste's heavily-stocked liquor cabinet.

On the sixth day Lucky Royal returned and burst in on them looking rested, well-fed, neat. He laughed delightedly as he told of escaping the quake and spending several days in Canada. "Only thing was, we couldn't fish. Something killed them. They were floating all over the lake. Smelled so bad we had to leave."

And the three laughed.

"We heard about it on the radio; the fish are dying all over the world," Douglas said. But no one was listening.

Royal indicated Francis with a nod of his head. "Have you told him anything?" he asked Madame Celeste.

"We have spent days talking. He has been a most apt pupil."

"What about him?" Royal jerked a thumb at Douglas.

Up to now Douglas had felt invisible. At Royal's question, they all looked at him and he smiled self-consciously.

"I have done absolutely nothing with him," Celeste said. "It would be a waste of my time. He's had too much Christian background."

"Does that mean he can't change?" Francis asked.

"No, but I prefer not to bother." She dismissed Douglas with a wave of her hand. "His Christian beliefs have little effect on the way he lives, but if I tried to teach him anything about our beliefs, a lot of resistance would rise up from his background. I've seen it happen too many times before."

Douglas stared at Celeste indignantly, while the others looked at him in a clinical way. "You're speaking about me as if I weren't even here!"

"Do you know what we're talking about?" Royal asked bluntly.

"I think so," Douglas answered. "She's a spiritualist and she learned about the earthquake before it happened. Now she's convinced Francis. But she says I'd never go along because I used to be a Catholic, and the church doesn't approve of spiritualism. Right?"

Royal turned back to Celeste. "Of course it's up to you, but Francis is so fond of him, maybe we ought to try."

Francis flushed. "Don't be sarcastic, Lucky. He does work for you, you know, and he's a pretty smart boy."

"Don't get your feathers ruffled," Royal laughed. "I don't care about your love life. But maybe he'd be useful, Celeste."

She gazed at Douglas with distaste. "I'm willing to try if you say so."

Douglas was aware of two simultaneous emotions: anger and

fear. He was angry at their patronizing attitude. He was fearful of losing a job that since the earthquake appeared more than ever the only desirable thing in his disintegrating world. Fear won out. "I don't think it's fair of you to exclude me just because I'm a Catholic. That's prejudice."

Celeste looked at Royal, then sighed with resignation. "All right, Douglas. But you need to know exactly what you're getting into. You used the word 'spiritualism,' and that's accurate as far as it goes. We do believe in spirits. But we go further than a simple belief that they exist. We believe they are active in human affairs; that they contact us, guide us, give us power. Is that clear to you?"

"Yes. And I believe you're probably right," Douglas assented magnanimously.

"So, because they do this, we feel and express gratitude to them. Do you follow me?" Celeste was watching Douglas alertly. He nodded.

"Now this gratitude leads to worship," Celeste continued. "We adore and glorify and praise—you know the words. We worship these spirits. Now, surely this disturbs you?" Her bright eyes glittered in the too-white face.

"Well, I don't know. Maybe not. Catholics receive a lot of criticism for worshiping saints. I don't know that they do really, but maybe it's the same kind of thing." Douglas fought down a sense of panic.

"You, of course, don't feel anything at all toward the saints. But let's get back to the point. We worship these spirits for what they can do for us. Do you understand?"

"I'm not stupid. I understand. People can believe whatever they want to. I'm not knocking it."

"All right then. If you can accept that, there is only one more point to cover. I need to tell you exactly what these powers are—these 'spirits' if you prefer that word. Why do you look so frightened?"

Douglas had leaned back instinctively, shaking his head in negation.

"You know, don't you?" Celeste persisted. "We are Satanists. It was by the power of Satan that you were saved from the earthquake, and it is in one of his dwellings that you have been sheltered these last few days. Now I challenge you. Can you really allow your sweet, baptized, confirmed little soul to remain here with us?" She stared at him, victoriously vindicating her opinion of his unworthiness.

Douglas looked desperately at Francis.

"Don't look at me," he said coolly. "I can't help you."

Douglas shifted his gaze to Royal who was observing the scene with amusement. "The way I figure it, Douglas," he said, "don't knock it till you've tried it. It isn't nearly so unappealing once you've started getting some returns on your investment."

Douglas's thoughts were in turmoil. I could starve if I leave this job, he realized, but I can't worship Satan. I've gone pretty far down lately, but I can't do that.

"See, just as I thought." Celeste sat back triumphantly. "He's absolutely worthless. He won't live his faith, but he won't renounce it either. And if he joined us, he would be as useless and namby-pamby for us as he is for them. Our powers can't stomach lukewarm people any more than their side can!"

"Wait a minute, Celeste," Royal said mildly. "You did spring it on him mighty sudden. I don't know how I'd have reacted if you'd thrown it at me that way."

"Yes," Francis agreed, "that was pretty rough. I think you're being unfair, trying to prove your point."

Douglas heard their defense with relief. Maybe he wouldn't have to make this impossible choice right now. He arose, shaken, and fixed himself a drink.

Francis came over and stood beside him as Celeste and Royal continued their discussion. "That really got to you, didn't it?" he asked in sympathy.

"Well, yes. It was a shock. Is she right, Francis? Are you really going to worship Satan?"

Francis chuckled softly. "Don't be a jackass, Doug. I don't worship anything or anybody. But there is something here. I don't claim to understand it, but you don't have to understand a thing to use it. Like electricity or atomic power—just use it."

Douglas nodded eagerly. Francis went on. "Just play along. We don't have to lose our heads. Can you see me or Lucky down on our knees, reciting prayers backward and worshipping an upside-down crucifix?"

"Well, I hoped that was how it was. I knew you had better sense than to believe in the devil." Douglas laughed, too, but there was a tinge of hysteria in his voice.

Francis patted his arm consolingly. "That's right, have a drink. Everything will be all right."

Douglas felt a glow of relief. He could fake it, say he believed anything, but inside he wasn't going to worship the devil. Inside is where it really matters, he assured himself. Yet inside he felt like a lost child—like a little boy who had run away from home and now night was falling.


Martha was furious with Hank. First it was Stubby Kraft. Craig suggested they take in the orphaned neighbor on a permanent basis and Hank had agreed without even discussing it with Martha. Now they were all being evicted from their home and Hank refused to protest. They were now packed to leave, yet Martha was still not reconciled.

"But this is our home, Hank," she wailed. "Can they really do this?"

"They can do anything they darn well please," he answered grimly. "We don't have running water, the sewer is still broken, so they condemned us."

"It'll probably be nicer, Mama," Susie said hopefully.

"That big house on Bayshore is a dream and Judge Redmond is a very distinguished man," added Craig.

"But how can we just walk into somebody else's home and start living there?" Martha protested. Her pale face was bloated from crying.

"We have an order from FML," Craig said. "Better to live with people like the Redmonds than total strangers."

"You may have met them, Craig, but I haven't," his mother reminded him.

"I think we're lucky," Craig continued. "When I learned we were being condemned, I asked Hastings if we could check with the Redmonds about our moving there. They had already been notified that they would have six people assigned to them. The judge was happy to accept all five of us."

"How big is their home?"

"Six bedrooms plus a garage apartment, and only three in their family."

"Four," Hank corrected. "The form shows they've taken in one already."

"Well, let's get it over with." Martha looked lovingly around the kitchen where she had prepared so many meals. The house was almost unlivable, true, still it was the home which had sheltered them for over twenty years and it hurt dreadfully to leave.

When the news of the new housing arrangements broke in the Redmond household, Molly stormed into the judge's study and brought forth all the weaponry in her arsenal: anger, logic, threats. In vain.

"There's nothing we can do. We're going to have this enforced billeting, Molly," the judge told her. "There are people sleeping in churches, office buildings, schools. What with the quake damage and the fires, thousands of homes are gone. And I'd certainly prefer having people we know at least a little about."

"How many are coming?" Molly asked.

"A family of four—the McKenzies—plus an orphan they've taken in. With Jason already out in the garage apartment, that makes nine of us in all," Judge Redmond said.

"Grandpa, if 75,000 people are dead and missing," Molly pleaded, "they shouldn't need as many houses. Granted that a lot were destroyed, but don't you see? The demand and supply ought to still be about equal."

"I only know they assigned six people here. And I was impressed with this young McKenzie that day he came here about the bees."

"You may like him, but I don't," snapped Molly. "He's a bore."

"You probably won't see much of him. I think we'll put him and the orphan lad, Stubby, out with Jason in the apartment. You and Mrs. McKenzie can work out a system about meals."

Molly glared at him in helpless frustration and strode from his room. For the second time in her life, she was up against a situation which would not yield to her charm, her stubbornness or her family money.

Craig settled for only three hours of sleep in order to help his family move. Susie's school was still closed for repairs so she also was on hand, but Susie could not concentrate on a packing project for ten minutes without remembering a friend she had to say good-bye to. Stubby meanwhile had been working for days to salvage what he could from his home. The McKenzies marvelled at the maturity of this fifteen-year-old boy.

It was late afternoon when the five of them climbed into the old Plymouth for the first of several trips to the Redmonds. Hank drove into the Redmond driveway and pulled around to the back. The judge greeted them at the back door. As they entered the kitchen, Martha gasped with surprise and pleasure. It was a large and cheerful room equipped with modern appliances. Two walls contained large windows, hung with bright yellow and white checked curtains, with counters and shelf space below. A large round table with eight chairs occupied the center of the room. There were a refrigerator-freezer, dishwasher, and a six-burner electric stove along the third wall, all in sunny yellow. On the final wall, a long counter contained a double basin sink, now overflowing with dirty dishes. Only the clutter and dirt kept the room from looking like a picture from a magazine.

Hank shook hands shyly with the judge as introductions were made. "I thought we'd let the boys have the garage apartment, if that suits everybody," the judge said. "Our other guest, Jason Brown, is out there now. He's a young black man who has been seriously affected by recent events. He saw his mother die in the quake, and possibly got a blow to the head himself. Quiet and obliging, though," he added hastily, catching Martha's look of alarm.

"There's a bedroom and bath at the head of the stairs which I thought would do nicely for you and your husband, Mrs. McKenzie," the judge went on. "Your daughter can have the blue room on the south side."

"Please call us Martha and Hank," Martha said, and Craig was glad to see his mother relax. She was obviously charmed by the old man.

Molly appeared and new introductions were made. "Well," she drawled, "we're certainly integrated, aren't we? I mean, we have our very own Jew now to match our resident black. I wonder what's coming next."

The group showed varying degrees of embarrassment, but Craig was angry. He had learned to respect Stubby in the short time they had been together, and it infuriated him that anyone could be so callous. "Maybe we'll get lucky," he blazed out at her, "and get a doghouse for the resident bitch."

"Craig!" Martha gasped.

"Watch your mouth, son," Hank said sternly.

Molly glared at Craig in fury and he felt suddenly shaken by the enormity of his indiscretion. "Listen, punk," she hissed at him, "I don't have to take that kind of crap from a pimply-faced high school dropout."

Craig felt himself reddening. It was out of character for him to behave so rudely and he wished heartily that he could take back the cutting words. Even in the midst of his chagrin, he had the thought that Molly's legs were really fantastic.

"Now, Molly. We've all been through a very trying period, and we need time to adjust." The judge spoke placatingly. "Why don't we get the McKenzies' things put away, and then we can have dinner." He turned to the newcomers. "It's very makeshift, I'm afraid. Molly doesn't cook."

"And doesn't intend to try," Molly added with a toss of her red hair.

"I'll be glad to do the cooking," Martha said as she and the judge started toward the hall. Hank and Susie followed, bags in hand.

# IV

For weeks following the earthquake most nations were in a state of shock and paralysis. As the losses were tallied up, the total dead and missing approached one-fourth of the world's population. Except in those nations where an entrenched dictator survived, there was either confused leadership or none at all.

The president of the United States, like most citizens, found himself in a state of numbness and indecision for days after the earthquake. His oldest son was among the missing; other close relatives had been killed. His son's wife had been an invalid; she died of shock during the quake. His vice-president, two cabinet members and an as yet undetermined number of staff and party leaders were missing. But only the president's wife suspected the real reason for his inability to take leadership after the global earthquake; some small vein had evidentally ruptured causing a slight stroke. The only effects were a barely noticeable slurring of his speech and a slowness to respond to decisions pressed on him. He saw as few people as possible in the weeks following the disaster.

One man he did see was Uriah Leonard. The two were closeted for several hours on Wednesday of the second week after the earthquake. The president then issued a short statement that he was taking upon himself emergency powers until Congress could convene and pass appropriate legislation. He paid tribute to the spontaneous response of the world relief organization "Feed My Lambs" and authorized this agency to take charge of the restoration of services on a national level, placing National Guard units under FML's control as needed. Looters and lawbreakers, the president added, would be tried under martial law.

The presidential statement was received with general relief. Only a small minority voiced incredulity that the president of the United States would grant such powers to a private organization. Strangely, in a series of bizarre accidents, these voices of protest were silenced one by one over the weeks that followed.

Dazed by the loss of many of its leaders, Congress could not agree on legislation to handle the crisis. Liaison between Congress and the president became almost nonexistent as the Chief Executive spent most of his days in seclusion at Camp David while repairs were made on the moderately damaged White House.

Meanwhile FML labored to bring some semblance of stability to the stricken nation. The world headquarters of FML had been announced as Zurich, Switzerland, but after the earthquakes, the power center seemed to shift back and forth between a large facility outside of Princeton, New Jersey, and an office building in Rome, Italy. Announcements of executive decisions came from

various FML officers, but the wielder of power was one man—
Uriah Leonard.

Dazed leaders of other countries were approached in much the
same way as was the president of the United States. Most countries
were willing, even eager, to have FML restore their devastated
communities even if they did have to grant this new organization
unprecedented powers.

In New York City the National Guard, under the direction of
Feed My Lambs, imposed martial law, and summary executions
of law violaters were carried out by this group. Thousands of
badly damaged buildings in the city were simply abandoned and
boarded up. The initial efforts were to clean up, make the streets
passable and guard the peace. The bodies of the dead were in-
terred in communal graves, bulldozers shoveling debris on top
of them. Medical care was coldly efficient: those who were dying
received none; those who would recover on their own were sent
away untended. Only people who required professional care in
order to survive were treated.

New York City, like Tampa, was classed as a "light" damage
area. Because of its importance to the country, personnel and ma-
terials for the restoration of functions were rushed in. Individuals
were unimportant; restoring the flow of services was done heart-
lessly but efficiently.

Royal Enterprises was one of the first businesses in New York
to reopen. The offices were open ten days after the global quake;
surprisingly over a dozen people showed up for work. No one
was more grateful for this return to normalcy than Douglas
Rymer. He resumed his work with an avid eagerness that would
have astonished him earlier. The office functioned as well as possible under the circumstances; the building generator was working, air conditioning and lights operative.

But a glance out through the wallboards which covered the
cracked or missing windows, brought home sharply the fact that
the world was far from normal. Royal's television stations were
still silent, the usually humming switchboard was dead. Royal
spent most of that first day at the newly established Communication Control Office, a new branch of Feed My Lambs, exerting
his considerable influence to gain preferential treatment for his
stations. He was leaving in frustration having only partially

achieved his objectives, when he spied a large figure in black crossing the entrance foyer. He rushed forward, hand extended.

"Bishop! How good to see you again."

Uriah Leonard's dark, handsome face glowed with pleasure. "Royal! You look fit. Wonderful! I need to talk with you."

"No better time than right now," Royal said.

"Wonderful!" the bishop said again, guiding Royal toward the back of the building. "This poor world has suffered a terrible blow. She needs firm hands at the helm now, hands like yours, used to power and not afraid of it."

Royal laughed without mirth. "None of my stations are working. I can't get a line on any of my foreign holdings. I don't know what's left, if anything. But I'll do whatever I can to help."

"We need your stations. That's a priority." The bishop opened the door to a temporary office and motioned Royal inside. It was small and poorly lighted, but as Uriah Leonard entered, the room took on importance from the strength of his personality.

"Now, tell me how you fared," the bishop began. "Were you here in the city when the quake struck?" His green eyes glittered as Royal launched into the tale of his flight from danger. When Royal mentioned going to Celeste's apartment, the bishop sat up straighter. "Madame Celeste, the seer? You know her?"

"Well, yes," Royal answered in some embarrassment. "I met her at a cocktail party a few months back and—"

"Don't be ashamed of that friendship, Lawrence. I count the lady among my friends, too." Bishop Leonard smiled at Royal's look of surprise, then continued. "We'll do whatever is needed to get your stations on the air again. Is electrical power all you need? What about damage? Do you have enough personnel?"

As they talked about the problems involved, the bishop showed a surprising grasp of the intricacies of television. Royal felt his tensions relaxing. Things were working out. He was still one of the favored few.

The bishop leaned back in his chair. "I want to get your stations operating again for a personal reason. I intend to make a televised speech on July 17th, and I would consider it a favor if you would help me with its composition."

Royal found this an unlikely request. The bishop's eloquence was well known. "I thought speeches were your specialty," he said.

Bishop Leonard chuckled. "I do have something of a gift there, but this speech is a little out of the ordinary. It is going to be broadcast all over the world with simultaneous translations into every major language. No one has ever before reached such a mass audience, and it needs to be a blockbuster."

"I'd be honored to be part of the planning."

The bishop thought for a moment. "Could we get together Thursday night? Privacy will be a necessity. We can meet at Celeste's apartment. We won't be disturbed there."

Royal found the choice of meeting place a strange one but he nodded. "I'll be there with my assistant. He's a genius at speeches and he can be trusted." Royal rose and offered his hand.

"I appreciate your cooperation," Bishop Leonard said. "When you accepted a position as director for FML, you probably expected the returns to be negligible. But the world is different now. What you thought an honorary post will be a position similar to that of cabinet member. I intend to save this poor old world and I have the power to do so. I may have to save man against his will. But save him I will."

Royal listened intently. He had seen power grabs before and understood the mechanism behind them. If Royal was to be a cabinet member, then the bishop must be planning something pretty impressive for himself.

During the first week the McKenzies spent in the judge's house on Bayshore Boulevard there were many attempts at adjustment. When rationing began, there was adequate food, if not of their choice. The running water was sufficient, but undependable and tasted bad. The word soon circulated: boil water before drinking. When Craig and Stubby tried the bay as a substitute for bathing, they found it warm, slimy, and stagnant. Dead, rotting fish floated on its surface. The small supply of soap and deodorant became precious. Finding long, greasy locks unmanageable, Susie mournfully cut her hair; each one lowered his standards of personal hygiene.

The lingering pollution, the merciless heat and the trauma of change tended to produce irritability and frustration. There were efforts toward social graces and consideration for others, but no amount of etiquette could smooth the conflicts between nine such different people.

The strangest behavior was Jason Brown's. When Craig and Stubby joined him in the apartment over the garage, he moved his cot bed down to the garage itself, claiming he needed the privacy for prayer and Bible study. He came to the main house three times a day for his food which he took back to the garage to eat despite invitations to join the others.

Craig McKenzie continued working the night shift and slept during the day. Most of his free time was spent in the garage apartment with Stubby Kraft. The two of them had begun an intensive study of the Bible. More and more Jason would drift upstairs to listen. As yet they had not shared their ideas with the others. Stubby was the most cheerful and thoughtful of the small community, evidencing a strength and serenity that surprised everyone.

Hank McKenzie left each morning for his work with FML. He had been transferred to the Disaster Center on Swann Avenue, nearer to his new home on Bayshore Boulevard. His written report on missing persons had not been satisfactory, and no further offers of responsibility were made to him.

With the move to the Redmond home, Susie McKenzie had withdrawn her services as a volunteer for FML. She had made one trip to the local center and found no males attractive enough to make it interesting. She spent her time at home, helping her mother when she had to, daydreaming and yearning for the excitement of her old life.

Scott Redmond commuted daily to the WTBA studios, his undisciplined body protesting the six-mile bicycle ride necessary to conserve fuel, also rationed. Broadcasting had not yet begun, but the staff was preparing for this eventuality. Scott's life-style had changed radically; there were no dates, no night clubs. He wondered vaguely what he would do when his supply of liquor ran out, but he refused to worry. All his life he had found a way out of every inconvenience. Scott had great faith in his ability as a wheeler-dealer.

Judge Redmond probably most enjoyed the merger of the families. He had been increasingly lonely as his grandchildren had grown up and away from him. He appreciated Hank's quiet companionship and Martha's dedication to the kitchen, essential with Carrie Lee gone, and he enjoyed talking with Craig and Stubby, finding their youthful viewpoints refreshing. He was distressed when Scott and Molly showed antagonism for the new household members.

In Martha and Molly, the conflicts of personality found their richest soil as they quickly began trading insults beneath a veil of amiability. The tension between Molly and Craig continued too, despite Craig's efforts at conciliation. Scott took a casual condescending attitude toward his new family as a subtle way of demonstrating his superiority. When Susie turned seventeen and there was a small birthday party for her, Scott eyed her mature body with appreciation but shrugged off her efforts to impress him. "She's sexy, all right, but just a kid," he concluded to Molly.

So the days passed, not in acute misery or danger which might have drawn them together, but in a ponderous boredom.

# V

Celeste's living room was quiet and dimly lit. Lawrence Royal tiptoed to the bar and poured himself a drink, annoyed when he lifted the glass to discover a smear of lipstick on the rim.

Uriah Leonard was relaxed in one of the tubular steel armchairs, eyes closed, apparently in deep reverie. Celeste was sitting cross-legged on the floor. Her eyes too were closed as though communing with some unseen force. She was dressed entirely in black this night and her face was very white through her make-up.

Francis Chapman joined Royal at the bar. "How long does this go on, Lucky?" he whispered petulantly. "I mean, we have better things to do than sit here while they meditate."

"Let's give them time to think—or whatever they're doing." Royal looked doubtfully at his hostess and the bishop. They seemed oblivious to their two restless companions.

While Francis mixed his usual Pink Squirrel, Royal wiped the
rim of his glass. "This place is filthy," he muttered. "It even
smells funny."

"That's the incense," Francis said. "Celeste never opens the
windows. The other night I had a miserable headache from it."

They turned as Celeste arose. She wore flowing black jersey
pajamas, the top cut into a deep vee, her ash-blond hair hanging
loosely to her shoulders. "I thought you'd forgotten about us,"
Francis told her sarcastically.

Celeste looked at Francis with disapproval. "Is it your beautiful
roommate? Is that why you're in such a rush to leave us?"

"I would hardly expect you to have old-fashioned prejudices
against someone else's life style," Francis returned icily. "These
are enlightened times, you know."

"I'm all for enlightenment," she replied. "And I could tell you
how we helped bring about this so-called enlightenment. But
let's not let playtime come ahead of more important matters."

"Don't downgrade Douglas, Celeste," the bishop spoke without
moving in his chair. "He is more valuable to us than you realize.
I have decided that Douglas should be a part of our little group."

"What do we need him for?" Celeste asked.

"He can be our sounding board, our own private poll right in
the family, to let us know how the common man is reacting." The
bishop spread his hands eloquently. "From what you tell me,
Douglas is average in intellect, skills, background and reactions.
He's the complete median. But he must not suspect we are using
him as a barometer. He must believe he is one of the inner circle.
Does this bother you, Francis?"

Francis was watching the bishop without expression, his drink
forgotten. "No, I guess not," he answered slowly. "So long as you
treat him decently. It hurts his feelings when Celeste is rude
to him."

"We will guarantee politeness from now on," Bishop Leonard
smiled. "Now let's go on with my speech. And we will speed
things up, Francis. You have made a legitimate request that we
be more businesslike."

Royal nodded in approval. He had been uneasy that Celeste
and the bishop seemed out of touch with reality. The results of
their continuing meetings would be surprising, astonishing at

times, but the road toward the results would always make him uncomfortable.

It was almost midnight when Francis returned to his apartment
to find Douglas waiting. "It wasn't necessary to stay up so late,"
he said genially.

"I was worried that something had happened to you," Douglas
said. "The streets aren't safe, you know."

Francis stared at his handsome roommate. "Would it really
bother you if something happened to me? I'm touched."

"Well, sure. I don't want you to get hurt," Douglas said.

Francis carried a drink to his favorite chair and sat down. "Are
you sleepy, or can we talk awhile?"

"I'm wide awake," Douglas replied.

"Well, he doesn't come right out and say so, but it is my personal opinion that the good bishop is shooting for the position of
world dictator." Francis shook his head. "It's absolutely unreal,
but with the world the way it is, it's quite possible that he can
do it."

"You're kidding," Douglas said. "How?"

"Look around you. There isn't a stable government left anywhere. If the economy hadn't wrecked them, the earthquake did.
The bishop not only controls distribution of the world's food,
he's now gaining control of communications. He has the charisma
and magnetism to sway people. Most important his organization
is organized. By the time people look around, they'll find that
FML has *de facto* power already."

"I can't believe it. People aren't that stupid," Douglas said
stoutly. "Not here in America, anyhow."

"In a crisis, people want a strong man to straighten things out.
And there is one other factor you don't know about. Celeste's
powers are in Leonard's corner, backing him."

"But he's a priest," Douglas protested. "How can he do that?"

"Easy. He says, 'Satan, help me.' " Francis' plump face was
amused.

"Something ought to be done about it," Douglas said in distress.

"If something is done about him, Douglas, it won't be by the
likes of you. Anyhow, the speech he's giving on the 17th sounds
great, but it's a lot of nonsense. It says absolutely nothing, but
when he turns on that resonance, it really gets to you. Even me—

and I wrote most of it myself. To show you how smooth he is, he insisted that the speech be based on a Biblical text. It won't be named, but all the time we were working, we had the Bible open right at the place."

"Well, good," Douglas said in relief. "I'm glad to hear that, at least. What part?"

"Exodus. Twentieth chapter. It lists the Ten Commandments. But I don't think you'll be so happy when you hear the speech. He changes every one of them."

"He changed the Ten Commandments! Why? People won't like that."

Francis waved his hand airily. "Nobody will even recognize it. It's done very subtly."

"But . . . if nobody's going to know, why bother?"

Francis shrugged. "I don't know. He said he had a reason."

"I think it stinks," Douglas said and pondered the feebleness of his description.

"Cheer up," Francis encouraged him. "As Lucky says, there will always be the haves and the have-nots. We're among the haves. So, count your blessings."

"Yeah, sure. If I take my time and make sure I don't miss any, it ought to take me all of two or three seconds."


Halfway around the globe from a devastated America was the small land of Israel, approximately the size of New Jersey. Without great wealth, with an unstable peace and few constant political friends, this tiny country maintained an immense importance in world affairs. Three events took place there during the earthquake which affected every life on earth.

For years Israel had been called holy by three great monotheistic religions. Within her boundaries one special city—Jerusalem —is even more holy, and within the city one area of ground is the holy of holies. Moslem, Christian and Jew have fought for centuries for control of this land and her shrines and symbols. She has been repeatedly destroyed, captured, trampled and razed, but she rises anew each time.

For the Jew, this holy city extends almost three thousand years back into history, from the time King David made his capital there in a conquered Canaanite city. The first temple was built by his son Solomon. This temple was destroyed in 587 B.C. by the Babylonians, but it was rebuilt by the returning exiles. As Christ predicted, this temple was destroyed also, in A.D. 70, by Titus and his Roman legions. For almost two thousand years, the Jews were dispersed from their land and their holy city. Their return to the land of Israel early in the twentieth century, and their rebirth as a nation in 1948, opened the way for the rebuilding of their third holy temple.

The Christian reveres the land of Israel as the site of Christ's life on earth, His ministry and His miracles. Christian shrines of all denominations dot the area.

The Moslem holy of holies, the Dome of the Rock, was built on the site of Solomon's temple in A.D. 691 as a part of their Holy Enclosure. It covers the Rock of Abraham (claimed as ancestor by both Arab and Jew) —the rock upon which Abraham was prepared to sacrifice his son at God's command. Moslems believe this is the site from which Mohammed ascended through the seven heavens into the presence of God.

At the time of the earthquake in June of 1988, Jerusalem was under Israeli control. The nation of Israel had recaptured the Old City twenty-one years before, but the mosque of Islam still covered the holy ground of the temple. However, with this mighty earthquake, worldwide in scope and unprecedented in devastation, the Dome of the Rock toppled, and the site of Solomon's and Herod's temples was razed again—for the first time in almost thirteen hundred years.

Within six hours, Israeli soldiers had control of the area, and heavy equipment was moved into place. Bulldozers worked under the shadow of tanks and guns, and the fighting between Jew and Arab reached new heights of ferocity and bravery. The sons of Moses, who said they had been deeded this site by the Almighty Himself, would not relinquish it. "The temple will rise again!" This battle cry rang out above the sounds of their equipment, and many died.

The second event of worldwide significance which took place in Israel at the time of the earthquake was the rise to power of the prime minister of Israel, Naphtali Seth Ben Daniel. Already an elected head of state, he was only the representative of the people at the helm of a constitutional democracy. The chaos resulting from the natural catastrophe and the tumultuous fighting in Jerusalem led him to seize considerable additional powers, and his role changed from that of an elected official with circumscribed authority, answerable to the electorate, to that of a dictator of a police state with almost unlimited power.

Ben Daniel, however, was devoted to his country and its citizens. He was an able and efficient administrator. Things progressed far better in Israel than they did in other, less tightly controlled, societies.

The third result of the earthquake was not apparent for some time. It came with a dawning awareness to the entire world, and there was heavy shifting of power and influence undreamed of a few short months before. Many Jews have laughed ironically at the wisdom of Moses choosing from all the land beyond the desert the single spot with no oil reserves. Deserts blossoming? Yes, after many, many centuries. Milk and honey? Yes, a decent standard of living for her energetic and willing workers. But the great, unthinkable wealth of oil, the power of life and death over the economy of the world—these were not a part of the heritage of Israel until the 1988 earthquakes moved and shifted the great subterranean plates. It was as though some giant hand had reshaped the stratae of the earth, both geologically and economically.

Simultaneously with the realization by the Arab states that by some freak of nature, their oil was gone, the realization grew in Israel that somehow they now had oil. With their usual efficiency and dispatch, the Israelis drilled wells that pumped unending streams of black gold. They shifted comfortably into their new role as a great world power. It was a fluke, an impossibility, undreamed of, a miracle. The people of Israel laughed in delight and divided their time between exploitation of this new wealth and defense of it. It was very difficult for them not to give some credit for their new status to their new leader, Ben Daniel.

# VI

Saturday July 16, like every other day, was hot, smoky and muggy. About noon at the Redmonds' house Susie was sitting on the front porch, recently rebuilt by Craig and Stubby, watching the bay where boats were hauling in the dead and rotting fish to be ground up and used as fertilizer. The stench hung sickeningly in the unmoving air. Martha appeared in the doorway, wearing a faded skirt and an old shirt of Hank's.

"I wish I could have seen this place before the grass all died," Susie commented to her mother. "I'll bet it was one of the prettiest places in Tampa."

Martha nodded, barely listening. "What's that?" She pointed across the bay.

A low, shimmering cloud was hanging above the horizon, silvery grey against the dirty brown of the sky.

"I don't know. You think it's going to storm? Oh, wouldn't it be great if it rained?" Susie stood up and looked eagerly at the cloud. It was approaching at an astonishing rate, glittering as it reflected the dim rays of sunlight.

"It doesn't look like a cloud, Susie," Martha protested. "It looks . . . I don't know . . . alive." She stepped outside, closing the door behind her.

They could hear a whirring noise now, a strange and disquieting sound coming from the cloud. The bay under the cloud was dark, the shadow line rushing toward them.

"I don't like it, Mama. Let's get inside."

As they turned to enter the house, the edge of the cloud reached them. The whir became a roar and the sky darkened. Through the din Susie heard a fainter sound, several soft thuds as though something were dropping from the cloud. She whirled to look, eyes wide and scared.

"It's bugs, Susie!" Martha screamed. "Grasshoppers!" She was hopping up and down, slapping at her legs which were covered by crawling insects.

Susie watched in terror as the creatures rained down from the cloud. The roar faded and they heard only the repeated plop, plop, plop of falling insects. Susie screamed as they covered her bare arms and legs, their horny feet marching relentlessly over her body.

"Get inside!" she shouted. "Hurry!"

Their cries and the strange darkness had brought Molly running to the front door. She stood stunned for a moment, watching the greyish silver mass that now covered the lawn. "Wow!" she gasped. "What is it?" Then she swung the door open. "Get inside! Quick!" She grabbed Martha by the arm and pulled her in. Susie was thrashing her arms and legs, trying desperately to clean off her body before going indoors and Molly grabbed at her too. "Come on, Susie! Hurry! They're getting inside."

Susie ducked into the house, slapping hysterically at her hair where several had tangled themselves. "Oh, help me, Mama! Get them off me!"

But Martha appeared to be in shock. Her pale face was contorted with fear, she only covered her mouth with her hands and whimpered.

Molly was striking out wildly at the bugs which had come inside. The insects seemed almost impossible to kill. Being knocked to the floor did not stun them. They simply marched down the hall, through the doorways, unaffected and orderly.

"Martha, step on them! Kill them! For the love of God, woman, move!" Martha was the only one wearing shoes.

Martha shook her head helplessly. Cursing, Molly ran toward the back of the house, moving as quickly as she could among the ranks of insects. She could not avoid stepping on some, and she moaned aloud as they squished between her toes. She reached the kitchen ahead of the marching army, and grabbing a broom, began beating at them with it.

Susie was right behind her. "What can I use?"

Molly shook off the insects which had crawled onto the broom handle. "Get a magazine, rolled up," she said breathlessly, and Susie grabbed one from the stack under the counter. She doubled it and together they lashed out at the swarming mass around their feet.


In his bedroom in the Redmonds' garage apartment, Craig had fallen asleep as soon as he returned from work Saturday morning. Those who were out in public as he and Hastings were each night knew that people were becoming frustrated at living in a state of upset. However, he found it hard to be involved with anything but the absorbing subject he shared with Stubby, and to a lesser extent with Jason. They had become convinced that the world had entered a period which the Bible called the Tribulation. It was to be a seven-year time of great hardship. They wondered if they would be able to meet the test.

He was awakened at noon by Stubby shaking his shoulder. "Craig, the locusts are here! Get up!" Stubby's dark brown eyes were enormous.

Craig sat up abruptly. "They're here?" he asked.

"Over the bay. You can see them from the window."

"Wow!" Craig looked where Stubby was pointing, hushed in awe at the sight he beheld. The shimmering, swarming cloud of locusts was descending on the ground, covering it like a blanket. Only the contours of the landscape were visible under the thin layer of grey. "Well, they can't bite *you*, Stubby. And they can't kill even the ones they bite," he said.

"We have to tell them, now, Craig. This is proof. This is one thing we can point to, right in the Bible."

"Yeah . . . maybe. Right now we better go to the house and see if they need us." The garage apartment was some fifty feet from the house, an expanse now covered with living horror.

"You better put on long trousers, Craig. And a long-sleeved shirt."

Craig quickly found them in a drawer, then pulled on socks and a pair of tennis shoes, and followed Stubby down the stairs. The yard was a solid mass of insects. There was no way to avoid walking on them, and the crunching sound was dreadful. Their legs and bodies were soon covered. Craig brushed at them mechanically: he was thinking of his mother and her almost phobic fear of any crawling thing.

Jason Brown's reaction to the advent of the locusts was typical of his behavior since the earthquake. Regular meals had restored him physically, and he now kept himself and his clothing scrupulously clean, but mentally and emotionally he still inhabited a world apart. He seemed not only to accept the new hardships of his life, but almost to welcome them. On the occasions he was asked to perform chores, he was unfailingly willing. He was accepted as a part of the little community now—a vague, fringe character who remained for the most part in the background. He spent all his free time studying the Bible.

For Jason, Saturday began as all his other days. He waked with the rising of the sun and spent some time in cleaning his garage home. At breakfast time, he walked to the back door where Martha handed him his meal. This morning it was especially good—eggs, some kind of white beans cooked to a soupy consistency, dried figs, a carton of fruit punch. He carried the food back to the garage, and after a prolonged blessing, he ate, discarding his trash neatly. His mother's Bible in hand, he then went outside and sat in a straight chair just within the shade cast by the garage. He read slowly but contentedly, rising occasionally to relocate his chair as the sun moved and the shadow changed.

It was almost time to return to the back door for his lunch when he saw the cloud. He knew immediately what it was. Unlike the others, he watched its approach with no trace of fear.

Jason took his Bible inside and placed it under his pillow to protect it, then stood in the doorway of the garage. The locusts dropped to the ground and began their march. They climbed his legs; they landed stingingly on his head. He stood, immobile. In a short while he saw Craig and Stubby stepping gingerly across the yard toward the house. He didn't call out to them. This was a private thing between him and God.

Saturday July 16 was a hectic time at Station WTBA. After many days of silence, they were going to resume broadcasting the following noon. Television stations around the world were to carry a speech by Bishop Leonard, live, at three o'clock Sunday afternoon.

To bring local residents up to date on the restoration of

services in their area, Scott Redmond and a crew of three went out early Saturday, filming shots of the city. Just before noon they finished a sequence on the mass typhoid-injection program.

"This FML outfit is incredible," commented one of the crew as they replaced their cameras in the truck.

Scott nodded. "They're efficient. When I did that documentary with Lawrence Royal, I had no idea that Feed My Lambs would be so big."

The driver gestured toward the bay. "Shall we film the fish operation? All those dead fish should produce some good shots."

The suggestion was greeted with approval and the truck headed out Bayshore Boulevard.

"I hope this fertilizer project works," Scott remarked. "I live here on the bay and the smell of those fish in this heat is something else."

"You don't have to live on the bay. I can smell them up in Palma Ceia," the driver retorted.

None of them saw the cloud of locusts approaching. Their first hint of danger was the sudden darkening of the sky. The driver swerved to a stop and quickly they rolled up the windows, slapping ineffectually at the pests which had swarmed into the cab.

"Grasshoppers!" shouted Scott.

"They don't look like any grasshoppers I ever saw."

"I thought grasshoppers liked big fields of grain."

"It must be the rotting fish which brought them."

Scott stared through the windshield at the underbellies of the creatures swarming over the glass. "Let's get some film of this. The networks will eat it up," he said.

"No they won't," said the driver. "That FML guy told us to film scenes that will encourage people. Upbeat stuff. They won't like this at all."

The others agreed and Scott sighed with resignation. And with some relief. He had no desire to get out into this mass of living fallout.

"Look," the driver said tentatively. "I don't know about you guys, but I'd like to go see about my lady. She'll go ape with this mess."

One of the cameramen shrugged indifferently. "I'm just staying with some strangers. It doesn't matter to me."

The other man nodded. "I don't have a family anymore. Just a cot at the Methodist Church."

"I'm only a few blocks from here," said Scott. "Why not drop me off first?"

The truck inched forward as the four men watched the scene through the laboring windshield wipers. The road ahead was a mass of writhing grey, discernible only by the contours of the curbing barely visible beneath the blanketing of insects.

The driver turned into the Redmond driveway and stopped at the back door. "Get out as quick as you can," he said. "And good luck. I hope your folks are all right."

"Thanks," Scott answered. "Same to you. See you tomorrow—I hope." He opened the door and shot from it as quickly as possible. The ground was covered as though a dirty blizzard had struck. He hopped first on one foot, then the other, shaking his legs to dislodge the locusts climbing his pants.

"Let me in," he yelled, pounding furiously on the back door.

Craig opened the door, pounding it with his fist to knock off a layer of crawling things. Scott swiped at his clothes before entering and Stubby and Susie brushed the remaining insects from him inside the kitchen. Molly was stuffing rags where the windows had only been temporarily patched after the earthquake. She stared at him, her eyes wide. "Glad you're home. You get bitten?"

"I don't think so," Scott answered. "Do these things bite? I thought they ate grain and stuff."

"They bite. Look here." Molly advanced and displayed an arm. On the skin there was a reddened raised area about two inches in diameter, a small puncture wound in the center. "It's like a bee sting. I was so busy I hardly noticed, but now it's beginning to ache."

"What's the matter with her?" Scott jerked his head to where Martha sat sniffling at the kitchen table.

"She won't talk, won't help, won't do anything but sit like a dummy and cry," Molly told him.

"Mom's always hated bugs," Craig said mildly. "She can't help it."

"Where's Grandpa?" Scott asked.

"Oh, Scott," Molly said anxiously, "he and Hank were out walking. They haven't come back yet."

Scott looked worried too. "And Jason?"

"Gosh, I forgot all about him. He must still be in the garage." Molly looked out the window, but it was covered by insects.

"Maybe I ought to go check on him?" Stubby suggested.

"He knows where we are," Molly said. "If he wants to come over here, he can. I don't want to open that door again unless we have to."

Scott sat down at the table and found to his surprise that his hands were shaking. "Anything about this on the radio?" he asked.

"Nothing but static," said Molly. "I don't know what you want to hear anyhow. We know they're here." She stepped back from the window and looked with satisfaction at her work. "Now what are we going to do with all these dead ones?"

Scott wasn't listening. "First a drought," he muttered, "then an earthquake, and now this. I wonder what's coming next? Maybe the black plague?"

The back door flew open and Hank burst in. His glasses were askew and his breathing was ragged. The others surrounded him quickly to brush off this new onslaught of insects.

"We have to get the judge," he panted. "He fell as we were running. Heart attack I think. Just beyond the oleander bushes. I couldn't carry him."

Stubby Kraft spoke up, his small face determined. "I'll go, sir. These things can't bite me."

For a startled moment the others stared at him. "Okay, Stubby," said Scott. "Just you and I. Two's enough."

They left, hunching their shoulders against the swarm at the door. Hank turned to Martha. "Do you know of anything for these stings? They're starting to hurt."

Martha sat up straighter and her sniffling stopped. "How about vinegar? Vinegar helps ant bites."

Hank nodded and Martha began fixing small compresses of vinegar, using the last remaining paper towels. The door thumped and Scott's voice called, "Open up!"

Hank leapt to the door and Scott and Stubby struggled in, the inert body of Judge Redmond between them. They carried him to the living room sofa, where Craig began to rub his limp hands and wrists.

"What's wrong with him?" Molly asked fearfully.

"Maybe nothing serious," Craig said reassuringly. "His color is okay. I think if he had a heart attack, he'd be bluer."

The judge's eyes fluttered open and Molly ran for a glass of fruit juice. Craig propped him up while he drank, then lowered him again to the cushions. By midafternoon he was sitting up, and by dinner time was well enough to walk into the kitchen.

Jason appeared briefly at the back door for his plate of food; he was so covered with bites he was almost unrecognizable, yet he refused to come in. The meal was a disaster as the locusts kept turning up in pots and serving dishes. The group sat silently, only pecking at their food.

"Say, Stubby," Hank said at last, "what did you mean about these bugs not biting you? Is that true? Didn't they?"

Stubby looked at Craig uneasily. "No sir, they didn't." He showed them his bare arms; the skin was smooth.

"How do you explain it?" asked Hank.

"Well, have all of you read the book of Revelation? It's the last book in the Bible."

"I know. I know. But what's that got to do with it?" Hank repositioned his glasses more firmly on his nose and peered at him more closely.

"Well," Stubby plunged in, "what Revelation talks about is happening right now. It says there that locusts will come for five months and that they'll sting like scorpions. It tells all about the earthquake and the fish dying and everything."

There was a moment's incredulous silence, then Martha spoke condescendingly. "I've read Revelation and it's an allegory, Stubby. None of it is literally true."

"No, Ma'am," Stubby said firmly. "It is true. Some of it may be symbolic, but a lot of it is literally true."

Hank smiled, using his most logical tone. "Even if you're right, Stubby, which I don't think you are, I don't see what good it does us. So what if it does mention locusts? We don't need the Bible to tell us about that; they're all over everything."

"Well, I guess it's supposed to make people repent of their sins so they won't lose their souls." Stubby felt his listeners stiffen.

"Well that takes the cake," Molly sputtered. "Where do you get off, telling us to repent? You're just a dumb kid."

"That's enough, Molly," the judge's voice was weak but steady.

"The boy is sincere. Listen, son, I know you mean well, but what you say is offensive to us. Most of us have been Christians all our lives. I don't want to slight anyone's religion, but don't you think it's possible we know a little more about it than you do?"

"I think it's lovely that you're reading the Bible, Stubby," Martha added. "I really do. And if you have any questions, I'll be glad to help you."

Stubby was fighting back tears of helplessness, but he pressed doggedly on. "It tells about the Rapture too. That's what happened six weeks ago, during the earthquake. All the Christians went to heaven. Don't you see? If you were really Christians who didn't need to repent, none of you would be here."

He sat in misery as the storm of anger rolled over him. Hank was shaking his balding head in amazement. "I can't believe my ears. With all we have to worry about, now we have a young Jewish boy telling us we aren't Christians."

Judge Redmond spoke sternly. "You've gone too far, son. I don't hold with youngsters criticizing their elders. It may be old-fashioned to some, but I believe in showing respect to older people."

"I don't mean to hurt your feelings. Honest. I appreciate all you've done for me. I'm just trying to help you," Stubby protested weakly.

"Help us!" Molly gasped in disbelief. "Now I've heard it all."

Craig had slumped in his chair, arms folded across his chest. Stubby shot a furtive glance at him, hoping for reinforcement.

Hank spoke again, more kindly. "Why don't we just forget about it? It's been a bad day all around, and you just got upset. Right, Stubby?"

"No, sir." Stubby squared his thin shoulders. "As long as I've started, I might as well tell you the whole thing. I didn't find out all this from the Bible. When the earthquake came, an angel came and talked to me. He told me a lot of things, and he asked me if I wanted to be one of the hundred and forty four thousand chosen Jews. Then he gave me a special mark. The mark keeps the locusts from stinging me." He finished in a rush, cringing from the incredulous looks.

"You are out of your head," Molly announced in disbelief.

Hank chuckled softly. "Oh, Stubby. I'm sorry to be laughing at you. But you can't expect us to accept all that. Now can you? Really?"

Scott rose from the table and left the room, a look of amused contempt on his face.

The judge shook his head. "You've really lost your audience, son. I could accept a statement that the world needs some changes, maybe even some repentance. A deeper dedication to mankind would be better. But angels and protective marks—sorry, son."

Craig straightened in his chair and Stubby looked at him with hopeful eyes. "I don't know if this will affect anybody's thinking or not," Craig began, "but for what it's worth, I believe him. I think he is one hundred percent right on every point. I think what happened was the Rapture—I saw a little girl disappear before my own eyes—and I've seen the mark on his forehead. It doesn't show all the time, but in a certain kind of light you can see it. As for repentance, I think we all need it. I know I do."

The room was completely silent. Craig's reliability and trustworthiness as a witness ranked vastly above Stubby's. Craig was an adult; he held down a job; he had proved himself rational, calm and dependable.

"Craig, you've been upset, too," Martha ventured. "You work so hard and you never get enough sleep."

Craig eyed her tiredly. "Mom, that won't wash. You know it won't."

Molly stood up abruptly. "I don't care who's seen what. There are dead bugs all over this house. I'm going back to work."

"I think you're right, Molly," Hank said. "We've had enough crazy talk for one day. Susie, get some of those cardboard cartons."

Everyone rose except the judge and Stubby, returning gratefully to activity.

The judge spoke softly. "I don't know what happened to me out there in the yard, Stubby. I'm feeling better now; still it may have been some kind of warning. I could be meeting my Maker any day now. While you were talking I remembered what the Bible said about a little child leading them. Maybe someday we can talk again about—about these ideas of yours."

"Oh, yes, sir! Any time you say!" Stubby joined the others with a lighter heart. One person had listened, after all. Maybe that wasn't too bad a start.

On Sunday, July 17, Martha awakened with a Christmas morning feeling of anticipation. Television was returning! She rose and dressed quickly. A number of the locusts had come into her room during the night and some had even crawled onto the bed. But even insects in close proximity could not dampen her good cheer. Television again!

Scott was in the kitchen when she got there, looking helplessly through the cabinets. "Can you find me anything to eat? I'm going to work as soon as I get some breakfast." He had been busy before her arrival. The floor was clear of insects. A pile of their writhing and dying bodies had been swept into a corner.

"There are powdered eggs," Martha said. "I could scramble some and fix you a few figs."

"Anything's all right. I'm hungry enough to eat those lousy locusts. Say, did you see? There aren't as many." He walked to the window and peered out. "They don't cover the ground now. I guess even a grasshopper couldn't live on that grass."

Martha looked relieved. "That's good news. Hank was mighty sick last night from the stings. Susie too. I thought locusts were supposed to be—what do you call it—things that eat plants?"

Scott smiled, superior. " 'Herbivorous.' And maybe they would be if there was anything 'herbified' left. You and I are lucky not to be sick." He attacked the figs. "Craig played it tough and went to work in that mess. And poor old Jason. I think he'll probably die. He's covered with bites. But Stubby says he won't."

"Wasn't that the silliest stuff you ever heard?" Martha said conversationally. "I felt sorry for Stubby, but I couldn't help but laugh."

"I missed most of that little sermon you all got yesterday. This religious stuff bores me." Scott watched Martha light the small alcohol stove they were using during the emergency. "Looks like our timing is pretty good. The alcohol's about gone and we get electricity today."

"Yes, and television." Martha sighed. "Remember how it was when we had power all the time?" She served Scott his plate and sat down opposite him with a cup of tea. "Is the station all set to broadcast today?"

"I think so, but I've got to get there early to help out." Scott thought a moment. "I'm taking the car today, gas shortage or no."

"I think it's wonderful that you've been willing to use a bicycle all these weeks."

"I'm getting used to it." Scott smiled at the thought of his pampered little body toughening up.

"I guess it's easy when you're young and strong," Martha giggled. She liked talking to Scott and considered him a television star—someone important and exciting.

Scott stood up. "Thanks for the breakfast."

"What time will the TV start?"

"About two o'clock. There'll be an hour of local stuff before the bishop comes on. I hope that film we got yesterday was processed okay. If not, I'll be ad-libbing for an hour and that might get a little old." He waved at her as he left.


To Martha's surprise nobody else in the household considered the return of television of monumental importance. They were happy about having electrical power again, but there were only three of them gathered to watch the first television show in weeks.

Scott, of course, was at the station and Hank at work at the Disaster Center. Craig was asleep, exhausted from his night's work. Susie was still too ill from the insect bites to be out of bed and Molly had taken four aspirin with her lunch and gone to her room. So only the judge, Stubby and Martha herself were waiting in the living room at two o'clock for the big moment.

The television set hummed, brightened, and Scott's relaxed, familiar face filled the screen. Martha felt a thrill of proprietary satisfaction at his attractiveness. He introduced himself, announced what was to follow, then spent the next hour narrating films taken of Tampa. Martha kept remarking on how good the program was. It proved things were getting back to normal.

"According to Scott, all that we've been through is a minor upset," Judge Redmond commented in disgust.

"I'm sure they're doing it this way to encourage us," Martha said.

"I think a little truth would serve us better than this pablum," the judge answered, shaking his white head.

There was a knock on the back door and a moment later Jason

hobbled into the room. "Oh, you poor thing!" Martha felt a
stab of guilt because she had not even missed him at meals. His
face was disfigured with bites, but she was relieved to see that no
insects had ridden in on his clothes.

He tried to smile through swollen lips. "I'm okay. Better than
I look. I want to hear the bishop's speech."

Scott was summing up his report. "It really makes you feel
proud to see how everybody in the Bay area is helping out. As
an old football coach back in the seventies used to say, 'When the
going gets tough, the tough get going.' That's how people in
Tampa are handling things. With hard work and respect for
authority, we'll have our situation back to normal before you
know it.

"And now it's time to bring you Bishop Uriah Leonard, the
worldwide director of Feed My Lambs. This man is the guiding
spirit behind an astounding organization which has taken on a
major responsibility for restoring our world. The bishop has
often been heard to say, 'The Lord helps those who help themselves.' Let's show him we believe that too. Let's do everything
we can to help ourselves. And now, Bishop Leonard." Scott faded
and the screen went blank.

Judge Redmond shifted restlessly. "Do you realize they didn't
even mention the locusts? Now, that's just stupid. They can slant
the statistics and gloss over facts but by golly, there isn't a soul
in Tampa who doesn't know we've got locusts."

Martha shook her head, disagreeing. "Maybe the locusts weren't
all over town, Judge. Maybe it was just right here by the bay."

"Don't be obtuse, woman. You saw that cloud. Can you ignore
your own brain, just because they didn't talk about it on television?" The judge looked at her sternly.

"Well, we don't know for sure. I'm certain if it was as widespread as you say, they'd have told us."

A craggy, handsome face appeared on the screen. Bishop Leonard spoke simply but earnestly. "My dear people, I come to you
in peace and in love. We have suffered a terrible earthquake.
Our world has been devastated. We have lost many loved ones.
As we begin the monumental task of restoring our society, we
need the full cooperation of all men. Our only hope of salvation

rests in brotherhood, my friends. I urge you now to face our task with hope and fraternal love, and trust in man's ability to shape his destiny.

"Six weeks ago we felt the foundations of our world change. This was a portent and a sign. Let us change our lives and our society as thoroughly as our earth has been changed. Let us fearlessly embrace change, so that, as we rise above this disaster, we mount even higher than before and turn this crushing blow into a blessing. I want to offer you some practical, concrete guides toward achieving a new heart and a new spirit—toward awakening a new hope for the new future.

"First of all, I want each of you to make the rebuilding of our society the prime objective of your life. There is absolutely *nothing* which should take precedence over this goal. In your common humanity, deny yourself personal pleasures and considerations in deference to the common good.

"Secondly, I ask you all to unshackle yourselves from the prejudices and bigotries of your past. Let us truly love all men, regardless of race, creed or color. No man should be hated or deprived because of his background. No one should be punished because of his father, his forefathers or his ancestors. Let us love all men as equals.

"Let all of us together right now pledge ourselves to this end. Let us each speak to the god he or she knows and vow to accomplish in the coming months what has been only a dream in the past. Let us promise our brothers our total effort, twenty-four hours a day, seven days a week, without rest or respite.

"Make your commitment to all men, not simply to those of your own nation or your own community. I tell you this, my dear people, that you owe no more to your family and kin than you do to the most distant, meanest citizen of this earth. Let us abolish the smaller interests; no longer will a man claim a greater obligation to his children or his parents than that which he feels toward all his brothers.

"And now, my dear people, I will propose guidelines to you that many will hear with shock. Many will find my instructions revolutionary, but a kind of revolution is what we need. Not in the earthly sense of taking over a government, but in the spiritual sense of changing our hearts and minds. I tell you now with all the earnestness I possess, *nothing* should supersede our commitment to building a new and better earth. In achieving our goals for mankind, we should consider ourselves at war with those destructive people and groups who want to continue their own selfish pursuits. Do not be dismayed if we are forced to use warlike measures to achieve our great goals. As a surgeon removes the cancer fearlessly, so we must fearlessly, exultantly even, remove from our society those cancerous elements which are destroying our chances for a new age of man.

"Place before yourselves the large picture of the whole human family—its needs and its possibilities. Let mankind be your family. Give to each man that which he needs without question. Let no man say, 'My family, my wife, come first . . .' Let him rather say, 'All men are my brothers; all that I have belongs to all men.'

"So I leave you now in peace. We have before us a marvelous opportunity, never before vouchsafed to the human race, to rebuild our society on new and revolutionary lines. Let each man give his all to his brothers, and the peace of man will be with us all."

The bishop's voice faded, and within seconds, the power went off. The four in Judge Redmond's living room stirred as though waking from a trance.

"It was so short," Martha complained. "I thought he'd talk longer than that."

Judge Redmond spoke dazedly. "I've heard great speakers in my time, but that man is on a completely different level. He had me absolutely mesmerized and yet I'm not at all sure what he said."

"I thought it was lovely, all about cooperating and loving your brothers. That was beautiful." Martha's wan face was aglow with emotion.

Jason had been silent since the beginning of the telecast. He looked at Stubby now, his black eyes glittering with fever. "You think he's the one in the Bible?"

"I don't know," Stubby answered thoughtfully. "He sure didn't sound like a priest. All that about using warlike methods—that's saying it's all right to kill."

"How can you say such an awful thing after that beautiful sermon on love?" Martha turned solicitously to the judge. "Are you feeling all right? Stubby and I can help you to your room if you're tired of sitting up."

"I'm fine, Martha." The judge straightened himself in his chair. "I think I'll stay here with the boys and talk."

The infestation of locusts was worldwide. While they did not swarm everywhere as they did in Tampa, there were few places on the globe where they did not appear in some numbers. Scientists reported that the locusts were evidently a strange mutant since they differed from their ancestors in many ways and appeared to be sterile. No medication or therapy was found to be effective against the stings. Opiates eased the pain temporarily and time eventually healed the wounds. The strange insects did not harm the few crops still available and no deaths were reported.

An assignment from Bishop Leonard to investigate these locusts was given to Douglas who discovered that the locusts mentioned in the Old Testament were short-horned grasshoppers belonging to the family locustidae *(acrididae)*. They had since been found on every major continent of the earth. Nonmigratory locusts were relatively harmless, but when their population increased beyond a certain point they changed: jaws enlarged, color changed and wing muscles grew for migration. At that point they began to swarm and become the devastating plagues that have occurred down through the centuries.

These migratory locusts could travel incredible distances. They had been seen as far as twelve hundred miles out to sea. In the early 1600s a swarm took three days to pass over the city of Lisbon, and in the late 1800s a migration, covering an area of about two thousand square miles, crossed the Red Sea.

Douglas was intrigued to discover that reports from early mankind often charged the locusts with being demon-possessed. A locust plague usually lasted five months and seemed impossible to eradicate or control, leaving the ground stripped and bare and packed full of eggs to hatch the next season.

Locusts belonged to the same general phyla as roaches which of all living things were most repugnant to man. Plagues of hard-to-kill insects were a particularly symbolic affront, Douglas discovered, striking at man when he seemed most vulnerable. The question haunted him: Were these locusts to play a part in man's final battle—the one which he will lose?

Douglas was included in the second speech-writing session and joined Bishop Leonard, Lucky Royal and Francis Chapman with a mixture of dread and pride. He was elated at being taken into the inner circle of power, disturbed that the meeting place was Madame Celeste's apartment. He selected a chair as far away from her as possible.

Francis sat at the marble-topped table, taking notes by the light of five candles in a tarnished silver candelabrum. Even generators in expensive apartment buildings only worked sporadically.

Bishop Leonard was pacing the room, ponderous and graceful as a lion, his magnetic personality drawing all eyes to him. Douglas, who had met the bishop only briefly at the office, was overwhelmed by the power of the man's personality.

"I think the time is ripe. People are ready for a savior." The bishop stroked his mane of dark hair.

"You're probably right," Royal agreed. "New York is fairly well off, but what we're getting over the wires from other places is close to anarchy."

"Many parts of the world aren't used to taking baths or having enough food," Francis pointed out. "They expect things to be bad."

"We'll have problems taking over America," the bishop pursued his thought. "But if I wait until things get worse, it may be too late. No, considering everything, I think the time is ripe."

"As I understand it, you want the political power first?" Royal asked.

"I prefer the word 'secular.' I don't intend to enter politics *per se*. The electoral process is not for me. I will work through the heads of governments." Bishop Leonard smiled smoothly.

"Wouldn't it be easier to get that kind of control after you're pope?" asked Celeste.

Startled, Douglas glanced at Francis, but his friend ignored him.

"That's a separate problem," Bishop Leonard said. "Becoming pope may well be the next step. But first the present pope must be declared dead. The Vatican is still concealing the fact that he is missing." He began to pace again. "These disappearances are quite interesting. Remarkable, even. I never really thought that part would happen, you know. But it's logical. It certainly will make our work easier, having all of the fanatics gone. I understand many of the cardinals are missing. Rome is in confusion, and that will facilitate my move."

"What you want us to do is help you write a speech which will make you the hero in the white hat, right?" Royal was coolly efficient.

"That's right," the bishop nodded. "I must appear as a veritable angel of light, the personification of good, so that anyone who opposes me will be completely ostracized."

"Brotherly love was a good start. That talk went over big last month," Francis said.

"Exactly. Nobody can claim to be against the brotherhood of man. That's the kind of thing we want." The bishop stopped by the table and stood looking down at him.

"What about provision?" Francis offered. "Bread and circuses —that sort of thing. What was that phrase in the 1930s? 'A chicken in every pot.' "

The bishop shook his head. "Can you see how it would strike people today if I made any specific, physical promise? With the world like it is, they'd laugh me off the air. It has to be a spiritual thing, an emotional uplift. Let them know if they'll follow me, heaven will come in their hearts."

"Their kingdom will come if thy will is done, right?" Douglas heard himself speak with horror. The last thing he wanted was to call attention to himself and he cringed as four pairs of eyes turned to him in surprise.

"Say, that's pretty good," the bishop replied. His green eyes glittered with amusement. "The kingdom of man. How does that sound?"

"People need to commit themselves to something greater than they are. I think we'll need the idea of God in it," Francis objected. "Lots of religions have this business of God coming down to earth," he continued. "Maybe not God Himself, but prophets and the like coming down among men to straighten them out."

"That's it. You've got it!" The bishop beamed on Francis. "Of course! We will say that with a change in man's heart, God will dwell in all of us." He stood erect, head thrown back, and he spoke ringingly. "I shall be fulfilling an old prophecy. I shall be speaking to all nations, and I shall be bringing them the good news that all power is ours. I shall bring peace, not a sword. My kingdom shall be of the whole earth." As his voice echoed through the room, Douglas felt goose bumps rising along his arms.

"Praise you!" Madame Celeste shouted. "Praise you!"

When the excitement died down, Francis spoke again. "We should ask people to make some sort of gesture of acceptance. Like Caesar's pinch of incense. That way, each person will know he's made a commitment."

"Like what?" Royal asked. "Ask them to send a donation?"

"No." Francis shook his head. "The mails are too undependable. Besides it ought to be something the person wants to do anyhow, and it ought to be fairly private."

"How about a prayer?" Celeste suggested. "A prayer to whatever each individual believes in."

The bishop considered this for a moment. "I don't think prayer is exactly the word we want. Maybe 'meditation.' Or, even better —'silence.' We could ask each person to spend a moment of silence considering how he can best help the new society."

"What about a whole day of silence?" Francis asked. "Tell people you plan to spend a day in prayer for guidance in bringing the world to its feet again. Ask everyone to join you in a creative silence."

"I like that very much." The bishop was glowing again. "And we'll use the FML symbol in all the publicity."

"Why don't we think of a symbol for you, personally?" Royal asked.

"I'll need a coat of arms when I become pope," the bishop agreed.

"It ought to be a simple one," Francis said thoughtfully. "All the old religious symbols were very simple. The cross, the star of David, the fish."

"What is the symbol for 'God'?" Royal asked. "Maybe we could show Him coming down to earth. God and man together at last —that kind of thing."

"The best-known symbol for God is a circle," the bishop said. "I like the idea of God descending into man."

Royal was sketching as they spoke: an arrow pointing down and at the bottom and immediately to the right of the arrow, a circle. "What's the sign for man? Maybe that would help."

Celeste took the paper from his hand and studied it in the candlelight. "You know, if you just curved the end of the arrow around the bottom of the circle, it would be almost like a six," she said. "That's very interesting."

"Why?" Royal asked. "What's so special about six?"

"Six is the Biblical number for man," the bishop answered. His eyes met Celeste's, and they smiled at one another in the dimly-lit room.

*Book Three*

# Exacerbation

*August 14, 1988*
*to*
*December 5, 1991*

# I

It was Sunday afternoon August 14, four weeks after his first worldwide broadcast that Uriah Leonard appeared again on television:

"My dear friends, I come to you again as the leader of an organization which is filled with love and concern for your well being. During the month since I spoke to you last, many of our brothers have suffered unspeakable hardships. Our hearts ache for them. We are determined to meet their needs.

"This past month, I have also thought at length about what changes I would work if I were god-like in my powers. Would I turn back the clock to the period before the earthquake changed our world? No, I would not willingly return you to those days of inequity when a privileged few enjoyed their wealth while many starved. My goal is to lead you into a new world of brotherhood and tolerance, a world without hatred, war or poverty. We must relinquish the old ways, work hard, discipline ourselves so that we can usher in a new and golden world, full of peace and plenty.

"My dear friends, before our latest hardships came, I asked you for one-tenth of your possessions. You gave generously. Not to me, but to your brothers. Now I ask more. Now I ask a major share of your hearts and minds and muscles. I ask the lion's share, not of what you own, but of what you are. And the lion can feed the lambs in the great millennial symbol of peace and brotherhood.

"We need a sign of our togetherness, an action that will unite us. Beginning at midnight Thursday, wherever you are, I ask you to join me in a day of silence. For twenty-four hours, we will commune with ourselves, seeking awareness and answers. To those of you who pray, I extend an invitation to join me in prayer to

155

whatever divinity you recognize. To those of you who do not pray, I say, listen in the silence to your own soul. For one day, let our spirits reign, controlling our bodies and our minds rather than being subject to them.

"I promise you, my dear children, there will be signs and wonders. Old creatures cannot build a new world, so let us open ourselves to the forces of the infinite. Let our feeble human souls be filled and possessed by larger life. And as God descends to mankind, man will rise up, renewed and recreated."


"Well, are we going to do it?" Martha asked brightly as she turned off the television. Every one but Scott who was at the station had gathered in the living room to hear the bishop's second speech.

"You mean not talk all day Friday?" Molly asked. "That's ridiculous!"

Judge Redmond, seated in his big reclining chair, was thoughtful. "I think he had in mind an interior silence. It won't do much good not to speak if our minds are chattering away."

"I don't see what good it will do," Susie said. "How will keeping quiet help us get gasoline or running water or anything?"

Hank shook his bald head seriously. "The bishop just feels the rebuilding of society will require sacrifice on all our parts."

"Well, what about it?" Martha asked again. She pushed her hair away from her damp forehead. The heat continued unabated, and the locusts' continuing presence meant keeping all windows shut.

"I'll be working Thursday and Friday nights," Craig answered. "I can't see not talking while we're at work. But that won't stop me from praying."

"Well, I'm not going to pray, and if I have something to say, I'm going to say it," Molly declared.

"That's simple stubbornness, my dear," Judge Redmond reproved her. "I don't believe it would hurt any of us to commune a bit with ourselves."

Molly tossed her red hair. "If there's anything I don't need, it's twenty-four hours of thinking about my problems."

"Molly, your grandfather's right," Martha said earnestly. "I plan to pray, too. Do you suppose we ought to get together, make a little group? It might be more fun that way."

"It's got to be fun, doesn't it?" Molly turned her scorn on Martha. "Maybe fix a few Baptist brownies and sing a couple of hymns. Well, count me out."

Judge Redmond shook his head. "No, Martha. That wasn't the suggestion. It is supposed to be a very private thing. I think I'll spend the day considering some of the things Craig and Stubby and Jason have been telling me—maybe read for myself some of those Bible passages they're always quoting." He smiled and the discord that flared so easily these days faded a little.

Jason got painfully to his feet. Although the others had long since recovered from the locust bites, Jason was still partially disabled by the number of stings he had received. "Thank you for letting me watch with you," he said. "I'll bring Momma's Bible over on Friday morning, Mr. Redmond," he added. "That would make Momma real happy, knowing you were reading it."

"And it will make me happy, knowing it was hers," the judge answered.

"No need asking if you're going to pray, Jason," Susie said with amusement. By now the group took Jason's new-found piety for granted, and had even developed a tolerant affection for him.

"I may have to work overtime," Jason replied seriously as he limped to the door. "Somebody'll have to make up for all the ones who don't know how to pray. Just asking spirits to fill you is risky business, you know. There are spirits and then there are spirits."

The room began to empty, Craig and Stubby following Jason to their little hermitage in the garage. Hank peered at the judge questioningly through his thick glasses. "What do you think, Judge? Strange suggestion by the bishop, wouldn't you say?"

"If you really want to know, Hank, I think we have a dangerous group running things, and it's just a matter of time before they start showing their teeth." Judge Redmond shook his snowy head in bewilderment. "I don't quite see how this silence business fits in, but I'm absolutely convinced he's after power, power, power, and there isn't a thing we can do about it."

"Well, he's a good man, wouldn't you say?" Hank asked. "I mean, he is a priest; he's dedicated his life to mankind."

"You know, Hank, a curious thing occurred to me as he was speaking. Maybe dedication to mankind isn't enough. Maybe he should have dedicated himself first of all to—to God. One thing I know; there never has been a truly benign dictator. Even if he started out that way, by the time he got to the top, he'd be changed. There's an old saying, you know, about power corrupting."

The two men fell silent, each lost in his own thoughts.


Craig had transferred to a more convenient FML center, Hastings moving with him so that the two could still be partners. Their new location, the Swann Avenue Center, was housed in the remains of a real estate office building. It was a three-mile walk from Bayshore Boulevard, difficult considering the heat and the insect population, but Craig was growing tougher. His lean body had become stronger from constant exercise. Despite a scanty diet and less sleep, he was healthier than he had been in years; even his acne was slowly drying up. Exposed to the raw reality of current life on nightly patrol, Craig might have become hard but for Stubby and Jason. Relating his experiences to them helped give him perspective. All three were finding in the Bible hints that the present situation was not simply an accumulation of unfortunate accidents, but part of a vast, long-foreseen climax of history, cosmic in its implications.

The night after Bishop Leonard's second speech, Craig arrived ten minutes early for work. Hastings was already there, sitting on a bench with a drink in a paper cup, ignoring the ever-present remnant of the locust plague crawling over his feet.

Craig grinned at him with affection. "Those locusts know better than to bite *you*. They'd die of blood poisoning if they did."

Hastings patted the bench next to him. "Sit down for a minute." He tipped the last of his drink into his mouth, then crumpled the cup. "Man, that tastes lousy. I'd give my right arm for a beer. Wonder how long it will be till we get cold beer back?"

Craig shrugged. There were many things he considered of greater importance than cold beer, but its scarcity was a real loss to Hastings.

"My idea of heaven," Hastings went on dreamily, "is all the cold beer I want. And a nice air-conditioned room. Then on Sunday afternoon I'd have a wall-sized TV, and I'd lay back and watch the Bucs beat the pants off Miami."

Craig laughed at his friend. "Sounds great. And before the game, how about a shave?"

Hastings had recently sprouted a face full of curly, reddish hair, explaining that shaving with cold water and old blades was too big a price for vanity. Now with his bushy beard and twinkling eyes he resembled a jolly pirate.

"Easy for a pipsqueak like you to talk," Hastings scoffed. "You probably don't have to shave more'n once a week anyway."

They laughed companionably. "By the way, we don't come to work on Thursday night," Hastings said.

"Really?"

"It's this silence thing. It starts at midnight, and we're supposed to be home meditating, or whatever."

Craig looked at Hastings in amazement. "That's crazy. Things are rough enough with us out patrolling. Imagine what it'll be like without us. Who made the decision?"

"FML. It's an order," Hastings answered. "Maybe the troublemakers will stay home and meditate too. Let's hope the bishop reached them."

"I thought it was a stupid speech," Craig snorted. "It sure didn't reach me."

"Well, kid, like they say, if you ain't tried it, don't knock it. Maybe it will help. Some say the bishop is a miracle-worker," Hastings said solemnly.

Craig was silent, thinking. Stubby, presented with an opening like this, would begin his quiet, serious effort to convince Hastings of the truth contained in the Bible. Craig wondered if he should do the same. It could be painfully embarrassing.

"I never did care much for preachers," Hastings was saying. "I got enough preaching when I was a kid to last a lifetime, but this guy Leonard isn't like that. He's really sincere. And if anybody had ever told me I'd say this about a Catholic priest, I'd have said he was crazy."

"What's so different about him?" Craig asked.

"The way he talks, for one thing. And the way he's influenced so many important people in politics. They say he's a buddy of the Number One cat in Israel. Now that takes some doing."

"You mean Ben Daniel?" Craig asked.

"Yeah, that's the guy. He was on TV the other day, laying the cornerstone for this big temple they're getting ready to build over there. Anyhow, he spent most of the time talking about Bishop Leonard. Called him the light of the world. It gave me goose bumps just to hear it. Why don't you like him, Craig? Is it because he's a Catholic priest?"

"Gosh, no, Hastings. I don't have anything against Catholics. I just think Leonard is dangerous. Doesn't it make you uncomfortable when you see how much power he has?"

Hastings shook his head. "Not particularly. The state the world's in, we need a strong man to run things."

Craig moaned softly. "Do you really think it's good for him to control so much, even the hours we work or don't work? He was never elected by the voters. He's just a regular citizen, like you and me."

"He may not be elected, but he's not like you or me," Hastings said.

Craig sighed. "Yeah, I'll grant you that. He's different all right. But do me one favor, Hastings. Try to keep an open mind about him. While you're meditating on Friday think about this: Instead of assuming he's good, imagine how it would be if he were evil. I don't mean just corrupt or dishonest—I mean really *evil.*"

Hastings looked at Craig in distress, his broad face concerned. "He hasn't done anything evil, boy. The bishop is a good, decent man, and if he doesn't save this world, who's going to?"  .

In their patrol car Hastings returned to the subject. "Why'd you want to say things like that about Bishop Leonard?"

Craig stared at the big man thoughtfully. "Okay, Hastings. I'll tell you what's bothering me, but you got to promise not to tell anybody. I mean, it's just between the two of us."

Hastings nodded and Craig went on. "In the Bible it tells about a brilliant but evil man who takes over the whole world after a terrible earthquake. He is called the Antichrist because he is working for Satan. Well, I may be crazy, but . . . there are things about Bishop Leonard that make you wonder."

There was a stunned silence. "I can't believe that," Hastings breathed. "I don't know anything about it, but you got to be wrong. People would know."

"Some people do, Hastings. People who know the Bible and believe in Jesus Christ. But you can't go around saying things like that about somebody who has the fantastic reputation Bishop Leonard has."

"Where in the Bible does it say all this?" Hastings asked.

"In Daniel and Revelation and a bunch of other books. It's hard to understand, but these two guys who live with me, they read and study all day. They're getting to know it pretty well and—"

They were interrupted by a voice on the radio. "An FML official has been shot in front of the Dixie Supermart on South Cypress. Two men escaped in a yellow Chevrolet, heading east. All cars in vicinity close in."

Hastings grunted. "That's us, boy!" He gunned the car foreward.

Only two blocks away they spotted the yellow car moving at high speed toward Route I-4. Hastings jammed the gas pedal down and they roared in pursuit. With quick twists of the steering wheel the big man shot in and out of the sparse traffic.

"Duck down, boy!"

Someone was firing at them from the yellow car. Hastings began zigzagging the car as much as he dared on the torn and uneven roadway. Then he shouted, "Can you hit his tires?" Craig took out his gun and rolled down the window.

"Don't fire yet. Keep down." Hastings flipped his gun on the seat beside him as he continued evasive action.

Craig was shaking on the inside, but found that his hands were steady. He hoped he would not kill anyone. Aim for the tires, he told himself.

"Try one volley, then duck down," Hastings barked.

Craig leaned his head out the window, took aim and fired six shots. Both cars were careening about so much that he was sure he had missed, but suddenly the yellow sedan lurched to the right, hopped the curb and ploughed full speed into the boarded-up window of a laundromat. Wood and metal flew over an area of a hundred feet while Hastings skidded his car to a stop.

He and Craig jumped out, guns ready, but there was no need

to use them. The fugitives sat dazed and bleeding in the front seat of the yellow sedan. Trembling Craig covered them while Hastings radioed in a report of the action and half a dozen other patrol cars closed in on the scene. They waited until an ambulance arrived. "Got him in the shoulder," the medic announced after a quick examination of the driver.

"Great shot, Craig," said Hastings as they drove back to head-quarters to start the paper work. "I didn't know you were that good."

Craig fingered his gun. "I was aiming for a tire," he confessed. "And there's something else you should know. When you told me to cover them while you called in, I kept my gun on them okay. There was just one thing wrong. I forgot to reload it."

Hastings threw back his head and roared with laughter.


In the New York apartment he shared with Francis Chapman, Douglas Rymer awakened early on the Day of Silence and groped his way to the kitchen to make coffee. As he sipped it, his mind was busy with many things that bothered him. This apartment, for example. It was getting dirtier by the day. The cleaning woman had never showed up after the earthquake—killed, he supposed—and Francis had made no effort to find a new one.

And the awful meals. Here they were, close to Bishop Leonard whose organization distributed most of the world's food, yet Francis made no attempt to get special consideration. He scarcely seemed aware of what he ate. This sensual man with his fondness for food and drink was now apparently indifferent to his palate and ate whatever was available without comment.

But the worst problem was the way both Royal and Francis had changed in their attitude toward work. They often stayed away from the office for days, spending long hours closeted with the bishop at Celeste's apartment. Douglas was upset by this; he wanted to succeed and make good money. He had made great sacrifices for his career—he had not seen or even heard from Molly Redmond since he left Tampa back in May, nearly three months ago. Even before the earthquake disrupted mail and phone service, she had refused to answer his calls and letters. The only way he knew she and her grandfather had survived the disaster at all was through a note from her brother Scott to Royal. And now it appeared that the job for which he had given up his girl friend and his self-respect, was crumbling before his eyes.

It was after ten when Francis joined Douglas in the messy kitchen. Although it was a Friday, a busy day at work normally, he wore a pair of soiled and rumpled dungarees.

"I take it we aren't going to work," Douglas said.

Francis remained silent, pouring a cup of coffee.

"Aren't you even going to talk to me?" Douglas asked petulantly.

"It's supposed to be a day of silence, remember?"

"You can't be serious. You mean we're supposed to mill around here together all day without even speaking to each other?"

"We have been asked to spend the day meditating," Francis reminded him. "Opening ourselves to a Higher Power and seeking new thoughts and ideas. Did you think this didn't apply to you?"

Douglas shrugged. "Well, I sure didn't think you'd let it apply to you!"

"I don't know why. I'm not above a little spiritualizing. But you, of course, already have a spiritual life. I keep forgetting. You hide it so well."

"Francis, why are you so sarcastic all of a sudden?" Douglas emptied the coffee pot. The idea of a whole day of enforced idleness bored him. "I sure don't want to hang around here all day. What are you going to do besides meditate?"

Francis smiled enigmatically. "Don't worry about me. You just run along and leave me to my own devices."

Douglas left the room in frustration. He had no place to go, and he certainly did not want to start thinking.


It did not occur to Lucky Royal that it was incongruous to be spending the much publicized Day of Silence in a strategy session with Leonard and Celeste. Nor did it occur to him to wonder why Francis and Douglas were not included. This was a special meeting, Leonard informed him; basic decisions were to be made.

Celeste greeted Royal affectionately and had him sit very close to her on the couch. Celeste's sexual drives baffled Royal. They were either strong or nonexistent. She and Leonard, it appeared, had been meditating.

"You can depend on the spirits," the bishop announced. "They are going to respond to this day."

Celeste closed her eyes. "The spirits are coming . . . they are here . . . we will rule with them," she murmured dreamily.

She took both of Royal's hands in hers, holding them tightly. But it was the bishop he was listening to:

"Vicar of Jesus Christ, bishop of Rome, successor to the prince of apostles, supreme pontiff, primate of Italy, archbishop and metropolitan of the Roman Province, sovereign of the state and the city of the Vatican, absolute monarch . . ." The words rolled ponderously off Leonard's reasonant tongue.

Royal cleared his throat. "There are a few problems to resolve first, Your Grace." He saw himself as the lone man of action in the company of two visionaries.

Celeste opened her eyes and smiled. "It may not be as difficult as you assume, Lucky. Did you know that the election of a pontiff can take place anywhere? The only requirement is that one-half of the College of Cardinals, plus one, be present for the voting. And there aren't many cardinals remaining, out of more than a hundred. They shouldn't be troublesome, darling."

"But can we be absolutely certain," Royal persisted, "that the present pope is dead? Maybe he's recuperating from injuries at some secret hideaway."

Bishop Leonard gave a mirthless laugh. "Maybe he's with all those cardinals and bishops who are also missing. He's dead, all right—or permanently removed from the earth, which amounts to the same thing."

"And there are other obstacles," Royal continued, determined to keep the conversation on a pragmatic level. Once more he reviewed facts they all knew well. Since 1378 only cardinals had been elevated to the papacy. For centuries no non-European had held this highest office in the Roman Catholic Church. The pope is an absolute monarch, answerable to no temporal power, holding the oldest administrative office in existence and managing the largest nongovernmental operation in the world. His power is absolutely unlimited save by divine law, and only death or his own will can remove him from office.

As for the bishop, he was too young, not yet fifty. He was considered an American radical, an outsider, too ambitious, an upstart. Before the earthquake his goal would have been laughable. Now . . .

"Now is the time to make my move," Leonard insisted. "My worldwide support will be hard to resist. I know the remaining cardinals pretty well. They are practical men who will look out for their own interests. Everything will be simpler now that the fanatics are gone." His eyes took on a faraway look. "There's another means of election. A pope may be elected 'per inspirationem,' inspired as it were by the Holy Spirit."

"What does that mean?" Royal asked impatiently.

"The United States of Europe is the key." Leonard's smile was knowing. The earthquake had finally done what statesmen could not. After years of bickering, ten European nations were to ratify a treaty in Rome in November, officially creating this new political entity. "Here's our strategy," Leonard continued. "You will arrange for me to address the ceremony as the director of FML. That will be my moment of 'inspirationem.' You know the pressures to use to bring this off. Once the treaty is signed, I will be urged to occupy the Vatican."

He met Royal's incredulous gaze. "It will all happen just as I say. You will see."


It was the first of September, nearly two weeks after the Day of Silence, and the airwaves were still filled with reactions to this special event from around the world. In many places unusual sights and sounds had been reported. The most common manifestations were man-like figures clothed in shimmering light, attested to by thousands all over the world. Sometimes the apparitions were accompanied by voices giving instructions for daily conduct or new forms of worship. Others reported hearing disembodied voices and many reported psychical phenomena: tables levitating, goblets moving through the air and the like.

Everywhere interest in spiritual matters was soaring. Schools for metaphysical study and psychical research were deluged with inquiries, and churches, spiritist organizations and meditation centers reported vastly increased attendance. The dawning of the true Age of Man had been proclaimed. World leaders now praised Bishop Uriah Leonard as the new messiah.

Martha and Susie had started supper and had gone out to sit on the porch while the meager meal simmered on the stove. Locusts still moved sluggishly over the ground, but in greatly decreased numbers, and even to Martha they seemed preferable at this moment to the heat indoors.

"What's that, Mama?"

Susie pointed toward the boulevard. As Martha turned, she saw a moving mass of animals come bounding up the Redmond driveway, a howling, barking, boisterous crescendo of noise.

"Dogs. Wild dogs!"

Horror struck them both as they realized the lead dogs—three of them—were dragging the body of a stranger, a man perhaps in his forties or fifties. The animals behind were yelping as they nipped at parts of the tattered body being dragged ahead.

"Oh, God!" Martha screamed.

"Mama!" Susie's voice pierced Martha's consciousness. "Get in the house!"

They ran inside, slamming the door behind as the dogs dragged their prey to the foot of the steps. Madness, volcanic madness, filled the pack as every animal fought, clawed, bit and hurled itself into the melee to get its share.

By the time Craig had awakened and appeared with his gun, it was all over. Most of the animals had been satiated. Craig fired one shot in their midst and they slunk away.

Martha and Susie remained at the window, clinging to each other as Craig gathered the remains of the man into an old blanket he had retrieved from the garage. Jason and Stubby appeared and the three of them took the blanket behind the garage for burial.

The scene she had just witnessed convinced Martha that she had to have more protection. Obviously a gun was the answer. With a gun she could scare off a prowler or a pack of dogs; even the rats which were showing themselves more and more boldly. Craig could help her get one. After his shooting of the murderer

of the FML official, Craig was in good standing with this organization. She approached him in the garage with determination.

"You could tell them that you lost your gun," Martha concluded her argument. "They'd give you another one, and we could
have your old one here."

Craig was appalled. His mother often demonstrated naïveté
about the world, but this plan was sheer stupidity. "It would be
the unpardonable sin for me to lose my gun. I'd be under suspicion from that moment on."

"Well . . . what about the black market?" she asked. "The
judge says there's a lot of trading on the black market, and some of
it right down on Hyde Park Avenue."

"Mother, there may be trafficking in guns, but not by amateurs
like us. If we got caught, well—some of the things I've heard about
the jails today—you wouldn't want to hear them. Just forget about
it, please," he pleaded.

"I don't see why you say that," she protested. "A black market
isn't really illegal. It's just the law of supply and demand."

"And what do you think you have that's negotiable?"

"Well," she mused, "we have whiskey. Quite a bit of it. And
there is some cash. If you think about it, this place is loaded with
valuable things. There's silver and a stamp collection that's worth
a fortune. And I think some of the paintings are quite expensive."

"Has it occurred to you that all these things belong to the
judge?" Craig asked. "And who cares about silver and paintings
now, anyhow?"

"Well, a gun would be for the judge's protection, too," Martha
said. "Him and his family. Of course, I wouldn't trade anything of
his without asking him."

The conversation ended. But Martha's thoughts did not.


It was the following afternoon that she slipped out of the house.
A half-hour's walk to Hyde Park Avenue, an hour for bargaining
and a half-hour's return walk with the gun should get her back in
time to prepare dinner. In the waistband of her skirt, she had
folded nine one-hundred-dollar bills, a healthy portion of the cash
reserves kept in the judge's desk. She told herself she was entitled

to the money because some of it had been contributed by Hank and Craig from earnings. It was a moist little wad next to her skin.

Martha moved timidly through the streets, her apprehensions increasing with every step. In her desperation to have a gun she was exposing herself to the very dangers she feared. Were the wild dogs still prowling? What about those reports of cat-sized rats, huge hairy things which were terrorizing whole neighborhoods? She darted fearful looks around every corner. When a tired-looking old man confronted her going around one corner, she barely suppressed a scream.

The streets and sidewalks were still dotted by thousands of crawling insects. Six weeks ago this would have terrified Martha; now she scarcely noticed them. Martha's middle-class training had conditioned her into thinking that life was meant to go well, that she had a right to food when hungry, water when thirsty and rest when she was tired. She had been led to believe she would be protected not only from life's dangers, but also from its unpleasantness. Now many of the things which she had considered hers by right were no longer available. She felt wronged. It was to make right one situation that she was now walking along a danger-ridden street in terrible heat, equipped with stolen money with which to purchase an illegal gun.

Hyde Park had once been a lovely street, with ancient oak trees and large, comfortable houses built during the 1920s. The old homes were now intermingled with funeral parlors, art galleries, and professional offices, and the earthquake had left gaping holes in the roadbed.

Martha found the building Judge Redmond had mentioned and stood for a moment examining it. It was a three-story grey frame house with a brick porch fronting on the street. Some of the windows were boarded up, and drapes had been drawn over others, giving it an air of secretiveness. Martha climbed the shallow steps hesitantly. At the door she took a steadying breath and knocked.

The man who opened it was dark and heavyset, his eyes guarded. For a while he simply stared at Martha. At last he spoke, "You want something, lady?"

"Can I come inside?" she asked. "What I want to talk about is private."

The man stepped backward, and Martha scurried past him. The hall was dark, and her eyes took a moment to adjust to the gloom. When she could see, she took in a surprised breath. The passageway was crowded nearly to the ceiling with boxes and piles of items which seemed to have no order. There were television sets, canned goods, lawn mowers, clothing, books, barbeque grills, and bicycles—an untold wealth of priceless bicycles. She stared in wonder.

The man coughed impatiently, and Martha turned to him. She found her nervousness increasing now that the actual negotiations were upon her. She cleared her throat, then spoke boldly, "I want to buy a gun. They tell me you have some."

"Who told you that?" The man's voice was expressionless but Martha felt a stab of fear.

"That doesn't matter, does it? Just let me buy a gun, and I'll leave." She watched for some reaction in his face. "I won't tell anybody where I got it, either."

"What kind of gun you want?" he asked after a pause.

"Well, something to shoot dogs and rats with, you know. Those awful packs of dogs." She waited for his answer. His flat black eyes raked her thin body appraisingly.

"You got something to trade?" he asked finally.

Martha spread her empty hands. "I didn't bring anything with me. If you want anything we have at home, I'll bring it. Or maybe you want cash."

"We take cash," the man nodded. "How much you got?"

Martha hesitated, then spoke craftily. "Five hundred dollars."

"Adios, lady. You don't even have talking money." He turned away, the matter ended. He was not bluffing, she knew. She had underestimated the value of a gun.

"Wait, no. I'm wrong. I have nine hundred." She spoke eagerly and reached out to grab his arm. He shook his head as he turned back to her.

"Lady, I could get two thousand for a gun if I had one, which I'm not admitting. You're not the only one afraid of rats. Four-legged and two-legged." He had lost interest in her. Nine hundred dollars was not enough even to begin the bargaining. She was crushed. And suddenly terrified of the trip home.

"Please listen. I can't go out there again without some protec-

tion! Please! I swear I'll bring you some more when I can get it."
She was pleading now, holding his arm desperately. Somehow she
had bolstered her courage for the walk here, but she had none left
to see her back home.

The man shook his head, a shadow of annoyance crossing his
swarthy face. "Lady, I don't have a gun, and if I did, I sure
wouldn't sell it for credit." He opened the door, motioning for
her to leave.

"You can't do this," she protested. She felt tears welling up.
"You have to do something to help me," she insisted.

He watched her in disgust, then abruptly closed the door.
"Okay, lady. I'll help you out. I'll make you less of a target for
the muggers." He reached for the neck of her blouse and ripped it
open to the waist with one pull. She shrieked in fear and backed
away from him, covering her body with both arms.

"Where's the money, lady? If I take it, maybe nobody'll bother
you. You sure ain't got anything else anybody'd want." His eyes
raked her nakedness with contempt.

Martha backed away. She bumped into a stack of boxes and as
they tumbled down she felt his fingers slip into the waistband of
her skirt. She pushed against him, feeling the skirt loosen as the
button popped off. As she grabbed for it, he stooped to retrieve
the little wad of bills which had fallen to her feet.

"Here we go," he said happily. "Now you're safe."

Martha held the skirt with one hand and clasped her blouse together with the other, watching him as he counted the bills. "You
can't do that," she said again.

"Sure I can, lady. I just did." He stopped smiling as he pocketed
the money. "Anyhow, money is worth less every day; you didn't
lose so much." He took her by the elbow, propelling her toward
the door.

"I can't go home without that money. It wasn't even mine!"
She was crying and felt a good case of hysterics coming on.

"Well, now it's mine," he said simply.

"Look at my clothes!" she protested. "I can't go out like this!
Don't you have any decency?"

"Not much. But I will give you a safety pin." He fumbled
through the stacks of boxes and produced a small cellophane bag
of safety pins. "Here, you can have the whole bag," he said.

She accepted the pins, turning her back to him to repair her damaged clothing.

"Don't think about coming back later to get the money," he said. "You come here again and you'll end up wishing you was out there with the rats."

Martha's hands were shaking so much it was difficult to pin her clothing. There was nothing left in her of the crafty wheeler-dealer who had come so optimistically to purchase a gun.

As she descended the steps toward the sidewalk she heard the click of the lock behind her. "I wish I could just die," she said to no one. And with that thought she summed up the torture of the times; to be forced to continue to live when life was unbearable.

*Effective Monday, September 12, 1988,* a curfew will be imposed between the hours of sunset and sunrise. All citizens not engaged in essential occupations or holding Class C Employment Cards are directed to be off the streets during these hours.
> Charles Stillman, Hillsborough County Executive
> FML International, Tampa, Florida

*Beginning at midnight, Saturday, September 17, 1988,* no vehicle traffic will be permitted on any state or federal highway without travel permits to be issued by FML offices of Transportation Control. Applications for permits are available at all local centers.
> Joseph Corella, Southeastern Coordinator
> FML International, Atlanta, Georgia

*Beginning October 1, 1988,* all members of building trade unions will work only through FML offices and on jobs assigned by officials of this group. Property owners who have repair work to be done should contact FML for priority assignment.
> John Tipitt, Regional Director of Housing
> FML International, Tallahassee, Florida

*Violations of the Energy Control Regulations* instituted July 6, 1988, will carry mandatory jail sentences as of October 1, 1988. Citizens holding Class C Employment Cards, including doctors, policemen, firemen, etc., will no longer be exempt.
> Samuel Peterson, Department of Conservation
> FML International, Washington, D.C.

As September passed and the heat continued unabated, the men often joined Stubby, Jason and Craig for evenings of conversation in the relative coolness of the garage. Generally the talk centered on the steady flow of governmental directives, all co-issued now by the ubiquitous FML, which it was one of Hank's duties to circulate through the neighborhood.

Or it dwelt on the increasingly stringent fuel and food rationing. Certain products had disappeared from stores entirely: coffee, tea, soft drinks and rubber goods. Others—tobacco products, alcoholic beverages, tools and hunting weapons—were in short supply with prices soaring and a flourishing black market. Martha's humiliating experience had had a sobering effect on the whole household.

Many people in America were actually hungry. Food reserves were gone and society was dependent on current production. Drinking water was another problem. The people of Tampa were fortunate to have the bay and the river available for washing and bathing. Selling bottled water for drinking was one of the few businesses that prospered.

Only the very wealthy and high officials of Feed My Lambs had their own transportation. With less traffic, it seemed pointless to repair the broken streets so this activity was abandoned. Horses had become valuable, more so than automobiles. The value of bicycles soared; in locations near water like Tampa, so did the value of rowboats and canoes. The vast majority of people, however, transported themselves as humans always had, on foot.

With the entertainment industry almost shut down and television operating only a few hours a week, people were spending their spare time reading; libraries were always filled, with long waiting lists for popular books. Family games were being rediscovered. Also conversation.

Jason surprisingly was becoming more vocal, although still preoccupied with unearthly matters. Only occasionally did he contribute anything to a practical subject under discussion, but at those times there was wisdom in his utterances. And he had made the garage pleasantly homey. Not one of the three cars which had once been housed there was still in running order; two had been pushed outside and covered up to make more room within. Jason had fitted out one corner of this free space as his home. He had a single cot, two plastic lawn chairs, his mother's old wooden rocker which Craig and Hastings had salvaged for him from the wreckage of her home, a small patch of carpet and a long low table on which he kept his books, a lantern and a small but flourishing collection of plants. Nothing matched, all items were castoffs, but they fitted together somehow, creating an area that was peaceful and secure, and it was here that the group met in preference to the hotter apartment upstairs.

"I guess we ought to take up whittling, Hank," Scott said one evening toward the end of the month. "Isn't that what men used to do to pass the time?"

"There's plenty to do, I guess, if we wanted to. Craig has been talking about starting a garden again." Hank had grown thinner, and his hands now had a gentle tremor.

"Nothing would grow unless it rains, and I think it's forgotten how," Scott mourned.

"It sure would be nice to have enough to eat for a change," Hank sighed.

"Go ahead and try, Hank, but you'd probably get it all planted and we'd get some more locusts or something," Scott said.

"No more locusts, Scott," Jason interposed. "They will only last five months and then be gone."

"Good. I won't miss them at all. And since you know all about it, what's the next misery on the agenda?" Scott grinned at Jason.

Jason smiled back. "A lot is going on in heaven. As for our earth, I guess it would be the desolating sin in the sanctuary. You know, the daily sacrifice and the host trampled underfoot. It's supposed to happen about seven and a half months from the beginning of the Tribulation."

"What's all this about hosts and sacrifices?" Judge Redmond asked. "You don't sound like a good old hardshell Baptist to me, Jason. That sounds Catholic."

Jason sat up straight, his face astonished. "That may be true, sir. There may be one Abomination for the Christians, another for the Jews." He turned to Stubby, eyes excited. "We'll have to check this out!"

Scott groaned in mock despair. "Anybody know what these guys are talking about? They're so wrapped up in that darn Bible they don't know what's going on around them."

"I wish I had something to keep me from knowing," Hank replied. "Things seem to be getting worse and worse. Now we hear that the schools won't reopen at all this fall. Too much civil disorder, they say; it would be dangerous for the young people."

"Getting those kids shut up somewhere under supervision would cut down on the civil disorder," Scott retorted. "They're half the problem."

"But . . . if the young are not educated," Judge Redmond said thoughtfully, "where will leadership come from in the future?"

The group in the garage fell silent. "Future" was the one word about which nobody cared to speculate.


# II


Once he had become prime minister of Israel, Naphtali Seth Ben Daniel moved quickly to consolidate his power. He combined an earthy eagerness for work with soaring intellectual achievements. A fifth generation sabra, he was a son of the land, the product of the Israeli army and years of living on a kibbutz. He also held a doctorate from the Hebrew University. With Israel now developing her new-found wealth of oil, Ben Daniel moved with dignity and aplomb among the leaders of the world. He was en route now to Rome to witness the signing of the treaty among the soon-to-be-formed United States of Europe.

Rome was alive with anticipation and excitement for the November 1988 event, the focus of all eyes. Even though the Italian government was in tatters and civil order was maintained by armed troops, once again Rome was the center of political activity. She welcomed her illustrious visitors like an aging courtesan, covering the ravages of time with shoddy disguises and smiling from behind a raveled fan.

The city was filthy; litter and debris accumulated appallingly. Ragged strips of billboards and posters dangled limply from innumerable buildings and graffitti marred even the most sacred shrines. Traffic was at a minimum: gasoline sold for $15 per gallon when available. With the decline of tourism, even desultory attempts to maintain ancient monuments were abandoned. The ruins of past glory, irreplacable buildings and treasures were being allowed to decay.

On arrival Ben Daniel was given an enormous suite in the most luxurious of the hotels used for the visiting statesmen. The building was over one hundred years old, its marbled halls still beautiful and its aging elevators, plumbing and wiring functional if inefficient. The rooms were superficially clean, the attendants dressed in formal attire, and the kitchen stocked with supplies rushed in from FML warehouses. Like the employees, hired and dressed especially for the occasion, certain areas of the hotel were prepared for show, others were left to the rats.

Once within his private quarters, Ben Daniel lifted the ancient telephone and rattled flawless Italian to the hotel's switchboard. The operator was apologetic: no lines were working to the Vatican. An inexcusable lack of efficiency, but not surprising. He called one of his aides into the room. "Please obtain transportation for me to the Vatican. Bishop Leonard is staying there, and I plan to join him for dinner."

The car was a seven-year-old Buick, spotlessly clean inside. It crossed the Tiber in a cloud of bluish exhaust and deposited Ben Daniel at the entrance to the Piazza of the Protomartiri, to the left of St. Peter's. From there he was escorted by a colorfully dressed Swiss guard into the Vatican palaces. Their steps sounded hollowly along the stone corridors. It was a long walk, but Ben Daniel kept busy observing the art work which lined the way, impressed despite himself with the value of such treasures. The place seemed deserted.

At last they reached the apartments assigned to Bishop Leonard. The guard knocked, then left in silence as the door opened.

"My first visit to the Vatican." Ben Daniel smiled without humor. "It has a certain style, I must say."

"Yes. It means a great deal to millions of people." The bishop led him into an inner room. The apartment was ancient, clean, ascetic. "Rome, the Eternal City," the bishop continued. "For nearly three thousand years she has hovered in maternal love over the affairs of mankind."

"That might be more impressive to another man, Your Grace," Ben Daniel observed drily. "I come from a city of even greater age, one which also considers herself a Holy City. Your palaces here are young to the sons of Abraham."

"Touché," the bishop laughed good-naturedly.

"I hope we can talk frankly tonight," Ben Daniel went on bluntly. "We may not have another opportunity for some time."

"We are quite alone," Bishop Leonard agreed. He poured two glasses of a pale wine. "You are aware of the plans, are you not? You approve?"

"Yes, yes, of course." Ben Daniel spoke impatiently. "We serve the same powers."

"Then I must caution you about two men in your country at this moment, two men who are our enemies."

"Who are they?" Ben Daniel asked.

"The first is a young man, oh, late twenties, early thirties. His name is, I believe, Elias Johnson—almost too apt a name. His mother was a Syrian, and his father a German, I think. This young man is involved in some kind of journalistic effort; he claims to be writing a history of some monastic order. It is almost certainly not true, but that makes little difference. He has several characteristics which concern us. He is intense and a loner. He spends a great deal of his time in the desert doing this research. Physically, he is tanned, lean, tough and leathery. He is a fanatical Christian. And hear this well: he is *not* a recent convert! He has been a devout and pious man all of his life, from what I can determine." The bishop cocked his head toward Ben Daniel and waited expectantly.

"If he were a believer before the earthquake, he should be gone," Ben Daniel said. "But we can't go by appearances. We might find hundreds of men who *appeared* to be good Christians before who are still around. But I agree, it is ominous. Anything else?"

"Nothing specific. Just the general characteristics, the area of the country, and of course the name."

"All right," Ben Daniel nodded. "I'll take care of it. You said there were two. What about the other one?"

"This man may just be a crackpot. He was a minister, some fundamental Protestant sect. He left his ministry and went to Egypt for some unknown reason and accepted a position with the Red Cross there. He was evidently quite a valuable employee, and he made a name for himself around Port Said as a man who could get things done. More recently, he served as a UN observer in the Sinai, and how he ever got that position I'll never figure out. He does have a flair for language, and that may have helped. At any rate, since the earthquake and the new regime, he has stayed in the desert for the most part, preaching. He's more the shepherding type than the evangelical. I'm not so sure of this one." The bishop trailed off.

"And his name? It might be of some value."

"Oh, yes. Of course. Amos Mozell. Another thought-provoking name."

"It is indeed. I will put my men on it," Ben Daniel spoke quietly. "Don't worry."

"Good." The bishop sat up straighter. "Now, what is your reading of the ten nations?"

"Three of them are shaky," replied Daniel.

"England, Switzerland and the Netherlands," Leonard supplied.

"That is correct. What is your plan?"

The bishop shrugged. "We control food distribution. It shouldn't be necessary to use a club."

"And you would like me to apply the same strategy with oil?"

"Only if they prove stubborn," the bishop answered. "The treaty ceremony will take place here day after tomorrow as planned."

Ben Daniel nodded slowly. "And your plans for the papacy?"

"There will be no problem. Another three months, and the plum will be mine for the plucking." The bishop's voice was a purr.

"Your Grace, I must be frank. I am aware of your illegitimacy. Is this not a bar to the papacy?" Ben Daniel studied the depths of his wine glass rather than the face of his companion.

There was no quick answer this time. Then the bishop spoke again, his voice smooth. "Your Excellency moves carefully. Not many people know the facts about my background, and even fewer that such a situation, if it exists, would be a hindrance to the throne. Please don't be concerned. I am just as much my father's son as any man and I will be protected."

"Very well. Now let us speak of other things." Ben Daniel produced a folder of maps and charts and the two men moved closer together.

"Every time you two start talking, I get a picture in my mind of an old man in a long robe, walking around with a sign that says, 'Repent, the end of the world is coming.' " The judge chuckled and both Stubby and Jason smiled in response. Then Stubby became earnest.

"We're not old and we don't have robes, but the rest of it is right. We are convinced that the end is near and with it the second coming of Jesus."

The judge settled himself more comfortably in the aging lawn chair which graced Jason's garage home. This was not their first talk and he was learning a respect for the two young men which surprised him. "I can remember the '30s very well. People said the same thing then that you're saying now."

"But the Jews were still dispersed," Stubby protested. "They had to return to their homeland before the end could come."

"Obviously people in the '30s were wrong," the judge continued. "But many situations were similar. The economy was shot. Men worked for as little as a nickel an hour and were glad to get that. I remember my father resharpening razor blades and Mother using 25-watt bulbs to save money. There wasn't enough money in the treasury to meet the federal payroll. When Roosevelt took office, he closed the banks. People had to use IOUs, bartering, foreign money, all sorts of things to do business."

"But there hadn't been earthquakes," Stubby countered. "And locusts. Or the freaky weather. Or drug abuse. Or blatant homosexuality and immorality."

"I agree. It's worse now, but there were some striking similarities," the judge replied. "There was this NRA, a Blue Eagle to put in your window. Folks were supposed to boycott places that didn't have a Blue Eagle—something like this FML thing today.

Some Christians wouldn't trade where there was an eagle because they thought it was the mark of the beast right out of the book of Revelation."

"I never knew about that," Jason said.

"Oh, there was more. Government agencies used the emergency to take authority over private lives. Commissions were set up and wielded power they had no right to. And the thing kept spreading—just like FML is now. If you have any influence with heaven I suggest you stop worrying about the end of the world and get busy seeing what you can do about the here and now."

Stubby shook his head. Despite his youth he spoke with authority. "That's not what we're here for. I believe we're to pattern ourselves after the New Testament church. The early Christians didn't try to change the political system which condoned slavery and dictatorships and injustice almost as bad as what we have now. They didn't try to change the social order; they tried to bring salvation to the people."

"I heard a preacher explain it very well," Jason said in agreement. "He said this world is a sinking ship. Our job is not to try to patch up the leaks but to get the crew off safely."

"There are other reasons why this period is more likely to be the end times than the '30s were," Stubby said, returning to their original subject. "We can show you in the Bible the prophecies that weren't fulfilled then which are now."

"All right, show me. I'm perfectly willing to listen." Judge Redmond smiled and once again the three bent over Carrie Lee's tattered Bible.


The United States of Europe.

A long-awaited dream had at last grown into reality out of the European Economic Common Market. England, France, West Germany, Italy, Spain, Greece, Belgium, Switzerland, Luxembourg and the Netherlands were forming a federal union.

With Israel as witness.

With her new oil wealth had come new power, and no important political event could take place without at least tacit recognition of the Jewish state. The treaty-signing ceremony, however, provided more than this. Israel would sign a separate pact once the formal treaty was a reality; a pact guaranteeing protection of Israeli borders.

The guest of honor would be the director of Feed My Lambs, Bishop Uriah Leonard. Although FML would not be an official party to either the treaty or the USE-Israeli pact, certain provisions were included in both which guaranteed FML's status as world provider and protector.

The morning dawned bright and clear, a blue Italian sky smiling benignly on the decaying city. Delegates, members of the press and several thousand invited guests from all over the world —business and religious leaders, statesmen and military men— jammed the huge assembly hall of the Borgia Palace, a large square orange edifice in downtown Rome.

As Uriah Leonard rose to address the gathering, the applause was a thunder of noise, a crescendo of adulation. For fully fifteen minutes the assembled dignitaries demonstrated their enthusiasm for the man they hoped would restore normalcy, order and plenty to the world. The man in command stood erect, barely smiling, eyes looking beyond the throng to some point in time beyond their comprehension.

At last the applause died down and the delegates were seated, the air electric. Leonard's appearance was hypnotic, his eyes seeming to pierce them all even though he looked at none of them. His words were more than spoken: they were intoned.

"The word of the spirit is confirmed today, the word first spoken by the prophet Isaiah. Today we can attest to its reality. Hear the word:

> The spirit is upon me;
>     For my lord has anointed me;
> He has sent me to bring good news to the humble, to bind
>         up the broken-hearted,
>     to proclaim liberty to captives
>         and release to those in prison;
>     to proclaim a year of my lord's favour
>         and a day of vengeance of my god;
>     to comfort all who mourn,
>     to give them garlands instead of ashes,
>         oil of gladness instead of mourners' tears,
>         a garment of splendour for the heavy heart.

The audience was transfixed as the vaguely familiar words flowed from Leonard's awesome visage. As he paused, they barely breathed for fear of disrupting the solemnity of the moment. When he spoke again, the bishop relaxed; his eyes began to scan the gathering, seeking personal confrontation with individual faces.

"This day belongs to my lord, the source of our strength, the giver of our insight; the one who has brought us together now to share this moment.

"He has anointed me! And no one can remove this mantle of leadership. On this great day, when the nations come together peaceably to seek solutions to our pressing problems, do not forget that our lord is supreme."

He continued, congratulating the ten nations on the formation of USE, lauding the presence of Israel at the ceremony, and emphasizing the all-encompassing activity of his own FML as it sought to relieve suffering.

"And now, dear friends, a more somber note. On this day of rejoicing let us not neglect to bring to our minds those who would trample and destroy what we are doing. I assure you, my people, we will not tolerate the subversive conduct of any who would attempt to detract from these monumental achievements. They will not be allowed to oppose our sacred mission—this I promise you!"

The audience was on its feet again, screaming defiance to all opposition, yelling their support for the bishop, applauding, stomping, in a great cacophony of sound releasing the pent-up tension and frustration of the past bitter months. Leonard's final words rose above it all.

"Hear, O mankind! Your savior is here!"

The green eyes were flashing now; the flesh on his face was taut, his arms raised, fists clenched, his smile triumphant.

The signing of the treaty was an anticlimax.

That afternoon Madame Celeste, Lawrence Royal, Francis Chapman, Douglas Rymer, Uriah Leonard and Naphtali Seth Ben Daniel met for a victory celebration at Leonard's quarters in the Vatican. It was Royal who attempted to put their thoughts into words.

"Bishop," he began tentatively, "I pride myself on being at least somewhat immune to the emotional pressures of propaganda or salesmanship, but you were something else today. It was— magnificent!"

As the others eagerly concurred, Douglas sat struggling with himself, awed by the power he had felt, sickened by his weakness to do anything but look on in wonder and amazement. A thought was forming in his mind which he knew he should suppress. But could not.

"You raped Scripture."

The words hung in the air like thunderclouds.

"What did you say?" Francis asked incredulously.

Douglas wished fervently he could take back his words, but something kept prodding him. "I said that the bishop raped Scripture. He took words from the Bible and twisted them."

He was staring intently at a point on the floor as he spoke, unable to face his accusers.

"Well, you'd better apologize, and quickly," Francis snapped. "You're here as Bishop Leonard's guest."

Celeste moved toward him, arms outstretched as though she wanted to strangle him. Abruptly she let them fall to her sides. "He's a waste," she said indifferently. "He's not one of them and he's not one of us. He's nothing. Why should we shelter him?"

"Precisely, my dear," said the bishop, "because he *is* a middle-of-the-roader. 'Lukewarm,' I believe, is their word. Douglas is a sort of cross section of humanity; a little bit of everything, a lot of nothing. He wishes to be strong, but shies away from the commitment which would make him so. He is more valuable to us than you imagine."

Ben Daniel had been sitting across the room, his cool eyes absorbing everything, the agile mind retaining all he saw. "You are right, of course," he said approvingly. "His value is in his lack of virtue. Now may I suggest we turn our attention to important matters. What was the reaction from the cardinals?"

Leonard sat down opposite Ben Daniel. "Positive. In fact, one word came voluntarily from every one of them. 'Inspired.' "

"Then there should be no problem?"

"No problem. The remaining cardinals and bishops met informally with me after the ceremony and agreed among themselves. Mark this—they did not agree on my assuming the papacy. They simply concurred that I was inspired. And as we discussed, this is the important point to have on record."

"It appears as if everything is in order then."

"Everything is in order."


Jason's various accomplishments began to impress the Redmonds and McKenzies. When Craig brought home a live chicken one day, no one knew how to kill or dress it. Jason appeared, quickly wrung the chicken's neck, then efficiently prepared it for stewing. When it was discovered that Jason was an amateur barber, his status rose even higher. Susie and Molly were his first customers, and the judge, Hank, Craig and Stubby also accepted his efforts gratefully. Finally even Scott, usually vain about his appearance, presented himself in the garage for a trim. As Jason snipped and combed, the two men talked.

Jason and Scott were close in age, and had known each other superficially all the years Jason's mother had worked in the Redmond kitchen. Although separated by class and race, before the earthquakes they had always had a lot in common, sharing the attitudes and prejudices of their generation. While Scott moved imperceptibly toward alcoholism, Jason had been ensnared by more lethal drugs. Both had embraced sexual freedom, both had acquired a patina of social conscience, spouting at length about 'rights' with little concern for responsibilities.

Jason, however, had gone through a searing process of regeneration following his mother's disappearance during the earthquake. In Scott he saw his old patterns of thought, his old hang-ups. It gave him a great burden for the judge's grandson.

"I'm no professional, you know," he warned as he brushed Scott's dark hair. "I can get it shorter, but I can't give it much style."

"With the company I've been keeping lately, it would be wasted anyhow," Scott reassured him. "I haven't had anything going for me in so long I can hardly remember what it was like." He laughed ruefully. "I'm hoping sex is like riding a bicycle, something you don't forget. Cause, believe me, it's been a long, dry spell."

Jason clipped a dark lock and stepped back to view his handi-
work.

"How do you manage?" Scott asked suddenly. "Don't you
miss it?"

"Honestly, Scott, I've never been happier. I don't miss a single
thing from that old life." Jason chuckled. "Even in the middle of
it, I had a hard time convincing myself it was satisfying me. Now
I know it wasn't."

Scott raised a dubious eyebrow. "Why the big change?"

Jason stood silent, thinking. "Something supernatural touched
me. Nothing else could have made a believer of me. I know
Momma tried just about every other way. I didn't want to change."

They were interrupted by the sound of a car in the driveway.
This was such an unusual event that Scott rose, shrugged off the
towel around his neck and they both walked toward the open
doors of the garage. Outside a police car bearing the FML emblem
had stopped near the house.

Judge Redmond was walking down the back steps toward the
vehicle and Jason laid a restraining hand on Scott's shoulder.
With his snowy hair and erect carriage, dressed in dark coat and
tie now that the weather was cooler, the judge looked very much
in charge of the situation.

Two large men in plain clothes stepped out of the squad car.
One remained silent, leaning against the front fender, while his
partner spoke.

"Your name Curry?" he asked gruffly.

"No, they live down the block. The tan stucco," Judge Redmond answered.

"You got some proof who you are?" the man asked.

"I have identification, of course, but I repeat, this is not the
Curry residence."

"Better watch your mouth, Gramps. We don't have to take no
lip off you." The man spoke without anger and made no move to
leave.

"If you have legitimate business with me, please state it," the
judge said. "I was interrupted in the middle of a book and I
should like to return to it."

"You ever hear of the Butcher Act?" the officer asked. "It gives
me the power to take you in, Gramps, if I think you're exhibiting

antisocial behavior. I stop off at some FML clinic and get a doctor to sign it, and you're in for 'observation.' What this does, it gets us to expecting polite answers. It's just amazing how people will go to almost any length to keep from being 'observed'. Isn't that right, Donny?" He turned to his partner for confirmation.

"And to what length must I go?" the judge inquired dispassionately. The two in the garage held their breaths as they watched the drama unfold.

"I figure that was about a fifty-dollar insult." The officer smiled for the first time.

The judge pondered this for a moment, then disappeared into the house. He returned quickly and counted out five ten-dollar bills, meticulously turning each bill in the same direction, green side up. As he finished he looked into the face of the officer. "Will you tell me something, please? Was I selected at random, or did you come here by design?"

The officer shrugged his massive shoulders. "It was just the breaks of the game, Gramps. We really do have a warrant for Curry, and you just happened to get in the way. No big plot." The officers then drove off.

When Craig woke up later that afternoon, he and Stubby and Jason met with the judge in the garage to discuss the police car episode. "From your description I can't identify them," said Craig. "But that's not surprising. There are hundreds of new men in the Protective Agency. Police control has become a big thing with FML lately."

Jason leaned forward from his seat on the cot. "I believe that organization is directly under the control of the Antichrist, and I believe Bishop Leonard is the one. The first beast in the thirteenth chapter of Revelation we were talking about last week, sir," he said to the judge.

The older man shook his head. "I find all that very hard to accept."

"I do too, Judge," said Craig. "But day by day I'm becoming more convinced that what we're going through is all spelled right out in Scripture."

"But why wouldn't more people be talking about this?" asked the judge.

"Because everybody who believed it has gone to heaven. The

people in the churches now never did see any reality in it," said Craig. "And the new Christians, the Johnny-come-latelys like Stubby and Jason and me—if we say too much, we get arrested."

"But even if we're in danger," Stubby put in, "don't we have an obligation to tell people what we believe? Shouldn't we say something?"

"I don't know," said Craig. "You're the one the angel came to."

"Yeah, Stubby," Jason spoke with affection. "Tell us what to do, glorious leader."

Stubby looked remarkably small and youthful, though he had just passed his sixteenth birthday, but now his face became resolute. "Well, if you really are asking me, I think we ought to tell everybody we can that the Antichrist is here. Tell them they should turn to God."

"Send us out two by two, Stubby," Jason smiled. "If we count the judge that would make two teams."

The little group fell silent, weighing their slender resources. One elderly man, not yet committed to the cause. One young Jewish boy. One black man, recently on drugs. One high school dropout.

"What good could we do?" Craig summed up the gloomy picture. "We can't even convince members of our own family."

"Well, I've just made a decision." The judge brought both hands down on the arms of the lawn chair. "I want what you boys have."

Scott appeared in the open doorway and the judge took him in with a sweeping gesture. "Scott, you might as well hear this, too. For weeks I have been reading the Bible and talking with these young men. I started with skepticism. Along the way has come belief. As of this moment I accept Jesus Christ as my Lord and Savior. I pledge Him my loyalty, my obedience, the use of my worldly goods, my life."

Scott blinked at his grandfather in bewilderment. "Now that may not be the dumbest thing you ever did, Grandpa, but it's got to rank somewhere up in the top ten."

The judge turned to him with utmost seriousness. "No, Scott. It's the smartest. If you want to participate or learn, please stay and watch somebody being born again. If you prefer to scoff, I'll ask you to leave. This is all new to me and I don't want to have to fight your disapproval quite yet."

Scott blinked again. "Sure, I'll take off. I don't want to make waves."

His elaborately casual exit was lost on the joyful group in the garage.


When Hastings dropped Craig off at the driveway early the next morning, Molly was waiting for him on the porch. "I'd like to talk about my grandfather," she said tersely.

"Let's do," he replied, dropping into the chair next to hers.

Molly stared at Craig for a few moments, surprised at her own uncertainty. She was aware of changes in Craig since that first encounter with him in this very driveway almost six months ago. His mouth was firmer, his eyes more direct, his body tougher. There was something else too that Molly couldn't identify, a quality of inner strength that went with the outer hardening of muscles and skin.

"I don't understand what happened to my grandfather," Molly began.

"He's asked Jesus to be Lord of his life."

"It seems utterly ridiculous to me and Scott—and we talked about this last night—that Grandfather would feel the need to do this. He's been a churchgoer and a good man all of his life."

Craig shifted position in his chair. "It's hard for me to understand, too. I went to Sunday School as a kid, but it was boring and I stopped. Then Stubby and Jason started making Christ and His teachings seem important to me, important and exciting."

"But you're normal and sensible about it," Molly objected. "Stubby and Jason . . . well, they're fanatics."

"If they seem like fanatics, it's because they both had such dramatic—"

Molly raised her hand to interrupt. "I've heard all that crazy stuff. Stubby thinks he saw an angel, and Jason swears up and down that Carrie Lee disappeared in a puff of smoke or something right in front of his eyes. He admits himself he was on drugs. And Stubby was probably hit on the head when his house caved in. You don't seriously expect me to believe them?"

"Maybe not, Molly. But my experience wasn't anything like that."

"Your experience?" she asked dubiously.

"Yes, if you can call it that. I mean, nothing sensational happened. It was more an inner feeling. You remember that Day of Silence back last August?"

"Day of Boredom, you mean. I didn't see any bright lights or hear any voices like those people claimed they did."

"I'm glad you didn't, Molly," Craig said earnestly. "I'm convinced that a lot of what people saw and heard that day wasn't coming from God at all."

"But you did hear from Him, of course," Molly mocked him.

Craig refused to be drawn into their usual sparring match. "Like I said, I didn't really hear anything. I just sat in the apartment over there, and thought about things. I was praying, I guess. I know Stubby was, in his room. Anyhow, I suddenly realized it wasn't enough just being honest, trying to help people like Hastings and I do. I suddenly knew that without God, it was all nothing. Worse than nothing. So I simply asked Him to take over."

"And that was all?"

"Well, the next day I told Stubby and Jason about it, and they'd done the same thing. In fact long before. But the three of us decided we should do something to sort of mark the occasion. We didn't have anyone to teach us what Christians are supposed to do, so we just got down on our knees around Jason's cot and told Jesus that we loved Him and wanted to do what He told us." He smiled at Molly's baffled countenance. "Now, does that make me a fanatic?"

"I don't know," she shrugged. "I guess it depends on what you believe He's telling you to do. I mean, shooting that murderer. That was really good. That was hardly what one of these nose-in-the-Bible nuts would do."

"I was aiming for the tires," Craig replied. "It was a lucky shot, or a bad shot, however you want to look at it. I would have felt awful if that man had died."

"Well, if you insist on being considered a fanatic," she flared, "that's your business. I just don't want to see my grandfather get that way."

"And if 'that way' brings him joy and peace of mind? What's more important, his well-being, or saving your precious self a little embarrassment?" Craig had to admit that something within him wanted to needle Molly. She attracted him enormously in spite of the fact that his rational mind told him she was selfish, spoiled and cold-hearted. Now he watched the color rise on her cheeks with a mixture of feelings.

"Are you insinuating I don't love my grandfather?"

"Of course not. But I've come to love your grandfather too. I think what happened to him last night was great. I think it would be great if it happened to you."

"There's no chance of that!"

"What makes you immune to God's love? Look Molly, I've heard you used to go with some guy named Douglas who walked out on you. I don't blame you for being sore. But it's obvious he wasn't right for you. Did it ever occur to you that God was watching over you—that He might have been protecting you?"

Molly was on her feet, eyes blazing. "What happened between Douglas and me is none of your business."

"I know that. I'm not trying to pry into your personal life. But I can see that you're hurting inside and I'd like to be helpful. Obviously I'm not."

"That's the understatement of the century." Indifferent to the sleeping household upstairs, Molly slammed the porch door behind her.

As Craig watched her go, he found himself breathing a surprising prayer. "Lord, please turn this selfish, angry, beautiful woman into one of your gracious children."


Life at the Redmonds' was becoming increasingly tedious for Susie McKenzie. With no school and no means of transportation, she had little to do except help her mother in the kitchen, watch the thin fare on TV, or read. None of this was fun. The coarseness of sex on the beach had not fulfilled her either, she admitted to herself. Yet now she found herself yearning for a physical relationship. But with whom?

Stubby and Jason were obviously out. Only Scott had potential. The twelve years difference in age made Scott seem absurdly old for her at first. But he was good-looking, sexy and above all, he was at hand.

She began trying to win his attention in subtle ways. They

did not work. Nettled, she considered the possibility that he simply was not attracted to her. That did not make sense: Susie knew her assets. She decided on a direct frontal approach.

But it was difficult to catch him alone. Scott worked during the day, and at night had other diversions both at home and away. By the time she finally caught him walking alone along the seawall after a swim, she was thoroughly frustrated.

"Was the water nice?" she began casually. Late November was a bit chilly for open-air bathing, but at least fish and other marine life were appearing again in the bay. With the decrease in manufacturing and mechanized transportation, the water was actually cleaner than it had been in years.

"Not especially, but it's better than smelling bad. I'd give my right arm for some deodorant." He smiled and she giggled nervously.

"I never seem to catch you alone," she complained. "You're always talking to Daddy or somebody."

"Oh?" He was waiting politely, but she sensed his eagerness to be gone.

"I wanted to talk to you alone." Susie's confidence was waning. She had dressed as attractively and as revealingly as possible, but he seemed not to notice.

"Well, here I am. What can I do for you? I can't offer you a career in TV anymore. I never could, really, but lots of girls thought I could." He chuckled, remembering. "The oldest line in the book, but it really worked."

"I don't care about a career. I just wanted to talk to you about us."

"Us? You mean—the McKenzies and the Redmonds?"

"Not our families. Us. You and me. That's what 'us' means, isn't it?" She was feeling more and more foolish.

"Well, what about us, Susie?"

"I thought maybe we could get together, meet sometimes, you know. Be together." She was floundering, unheard of for Susie. Finally, in a rush of irritation, she finished: "Make love, stupid."

He was standing very still, watching her. He did not laugh and she realized how afraid she had been that he might. Laughter would have destroyed her. "Do you do much of this sort of thing?" he asked finally.

"Well, I used to, but I never see anybody now. That's why I picked you."

"Very flattering." But his voice was more amused than sarcastic. He put his hands on her shoulders and leaned back against the seawall, examining her at arms' length. "How old are you, Susie?"

"Seventeen. Mama gave me a birthday party, remember? Look, if you're worried that I'm a virgin or anything, forget it. I was thirteen, the first time."

"All the same, we'd have to be careful. I wouldn't want your folks to know."

"Don't worry about them. They never see anything." Susie moved closer to Scott, snuggling her head against his chest. It had been no problem at all. Even at his age, and coming from a well-to-do family and everything, he was just like all the rest.


"I thought your attitude toward the bishop was childish and insulting." Francis and Douglas were back in their New York apartment. It was a cold December night and for the first time in weeks they were alone together. Francis had been manicuring his nails. Douglas was working on a jigsaw puzzle.

"Keep it up," Francis continued his verbal assault, "and you'll be out of a job."

Douglas poured himself another double bourbon over ice and stood at a window looking out on the street below. He did not trust himself to answer his companion of six months. If he had he would have told Francis to take the job and stuff it. He drew a deep breath. "You know what's happening, Francis. Doesn't it bother you? You grew up in the church just like I did. Deep down you still must care a little."

"No, I don't know and no, I don't care! What I do know is that your behavior was inexcusable."

At last Douglas turned and looked at him. "Francis, take a look around you. Leonard is trying to take over the world. He's taking over people's minds. You were there, you heard it."

"Doug, most people in this friggin' world are starving. If Leonard takes over, don't forget we take over with him. We've got power—real power, almost in our hands, and I'm not going to let you screw it up."

They were glaring at each other now with the intensity that comes from a too close relationship.

"Francis, that man stood there before all those people and blasphemed. There's no other word for it. He took Scripture and made it into something it's not."

"He took the Scripture and interpreted it the way he saw it. It's been done for centuries."

"Not like this it hasn't."

"Look, are you on the winning side or not? If not, you can leave tomorrow and go back to your girl friend."

"She wouldn't have me now." It was true, Douglas thought. He had nowhere to go. He was stuck with Francis and both of them knew it. With a quick gesture he downed the remainder of his drink and retreated to his room.

There he paced up and down, breathing hard, eyes bright. A fantasy scene grew in his mind, soothing his humiliation. Some daring assassin crept into Leonard's rooms, drew a gun, fired! As he toyed enjoyably with the picture, the assassin became himself. He, Douglas Rymer, would destroy this evil man who was corrupting God's world. He would save the world from this power-mad would-be pope. For the first time in six months Douglas contemplated himself in a hero's role and it felt good. He was strong, clean, and a bit giddy. "Molly," he said aloud, "this will be for you. The first good thing I've done since I left you."

Even as the melodramatic words came out, he knew it was the bourbon speaking; tomorrow's hangover was going to be a beaut.


Christmas of 1988 would have been dismal if it had not been for Stubby. He was so thrilled about his first Christmas since becoming a Christian that he infected them all. There were projects and gift-making and secrets. There was the seven-foot aluminum tree which the Redmonds had owned for years. It was set up in the living room and decorated with strings of tinsel and shiny balls. The large plastic wreath that adorned the front door was a touch of bright green amid the decaying foliage of the yard. In the attic Molly found a battered plastic Santa that she had loved as a child. Several washings and a few dabs of paint made it look presentable enough to adorn the front lawn.

For weeks Martha racked her brains for an inspiration for Christmas dinner. She longed to come up with something special to offset her terrible chagrin over the nine hundred dollars. The judge had been gracious about it, but Martha had lost face with everyone. What could she come up with for a holiday treat? Almost everything they ate now was canned, dried or salted. She had served meat a few times during the fall; none of it tasty enough to be festive. Fish was a possibility, but not traditional. "It just won't seem like Christmas without a turkey," she said many times.

Susie was busy sewing. As no one in the family had purchased store-bought clothes since the earthquake, mended and remade garments were as welcome as brand-new ones used to be. Craig and Hastings were designing and building a fish trap. Hopefully, it would increase their food supply without needing too much time or attention and it was to be a gift for the entire family.

Jason had whittled small plaques of wood from one of the dying trees in the yard and glued on them small bits of Scripture. Stubby was horrified that he would cut up his Bible, but Jason explained happily that he knew all the verses by heart. Hank managed to get some varnish to cover the little gifts and Jason worked on them lovingly.

Only Stubby had no gifts for anyone and only one way to obtain any. He felt grateful to each of the people who had taken him in and yearned to show how much he loved them. So he prayed for a miracle. Two days before Christmas he was walking home along the boulevard when a brightly painted truck belonging to Feed My Lambs raced past him. It was going too fast, considering the condition of the street, and he watched it bump violently over a jagged crack in the pavement. An oddly shaped package flew off the end of the truck.

"Hey, Mister," Stubby shouted. "Mister, you dropped something!" But the truck sped on, never slowing down. As he walked toward the fallen package, he knew immediately that it was meant for him, personally—a gracious gift from God. The wrapping had split open as the package hit the ground. Inside was a cleaned, dressed, frozen turkey.

Christmas dinner was a glorious success. Martha had devised a dressing of sorts for the turkey, and everyone pronounced it a gourmet's delight. In addition, there were vegetables, gravy, some rice and sweet syrupy canned peaches, more than enough for everyone. After dinner they sat around the tree and unwrapped their gifts, then sang the old Christmas carols. Outside the sky had darkened, the temperature dropped and snow began to fall, a rarity for this part of Florida.

As the last song died, Stubby joined Martha in cleaning up the room. Never had his heart been so filled with love for his new family. Then struck by a thought as he was carrying a trash-filled wastebasket to the kitchen, he whispered softly, "I hope you enjoyed Your birthday as much as I did, Jesus."


Later that Christmas afternoon Molly stood by the long living room windows and watched Jason, Craig and Stubby throwing snowballs, faces shining with youth and good health. Jason had on a ragged sweater. Stubby and Craig summer-weight jackets, all inadequate for the weather but the young men seemed unaware of this. They rounded the house and headed for the kitchen. Molly found herself drawn to the kitchen too and met them as they entered, laughing and shaking snow from their clothes.

"Your mother'll have a fit if you mess up this floor," she warned Craig.

"She couldn't be upset on a day like this," he grinned. "It's too beautiful." He walked toward the windows and looked out. "That's really incredible, isn't it? We've had snow before, but this is something else. Some of those flakes must be two inches in diameter."

"What always amazes me," Jason said, "is that each flake is a different shape and totally unique."

Molly sat at the table and hugged her own body. "Snow's pretty, all right, but right now I'd settle for a little of that heat wave we had last summer."

Craig shook his head in amusement. "The Lord has given us a special Christmas gift of a million snow flakes to look at, each one different, and you ask for the sun."

Jason stood quietly deep in thought. "God's amazing," he mused. "He made each human being different too, each with a unique genetic pattern. The same with animals. Did you know that dogs and cats have distinct swirls and markings on their paw pads much like our fingerprints?"

"Where do you find all these little gems of trivia, Jason?" Molly asked. "You'd be a whiz at cocktail parties if you drank and if anybody still had parties."

"Do you know the origin of the word trivia?" Jason countered. Molly shook her head.

"It's from the Latin words *tri,* meaning three, and *via,* meaning way or road. Years ago there was a place near Rome where three roads met called 'Tri via.' People used to gather there to gossip. Later someone would ask, 'Is it important?' and another would answer, 'No, it's just from the Tri via.' In time all idle talk was called 'trivia.' How about that?" Jason grinned at her.

"I wish I knew when to believe you," she complained.

"There's one subject about which you can always believe me." Jason became serious and Molly groaned.

"Here it comes," she said. "I knew it."

"Molly, don't leave. We won't preach," Stubby shook his head warningly at Jason.

"Right," Jason agreed. "This is not the time. But 'out of the abundance of the heart, the mouth speaketh.' And sometimes I speaketh even if it annoyeth. Sorry, Moll."

The four fell silent, watching the enormous flakes drift past the windows. "The old people are in there talking about how the weather's changing." Molly jerked her head toward the living room. First Susie and then Scott had wandered off during the carol singing and no one had seen either one since, but Hank, Martha and the judge were still sitting around the Christmas tree.

"Grandpa thinks the meteor knocked the earth off its axis and that changed the jet stream or something," Molly went on. "And I heard your Dad, Craig, say that another ice age is coming."

"That's not logical if they're dying of the heat in Africa," Craig said.

"Floods in some places and droughts in others. Weather has gone crazy," Jason said thoughtfully. "I'll bet if we got worldwide news like we used to, we'd see patterns that would really shake us up."

"I suppose this is another sign of the end-times you're always talking about," Molly said.

"It sure is. That's why I feel like jumping up and down and laughing." Jason's dark face was radiant.

"You see, Molly, the end-times means good news to Christians. It means the return of the Lord is not too far away." Stubby's face mirrored Jason's joy.

"You three think you've got it made, don't you?" she asked, frowning. "No matter how bad things get, you've got it made."

They smiled at her. "Come on, Molly, it's Christmas. Let's build a snow man!" Craig jumped to his feet.

"I'd freeze out there," she protested.

"It's no colder out there than in here," Craig said. "Come on, join us."

Molly rose to get a jacket, her spirits lifting despite herself. They continued to confound her. Craig, she knew, had slept only a few hours. All three seldom ate enough. But they were always full of joy. She recalled a comment Jason had made one day when she had mentioned how cheerful he seemed under the circumstances. "A Christian doesn't live under the circumstances but above them."

What did he mean by "Christian," she thought suddenly, her old haughtiness reasserting itself. A black, a Jew, and a kid her family had taken in off the street—were they insinuating they were better than she was? "No thank you," she said stiffly. "I have more important things to do than play in the snow."


For almost two thousand years the eyes of the world have watched each time a small handful of men in red chose from among their number a new pope. For a good portion of the world's Christians, the words *Habemus Papam* shouted from the sala of the benedictions above the doors of St. Peter's meant a new father in the faith.

The morning after his election to the chair of Peter, Uriah Leonard awakened early. His Holiness, Sixtus VI, Pontifex Maximus, 265th pope, smiled as he contemplated the city through the curtain hanging limply in front of his tall windows. The day would be full; each moment was allocated and assigned; he would spend it in the presence of thousands. Yet he felt totally alone. He was removed by an enormous gap from all his fellow men. He always had been different inside from the outer face he presented to the world, and as his power and strength grew, these two halves grew further and further apart, the outer man unchanged, the inner man growing more distant each day. As the long, dizzying day progressed, he remained aloof inside himself.

In the Sistine Chapel, he sat enthroned in front of the altar while he received the obedience of the College of Cardinals; a sadly reduced number. The cardinals knelt before him in humility, kissing the small cross on his slipper, then returning to their seats along the chapel walls.

Afterwards the procession formed in the Sacred Apostolic Palaces. The cardinals led the way, and he followed, enthroned in the *sedis gestatoria*. Behind him followed the vast crowd of dignitaries, an endless, splendid file of homage to him. He was crowned in the Basilica of St. Peter's. The choir pealed, *Tu es Petrus,* and as the words rang out, "Thou art Peter and upon this rock I will build my church, and the gates of hell shall never prevail against it," he thought, suddenly and unexpectedly, of Douglas.

The ceremony droned on. "Holy Father, in this way shall pass the glory of the world." Three times there came the brightly consuming flame symbolic of the brief span of man's temporal existence. *Sic transit gloria mundi* . . . yes, nothing worldly was eternal. Pope Sixtus VI knew that as did none of his predecessors. "Receive the tiara adorned with three crowns and know that you are the father of princes and kings, rector of the world, and vicar on earth of our Lord Jesus Christ . . ."

Back in his apartment the pope donned a simple white garment. It was the moment to show himself to the people and bless them. He moved slowly toward the window. The crowd that waited in the piazza below for his appearance resembled a sea. So many souls, he thought . . .

And for a moment Uriah Leonard, who never forgot anything, forgot that the church no longer existed on the earth. The church had served her function: she had brought souls to God; for centuries she had preserved the faith and the Scriptures, and now she was receiving her reward in heaven. Pope Sixtus VI was head of an abandoned shell. He stepped onto the balcony to earshattering cheers. He raised his hands and spoke.

"Beloved children," he said, "we greet you with deep humility, yet with pride also. Humility which makes us small before the enormity of the task we face; and pride that we have been chosen by the spirit for our role as pastor to the world. We pray that we may bring the kingdom closer in this generation.

"We pledge our unstinting effort to achieve unity among men. We have made great progress in establishing unity with our non-Christian brothers .They see in us seekers of truth and we will no longer offend them by arrogantly claiming a sole proprietorship of that truth. Let us, in all humility and charity, admit the possibility that we have made mistakes in the past. What can we poor mortal men know of the eternal truths? Let us assume the role of seekers, learners.

"Closer to home, we shall try to bring greater harmony among the various denominations of the Christian faith. What a scandal this must be to others that we have differences within our own family. We well know that much of our Catholic doctrine gives offense to our Protestant brothers, and we vow to spend our reign bridging those barriers. We feel that accord within the Christian church is far more important than a reactionary clinging to outdated myths and old formulae. For that reason, and with that great goal in mind, we pronounce this truth to be an article of faith:

*Nos, Sixtus, etiam nunc fideliter adhaerentes memoriam receptam ab initio persuasionis, tenetes memoria explicandum Revelationis—aspicientes in gloriam Dei et Hominis, elationem religionis, et salutem gregis permissam custodiae nostrae (Concilio Sacro approbante), dogma divine patefactum docemus et definimus, quandoquidem unum Corpus in Societate Hominis simus, disciplinam Transubstantiae Panis et Vini in Corpus et Sanguem Christi, prius firmiter et religiose obtentam et creditam, ut in illa Praesentia Praesentiam efficacem Omnium Hominum in Elementis Sacris ascribat emendari et augeri. Homo ad solium mundi escendit; Aetas Pacis praedicta a vatibus emersit. Si quisquam hanc finitionem nostram contradicere audebit, anathema sit.*[1]

---

1. "We, Sixtus, still adhering faithfully to the tradition received from the beginning of the Faith, keeping in mind the unfolding of

"We are, of course, aware of the normal channels for an infallible pronouncement on Faith and Morals, but this involved mechanism strikes many of our brethren as medieval and is an offense we need not perpetuate. This change will be effectual immediately. The words of Consecration no longer will be: 'This is my Body,' and 'This is my Blood,' for this is not applicable to the new intent and direction of our church. All priests will, from now, spread the joy of universal brotherhood by proclaiming the words: 'This is our body; this is our blood.'

"And so, beloved children, we bless you. Our paternal love extends to all mankind everywhere, and we wish for each man the peace of tolerance for all men."

While Pope Sixtus VI spoke his first pastoral words to the throng in St. Peter's Square, Royal, Francis and Douglas waited inside the papal apartments where microphones amplified without distorting the magnificent voice. Douglas was like many American Catholics in the late 1980s. The catechism he had learned as a child had been watered down until almost nothing was left but for the individual to try to live a decent life. Nothing was clearly defined as either good or evil. Yet even with this weak and threadbare faith, Douglas could see the fallacies in the pope's speech.

For one thing, Sixtus kept saying "spirit," instead of *Holy* Spirit. And instead of defending the faith, the pope made it sound sinful to believe anything specific. The part in Latin was completely over Douglas's head, but he understood that somehow the Mass had been changed. Nor had Leonard once mentioned God in the English segment of the address.

"I have never heard a man who can speak so well," Francis was saying. "You'd think I'd get used to it, but I don't."

Revelation—with a view to the glory of God and Man, the exaltation of religion, and the safety of the flock committed to our charge (the Sacred Council approving), do teach and define as a dogma divinely revealed, that inasmuch as we are all one Body in the Brotherhood of Man, the doctrine of the Transubstantiation of the Bread and Wine into the Body and Blood of Christ, heretofore firmly and piously held and believed, is amended and augmented to include in that Presence the effective Presence of all Mankind in the Sacred Elements. Man has ascended the throne of the universe; the Age of Peace foretold by the prophets has issued. If anyone shall presume to contradict this, our definition, let him be anathema.

"He's really gifted," Royal agreed. "What do we call him now? 'Your Holiness?' 'Holy Father?' "

"What about 'Sixtus?' That's his name now. We could say 'Sixtus the Sixth.' That's catchy, isn't it? But we'll probably just call him 'Father.' "

The doors to the sitting room opened and they were joined by the pope.

"Great speech!" Royal said enthusiastically. "Will there be much flak about your speaking in English?"

"No. There will be no trouble about anything." The pope's floor-length white cassock accentuated the deep tan of his handsome face.

"Well, another step accomplished," Royal went on. "It's beginning to look as if nothing can stop you."

"Yes. There is much to be said for the satisfaction of fulfilling destiny." The pope seated himself on the Louis XV sofa. "Let me ask you something; you are out in the world. You hear what is going on. What do people say about me?"

"You have a fantastic reputation," Royal answered eagerly. "People are saying you saved the world after the earthquake."

Francis was nodding agreement. "They're saying you're the greatest world leader since Julius Caesar; that you can get things back to normal if anyone can."

"And you, Douglas?" The pope turned his burning green eyes on the last of his three companions. "Who do you say that I am?"

Tense and lonely, badly wanting a drink, Douglas steeled himself for his moment of greatness. "I say that you are the Antichrist, the son of Satan."

There was a moment of surprised silence. Then the pope burst out laughing, rocking from side to side with helpless mirth. Douglas felt himself go red as the others joined in the hilarity.

The pope was wiping his streaming eyes. "Oh, Douglas, you are absolutely priceless. I don't know what we would do without you. But come now," he said to Royal and Francis, "it isn't very tactful of us to laugh at the poor boy."

Douglas was totally nonplussed. For a heady moment he had felt himself capable of withstanding anger, danger, heated arguments . . . anything but ridicule.

"Douglas, my son," the pope's smile radiated forgiveness, "I know your problem stems from my friendship with Celeste. But, consider my responsibility; Celeste is an old and dear friend. When she left the faith to become a spiritualist, was it right to abandon and ostracize her? Our Lord Himself dined with sinners. I regret offending you in this matter, but the care of many souls is entrusted to me."

Douglas stared back in confusion. Was he indeed guilty of judging too harshly? Those parts of the address from the balcony that had troubled him—maybe the pope had simply chosen his words so as not to offend non-Christians. After all he had often stated his desire to relate to all mankind, not just to Catholics.

"Let's forget the whole episode, shall we?" the warm, resonant voice was saying. "And try to have a little more faith in me in the future. I need your faith. We have mountains to move."

Douglas nodded, all his resolution lost.


Stubby was becoming more and more concerned over the fact that he was not a regular contributor to the family welfare. He was aware of the scriptural injunction to work and made every effort to be productive about the house and grounds. But he wanted to bring in something tangible as well.

At sixteen he was too young to qualify for the work permit required now for all forms of salaried employment, but he learned about volunteer work crews being organized by FML to harvest local vegetable crops as they came in. Pickers were not paid in money, but were permitted to take home a half-bushel of produce at the close of each day.

Stubby waited in line at the volunteer center for hours on his first two efforts, but was not selected to go along with any of the crews. Then came a rainy, dreary day when fewer men reported for work. This time Stubby found himself in the back of a pickup truck bumping over the uneven roads to a farm collection point about twelve miles out of town. Some of his fellow volunteers were teen-age boys like himself, but most were men in their thirties and forties, probably, Stubby guessed, with families to feed.

Rain was still coming down when they arrived. Stubby jumped down and looked around. A long shed, open on one side, was stacked with crates of tomatoes, peppers, beans and lettuce. Armed guards paced around the shed and two lean, nervous guard dogs strained against chains, their barking a constant irritant. Picking had apparently been completed the week before; the present job was to carry the boxes of produce from the collection shed to a waiting row of tractor-trailers.

It was unnecessarily hard work. The trucks which were to be loaded were almost five hundred yards from the shed, but the drivers either could not or would not move them closer. There were no dollies or fork lifts, and it was a backbreaking job to carry the heavy crates over the soggy ground. There was little super-vision; each laborer did as he saw fit, with no incentive for either efficiency or speed. Some of the vegetables had already spoiled, and the sullen rain added to the sense of futility.

Stubby, as usual, worked as though Jesus Himself were the boss. He walked as fast as possible. He piled his boxes as neatly as he could, consoling himself by recalling his ancestors. The Hebrew captives in Egypt had been forced by Pharaoh to make bricks without straw, so Stubby could load overripe produce on a poorly parked truck without complaint for the glory of God.

As lunchtime approached, men began stopping to eat. Stubby at last concluded that no formal break would be called. He sought shelter at the side of the shed and took his lunch from his shirt pocket. He had a hard-boiled egg and one of the home-baked rolls Martha somehow contrived to turn out with neither shortening nor milk. He said grace, then ate as slowly as he could: the longer you chewed, he and millions of others were discovering, the fuller your stomach felt.

He was still eating when he saw a group of tall, muscular-looking women approaching from the road. There were ten or twelve of them, and they were still some distance away when he realized they were not women but men wearing women's cloth-ing, their high-heeled shoes clotted now with mud. As they came closer he noticed wigs, nail polish and false eyelashes on several of them. They reminded Stubby of people wearing Mardi Gras and Halloween costumes.

The laborers watched in silence as the transvestites marched boldly up to the guards who were standing just inside the shed. They spoke to them with an easy familiarity.

"Any prospects?" The speaker was a tall, bony man of about thirty, wearing black mesh stockings.

The guard shrugged. "Take a look for yourself."

As the bizarre group fanned out among the resting workers, Stubby shrank against a tree, praying for invisibility.

"Oh, look here. I found something!" One of the gang pointed toward a thin, delicate-looking boy, even younger than Stubby, with a long, sensitive face and enormous brown eyes.

The guard sauntered down to join them. "He's pretty enough, okay, but he can't speak English."

The man in the mesh stockings laughed without humor. "We weren't planning to do much talking. He'll do fine."

He moved closer to the boy who was obviously terrified by the crowd of leering men. "What time do we have to bring him back?"

"They're working like snails so we'll be here for hours yet. Have him back by five." As the guard began a bargaining session with the gang leader, Stubby started to cry. The full truth had finally penetrated his innocence: he recalled a similar situation in the Old Testament when angels had visited Sodom in the days of Lot and depraved men had sought to abuse even heavenly bodies.

There was an exchange of money between gang leader and guards and the strange group left, hobbling awkwardly across the muddy ground. In their midst, small and lonely, was the young terrified Cuban boy. In the entire work force not one voice had been raised in his behalf. Blinded by tears Stubby stumbled to his feet and mechanically picked up the first produce crate his hands encountered. As he started across the yard the smell of rotting tomatoes assaulted his nose.

"I hate this world," he muttered. "I hate it!"

He trudged toward the truck, misery settling down upon him. Then a consoling thought came to him, and some of his peace returned. He belonged to a different world. Thank God for that.

# III

As the months passed life settled down into a grim routine for the nine people living in the Redmond house-garage complex. The basic issue was survival. The worldwide earthquake, the loss of a third of the earth's population, and the freakish weather and plagues that followed this disaster resulted in economic chaos and, in much of the world, actual famine.

Feed My Lambs, well organized as it was, was unable in many places to solve problems of food production and distribution. What it could and did do all over the globe was to move into political and governmental vacuums, helped in most cases by the decrees of existing political leaders who capitulated to expediency, persuasion and in some cases duress. Above all, responding to the fears created by the gangs of thieves which had sprung up everywhere, it held out to ordinary citizens the hope of strong law enforcement. In the United States alone hundreds of thousands of men and women were recruited into new local FML-directed police units.

Immediately after his shooting of the murderer of the FML official, Craig had been promoted to sergeant. A year after the earthquake all vigilante groups in the Tampa area were absorbed into a new organization called the General Corps which also included regular police, highway patrol, sheriffs' departments and law enforcement branches of the military. In the general shuffle Craig and Hastings were transferred to the day shift.

Craig was deeply distressed by many of the new men and women taken into the General Corps. He quickly discovered that they were using positions of authority to commit a wide variety of crimes. Protests were mostly ignored by top officials and supervisors; he observed that the one crime not ignored by FML leaders was political activity against FML itself. This was dealt with harshly; the priority for new construction focused on detention facilities for resisters of FML activities.

Since his failure to write acceptable publicity copy for the organization, Hank had received no further opportunities for advancement. He remained at the lowest echelon of the local center, his take-home pay hardly enough to provide food for himself and Martha. Scott's situation at the television station was even worse. Royal had cancelled his contract to purchase the facility; instead it had been taken over by FML through a new communication decree that put all the media under government supervision. When told to take a fifty percent reduction in salary or get out, Scott took the pay cut. He had no other job qualifications.

As it became obvious that the combined income of Craig, Hank and Scott barely provided subsistence for nine people, the judge organized a Survival Program which included gardening (depending on what seeds could be obtained), raising chickens and fishing in the bay. Susie volunteered to take charge of the chicken coop Jason had built in the back of the garage, and to her surprise she enjoyed it. Jason and Stubby monitored the fish trap which Craig and Hastings had presented to the household on Christmas, and by the fall of 1989 fish—mainly grouper, mullet and mackerel which had made a comeback since the earthquake—had become an important food staple at the Redmond complex.

Molly's inner conflicts continued. She tried to maintain her image as the lady of the house, but her imperious arrogance fell more and more on deaf ears. The skills she had acquired in sports and as a socialite were almost useless. She was forced to share the work load, but when she discovered that this meant doing the laundry, she rebelled until sternly rebuked by her grandfather.

Hastings had become a regular evening visitor. His strong pro-Leonard stand weakened as he became disillusioned over FML policies and as his respect grew for the judge, Craig, Jason and Stubby. Hastings was a simple, uneducated man with a tender heart. It grieved him to see people assume the role of public protector, then harass and rob the very ones they had pledged to look after.

The judge's change was the most astonishing to the others.

From a neutral and indifferent position toward religion, Judge Redmond had in the space of a few months become as fervent a believer as Jason and Stubby. He spent hours every morning absorbing the Bible, enthusiastically reporting his discoveries to a mixed response at mealtimes.

Judge Redmond not only became a vocal disciple of Christ in his household, he began to share his new faith with neighbors, friends, even total strangers. When cautioned against this one night by Scott, the judge was indignant. "It took me over seventy years to realize the truth. Since I don't have much time left, I'm going to use as much of it as I can to pass the Good News on to people who need it."

"Grandpa, it just isn't smart to have one-sided opinions today. Everything I talk about on the air is supposed to emphasize brotherhood, unity, the healing of our differences. The things you've been going around saying could be interpreted as divisive."

"Sometimes the truth does divide people."

"Just don't get a reputation as a troublemaker, Grandpa, that's all I'm saying. Things are tough enough as it is."


The reconstruction pattern in New York City was similar to Tampa's. Citizens demanded protection and strong leadership; FML moved into the breach. Businesses that cooperated survived, those that resisted went under. For a while the unions maintained a solid front against the FML takeover. Then an odd trend developed. Union leaders began to resign, leave town, die or disappear. It happened over a period of months so that there was no hue or outcry. FML men moved into positions vacated by union leaders. One by one the unions were then dissolved by vote of the membership. Two years after the earthquake FML was in complete control of New York City.

After Pope Sixtus VI was installed in the Vatican, Royal, Francis and Douglas returned to New York. Lawrence Royal spent the next year reorganizing his enterprises. Half of his divisions were folded; the other half were restructured in conjunction with FML activities. Royal took the title of Board Chairman of FML and installed three FML men on the board of Royal

Enterprises. Through a deft legal maneuver Royal Enterprises then gained stock control of a new worldwide television network which was then granted exclusive coverage of all major world events in the United States of Europe and forty other nations, including the U.S.A. Behind all the maneuvering was one man: Royal's powerful patron, Uriah Leonard.

As Pope Sixtus VI, Leonard was the world's most powerful man. He seemed to be everywhere. His private jet, *The Morning Star,* covered the world's capitals, and each improvement in the international situation was attributed to him. There was, for example, peace. It came as a result of reduced military resources, true, but it was still peace. With industry and mechanization greatly depleted, pollution of air and water decreased. The reduction of transportation released a greater supply of power for private use. With a third of the world's population dead or missing, there were fewer people to feed, or the famine would have been worse. The pope took credit for all of these bright spots.

The relationship between Leonard and Ben Daniel continued close. The Israeli premier had become the strong man in the Middle East, forcing on the Arab nations an uneasy peace which had continued for three years after the earthquake. It was Ben Daniel who came up with the idea for a Day of Brotherhood. It would serve two purposes: celebrate and reinforce the peace, putting war in the Middle East on a plane with fratricide; and honor him as the author of the new-found harmony.

He discussed the prospect with Leonard who saw its possibilities immediately. The Day of Silence back in '88 had been popular; why not follow it now, three years later, with a Day of Brotherhood? Royal, Francis and Douglas were asked to come to Israel to be a part of the planning committee.

It was Douglas' first visit to Israel and he was overwhelmed by the country's vigor. Israel was one of the few areas in the world of 1991 which was growing and prospering. The visitors from New York were housed in a clean, modern apartment in Jerusalem and the meetings were held in Ben Daniel's home— a large townhouse furnished in a comfortable efficient manner, without excesses or elegance.

Pope Sixtus VI was present when they arrived, dressed in a

plain black suit and Roman collar. He had been lounging in a deep armchair, but moved forward gracefully to welcome the newcomers. The room in which they met was spacious and quiet, with floor-length windows opening onto a neatly trimmed garden. Ben Daniel opened the meeting without preamble.

"Let us get to work, gentlemen. Will you recapitulate the basic ideas, Your Holiness?"

Leonard nodded. "We plan to set aside a day sometime this fall or winter to honor Ben Daniel and his country's role in this new world. We think it might be called a Day of Brotherhood. We also want to direct world attention to Israel's accomplishment in completing the largest construction project undertaken anywhere since the earthquake." He turned to his host inquiringly. "I believe the new temple has been open for two months now?"

Ben Daniel nodded. "The daily sacrifice has been offered since the Passover last year."

"What we really want to say is that we have peace, progress and growing prosperity in the world, and it could never have happened without the prime minister, right?" Royal smiled agreeably.

"You have accomplished much, sir," Francis said. "You have the highest standard of living in the world. There is no trace of the ghetto in Israel. You supply much of the world's energy needs."

Douglas spoke for the first time. "But if you get up and talk about these things, won't you sound self-centered?"

Ben Daniel looked at him gravely. "The psychology of that has not escaped me, Mr. Rymer." He turned to the others. "I think the pope should speak and possibly from the temple. That way it won't look political."

"I like that idea," Leonard said. "Maybe we could use a text which would embrace both our faiths. Something that combines brotherhood and peace."

"How about that thing about swords and plowshares?" Francis was sitting on the edge of his chair. "Take a big sword and beat it into a plowshare right in front of the camera. That's got visual intensity."

The pope beamed. "Very scriptural."

"I think it would appeal to everybody," Royal said. "What's your reaction, Your Excellency?"

Ben Daniel was nodding slowly. "It has potential as a basic theme. How difficult will it be to arrange the temple for telecasting?"

Royal answered, "It shouldn't be a big problem, but if we're thinking of early December we'd need to get our crews in there by mid-November at the latest."

"You'll have to keep your camera angles away from the altar area," Leonard cautioned. "Not every religious communion, my dear Ben Daniel, shares the Jewish zest for blood sacrifices."

"So I understand," the prime minister murmured drily. "Do not worry, Holy Father. We have included a prayer hall in the new building which will cater to the most modern sensibilities."

"I suggest you stop your services for a while," the pope said. "Only temporarily of course."

Craig pulled the squad car into a parking slot and thought again how nice it was to have parking spaces available. It was one small benefit from the major disasters which had curtailed traffic so severely. He reviewed his shopping list. Susie had requested shampoo, seldom available. His mother always asked for toilet paper. The more practical items included water purification tablets, charcoal, lighter fluid, jellied alcohol for the cooker, yeast, and paraffin for sealing the jars of jam which Martha was putting up with some of the beet sugar he had been lucky enough to find last week.

As Craig climbed out of the car he realized what a challenge shopping had become. He was often elected for the chore because he had use of a car.

The shopping center had changed considerably in the three years since the earthquake. The parking area was cracked and uneven, with weeds growing where the concrete was missing. Many of the glass storefronts had shattered; most had not been replaced. Sheets of plywood covered most window areas and added to the interior darkness. Commercial establishments rated power ahead of homes, but stores were still often without electricity. Craig more than anyone else in the Redmond-McKenzie household was aware of the extent to which FML had squelched private enterprise in America as it had worked its way from consultant to supervisor of the business world. As Craig approached Greene's Discount House, he realized that only the name and the building remained the same. The control and the profits, if any, were under new management.

A small stirring of activity near the entrance caught Craig's attention. A dozen or so shoppers had gathered to listen to a white-haired man who was addressing them in ringing tones. With dismay Craig saw that the orator was the judge. He well knew the subject matter of the speech and that as a law-enforcer he would be expected to break up the gathering and arrest or warn the speaker. Yet he also wanted to cheer the judge on, to stand up beside him and be counted.

"We're lost sheep, that's what we are," the judge was saying. "We accept what we're told without question. We're told where to live, where to work, what to think, and like stupid sheep, we obey."

There was growing attention. Judge Redmond was a good speaker and he was only getting warmed up. "I'm aware of the hard times we've been through the past few years. There was a need for leadership and for direction. At a time of crisis, hard decisions have to be made. But three years have passed since that crisis and I believe it's time that we citizens regained control of our destiny. When was the last time we had an election? You, sir, when did you last vote?"

The judge had them. His listeners were completely silent.

"Let me tell you what I think is wrong with us," the judge continued. "I think we have lost our spiritual bearings. I think we have forgotten the one true Shepherd who can be trusted with the guiding of the sheep."

The judge raised the black leather Bible he had been holding in his hand. "In this book is the direction and help we need to become strong men and women again. God wants His people to be free of the manipulations of selfish, ambitious men. He wants us to find that freedom in His word. He wants us to follow His Son, Jesus Christ, the good Shepherd of the sheep. The Lord

Jesus will be coming again soon and God wants us to be ready for Him."

At the mention of Jesus, Craig sensed a stirring of restlessness in the little group.

"You christers make me sick," one man said. "You think you're the only ones who have any answers. We all believe in something."

"Yes, my friend, but it makes a great deal of difference *what* we believe in," the judge responded.

"It doesn't matter what you call it," the man came back. "It's just different names for the same thing. Maybe you call it 'God' and I call it a 'life force.' What's the difference?"

"All the difference in the world," the judge said earnestly. "God is not some vague, impersonal 'force,' and He's not an 'it.' He's a Person and some day you will look Him in the face."

"My beliefs are just as good as yours," the man repeated.

"Beliefs aren't enough. Satan believes in God, but he will burn in hell."

"Are you saying that's where I'm going?" The man leaned forward, fists clenched, face distorted.

"Only God can answer that," the judge answered evenly. "Of one thing I am sure. Jesus Christ is our Savior and He is the only One who can save us from this messed-up world."

Too late Craig saw the knife in the other man's hand. With a snarl the man lunged at the frail-looking judge, eyes narrowed in hatred. Craig heard the judge gasp as the knife sank into his abdomen, saw a dark red stain appear on the tan linen suit. Craig fought through the gaping bystanders. "Lord, help him!" he whispered.

A sudden sound pierced the air, a wailing police siren, and the little group melted away. Craig guessed that someone had reported a gathering of more than ten people without a police permit. He reached the judge and knelt by his still body.

Judge Redmond was lying on the broken pavement, unconscious, a pool of blood collecting beneath him. Craig tore at the judge's clothing to examine the wound. It was five inches long, running from his waist to his lower abdomen. Craig began weeping in fear and grief.

The siren drew closer. Impulsively, Craig gathered the judge in his arms and staggered to his feet. He stumbled to his car, and placed the judge's limp form on the back seat. Then he jumped into the driver's seat and gunned the motor. He had just turned the corner when the police car roared in. Shaking with fear he drove rapidly home.

Jason and Stubby helped Craig place the judge's unconscious body on Jason's cot in the garage, then closed the garage doors. The dim light cast an additional pall over them as Craig knelt by the cot trying to staunch the flow of blood. Through the silence of the room, they could hear the steady plop, plop, plop of blood which seeped through and around the folded towel placed over the wound. The judge was dying, and they did not know what to do.

If they took him to a local clinic, there would be questions and reports, and they would all surely be arrested. Such a risk was not worth taking when the cure rate at the clinics was so low. Even those with nothing to fear from the law had much to fear from the quality of medical care given nowadays. The judge's pulse beneath Craig's fingertips was weak and thready, his breathing erratic and shallow.

"Without a doctor, I guess we're on our own." Jason placed a gentle hand on the judge's forehead. "Or, on our own with the Lord's help."

"The Lord sure got us out of that parking lot. When I prayed for help, that siren started right up. That guy was going to carve him in little pieces." Craig paused to stare down at the wounded man. "If I'd only asked for help a little earlier."

"Don't we have to get Molly? And send someone for Scott at the TV station?" Stubby addressed his question to Craig. "If he dies before they see him, they'll never forgive us."

"What do you mean, if he dies? Are we going to just sit here and let him die?" Jason asked them. "We haven't really prayed for a healing, you know."

Craig watched him cautiously. Surely Jason didn't expect a miracle of that magnitude!

"Well, no. We haven't." Stubby looked dubiously at the still form on the cot. "Do I have to believe it's going to happen before it does?"

Jason was pacing now, growing more determined as he spoke. "The Bible says, 'Be it done unto you according to your faith.' Maybe we do have the faith. Faith is more a decision to believe than a feeling."

"But . . . how can we believe something impossible?" Craig objected.

"You had your appendix out, didn't you?" Jason asked him. "Who healed that incision? The doctor? Your own power? If God didn't restore that tissue, who did?"

"Well, sure, it was God," Craig agreed. "But I was in a hospital. I had medicine and nurses and all."

"You're saying that God can heal, but He needs doctors to help Him."

"There's nothing wrong with doctors," Stubby broke in. "Luke was a doctor."

"Sure, but did Jesus ever heal by sending people to Luke's office?" Jason demanded. "I can just see him with the blind man. 'Make an appointment with Dr. Luke for next Tuesday.' "

"Then . . . you think we can ask God to heal the judge? Just like that? No blood transfusion, no sewing up the wound? Just Jesus?" Craig was not belligerent, but as he rearranged the towel to check the judge's bleeding, he felt breathless with the temerity of the idea. No human agency at all, nothing but pure, naked faith. No one to receive the glory but God.

"Yes, just Jesus," Jason answered.

"You do it, then. I hope it works." Craig stood back, making room at the bedside for Jason.

"The prayer of hope won't do it, brother. It's the prayer of *faith* that heals the sick."

"Well, how do I get faith if I don't have it?" Craig asked. "Do you want me to lie and say I believe when I don't?"

"I have the faith," Stubby said suddenly. "While you were talking, I suddenly knew God would heal him. Pray, Jason! God is just waiting to heal him."

Craig felt goose bumps rising on his arms. From his Scripture reading came the picture of four men removing a roof to let their friend down to Jesus through the crowd, and he was healed on the basis of their faith.

Jason knelt by the bed and placed two thin brown hands on

the judge's body. He spoke in a reverent but natural way, speaking to Someone he knew well. "Lord, we have a need. You said You'd supply all our needs, and You told us to lay hands on the sick and they would recover. I'm obeying You. I believe You will heal this son of Yours because You said You would, because we ask You to, knowing that our health is Your will. Please heal him, Jesus. Thank You."

He stood up slowly, and they waited in silence. Craig felt a desperation suddenly. What if it did not work? What if the judge died? What would become then of the wild hope he felt stirring inside him? "Oh, God, *please!*" he muttered.

"Don't try to talk God into something, Craig," Jason said gently. "Trust Him. He's on our side."

"Just keep thanking Him for the answer," Stubby urged.

Craig closed his eyes and joined in the praises of the others. As they prayed, he listened to the soft dropping of blood. It seemed to be slowing down. He stopped his whispered thanksgiving to listen more carefully. No doubt about it. It had stopped. His mind flew back to the woman slumped dead over her kitchen table, his first night as a vigilante. Was Judge Redmond too . . . dead?

He opened his eyes and with trembling fingers felt for the judge's pulse. His hand closed around a warm, pulsating wrist, the blood throbbing strongly through the gnarled old veins. In disbelief he watched the old man's chest rise and fall with deep, regular breaths.

"Jason! Stubby!" he cried.

Gently he lifted the bloody towel from the judge's abdomen. The edges of the wound were almost touching. That gaping tear, the gray intestines hideously visible, was nearly closed. "Praise God!" Jason howled in glee.

But Craig kept staring at the wound site. It had happened, and he felt weak-kneed in the presence of such a miracle.

Afterwards he joined the other two as they danced and hugged each other and praised God. They piled blankets on their patient and followed his restoration which was almost, but not quite, rapid enough to observe with the natural eye. Within thirty minutes, the judge regained consciousness. He opened his eyes, then sat up with alarm at the sight of his three friends.

And well he might have been concerned: their faces were stained with tears, their voices hoarse from their shouts and songs. "What's the matter!" the judge asked anxiously. "What's happened?"

"Lie down, dear brother," Jason rasped. "We have a lot to tell you . . ."


"So, welcome to my humble dwelling, Your Holiness." Ben Daniel smiled easily.

Leonard strode toward the fire and stretched out his hands. "It has been a long time. I have missed our little talks." The two men were alone for the first time since the pope's arrival in Israel for the Day of Brotherhood ceremony in the temple the following month.

"Tell me," Ben Daniel began, "I've been meaning to ask you for years: why Sixtus? I thought you might pick the name Leo, since you ask so often for the lion's share."

The pope chuckled, his green eyes flecked with amusement. "Do you know what the lion's share is? According to the old fable it is *everything*. The lion's share is all. And we will get it, too. But to answer your question, I was told to use Sixtus. The first three Sixtuses were saints, all back in the early centuries. Sixtus V lived in the 1500s. He was also elected by acclamation. He too was an innovator, and he was from humble beginnings just as I am."

Ben Daniel smiled. "Was he the one who was a swineherd?" he asked innocently. The room was very still, warmed by the fire and the thin winter sunlight.

When Leonard spoke again the moment of cordiality had passed. "I continue to hear distressing things about those two men, Johnson and Mozell. I was under the impression you were going to attend to them long ago."

Ben Daniel's face hardened. "They seem to be untouchable. I have made repeated efforts to eliminate them but something always goes wrong. They have some remarkable talents. They've been doing something to control the rainfall in their areas and this has really impressed the local population. What's more serious, some of my own people have gotten superstitious about them —think they've actually brought about the accidental deaths of a number of my agents. All just unfortunate coincidence, of course. Several of my top men are unstrung by these two fanatics. Three or four have even defected and now work for Mozell. You wouldn't believe the problem these two men have caused me."

"Don't let it upset you," Leonard said soothingly. "We now control all radio, television and newspaper outlets. They can't accomplish much without publicity, can they?"

Ben Daniel shook his head. "They recently claimed to be able to turn the sea to blood. Have you ever heard of anything so ridiculous? Yet people believe them." He was silent a moment, facial muscles working. "The last men I sent were killed, like all the others. And do you know the story that is circulating? They were killed by fire from Johnson's and Mozell's mouths! Now how do you like that?"

Leonard laughed softly. "Even if it's true, it doesn't bother me. So they've learned to do tricks with fire. That doesn't impress me; you will be able to do the same, you know." The pope smiled placatingly. "Forget that I was worried about these two men. They will die. Even their own prophesy says so. It won't be long now. How many nations are sending representatives to the ceremony next month?"

With the change of subject, Ben Daniel relaxed. "There have been no refusals. There never are. Lawrence Royal is completing arrangements for telecasting from the temple. We will transmit worldwide by satellite. You will talk about the glories of peace and show a sword, which will be placed under the lectern. As you explain how it is to be beaten into a plowshare, you will simply lower it behind the podium again and switch implements. We'll have a hand plow of some sort placed there."

"Sounds good, but this time we must be sure there is no way for subversives to exploit the occasion." It was Leonard's turn to be agitated. "Where we slipped up on the Day of Silence I'll never know. And by and large, of course, it went exactly as planned. The spirits were pleased; they told me so."

"What's bothering you?" queried the premier.

"I'm not sure," Uriah Leonard said slowly. "There are rumors —nothing you can put your finger on—unsubstantiated stories of priests starting to say Mass the old unenlightened way. Bibles selling out of bookstores all over the world. Little groups calling themselves Christians, meeting in basements and attics in scores of countries. All nonsense of course. That sort of thing came to an end once and for all the day of the earthquake. Still . . ."

Leonard poked restlessly at the fire. "Still, whenever my peace officers question one of these lawbreakers—if they don't die under torture, that is—they trace the trouble back to some slippage on that Day of Silence. That's why I say again: we can't be too careful."

At eleven-thirty when Hastings arrived everybody was asleep. He climbed the stairs to the garage apartment as quietly as possible and knocked. "Craig," he called softly. "Wake up, boy. We got trouble."

Craig and Stubby were both on their feet in seconds. Craig opened the door for Hastings, apprehension spreading across his face.

Hastings entered the apartment and shut the door. "Where can we talk?"

"We're safe here," Craig replied.

"It's the judge," Hastings said, his gruff voice barely audible. "They've got a 'pick up and hold' order on him."

"What's the charge?" Craig asked in dismay.

"Speaking against the public welfare," Hastings answered. "Somebody recognized him there at the shopping center. And that's a charge the magistrate can hear immediately. He could be on his way to a prison farm before morning."

Craig nodded. In a widely-heralded court "reform" a number of offenses could now be tried at the time of arrest, a judge, a prosecutor and a public defender being available at all times for such cases. In theory, it unblocked overcrowded court calendars; in practice Craig and Hastings were aware of the potential for injustice in the new twenty-four-hour courts.

"Can he run away?" Hastings asked. He glanced over his shoulder at a sound and grunted in relief as Jason appeared to join them. "I've got the car outside," Hastings went on.

"Where would he go?" Craig said. "You can't cross the street nowadays without a permit. The minute someone asked for his papers, or he got out his ration card to buy a carton of milk, the game would be up."

"The judge isn't a child," Stubby said. "Let's ask him what he wants to do."

The four moved silently toward the house. Craig used his key to enter the back door and climbed the stairs to the judge's bedroom while the others waited in the kitchen. On the top step he stumbled in the dark. In an instant a light turned on in the nearest room. Molly opened the door and stood there in her nightie, her red hair tumbling about her shoulders, eyes wide and frightened. When she saw who it was the fear left. "What's wrong?" she whispered.

"I need to talk to your grandfather, Molly."

"In the middle of the night?"

"I'm afraid he's in trouble with the authorities."

The fear was now back in Molly's eyes. She and Craig tiptoed to the judge's room and Molly knocked softly. As they waited Molly suddenly clutched Craig's hand.

The judge opened the door; in a whisper Craig explained the situation. After a moment of silence the old man said quietly. "I don't suppose there's anything we can do?"

"Let's go down to the kitchen and talk to Hastings. He's the one who brought the news," suggested Craig.

Molly and the judge put on bathrobes and slippers and walked quietly down the stairs. The judge looked at Hastings. "Do you have any idea who it was who reported me?"

"No, sir, I don't," he replied. "Does it matter?"

"No, I guess not." The judge reflected a moment. "We're supposed to forgive our enemy. I sort of wanted to know, so I could do it right."

"I think shooting him would be a better idea," Molly raged.

Stubby's dark eyes glistened with tears. "Maybe they'll just put you on the prison farm and let you work out your sentence. Maybe that's all there is to it."

"I hope you're right, Stubby." The judge looked around the row of faces. "I won't run away. I will simply wait until they come for me."

There were pleas from Molly to resist, to hide the judge in the attic, to seek shelter for him with friends. Emphatically the judge refused each suggestion. He had done nothing of which he was ashamed. He would meet his accusers face to face. He would implicate no one else. "Now quit worrying," he told her, patting her hand. "And go wake Scott. He'd want to know right away."

The judge turned to the others. "Do you know anything about how I will be treated? It might strengthen me if I knew for sure, one way or the other. The uncertainty is most unnerving."

"I honestly don't know a thing about it, Judge." Hastings shook his head, distraught. "I make a point of not finding out. I don't want to know."

"I see," the judge said soberly. "That explains something I worried about after World War II. I wondered how six million Jews could vanish in Europe with so little disturbance. Just swallowed up, so to speak, with no hue and cry raised, no questions asked. If the police don't know what's going on, the general population certainly won't."

Craig swallowed the lump in his throat. He noticed with surprise how gaunt the judge's tall erect body had become, how thin the white hair. He was shaken by the depth of love, real love he had for the stately and kind old man.

"Oh, Craig, I wish I knew that they were just going to kill me." The words were wrenched from the depths of the judge's being. Then he put his arm around Craig's shoulder and laughed. "I'm quite a strong Christian, you know. I can go singing to a martyr's death—if only it doesn't hurt!"

# IV

Douglas was excited at the prospect of a whole day alone to wander about Jerusalem. He realized that a part of his enjoyment was due to the fact that he was in Jerusalem and the pope in Tel Aviv. It was an extra dividend that he had been able to slip away from both Royal and Francis too.

The day was nippy. The chill late November wind scurried the crowds along, and Douglas put both hands in his pockets to keep them warm. It was hard to believe that he had been with Royal Enterprises for three and a half years. At times he felt almost like a prisoner. But today was different. He was free. He discovered to his surprise that there were more cars here than in New York, and the crowds were remarkably well-dressed. It made Douglas realize that as an American he was now a citizen of a second-rate nation and he was startled at how much he resented this. But even the obvious contrast between Jerusalem and New York could not depress him today.

He noticed a plan and a symmetry about the city. All buildings were constructed of the same stone. Architects had managed to blend ancient, centuries-old landmarks and brand-new condominiums into a visual oneness; the city had a wholeness and integrity unmatched in the world. The gentle hills and deep ravines were covered with a soft foliage of deep green, a beautiful contrast to the golden stone buildings. Whatever direction he faced, he saw breathtaking vistas.

Dominating the scene were the soaring domes and spires of the new temple, built on the site of the mosque which had been completely destroyed by the earthquake. Arab hostility over this action had diminished, according to news reports, thanks to the pope's peace efforts. As Douglas circled the streets around it, the contrasts delighted him: camels and Cadillacs, burros and sleek European tour busses, Arabs in burnooses and models in the latest fashions, bearded scholars and the armed boys and girls who comprised the Israeli army. The color and excitement and activity were almost intoxicating.

And everything was so clean. The streets, the buildings, the very air was pure and bracing. He was surprised at the hills, having forgotten, if indeed he had ever known, David's song. "As the mountains are round about Jerusalem, so the Lord is round about His people henceforth and forevermore." From research for the pope's speeches, Douglas knew that the city was the site of fifty wars, that it had been besieged thirty-six times and destroyed ten times. He marveled that it could still appear young, dynamic, beautiful.

Lunchtime found Douglas in the Old City, and he bought fruit from a vendor. He was resting under a stone arcade sucking on an orange when he became aware of a disturbance. There was a babble of excited voices as people swarmed toward a large, rough-looking man mounting a flight of stone steps. Douglas looked at him with interest. Although poorly dressed, he was evidently a young man of some importance. He was obviously an orator too, although Douglas could not understand Hebrew. While he turned and addressed them, the people appeared mesmerized.

It was a small episode, and Douglas might have forgotten it completely if he had not encountered the man again only a couple of hours later. Douglas had stopped for a drink in an open-air cafe—his first of the day, he noted proudly, although it was already three in the afternoon—when the young orator suddenly appeared, walking directly toward him.

"Are you Douglas Rymer?" he asked.

"How do you know my name?" Douglas asked with astonishment.

"I am Elias Johnson. So now you know mine," the other replied with a smile. "I would like to talk to you. Will you come with me?" As he spoke Douglas noticed that he watched the crowd alertly.

"Can't we talk right here?" Douglas was suddenly wary.

"It may be dangerous for you to be seen with me," Johnson said. "I have a car nearby."

"I'm sorry, but I don't even know you," Douglas answered.

Johnson leaned closer and spoke urgently. "I was told you are a decent man. I find it hard to believe, considering the company you keep, but I'll give you the benefit of the doubt. If you aren't, then we are both wasting time."

Douglas gulped his drink. "Who told you about me?"

Johnson shook his head. "I cannot stay in a public place any longer. Will you come with me?"

Every ounce of Douglas' self-protectiveness argued against this insane proposition. He could be kidnapped. Robbed. Murdered. And yet something in the eyes and bearing of this tanned, roughly-dressed stranger told Douglas he could be trusted—trusted as Douglas had never before trusted anyone.

"I will come," he heard himself say.

Out of sight of the small cafe, Johnson led the way. Douglas followed, feeling uneasy but excited in spite of himself. They entered the back seat of an old dirt-streaked sedan and Johnson spoke in rapid Hebrew to the driver. For the first few blocks he checked behind them for possible pursuers. At last he relaxed and stared at Douglas with satisfaction.

"I'm glad you came," he said. "I didn't think you would."

Douglas nodded uncertainly. "I still don't know why I did. What's it all about?"

Johnson leaned back against the stained brown upholstery. "I have some friends who plan to add a surprise ending to the sword-into-plowshare ceremony. They are convinced the pope is the embodiment of evil, the Antichrist as a matter of fact. So, they plan to murder him. How do you feel about that idea?" He watched Douglas.

Douglas flushed, recalling his own short-lived fantasy, wondering if the man beside him was also a mind reader. "They'll never get away with it."

"Probably not," Johnson agreed. "But it is the remote chance that they might which worries me. We don't want the man even wounded."

The car stopped in front of a plain, seemingly deserted stone house. Untended shrubbery surrounded the building; the windows were shuttered. Inside it was only slightly warmer than outside. Furnishings included several threadbare rugs and some unmatching chairs.

"Have a seat," Johnson said. "Want something to drink?"

"No thanks," Douglas replied. "I can't be gone very long. You don't think Pope Sixtus is the Antichrist, then?"

"As a matter of fact, I do. I just don't believe in using carnal weapons in a spiritual battle." Johnson seated himself in another chair and rubbed his large hands across his eyes in a gesture of fatigue. "This may come as a surprise to you since there has been no publicity about it, but there is a great move of God under way in Israel. A fourth of our population is now Christian. Those of us who are known are being persecuted."

"Persecuted?" Douglas asked in surprise. "But there's universal religious freedom now!"

"What you read in the press or hear on television has little connection with what's actually happening. This should surely not surprise you, of all people. At any rate," Johnson continued, "in times of persecution, feelings run white-hot. It is hard to reject force, to turn the other cheek, when your friends are tortured and killed. Do you know what spiritual warfare is?"

Douglas shook his head.

"The group around the present pope is allied with evil spirits. We call upon the Holy Spirit for help. These two forces are now locked in the final conflict. But some of our people don't think this is good enough. They want to get right in there physically. And we're specifically told not to fight our battles this way."

"Where do I come in?" Douglas asked.

"We have been told you are not an evil man. Weak but not wicked."

"Thanks a lot," Douglas said sarcastically.

"Sorry to be so blunt, but we are not here to play games. We want you to help us see that the assassination does not take place."

"You won't need me for that. Every person entering the temple will be x-rayed, searched, and sonar-scanned. A mouse in tennis shoes couldn't get past that security."

"I'm sure that precautions will be great," Johnson agreed. "But suppose something goes wrong? You will be close to him, on the platform. You can keep your eyes and ears open—be on your guard."

"It seems funny," Douglas mused. "You, going to all this effort, running the risk of telling these things to me, to save the life of a man you believe is the Antichrist."

Johnson got to his feet. "I believe it's time for you to meet somebody else. His name is Amos Mozell. He might say the very thing you need to hear."

"What time is it?" Douglas asked uneasily. "I have a dinner appointment at seven."

"It's not even four yet. There's plenty of time."

Feeling foolish and sheep-like, Douglas followed him to the car. It seemed he was always responding to a stronger personality. Why was he so spineless? But Johnson was different somehow. He would meet this man Mozell and learn what he had to say. That much would not involve any commitment.


Breakfast following Hastings' midnight visit was tense and emotion-packed, everyone watching the driveway for the arrival of the officers to arrest the judge. Eight-thirty came and Scott and Hank reluctantly left for work; Craig had decided to take the day off to be on hand for whatever might happen.

The dishes done, the three women sat down by the radio for "Celeste Sees," while Craig, Stubby and the judge joined Jason in the garage for prayer. The small blue transistor radio owned by Martha had come to dominate the kitchen from its position on the side counter. It was Martha's most prized possession; she bought batteries for it at the sacrifice of other things. Its thin electronic voice was almost the breath of life to her, a voice from outside.

Martha particularly looked forward to the pope's monthly broadcast from the Vatican, "Chats With My Children." "You can just *feel* the love when he speaks," she'd say. "I could almost be a Catholic nowadays," she confided once to Hank. "When you and I were young I used to think Catholics were silly. All that parading around reciting a lot of gibberish. But this man is really doing something for people."

Her favorite program, however, came at nine o'clock each morning: fifteen minutes of philosophy, advice and prediction by Madame Celeste. Martha had followed Celeste's newspaper column for years, insisting, "I don't really believe in it; I just read it for fun." With newspaper production now sharply reduced, Celeste was reaching her millions of fans by radio, and Martha was one of the most ardent.

Molly and Susie, too, had been hooked by the promise of secret revelations from Celeste. There was a studied cliff-hanging suspense to the various predictions made, and the women joined together in an unofficial scorekeeping, feeling a sense of mutual excitement when the prophecies proved to be true, quickly forgetting those that did not. It was the only activity in which Martha and Molly could share without bickering.

This morning the prediction was more specific than the usual ambiguously worded "message from the larger world." More exciting too: Madame Celeste foretold the imminent assassination, "before the month is out," of a major world figure. Grateful for anything that could keep their minds off the judge's danger, the three returned again and again during the morning to the spiritualist's words, speculating about which business leader or head of state was meant.

It was early afternoon before two policemen arrived to arrest Judge Redmond. Craig answered the doorbell. Being a member of the Corps himself, he felt there would be no attempt at intimidation if he were present. Perhaps as a result of this, all was routine and politeness. Craig certified that the arrest order was legal. The judge appeared, shook hands with the boys and hugged Molly. Stubby carried his suitcase to the police van, then they all waved good-bye.

When the wagon was out of sight Molly flung herself angrily on the porch steps. "If anything happens to Grandpa, I don't want to go on living! He's the only one who ever loved me, except maybe Carrie Lee."

"Wait here, Molly, will you?" Craig said suddenly. He trotted off to the garage, then returned with a furry orange object cradled in his arms.

Molly sat up, startled. "A kitten! Where'd he come from?"

"I found him in a vacant lot. We've been feeding him in the garage. You like cats?" Craig held out the kitten and she took him eagerly.

"I adore them. They have so much more character than dogs. They may look soft and cuddly, but they have pride and independence. Nobody can walk all over them like you can a dog."

Craig nodded, thinking that the description fitted her as well. "You can have him," he offered.

"Oh, thank you! What's his name?" She was nuzzling the fuzzy orange face.

"Ragtime," he said.

"Ragtime? That's a dumb name. Why Ragtime?"

"Why not?"

And they laughed together.

"He needs something to eat. Let's go, Ragtime. It's a tough old world, and you'll need to grow if you're going to make it." She smiled at Craig. "You can be nice at times."

Craig watched her cuddle the kitten close. Ragtime, he felt, was one lucky cat.


For the next several days Scott skirted gingerly around the fringes of the power structure at FML headquarters and found himself firmly repulsed. The judge had been given an in-

determinate sentence and committed to one of the new institutions which combined jail, hospital and rehabilitation center.
To cure him of his antisocial tendencies, a variety of methods
would be used, including drug therapy, psychic reeducation and
behavioral conditioning. No visitors were allowed.

Craig tried from his side, too, to see what he could discover
about the judge's welfare. He too was frustrated. The judge had
dropped completely out of sight. All attempts to locate or visit
him, or try for an appeal, were in vain.


The Day of Brotherhood dawned crisp and cold in Jerusalem.
Guests of honor from all over the world had arrived and been
quartered comfortably. The pope had been driven by automobile
from Tel Aviv, his entire route lined with sightseers who cheered
wildly as his car sped past.

The broadcast was to begin at noon. Douglas and Francis left
their hotel at ten. As they walked through the noisy holiday
crowd, Douglas found himself seeing people for the first time in
years as individuals, wondering if any were followers of Mozell
and Johnson. His brief meeting with Amos Mozell, several days
earlier, had left him changed. Mozell had turned out to be a big
bear-like man who exuded more love than Douglas had known
existed.

He had made things sound so simple, so easy. One had only to
make a decision about Jesus Himself; was He God or not? And if
not God, then what? Madman? Devil? Certainly not merely a
good man, teacher, prophet. That choice was not available since
no good man and moral teacher would swear under oath, as
Christ had, that He was God. Not if he were sane, at any rate.
So, according to Mozell, either Jesus was God or He was not, and
the only important thing in life was the decision each man made
about that one question. No duty, no human love, nothing could
equal the importance of this choice.

There was much more talk, but no exorbitant emotionalism to
sway Douglas; it was simple and logical. By the end of the day,
Douglas was committed, a new man. He was inspired, fired up and
full of eagerness. Mozell had laughed gently at his enthusiasm.

Douglas had left the man's small apartment in a daze of warmth and acceptance. He felt that once again he was a soldier in good standing, fighting on the side of right. Words from long ago had come to his mind, "Oh, my God, I am heartily sorry for having offended you . . ."

Francis and Douglas were checked three separate times before being allowed to enter the temple area. Their identification, pictures and thumbprints were examined exhaustively; they were body-searched and x-rayed. Douglas felt sure there was no need to worry about Johnson's radicals; no weapon could be smuggled past this screening.

The two found their seats at one side of the stage. As they took their places they could see that the two-thousand-seat auditorium was rapidly filling. By eleven-thirty all the guests were in place, the director and stage crew moving toward air time. At eleven forty-five there was a sudden flurry of activity and the pope entered, his white garments making a stunning contrast with his dark coloring. He was followed by Ben Daniel, conservatively dressed in a dark business suit. Leonard moved toward the front of the stage and spoke pleasantly to the director. An assistant trotted over to him with a script, and he began to study it quietly.

"We really graze in the tall corn, don't we?" Francis asked, his plump face flushed with excitement. "Aren't you glad now that you decided to throw in with me instead of settling for marriage?"

"Funny you should ask that," Douglas replied. "I was wondering last night where I'd be if I'd refused your job and married Molly."

As the clock inched toward noon, Douglas studied the ranks of VIP's in the audience, the special guests on the stage, the long table of translators behind their glass partition. No one here but friends and supporters of Uriah Leonard. The whole affair had the aura of a major international event. He peered into the control booth, searching unsuccessfully for Royal among the crowd of milling men inside. The "on the air" lights flashed; the director pointed his finger at the announcer.

It was slickly stage-managed. The master of ceremonies handled the introductions, then turned the microphone over to a shriveled little rabbi who spoke interminably and unintelligibly. Television audiences around the world would be receiving a translation in their own language, but the people in the temple itself heard only the speakers, both of whom had spoken Hebrew. Ben Daniel took the rostrum. His smooth voice flooded the large room and Douglas knew he was introducing the pope.

Leonard finally rose to thunderous applause. He smiled at the crowd, his dark regal head bowed modestly, his green eyes hooded. He strode forward to take the microphone and Douglas sat up straighter. The pope would speak in English as always. The tall handsome figure in white stood quietly until the applause died, then spoke.

"My beloved children. How glorious it is to meet here in this cradle of human faith and join our brothers from around the globe. We celebrate the first reign of peace known in this em-battled land in half a century and honor the man who has made this possible." He turned and bowed to Ben Daniel who had re-sumed his seat.

The pope reached below the lectern and with a dramatic gesture withdrew a long, shining sword. He held it aloft, the sleeve of his garment falling back to reveal a strong, muscled forearm. He waved the sword, and its gleaming shaft reflected the television lights.

"I hold here a sword, ancient instrument of war and hatred. In these advanced times, we have more sophisticated methods of maiming and killing our brothers. But here it is—the symbol of our inhumanity to man, the symbol of our lack of brotherhood—the sword!" He thrust it aloft again and stood in a martial pose, eyes flashing and body erect. The crowd was hushed, breathless.

And at that moment two men converged on the pope. One came from behind the cameras; he appeared to be one of the crew, possibly a stagehand or lighting technician. The second man had been standing next to the soundproofed booth where the trans-lators sat, a clipboard in his hand. Like the other man, he seemed a perfectly natural part of the scene.

The two men reached the pope before anyone was aware of them. The first, coming from behind Leonard, struck him sharply across the base of the neck with the side of his hand. As the pope fell, the second man grasped the sword from his nerveless hands. The pope's body hit the floor; the man who held the sword raised it in a strong two-handed grasp, then swung it down whistling, to strike the pope across the side of his head. He shouted aloud, in

English, "Death to the Antichrist!" He was raising his arms to strike again when he was shot; he crumpled immediately, his body falling on top of the still and bleeding form of the pope. Security agents, recovering from their momentary shock, had already swarmed over the other assailant.

The vast room was in pandemonium. The stage crew, shocked and bewildered, swung the camera to the shaken master of ceremonies who had moved to the front of the stage and was asking the audience to remain calm. The entire audience was on its feet, struggling and pushing toward the end of the rows. The doors had been shut and locked immediately after the pope had fallen, and the room seemed suddenly too small for the number of people inside it.

Two men had moved quickly to the pope's side, the pope's personal physician and a second doctor from the audience. They examined the fallen body and exchanged looks of dismay.

Douglas and Francis had looked on the scene in stunned amazement. "Is he dead, do you think?" Douglas asked. Francis was standing on his chair, trying to see.

"He has to be. That was a terrific blow."

A small man in the long black gown and flat, broadbrimmed black hat worn by the clergy of the city of Rome had pushed his way frantically to the fallen pontiff. As he sank beside the body, he kissed a stole and placed it around his own neck.

Douglas nodded. "The Sacrament of the Sick. Used to be called the Last Rites." He wondered if he should be praying for the pope. He had spent more time in prayer during the past few days than he had in years, but it seemed wrong to pray for this man to live. Yet he was also sure it was wrong to pray for him to die. A solution occurred to him, and he prayed, "Thy will be done."

As the master of ceremonies voiced calming words in various languages over the microphones, the onlookers numbly resumed their seats and watched the activity on the stage. Several men soon entered carrying a basket-like stretcher. They gently, reverently lifted the large body and carried it out. The body of the assassin too was taken away. The prisoner was handcuffed and led off. After what seemed an interminable wait, ushers began to clear the sanctuary, starting with the more important guests.

Douglas and Francis were still on the stage, perhaps two hours after the assassination, when they were approached by two quiet men in uniform. "Please come with us, Mr. Chapman and Mr. Rymer."

As they followed the uniformed men, Douglas felt a spasm of fear. Had someone discovered his talks with Johnson and Mozell? He began praying in earnest.

The security officers led them to an office in the rear of the huge temple complex. Ben Daniel looked up from a desk as they entered. "Our friend is dead, the victim of the sword he hoped to forge into an instrument of peace. We failed to protect him, but I shall have vengeance upon the men responsible for this." Douglas was astonished to catch what he thought was a hint of real affection for the late pope.

"I have asked you here to help me. The body will be taken to Rome and I would like Mr. Royal and the two of you to accompany it. Will you?"

Douglas and Francis nodded without speaking, and Ben Daniel looked up at them suddenly, piercingly. "Did you know he was a Jew? Very few did."

"A Jew?" Douglas protested. "He was a Catholic."

"Yes, but he was originally a Jew. Do you know where he was born?"

"In Pennsylvania somewhere, wasn't it?" Francis asked.

*"Bethlehem,* Pennsylvania." Ben Daniel looked at them in triumph, as though he had proven some point. "I was positive he was the one. Now he is dead, and we will have to start over completely." The premier stood up in dismissal. "My aide has arranged your transportation."

The colonel who headed security for Ben Daniel led them out of the building to a dark green sedan, one of the many in a row near the temple. He spoke swiftly to the driver, then said to Francis and Douglas, "The body is being transported to Haifa by hearse and from there by ship to Rome."

Francis and Douglas climbed into the back seat and the driver sped rapidly away from the temple north toward the port of Haifa.


Martha was the only one who was downstairs before 5:00 A.M. to watch the pope's worldwide telecast. It was chilly and she tucked her feet under her as she settled back on the sofa to sip bitter artificial coffee and watch. Ragtime jumped into her lap and Martha stroked him unconsciously. Madame Celeste had predicted bad news from the Holy City this week. When the pope rose to wild applause, Martha clapped too.

Television viewers were shown a banner hung behind the rostrum while the applause continued for almost a minute. The pope's own sign, the schematic "six," was displayed on a field of red, with the words "God Descends, Man Ascends" in many languages, surrounding it in a circle. The pope stood modestly while the applause flowed over his bowed head. Then he raised his hands for silence and began to speak.

As always Martha listened as though hypnotized. It was wonderful to have a world leader who really, truly cared about people and —she stirred as though waking from her worshipful trance. Surely that cameraman was not supposed to be there! Or that other man! Martha screamed and the cat jumped from her lap.

The camera shifted to a shocked announcer who mouthed some meaningless words. Then the television set went blank. Martha sat without moving, stunned, for several minutes, then raced upstairs to wake the others with the terrifying news. The TV did not come on again and she turned on the radio in the kitchen. Over an hour passed before a solemn-voiced announcer reported that the pope was dead. Martha shed tears for the man she had admired so much.

Scott, Hank and Craig had left for work when Jason came to the house about ten-thirty smelling of the fish he and Stubby had found in the trap. He heard the news of the pope calmly. Martha and Susie were chopping vegetables while Molly folded towels; all were waiting for more news.

"I suppose you and Craig and Stubby are glad he's dead," Martha accused Jason. "And what do you say now about Madame Celeste? You're always running her down, and yet she predicted this!"

"What exactly did she say?" Jason asked.

"She had predicted that a world leader would be assassinated within the week. Yesterday she said that bad news would be coming from Israel today," Martha replied triumphantly.

"That's really hitting it dead center," Susie pointed out.

"How would the three of you like a prediction from me?" Jason asked. "And I'll make mine even more specific than Madame Celeste's."

"Okay, Jason. Go ahead," Molly said.

"I predict that the pope will be alive by tonight. Or maybe sooner." He spoke quietly, but his words electrified the room.

"You think—you think they're wrong?" Martha asked. "You think he isn't dead?"

Jason was smiling at them all. "I won't say whether he never died and they made a mistake, or that he did die and came back to life. I just predict he will be alive—and soon."

He turned to Susie. "If I'm right, will you give me five minutes to show you how I did it?"

"I suppose it's something in the Bible," Susie said defensively. "That's all you ever read. But, gee, yes, if you're right on this one, I'll listen to you as long as you like!"

Jason rose and made his usual, formal thanks to Martha for the breakfast.

"Jason, why'd you want to say something so crazy? Seriously now, why?" Martha asked.

"I honestly think he'll survive, that's why. I don't mean to annoy you with my preaching, Mrs. McKenzie. But if it's prophecy you want, Madame Celeste isn't the only one with power."

Molly stared at him somberly. "Jason, you kill me. You're so darned cocky—you and Craig and Stubby, all of you. Madame Celeste has experience and a proven record for her predictions. You and your garage buddies have—what? A lot of gall."

Jason smiled and left, cheerful as always, and Martha turned up the volume on the radio. The announcer's tragic tones filled the kitchen. ". . . body will be transported to Rome today and placed in the Sistine Chapel. The late pope will lie under the fresco of Michaelangelo's *Last Judgment*." He went on to explain in detail the protocol involved in burying a pope: the three days of veneration by the crowds, the three coffins, the three bags of coins to be placed at his feet.

The door opened again and Stubby burst in, having heard the news from Jason. He grew even more excited as Martha described the tragedy. Totally unlike his usually respectful self, he grabbed both her shoulders in a viselike grip: "You mean he was actually wounded with a sword? A real sword? In the head? That's just incredible! I thought 'sword' just meant violence of any kind. Wow! Now all we have to do is wait till he comes back to life."

"Not you, too!" Martha said, shrugging off his grasp. "Where do you and Jason get these wild ideas?"

"It's in the Bible," Stubby explained. "Wait, I'll show it to you!"

"I don't want to hear any more crazy talk. Believe what you want to believe, but leave us alone." Molly's voice became shrill.

The radio continued to detail the plans for the papal funeral. Martha put the vegetables in a pot for the fish chowder she planned for dinner. Stubby, who had been up most of the night fishing with Jason, finished his breakfast and left for the garage to get some sleep. "If you hear anything about the pope being miraculously cured, will you wake me up?" he asked eagerly.

"Sure," said Molly sarcastically. "And if he isn't, we'll wake you up for supper. Whichever comes first."


The city of Haifa was spread out like a jeweled cloak along the hilly coastline of the Mediterranean, curving luxuriously around its natural harbor. But the beauty was lost on Douglas; his mind whirled with recent events and he viewed the green hills and sparkling sea with unseeing eyes. The ship they boarded was long, gleaming and spotlessly clean. A dapper uniformed man greeted them as they boarded and led them to a lounge area where a buffet was set out. While they ate, the room gradually filled with the pope's entourage who were speaking in subdued voices. After the meal Douglas tried to go on deck, but an armed guard in the companionway informed him they were restricted to the below deck areas.

Lawrence Royal arrived shortly before the ship departed at 5:30 p.m. and Francis and Douglas greeted him eagerly. Royal had spent hours with the security forces and reported that the surviving assassin was under intense interrogation. All involved in the murder plot would be quickly rounded up and shot. Douglas was alarmed by the next bit of news.

"The men who did the killing are just hatchet men," Royal continued. "The real villains are those two fanatics, Johnson and Mozell, who've been speaking against the pope all along. They've both been picked up. There's so much popular feeling against these two, the police are afraid they'll be lynched before the night is over."

Douglas shuddered. He felt grieved that Johnson and Mozell were to die for a murder they had tried hard to prevent. Then came a sneaky little thought: if they were dead, they could not name him. He felt suddenly shabby for thinking it and he was so very tired of feeling shabby.

Royal had served himself from the buffet and was eating mechanically. Fatigue and shock lined his face. He looked up and groaned as a Vatican official entered the lounge and announced that he was assigning various people to serve as "an honor watch" over the body during the night. Royal, Chapman and Rymer were to comprise the first two-hour watch from six to eight o'clock.

Royal slumped back in his chair. "I don't know if I can stay awake even one hour, let alone two. It'll be bedlam when we get to Rome. Let's finish our coffee anyhow."

The body was lying on a hospital bed in a small, chilly room. They were admitted by a doctor who relinquished his vigil with evident relief. The room contained the bed, a small table and three chairs. When the doctor had departed, the three men looked at each other uncomfortably, then at the large body lying so still, yet dominating the room.

"It's hard to believe he's dead. He's still awe-inspiring," Francis whispered, his chubby face even paler than usual.

Douglas found himself wondering where it had gone—all that vitality, that power, snuffed out so suddenly. The chill in the room began to penetrate their bones. Two hours could be a very long period, thought Douglas. Then he stared. A flicker of movement had caught his eye. Hardly breathing, he riveted his eyes on the long, ropy muscles along Leonard's neck. Yes, there *was* motion, faint, fluttery and pulsating weakly.

At that moment Francis screamed, "He's alive! His heart is beating!"

Royal placed two shaking fingers against the pulsing artery. He turned to the other two, staring wild-eyed. "He's alive! I can feel a pulse." He placed his other hand on the pope's chest. "I don't think he's breathing, though. Quick, get the doctor!"

Released from his trance-like state, Douglas dashed from the room toward the small sick bay where the doctor sat writing at a desk. "Doctor, come quick. The pope isn't dead! His heart's beating!"

The doctor looked up, irritated. "That's impossible!"

Even as he argued he was hurrying with Douglas along the narrow passageway. Inside the stateroom he placed his stethescope against the pope's chest and listened. Then his body stiffened and he moved as though stung, dashing to the door and shouting for his technician.

"Get the crash cart! Quick!" He moved back to the body and peeled back one of the pope's eyelids.

The assistant arrived almost immediately, dragging a small wheeled cart behind him. As the two men worked over the body, Royal, Douglas and Francis stood aside, watching.

The doctor grabbed a blood pressure cuff from the cart and wrapped it around the pope's upper arm while he spoke quickly to his technician. "There's a pulse, no doubt about it, and he's breathing. Get an EKG, stat." He listened briefly to the blood pressure and nodded in amazement. "Ninety over fifty. He's alive!"

They began tearing Leonard's clothing off, placing electrodes on his wrists, ankles and chest. The machine hummed as the technician moved the electrodes and took the tracings. The doctor followed the strip avidly as it ran out of the machine.

"Strange," he kept muttering. "Look at this! And over here! I never saw a complex like that! It doesn't look like any heart I ever saw . . ."

"But it's beating," Royal broke in impatiently. "That's the important thing! Who cares what some mechanical contraption says?"

"I do," the doctor said shortly. "This 'contraption' can prove he's alive. You can be wrong about a pulse, even a blood pressure, but they can't argue with an EKG or an EEG." He followed the strip again, his face a picture of bewilderment.

The technician finished his work and began removing the electrodes. The doctor rechecked the blood pressure. "It's 104 over 80 now. And the pulse is down to 96." He looked at the now smoothly-breathing pope in desperation. "I'll have to announce this. What do I say?"

Royal spoke authoritatively. "Just tell them he's alive. It's very simple. The doctor who said he was dead made a mistake."

"*The* doctor?" the man shouted. "There must have been twenty-five doctors there! They rushed him straight to the medical center at Hebrew University. There was no mistake. That man was dead." The doctor's voice had a tinge of hysteria and Royal spoke soothingly.

"Then you will be the hero. The pope is the most important man in the world and you'll get the credit for saving him."

"I didn't do anything," the doctor protested. "He just came back to life and I'll have to try to explain it."

"Shouldn't you be giving him some kind of medication?" Francis asked anxiously.

"What would I give him, when I don't know what's wrong with him?" The doctor shook his head. "Or I should say I don't know what's right with him. I've had patients get better, but this . . ."

"What did they list as cause of death?" Royal asked.

The doctor looked at him blankly for a moment, then turned to his assistant. "We have the preliminary report. It's in on my desk." The four of them watched the pope's quiet breathing as the technician left the room.

He returned shortly, a thick, official-looking paper in his hand. The doctor scanned it, then read aloud.

"Depressed fracture of the left temporal bone with massive sub-dural hematoma."

"Did you see the wound?" Royal asked.

"No, it was bandaged. But I assume they did some kind of repair to make it easier for the mortician since the body would be viewed." He turned to contemplate his patient, while Royal, suddenly spent, sank into a chair.

"Can you imagine what a stir this is going to cause?" he asked. "The whole world will go wild."

Francis nodded. "It's probably the biggest thing that's happened this century."

The doctor faced them suddenly, as though he had reached a

decision. "We ought to get him to a neurosurgeon. They'll have to reduce that hematoma, and we sure can't do it here in this little clinic. I think we ought to put back into Haifa and have them fly him to the medical center. Let those same boys who said he was dead have the pleasure of attending him."

Royal left to radio Ben Daniel, while Francis was delegated to notify the captain. Douglas and the doctor watched the form on the bed uneasily. "You think he'll be . . . all right after they operate?" Douglas asked.

"I have no idea," the doctor answered. "Right now, according to his vital signs, he has an excellent chance of surviving. But that's not saying anything about his mental condition if he does."

"You mean, even though he's physically normal," Douglas said, "he might have brain damage?"

"Not everything is normal," the doctor corrected. "That cardiogram was the wildest thing I ever saw. There's always a certain pattern to the tracing. It can vary, but there is still a basic pattern to deviate from, if you follow me. An interval can be too long or too short and a complex can be normal or inverted. But this cardiogram had no recognizable rhythm at all." He blinked, recalling the undecipherable strip. "It was like nothing on earth I've ever seen . . ."

Royal returned. "We're turning back," he said, looking at the still form on the bed. "They're going to meet us with an ambulance which will take the body—er, the pope, rather, back to Jerusalem. You're to accompany him, Doctor."

"That's good," the doctor said, shaking off his mystification. "Well now, there are a good many things to do. For one thing, we need to get some heat in here. It's not a body anymore; it's a patient. Where's the tech? We need to mount that EKG." He bustled from the room.

"Do you think he'll really recover?" Douglas asked.

"I don't know," said Royal.

"And things could go on, just as they were before?" Douglas posed it as a question.

The look of uncertainty deepened on Royal's face. "Who can possibly guess what the future will bring?"

# Book Four

# Crisis

*December 5, 1991*
*to*
*September, 1992*

# I

As news of the pope's return to life spread throughout the ship, the reaction was one of stunned, incredulous joy. Passengers gathered in small groups to discuss this unbelievable development as the ship turned around and slipped back toward the harbor at Haifa. Meanwhile the officious doctor was hovering over Uriah Leonard checking and rechecking the vital signs of his patient.

Ben Daniel and scores of police were awaiting when the boat docked. The Israeli prime minister went directly to the ship's sickroom where the pope had been transferred to a stretcher. Douglas, standing beside the doctor, saw the still form on the stretcher beginning to move. One large, white hand lifted up.

"I am here, Leonard." The prime minister stood beside the stretcher. "Leave us alone," he said to the doctor.

The doctor backed a few steps away, but both he and Douglas remained close enough to hear the conversation which ensued.

"You are the one. We do not need to seek another," Ben Daniel whispered.

The pope's eyes opened. "It is completed. I am filled. This body will be healed." Leonard raised his head slightly. "Do not let them take it to a hospital. Take me to your home. And those two —Johnson and Mozell—they must die tonight! I will never forgive them! They knew what they were doing when they opposed me."

"It will be done," Ben Daniel answered. He hesitated, then asked. "Is it really you, Master?"

"Don't you recognize me?" The pope's voice sharpened. "I know my friends and I expect them to know me."

As the pope's head fell back, Ben Daniel turned and walked

toward his officers and began barking orders. Several moved forward and picked up the stretcher.

"He needs medical care," the doctor protested. "There is a blood clot on his brain!"

Ben Daniel ignored him, and within minutes the room was cleared. The pope's body was placed in an ambulance. Ben Daniel climbed into a military vehicle, while a chauffeured limousine was provided for Royal, Francis and Douglas. As the cars sped back to Jerusalem, Douglas wondered if he would ever see New York again. Every nerve in his body cried out to put as much distance as possible between himself and the creature who had been Uriah Leonard.

The news that the pope was alive caused even more amazement than the report of his death. Most people assumed that there had been a mistake in the original examination. Tests done at the Hebrew University Medical Center which had certified the pope's death were suppressed by order of the prime minister. Those who had seen the wound, a long, deep gash which had broken the skull, were told to keep quiet about it.

The pope began recuperation as a house guest of Ben Daniel where he saw no one but close friends and advisers. Press releases informed the public of his return to health; Leonard promised a speech soon with full details.

Most of the world was enthralled, jubilant. The few who had doubted his divine calling as world leader were persuaded that this miraculous event somehow put the stamp of approval on all that Leonard had done. There was so much demand for more news of their beloved leader and so many requests to see the proud, regal head unbloodied and healed, that Ben Daniel appeared on television to make a report to the world. He had the largest audience ever reported as he announced that the pope would appear on television at noon the following day, again from the temple in Jerusalem.

Ben Daniel also announced that the two militants they considered responsible for the planning of the assassination—Elias Johnson and Amos Mozell—had been executed. The bodies of these two plotters had not yet been buried, the prime minister continued, because the pope had asked for permission to officiate at their funerals personally. This further increased public adulation of Leonard. It was so like the pope, this man of charity and forgiveness.

So the world rejoiced that the Lion of Rome, their good shepherd who had fed his lambs for three difficult years, was returned to them. People laughed, celebrated and enjoyed a holiday atmosphere natural to those who feel they have escaped by a narrow margin from a horrible tragedy. And they waited with eagerness to see him again via television.

If Jason and Stubby expected a sharp rise in esteem from the household after their prophecies about the pope's recovery had come true, they were in for a disappointment. Hank was annoyed, while Martha's reaction was anger. "Young people who think they know more than adults make me sick," she snapped.

Hank scolded Stubby. "I don't want you upsetting my wife any more. She's got enough troubles already."

Molly was irritated at their attempts to discredit Madame Celeste. "She helps people. Why must you try to tear that down?" she asked.

"Molly, that woman is a fraud. The Bible can give you so much more than she can," Stubby said. Molly just shook her head.

Scott found the whole thing amusing and not terribly important. He had a new interest—an undercover night club where he and some old friends were meeting nearly every evening. Susie's pleasure at being taken there, the nights when he remembered her, was touching to see. To Scott the place was a stopgap, a shabby imitation of the lively discos of the '80s. To Susie it was new and thrilling, a first taste of sophistication.

And yet, strangely enough, it was Susie alone in the household who was genuinely impressed by the prophecies. Until this episode the Bible had bored her. Now suddenly it was a book to consider.

Stubby, Jason and Craig met briefly to discuss the new situation. "Their reaction doesn't surprise me one bit," stated Craig. "Now that the judge is gone, our household is divided into two camps: nonbelievers and us fanatical kids."

"How can they think of you and Jason as kids?" asked Stubby. "Jason's 34; you're 22."

Craig shrugged. "It's easier to dismiss what we say if they can think of us as religious nuts."

"We have to quit trying so hard to convince them," said Jason. "We just can't do it. Only the Holy Spirit can change people's hearts."

"It looks like this has happened with Susie," said Stubby. "She's interested in joining our Bible sessions."

"She might be ready," admitted Craig. "Let's let things happen slowly with her. No pressing."

"It's difficult for Susie and the others to understand the supernatural events of these times," said Stubby.

"It's all there in the Bible," said Jason.

"Of course. But people today don't believe in Satan as being a real personality anymore than they think of the Holy Spirit as a Person," continued Stubby.

"And the few Christians who do speak up, like the judge, are arrested," added Craig. "All we can do is to keep praying for the others. The Bible is our base. They can sneer at us, but it's harder to dismiss that book."

"Things are going to get worse. The numbering will come next," said Stubby.

"You mean the mark of the beast?" queried Jason.

"It's bound to happen," said Craig. "Christians are forming small groups and communities to avoid persecution. One group is hiding out in the stadium. I've been bringing them a few supplies."

"Be careful, Craig," said Stubby. "With the judge gone, your leadership is important to this household."

This idea was a bit of a shock to Craig. He had sensed a gradual change of attitude toward him by everyone—his opinion was sought more often, he was asked to mediate disputes. It was true, he admitted to himself, that he had taken over many household responsibilities—purchase of supplies, repair of equipment, decisions about security matters. Had he really become a leader?

"Good morning, Your Holiness," Ben Daniel said softly. "May I join you?"

The pope was reclining in a massive bed, his body propped up on pillows, intently reading the scores of accounts of his healing. The Israeli prime minister studied his friend with slightly narrowed eyes. The pope had not been an easy guest; Ben Daniel's staff complained of Leonard's peremptory orders, his blazing anger at the slightest mistake.

"Is the telecast prepared?" Leonard asked.

"Everything is ready. But there is one problem about which I must be frank." Ben Daniel's tone was respectful and he made no move to pull up a chair.

"What is it?"

"The fact that you have no scar where you were wounded. People will notice this. No normal body would have healed so completely in such a short time as yours has. If you wear a bandage, it will save many questions."

The pope nodded. "Very well. Now, have you arranged the subliminal message I requested?"

Ben Daniel frowned. "Those split-second messages you wanted flashed on the screen? My staff is puzzled about them. Subliminal advertising has never amounted to anything. Why is it necessary?"

"Do you question my commands?" The pope's voice was harsh and Ben Daniel blinked in surprise.

"How are plans developing for installation of the numbering system?" the pope continued. "I gave you the credit for this, you know. I didn't have to do that."

"I appreciate that," Ben Daniel said. "We have about forty countries with us now. I expect Russia and China to cooperate. Some of the African nations are resistant, but I predict they'll all join. The idea of a cashless society has to be sold."

"You see the beauty of it, don't you?" The pope leaned forward. "There was a census before, too. They had to be numbered then, and that's why they were in Bethlehem."

"The numbering system goes back to King David and before," Ben Daniel replied drily. "And it usually caused trouble. But the ease of setting it up with modern computers will knock out most of the resistance."

Leonard's green eyes were glistening as he shuffled through his papers. "We must begin notifying the various heads of state that we plan to change the calendar."

"The calendar?" Ben Daniel looked surprised. "In what way?

I remember we talked about it once, but don't recall any decision."

The pope's face suddenly flushed, his neck corded with tension, and his fists clenched tightly. "I will not have it! I have endured this 'B.C.–A.D.' outrage for almost two thousand years and I will have no more of it."

"I don't know what you're talking about." Ben Daniel was perplexed by the outburst.

The pope's anger subsided. "Perhaps I have sensitivities which you don't. I will not tolerate the way they use 'A.D.' as 'the year of our Lord.' That this carpenter Jesus could be important enough to split history in two offends me. My hour has come. Old customs must pass away. No more Anno Domini. I don't care what we call it—year of man, year of peace, anything will do, anything else. You must support me in this." The pope lay back on the pillow breathing heavily.

"I'll support you." Ben Daniel bowed slightly, turned and left the room.


The institution where Judge Redmond was taken following his arrest had become one of America's largest "conditioning" centers. It was a huge grey building, windowless, its rectangular shape unsoftened by plantings or landscaping. Located southeast of Tampa off Route 301, it loomed menacingly, amid patchy grass behind cyclone fencing and "No Trespassing" signs.

The judge's admission was processed routinely and he answered questions mechanically, watching in silence as a smock-clad man took blood pressure, temperature and pulse. He was fingerprinted, stripped and his white hair shorn. Then he was handed drab, ill-fitting clothing. Finally, he was led to his "interrogation" area, a bare, antiseptic-looking waiting room. Inside were several plastic and chrome chairs and one small table. There was no reading matter. The walls were bare; the lighting came from flourescent strips in the ceiling. A uniformed woman sat at a desk near the hall door engrossed in paper work.

The screams startled him. They came at intervals from rooms nearby and as time passed he recognized at least three tonal qualities indicating that pain was being inflicted upon a number of people in different locations. The woman at the desk never raised her head from her paper work. When the judge's hands began trembling, he clasped them together tightly.

What did he know of torture, he asked himself? First, that it was a device of cruel men from the beginning of civilization. He had read of its use in China, Russia, Chile, even in nearby Cuba. But it was fairly new to America. The main purpose was usually to extract information from unwilling prisoners. A second more chilling objective was to reduce prisoners to the mental and physical level of animals. Judge Redmond decided that this latter was more to be dreaded.

The prospect of pain was what made him tremble. But he knew it was not this alone that he feared. It was the fact that they wanted him to feel pain, that they would put a great deal of effort and technological skill into making him feel pain. This was an obscenity, he thought angrily—to delight in mutilating the divinely devised tissues and systems of the human body, and in destroying its lovingly designed organs. The judge began to rock back and forth in misery. There was also the dreadful fear of loss of dignity, loss of control. Would he cry? Would he beg for mercy, appealing to some humanity they did not possess?

In the midst of his anguish, the thought came, "I will fear no evil, for Thou art with me." But it was not true. He *did* fear, and he found it impossible to feel God in this cold, dingy, frightening room.

He found there was a rhythm to the screams which filtered through the doors and walls. Since he began tensing up just before the screams were heard, there must be a predictable pattern to the torture. This frightened him; anything so regimented must be mechanical and not human.

The hall door opened and he looked sharply at the man who entered. He was obviously another prisoner, small and bent and old. He sat down by the judge slowly.

"You realize, don't you, that this is part of the process?" He rubbed his hands along his thighs, and the judge was aghast at the sight of fingers so twisted and gnarled that some joints appeared to work backwards.

"You mean the waiting?"

"Yes," the man nodded. "They want you to sit out here and worry and face them terror-stricken."

The judge was so grateful for this human contact that he felt his eyes misting. "Who are you? Why are you in this place?"

"I was a teacher years ago. I spoke out against the new system. Now I'm an experiment. It has been painful, but also educational. For example, I've discovered that the prisoners are not the only unfortunate ones here. I honestly think I'd rather be a prisoner than an employee. You don't believe me? Well, look into the eyes of the man who interrogates you. Then ask yourself if you would trade places with him."

The door in the back of the room opened. The judge looked up, talk forgotten, to face the man who stood in the doorway. He was medium in height and build, dark, about thirty years old. His uniform was sweat-stained and he seemed tired. The judge wondered, was it fatiguing to torture someone?

"Okay, Pops," the man said.

Judge Redmond stood up, not surprised to find his legs unsteady and his breath shallow. The aged teacher extended one of his pitiful hands to touch the judge sympathetically. He followed the uniformed man out the door and down a long colorless hall.

They entered a room about the size of a doctor's small examining room. It contained a console of electronic equipment with a stool in front of it. The only other piece of equipment was an armchair riveted to the floor in the center of the room. There were leather straps on the arms and on the front legs, and a strap attached to the back.

"Sit down," the interrogator said, indicating the chair in the center of the room. He adjusted the leather straps over the judge's chest and did the same with his arms and legs. Then he attached electrodes to his wrists and ankles.

"This conditioning is not to be considered as punishment; it is for your ultimate good as well as the good of society." The interrogator spoke without emotion, addressing the wall above the judge's head. Then he moved to the console which was equipped with knobs and buttons.

So, it was to be electric shocks, the judge thought. He slowed his breathing consciously and tried to force his mind to prayer, rather than futile thoughts. He began to concentrate on the Person of Jesus.

A knob was turned slowly, and the judge suddenly felt an assault of pain, a growing fire along his limbs. His body arched in agony and his eyes blurred. All his long muscles contracted in spasm, and he felt the back of his head slam against the chair. His body was a flame of pain, almost unendurable pain, but still it lasted and consciousness remained. Finally, it faded. He sagged in utter exhaustion, breath rasping, torn asunder by fear and misery. He saw with despair that he had emptied his bladder and the odor offended him.

"What's your name?" came the bored voice of his tormentor.

"Lucius Redmond."

"Address?" The questions came quickly, routinely. No notation was made of his answers; he was merely being conditioned, trained like an animal to respond without thought to the other voice.

There was the sudden onset of pain again. He had not delayed his answers. He had done his best to placate the other man. This was merely an attack against his self-control. It seemed to last longer this time. Would it always grow worse? How long would he maintain consciousness?

"Have you ever engaged in activities against the public welfare?"

"No!" It came out in anger.

"Have you spoken against the duly-appointed authorities or their ordinances?"

"No!" His mind made excuse against the lie; they weren't "duly-appointed."

The pain returned. He yearned for unconsciousness. Could he not pass out quickly? He was, after all, an old man. "Lord, help me," he breathed.

The fear receded a bit. "Lord, I submit it all to you," his mind whispered. Again the fear seemed to withdraw, and to remain away, this time a little longer. Then he felt peace, comfort nearby. The same Jesus who had died under torture, who had been abused, hated, mocked, tormented and killed, was beside the judge at this moment. His love flooded the room, and the judge was buoyed up by it. The words Jesus had spoken were really true: "I will never leave you nor forsake you." And as his need grew greater, so the love and grace grew greater.

The pain came again, lasted longer, then receded. The questions continued, the answers followed obediently. But the judge was only dimly aware of all this. He was suspended high above his body somewhere, high above the room, the building. He was seated with Christ in the heavenlies, being held in love and power, safe from the grasp of the evil one. Joy welled up in him as he realized that the suffering was nothing compared to the prize.


"My beloved children," the pope's voice flowed from television and radio speakers all over the world, "I greet you again only through the miracle of a strong and awesome spirit, which saved me from death at the hands of assassins. To have faced death and seen judgment waiting can sober a man, shatter his complacency and bring to his mind the eternal values often forgotten in the hustle and bustle of daily life. I feel many truths have been revealed to me by my brush with eternity. My task is clearer than ever. I have been chosen to lead you to a new destiny, a new level of spirituality. I was saved from death to fulfill this great mission.

"I have spoken with you many times before and always asked you to love your brothers, to live in peace and harmony and in tolerance with all men. And a good leader must always be willing and able to do whatever he asks of his followers. So today, I will demonstrate my own capacity for love and forgiveness by officiating at the funerals of the two men who persecuted me. These men have incited others to use violence against my person. But I forgive in true fraternal charity. And I will commend their spirits to eternity with no hatred.

"We have accomplished so much together, my children. We have gained religious freedom and have merged our faiths in ways that would astonish our ancestors. We have achieved a one-world government, with justice and equality. We have brought about a new security as we blunted the fangs of war and made peace a reality. We will see within the next month another step forward, the implementation of the cashless society, with each man's productivity and his prudent stewardship protected forever from the age-old scourges of theft, mismanagement and accidental loss.

No longer will productive time be spent in repetitive paperwork and the red tape of conventional banking procedures. What a glorious advancement! Our treasures will be protected for us within the incorruptible brain of the world's largest computer.

"There will be a great advance in medical care," the pope continued. "Your blood type, health record, the complete history of your medical care will be recorded in this giant computer, instantly available in case of an emergency. What a tremendous saving of lives this will bring!

"So we face the future with a unity of purpose and a harmony of action never seen before in history. Much of mankind is joining us in the glorious upward surge of our species, at last to realize our potential and fulfill our destiny. So mankind ascends the throne of the universe. God descends, man ascends, God and man meet in a glorious hypostatic union that yields a new creation, the God-man, the new king of creation.

"And we will celebrate the dawning of this new age, the messianic age of man, with the adoption of a new calendar. We will begin now with the year One. The Year of Man. A new method of reckoning time to celebrate the new ways of life. So join me, my dear children, in greeting the new era. Reach out to seize your destiny and your place as master of creation. I tell you truly, my children, you have earned this glory."

# II

Fishing was now the big topic of conversation in the Redmond household. What began as a rather desperate effort to provide needed food for the household had expanded into a small business. The fish had returned to Tampa Bay and the boys' ingenious traps, set up at a nearby point, were paying rich dividends. An old flat-bottom skiff, several nets placed at strategic places, and a sense of timing were the key factors.

When Hank asked how they knew when and where to drop

the nets, Jason replied simply, "I ask the Lord and He tells me."

Hank felt rebuffed by this, but no one resisted the steady flow of very edible seafood. Nor the growing income that came from their catch.

Most of the fishing was done from 4:00 to 9:00 A.M. by Stubby and Jason. The selling area was comprised of a card table, styrofoam boxes and several small chairs. Susie, and Craig when he was off duty, offered their catch for sale to the thin stream of traffic on Bayshore Boulevard.

"I think we ought to consider smoking some of our catch. Then we could sell it ready to eat," Jason said one morning as he, Stubby and Susie were sitting around their small table.

"Is that hard to do?" Susie asked.

"Not really," Jason said. "We'd need a small smokehouse. I think we could use one of those old beehives."

A man on a bicycle stopped and approached their table. Susie smiled winningly and made the sale. She pocketed the money and grinned. "This is a good job for me. I can practice my techniques."

"What techniques? Flirting?" Jason asked.

"Don't argue with her," Stubby said. "If it sells fish, let her flirt."

"I'll do some figuring on this business of smoking fish," Jason said. "I think it should be our next move."

"If we get too successful, we'll be hassled by FML," Susie said.

Jason nodded. The more ambitious and successful small businessmen who had launched original ideas since the earthquake had run into many obstacles. They were harrassed continuously about their records, their permits, their employee relations. The more successful the operation, the more harrassment it faced.

A car stopped nearby. Three men got out and walked toward their table.

"Do you know what day this is, Cutie?" The speaker was heavyset with a double chin, about 35 years of age. He exuded an odor of stale sweat.

Susie nodded brightly. "Sure. It's December sixth. And I even know the year. It's 1991. Do I get a gold star?"

The man laughed. " 'Fraid not. You forgot the most important thing. It's my birthday."

Jason and Stubby watched uneasily. There was something disquieting about these men. Their laughter was humorless.

"Don't you think you ought to give me a present for my birthday?" the man asked.

Susie nodded. "We sure will. You pick what you want, and we'll throw in something free for the birthday boy." She indicated the fish floating in cool water.

The man looked at the catch with distaste. "No, I don't like fish. I had something else in mind. Like maybe you." He smiled and no one spoke.

"Me?" Susie laughed nervously.

Jason rose slowly and faced the three men, his expression calm. "Let's not start anything, Mister. Please."

The man looked scornfully at Jason. "Don't mess where you're not wanted, boy."

"It's all right, Jason," Susie said quietly. "I can handle it."

Jason shook his head firmly. "I'm asking you people in a nice way to leave." He stood close to the first man and spoke quietly. "We are peaceful people; we love the Lord; we do not want trouble."

The man laughed softly at Jason's words. He glanced at Stubby, still undersized at eighteen. Then he looked at his own friends who were large and muscular.

"You're going to make us leave, eh? That'll take some doing."

Susie tried some small chatter, but there was a note of hysteria in it. Jason knew she was accustomed to handling most situations with her bright personality, but this was different. He spoke again, more firmly. "I mean what I say. We want you to leave us alone."

The heavyset fellow ignored the slender black man. "Now, Cutie," he said to Susie, "I've ridden by here many times and I like your looks. You are prime stuff and I'm willing to take you on. But I don't want any of this nigger's mouth to go along with it. Can you make him shut up so we can discuss our business?"

"We don't have any business," Susie said weakly.

"Sure we do, baby. And I usually get what I want."

"Well, you won't this time," Jason said firmly. He stepped in front of Susie and folded his arms across his chest.

The other man chuckled softly. He moved forward lazily and looked at Jason. He was at least six inches taller than Jason and probably fifty pounds heavier, but Jason showed no fear. Stubby walked up behind him.

"Jason, don't," Susie cried.

Jason shook his head and inhaled deeply, then spoke again. "I command you in the name of Jesus, leave us alone."

His voice rang out with such strength that the threatening man looked startled. He turned to his friends.

"Did you hear that? He's calling in reinforcements." He laughed uncertainly.

Jason stood perfectly still and said nothing more. He was praying there would be no fight. He had never been much of a boxer, and now that he was a Christian he would have to fight fair. He was not sure he knew how.

The silence was taut with suspense. The belligerent man grew more and more ill at ease. At last he shrugged his shoulders impatiently and turned away. "Let's get out of here," he said to his friends. "She's not worth all the hassle."

The three walked to their car and climbed in, talking loudly. As they drove away with squealing tires, Susie laughed and hugged Jason.

"You're fantastic," she said. "I was sure they'd clobber you and Stubby."

Jason's knees began to shake and he sat down suddenly. "I knew it was supposed to work," he said. "But knowing it in your head and putting it into practice are two different things."


For three years the U.S. Postal Service in America had ranged from nonexistent to poor. Service had been partially restored to Tampa in 1990, but the main post office had not been rebuilt since the earthquake, and home delivery was no longer attempted; what little mail got through had to be claimed at a "temporary" sorting station downtown.

So Scott was surprised to see a postman ride up to the front entrance the following afternoon on a bicycle. He wore faded jeans with his uniform shirt and was equipped with a leather mail bag as in the old days. Scott opened the front door and waited.

"Got a registered letter for Scott Redmond," the man announced.

"That's me." He took the letter and glanced at the return address. He felt his stomach knot as he read the address of the local FML security division. Numbly he signed the postman's book.

He carried the letter toward the kitchen where the three women had been working with rare good humor. There had been electrical power all morning and the ladies had bustled about domestically, vacuuming carpets, washing in the machine, cooking on the big stove and luxuriating in hot showers. Scott feared he was the bearer of bad news.

Martha, Susie and Molly were relaxing at the kitchen table, chatting. Ragtime, the cat, lay contentedly on the floor in the golden rays of a warm sun.

"It's nice to have electricity," Martha was saying. "You just can't clean carpets by sweeping. Especially shag."

"Want some iced tea?" Susie asked, holding up her glass. "There's no sugar, but it's cold."

"I don't think so, thanks." Scott turned to Molly and noticed her questioning eyes.

"What's wrong with you?" she asked. "You look funny."

"I'm afraid I have bad news," he answered. There had been so many blows to take and absorb. There was a limit to their resilience.

"What kind of bad news?" Molly asked.

"There's a letter here from FML headquarters. I haven't read it, but I'm sure it's about Grandpa." He examined the letter again, still reluctant to open it.

"Well, read it," Molly said impatiently.

Scott tore open the letter, breathed deeply, then read aloud: *"This is to inform you that your relative, Lucius Redmond, died of natural causes on December 6, 1991. Arrangements were made for burial. Personal effects will be forwarded to you as soon as processed."*

Molly shook her head in agony while Martha sobbed openly.

Scott spoke again, harshly. "It's not even a letter. Just a form with the name and cause of death and date filled in. No signature. You get chewed up by the system and spat out. All that's left is a form without a signature." He was trying valiantly to let anger replace his grief, but in spite of himself he felt the tears coming.

Molly ran to him and clung to him silently. After a while, he patted her awkwardly on the shoulder. "He's better off out of it, you know," he offered.

"But it was so stupid!" Molly cried. "He didn't have to die! He just wouldn't keep his mouth shut."

"That religion business gave him something to live for," Scott pointed out. "It was the only thing he cared about toward the end, except us."

"But did he have to die for it?" Molly cried.

"It was his choice, Molly." Scott folded the letter and put it back in the envelope. "There's nothing we can do now anyhow."

Molly stared at her brother stonily. Susie's eyes were wet and Martha was still sobbing. Scott walked out the back door to find the others.

He approached the garage aware that his spirits were lifting a little. Craig, Jason and Stubby would mourn the judge's passing. But they would see the joy in it. They found joy in everything.


Douglas was determined to attend the funeral of Mozell and Johnson. He was surprised at how deeply he mourned their passing.

The pope had decreed that the ceremony was to be private and held in the Jewish Temple at noon the day after his worldwide speech. "I didn't know he could speak any other way than on live television, worldwide," Francis remarked facetiously.

Douglas and Francis arrived at the temple early to be sure of a seat near the front. Douglas had a sense of expectancy he did not understand. All he knew was the debt he owed these two men. They had rekindled long-forgotten feelings of self-worth. Where it was to end he could not tell. But he knew he was different.

He recalled attending church as a child and yearned to receive the sacraments again. He knew of no service more moving than the funeral Mass of his church. He felt sad that it was seldom used now. Since Pope Sixtus had decided that differences of belief caused divisions, the joint committee of all faiths had written new services, eliminating all controversial tenets. Undoubtedly the pope would use this universal form today.

The pope arrived and walked directly to the small lectern
which stood center stage. He was dressed in simple garments,
nothing priestly or pontifical, and he spoke quietly without ora-
tory. "My dear people," he began, and Douglas thought, *Now he's
going to tell us how forgiving he is.*

The sanctuary was crowded and the atmosphere charged. It was
more like a political meeting than a gathering to pay respect
to the dead, thought Douglas. He intensely disliked the temple
auditorium, its lofty ceiling, the modern design, the convention
hall motif. The platform in front resembled the stage of a modern
theatre.

The two open caskets had been placed on the right side of the
stage; they were open and inclined so that the two bodies were in
full view of the audience and surrounded by flowers. On the left
side, to balance the picture and to flank the speaker in the center,
were the honored guests, including several dozen religious leaders
from all nations. Most of them had come for the sword-into-
plowshare ceremony and were still in Jerusalem to attend the
funeral on December 8th.

The pope was warming up now, speaking with more force.
"They lived in hatred. These men failed to join the human
family and this is the tragic result."

*It's the result of your ordering Ben Daniel to kill them,* Douglas
said to himself. He moved restlessly in his seat, anger and a strong
sense of injustice suddenly bubbling to the surface. How could
people swallow that man's lies?

"So we will commend the souls of these men to the hands of
the spirits, to be taken to the place of rest . . ." The pope's deep
voice rolled on, and Douglas noticed again his use of the word
"spirits" instead of the Holy Spirit. And what was that "place
of rest" supposed to be? A priest was supposed to commend the
soul to God, Douglas thought, and to heaven as its destination.
The two strong, stalwart Christians whose bodies lay before this
huge crowd were almost certainly with the Lord, martyrs for the
faith.

". . . in the grave sin of intolerance. Each man is entitled to
his own faith, his own way to eternity. How can any man dare to
preach that his way is the only way? What a monstrous pride that
would indicate."

Crisis: December 5, 1991 to September, 1992

Douglas shook his head. Christ said He was the only way to the Father. He could not remember it all, but he knew there was such a quote.

His mind was so busy analyzing the pope's talk that he missed the first stirrings in the audience. Suddenly he saw Francis stiffen, his eyes fastened on the twin coffins among the banks of flowers. "What's the matter, Francis?" he whispered.

Francis said nothing and seemed to be in a trance. Douglas noticed others staring at the stage with looks of awe and fear; a growing murmur from the audience began to compete with the pope's speech. Leonard continued to talk, but he had lost some of his poise. He shot little darting glances around the audience, aware that something was wrong. Then Douglas saw the reason and his body began to tingle. There were movements inside the coffins!

Suddenly Elias Johnson sat up in his casket, wide-eyed and wondering. A loud gasp burst from the audience. Then came pandemonium, as people screamed and shouted. Some fainted, others rushed for the doors. Dozens fell and were trampled amid the panic that ensued.

The pope stopped speaking and turned around. He found himself staring into the radiant face of the evangelist. The two gazed at each other for an endless moment. The contrast was startling.

Johnson's face was aglow with joy; Leonard's flushed with fury. His hands moved forward, fingers curved like claws, as though he would tear his adversary limb from limb. Then the deep red face, with its white bandage across the temple, turned a dark purple. The pope threw back his head like an animal and howled. This inhuman sound increased the hysteria of the onlookers who scrambled more frenziedly to escape the hall.

Mozell, too, then sat up suddenly, a broad smile splitting his face, and climbed clumsily from his box-like resting place. He stepped onto the floor of the stage, then turned to help Johnson climb down.

"What is going on?" Francis asked panic-stricken. "What makes all these dead people come back to life?"

"They are good men. Be glad," Douglas said, and he laughed. He felt exultant. "Yes, Francis. Be glad. We are seeing a miracle of God!"

Mozell was standing at the foot of the coffin that had contained his body, handkerchief in hand, wiping off the make-up applied by the morticians. Johnson walked toward the edge of the stage and raising his arms in a wide "V," shouted to the dazed, retreating audience, "Praise the Lord!"

To Douglas' amazement, a number of persons turned in their tracks and shouted back: "Praise the Lord!" Many began to sob, several raised their hands, others appeared terror-struck. A number seemed to be praying.

Most of the religious dignitaries on the stage had fled. The pope stood in lonely rage by his microphone staring helplessly at the two men who began to praise God with upraised hands.

Then the building trembled. "Earthquake . . . earthquake!" came the cries. The remainder of the crowd surged toward the exits. Francis fled, but Douglas stayed rooted to his spot, determined to follow Mozell and Johnson wherever they went.

What happened next amid the bedlam of noise was disputed by the witnesses left in the sanctuary. The building trembled again. Then a voice was heard. Some thought it was the pope who spoke, since he was still standing near the rostrum. Others said it was the voice of God. None could agree what was said. All were in accord on only one fact: after the voice Mozell and Johnson disappeared.

Douglas had been watching the stage closely. He heard the voice clearly. It was not the pope's voice. He was sure of that. The tone was deeper, more resonant. The words he heard were: "Come up here." Then the two men on the stage vanished.

Even before the aftershocks of the earthquake had subsided, security forces had taken over. The room was cleared. The caskets were nailed shut and buried as planned. Guards were posted at the grave site. A news release was later issued which stated that a disturbance had occurred at the funeral when, in the confusion created by the earthquake, two followers of the dead men had raced onto the stage claiming to be Mozell and Johnson. It stated that the imposters had been arrested and would stand trial, and that the dead men had been buried according to plan.

Douglas scoffed at the news release. He was convinced that Mozell and Johnson had gone directly to the Lord and wondered what bodies—if any—had been substituted in the caskets. Then the thought struck him—if he was determined to follow Mozell and Johnson he would have to go to heaven to do it.

The day was bright and clear. The sun shone into the kitchen, making it homey and cheery. Stubby and Craig were cleaning the night's fish catch at the sink, while Jason at the kitchen table was designing a trap. Some animal had been raiding the garden, a disaster in these days of famine, and Jason had taken upon himself the job of trapping it. He was sketching, erasing, sketching again. "It would help some if we knew how big the thing is," he commented.

"Growing bigger every day," Craig grinned. "He's eating better than we are."

Molly entered the back door, arms full of clothing from the line. She smiled at them as she dumped the clothes on the table. "Even if we don't have soap, they smell good from being out in the sun," she said.

"Maybe the sun sterilizes them," Craig responded. He was always warmed when Molly was in a good mood.

Molly glanced at Jason's drawing. "What is it for?"

"I'm hoping to trap whatever it is that's raiding the garden," Jason answered.

"If you catch it, can we eat it?" she asked. "Wouldn't it be great to have some meat? I mean real, red meat, instead of fish?" she smiled dreamily.

"Don't get your hopes up," Craig warned. "He's not caught yet, whatever he is."

"Anyhow, Jason," Molly said with a return to her habitual sarcasm, "I don't see why you're going to all this trouble. Why don't you just take control of this animal and command it to stay away? You did that with the man you told us about, the one who wanted to take Susie off in the car."

Jason and Craig exchanged looks. Craig nodded slowly. "Why not?"

"Don't misunderstand me, Molly. I didn't say we had control of everything," Jason corrected. "But it does say in Genesis that man has dominion over animal life." He turned to Craig, "What do you think? Maybe Molly has a word for us from the Lord."

"Me?" Molly asked in surprise.

"The Lord can use anything or anybody, Moll," Craig told her. "He used a jackass to speak to Balaam."

"Thanks a lot."

"I believe you're right, Molly," Jason said reflectively. "I've been too trusting in my own devices." He crumpled his paper joyfully. "I'm going out there right now and claim that garden for the Lord and rebuke anything that might be trying to take food away from His children."

"Does that mean we won't have to guard it any more?" Molly asked. "If you guys don't have guard duty, you can help with some of the other work."

"We'll still have to stand guard some, Molly," Jason replied. "We don't have authority over other men, only animals and demonic forces."

"That's a shame," she said.

"You don't mean that," Craig smiled. "If we tried to take authority over you, you'd scream bloody murder."

"Amen to that, brother," she agreed. "Maybe you can explain it to me, very simply, exactly what your powers are. I'd like to know when you can take care of things yourselves, and when you use the supernatural."

Molly's tone was mocking, but they sensed an interest underneath. So Jason drew a deep breath. "The Lord gives us all kinds of weapons and authority," he began. "One of the strongest lies in the use of the name of Jesus. In the Bible, names were more than just a label to identify a person. The person's name had a lot to do with the type of person he was. When the situation or the person's character changed, so did the name. Like Abram became Abraham, Jacob became Israel, Simon became Peter, Saul became Paul. Well, the name of Jesus identifies His character, all His power and authority. Most people in our world don't realize this or accept it, but animals and nature and Satan and his evil spirits know that Jesus is the Lord of everything. When we use His name, we call to our aid a powerful Helper."

"It's like a power of attorney," Craig explained.

"And the guy bothering Susie at the fish booth recognized this?" asked Molly.

"Not the man, but the demons that were influencing him did."

Molly shook her head. "I'm sorry. It just seems like a lot of hocus pocus. Little red men with pitchforks. I've never believed that stuff."

"Let me give you one example of what happened when Jesus

Himself used the name of Jesus." Craig watched Molly carefully, judging the affect of his words, "When Jesus was being arrested in the garden, He was probably a pretty ordinary-looking person because when the soldiers appeared they had to ask which one was Jesus. There wasn't any halo or any physical sign. He answered them using one of the names of God. It's translated in our Bibles, 'I am he,' but it was the name God used when He spoke to Moses from the burning bush—'I am that I am.' When Jesus spoke from His own mouth the name of God, the Bible says the soldiers 'fell back'—they literally fell to the ground. Now this Jesus was an unemployed street preacher, but when He said that name, the might of the Roman army couldn't stand against it. There is power there. No doubt about it."

Molly was watching him intently, the clothes forgotten. "That's really heavy," she said slowly. "Then you have it made, don't you? You can just command things to happen."

"Not exactly. It's not magic, you know." Jason said seriously. "Christians have this power if they're in a position to use it, if they have no unrepented sins, if they are at peace with their brothers, and if they are so guided by the Spirit of God that they know how His name should be used."

"I should have known there would be a trick to it," Molly shrugged. But watching her, Craig was encouraged. She had shown less resistance. There were subtle changes in her nature: the pout was gone from her mouth; she was becoming more productive with household chores; there was a relaxing of her imperious, arrogant spirit. Craig sensed, too, that Molly was seeking him out more and more. This excited him. It also troubled him in a way he did not understand.

As he went with Jason outside to claim the garden as God's territory, Craig found himself praying for Molly too. "Save her, Lord. She is one of those You died for. And help me not to want her so much."


For days after the earthquake Jerusalem was a city in a turmoil. Although the quake was listed as moderate, there was widespread damage and the death toll of seven thousand was high. Most of the fatalities occurred at a large convention hall where over

15,000 people had gathered to see the Mozell-Johnson funeral on closed-circuit television.

While earthquake damage and casualties preoccupied the media, the strange occurrences in the temple dominated the conversations of the people. One story circulating was that a small group of zealots had stolen the bodies and disguised two confederates to take their places in the caskets. This explained their dramatic emergence from the coffins, but not the subsequent disappearance.

The explanation which most people accepted was that the disappearing act was a trick of magic, carefully rehearsed. Ben Daniel's public relations staff circulated an official report to explain and debunk the event, but they could not squelch the sudden surge in Christian activity.

As the days went by, Douglas felt more and more a prisoner in the apartment he and Francis occupied. He longed to get out, to meet Christians, to talk with them, and he dreaded the get-togethers with Leonard because he was finding it harder and harder to mask his true feelings. At every spare moment he dug out the Bible Mozell had given him, finding his soul nourished and his spirit empowered by the words. New and strange attitudes were developing, too, and new requirements of charity. One afternoon, he surrendered to one such urge. He sat down at the desk in his room and began a letter.

"Dear Molly . . ." He made several false starts, then the words began to flow, and he felt a release as he poured out his feelings to her. In one way it was a foolish endeavor; there seemed no safe way of transmitting the letter to Tampa. Mail was unreliable and strictly censored. Such a subversive missile as this would certainly bring swift destruction on both sender and recipient, but Douglas continued to write. Contrary to all logic, he felt certain Molly would someday read these words.

He signed it with a flourish, and read it over with some satisfaction. Then he put it in an envelope, addressed it, and slipped it between the pages of his Bible. It seemed a fitting place to keep it until he could arrange to send it to Molly.

# III

The sun was warm, the breeze was gentle. Susie sat on the ground beside the chicken pen and leaned against the trunk of a small tree, alone with her chickens. The hens clucked contentedly, scratching in the sandy soil for food. Susie felt a real affection for them. They were so small and helpless, so comical in their complete absorption with the acquisition of food, with the establishing of a pecking order and with the egocentric life of being a chicken. Idly she reflected on the fact that they had no knowledge and little awareness of the humans who fed and cared for them and eventually brought on them swift destruction. The chickens dwelt daily in the shadow of death, but were unaware of it. She smiled with superiority, feeling godlike in her vast knowledge compared to the mindless chickens.

Then she stiffened in astonishment. She was hardly superior; she saw in herself a reflection of the ignorant, egocentric chickens. Like them, her thoughts and vision were directed downward into the dirt. Like them, she spent most of her time and effort in trivial concerns, living an aimless life. Was there a Higher Intelligence which sadly watched her unawareness of larger matters? Her mind whirled with the idea. She was sitting erect, face tense with the effort of her thoughts, when she noticed Scott approaching across the overgrown lawn. She saw him objectively for once, thin form, poor posture, slouching walk.

An hour ago, she would have been excited by the prospect of a tryst alone with him. Now the physical desire was gone. In its place was a sudden hunger for communication as Scott dropped to the ground beside her, sitting on one heel and smiling languidly.

"I got off early," he said quietly. "Where can we go?"

The bluntness of his question irritated her. "Is that all you can say? No 'hello'; no 'how are you, Susie?' Just 'let's go jump in the sack'."

"Hey, what's bugging you?" he asked in surprise. "I came home early to be with you. We better hurry. Your Dad will be home soon."

"Today I don't feel like it," she answered.

"Okay, okay. I understand."

"No, you don't. It's not what you think."

Scott peered at her and Susie understood his bewilderment. She had instituted their relationship and had never before expressed any desire to change it. Now for the first time a half hour of sex in some hidden corner with Scott was distasteful to her. She picked at her thumb nail and tried not to cry.

"What's wrong? Are you, uh, is there, uh, any problem?"

"I'm not pregnant, if that's what you're worried about. I'm just . . ." she paused, suddenly overwhelmed, and finished in a burst of anguish, ". . . miserable."

"Why?" Scott was glancing surreptitiously at his watch. She could see he hoped to calm her down and still have a time of privacy.

"It sounds so dumb, but suddenly I realize I'm just like a chicken."

"A chicken?"

"I know it's silly, but it's true. We're like those chickens, both walking around blind to what's really going on. We're living on worms and pretty soon we'll die, too. There isn't anything real or important or good in either one of our lives."

He was silent a long while, and she glanced at him through her lashes. His face was clouded. He shifted his weight and poked idly at the ground with a finger. "What is it you want, Susie? Is this a way of saying you want to get married?"

"No, Scott, that's not what I'm after." The vehemence of her reply surprised him and his face went blank. Susie took a deep breath. "I'm troubled about life . . . about what's going to happen to us. Things keep getting worse, people get meaner and each week there's less food. I guess what I'm saying is that I've been just living for pleasure, and it hasn't made me happy. Do you understand?"

"Yes," he nodded thoughtfully. "But I can't see much of anything else to live for either."

"Scott, I really don't know what I'm saying. I just know I'm miserable." She reached out and touched his face. "I like you. But I think we ought to stop these secret meetings, at least till I get things straightened out in my mind."

He looked at her thoughtfully, viewing her as a person for perhaps the first time, not merely as a body, available and now familiar.

"I guess that's okay," he answered. "I'm sure not going to force myself on you."

"You're important to me, Scott." She realized as she spoke that it was true. He was more than a conquest or someone to prevent loneliness. He was Scott—skinny, selfish, sexy, thoughtless, witty Scott. "I have to think," she explained. "I want to see why I've been a chicken and how to stop."

"Well, if you get any shattering revelations, let me know." He walked away stiffly.


"What in blue blazes is an Oriental Thought Form?" Hastings asked in annoyance. He replaced the microphone on the dashboard of the squad car and looked at Craig.

"I don't know, Hastings," Craig replied. "Must be one of those new FML study groups. Why?"

"There's a report of some deaths there. We're to check it out."

Craig sighed. It had been almost quitting time. Now it might be hours before they could clock out.

"These groups are bad news," Hastings fretted. "If there is trouble we can't do anything about it." Silently the big man drove a circuitous route around badly broken streets to the Institute for the Study of Oriental Thought Forms.

A series of new institutes had sprung up, encouraged by FML and supported by public funds. Protests over such favoritism had been harshly squelched. One of the institutes was on "Alternatives to Marriage," which spawned several private clubs that Scott occasionally attended. There was an institute for "The Study of Psychic Phenomena in Everyday Life"; one to investigate "The Effects of Controlled Drugs"; another to delve into "The Relationships of Music to Sexuality." The list of ever-increasing organizations which scientifically explored almost any possible alternative to the old and the traditional and the accepted was nearly endless.

The location of the disturbance was a large, U-shaped, three-storied white stucco structure. After Hastings and Craig had parked their patrol car in front, they entered a courtyard peppered with dry and spiky plantings. On the ground they saw seven male forms. On the porch above the courtyard several dozen bare-footed and robed young people milled about chanting and ignoring the still bodies below.

Hastings glared at the chanters. "Who's in charge here?" he shouted.

There was no answer and the chanting continued unabated. Hastings and Craig quickly confirmed the fact that the seven males, apparently under 35, were indeed dead. Craig was struck by how well nourished the bodies were.

When Craig and Hastings climbed the stairs up to the porch, the chanting stopped. They were met by a tall youth whose black hair hung down his back in a long ponytail. High on drugs, Craig told himself as he noticed the young man's pinpoint pupils.

"What happened?" Hastings asked calmly.

The young man giggled. His companions stood nearby, swaying unsteadily, their blue robes moving gently with the motion of their bodies.

"I suggest we go to the Center," Hastings said mildly. "We need to hear the truth about this."

"What is truth?" the youth countered.

"Truth is seven dead bodies. My job is to find out what happened." Hastings was more aggressive now and the young man steadied a bit.

"They all wanted to go," he said, "but they will be back soon in another incarnation. They weren't satisfied with this life so we just released them a bit early." The young man became more emphatic. "It's not murder to release a soul from an unhappy incarnation."

"You mean they wanted to die?" Hastings asked.

Crisis: December 5, 1991 to September, 1992

"Certainly," the youth replied. "They cooperated fully, took the drugs themselves and then we all joined in a celebration of life while the drug took effect."

Craig studied some of the faces of those nearby. Most shared the dazed, blank look of their spokesman, but on one or two faces, he saw fear and uncertainty. "Do you all believe in reincarnation?" he asked.

There was a general murmur of agreement, but he noticed the bewildered face of one girl who seemed different from the rest. She resembled Molly, slender but strong, and her hair was also red. Craig saw that her nod in response to his question lacked conviction. He spoke directly to her. "The Bible says that it's 'appointed to man once to die, and after that the judgment.' So your friends are facing the Judgment right now."

"We don't have to listen to that," the spokesman interrupted. His bland smile was gone. The emotion in his voice now was anger.

"Are you willing to hear the really good news about life after death?" Craig countered.

"We're not trying to push our beliefs on you," the youth snapped back. "Why are you trying to do it to us?"

Craig looked again at the red-headed girl. She too was now angry and Craig surrendered. No sense bringing on trouble if there was no hope of success. They all were brainwashed by Leonard's teaching that any belief was permissible so long as its adherents did not attempt to proselytize others. He would be reported to headquarters if he tried to talk about his own faith.

A feeling of sadness passed through him as he saw with sudden clarity that he and others like him would soon be forced out of society. Already a group of Christians had gone into hiding in the ruins of the Tampa stadium. This sports center had been destroyed by the earthquake which had toppled the massive concrete stands and opened giant cracks on the playing field and surrounding areas. The huge piles of fallen concrete had formed a number of caves and tunnels in which dozens of people lived.

Craig walked down the steps, defeated by the encounter. Hastings turned to him. "What'll we do about this, Craig?" he asked.

"Call the meat wagon to take the bodies away. Then write it up as a mass suicide," Craig said with a shrug. "Why try to protect this society from itself? They've been saying for years that what they do is nobody else's business. So let them play by the rules they made up."

"It'll save us a lot of trouble," Hastings agreed.

"This outfit will break the hearts of some parents," Craig said sadly as he glanced again at the red-haired girl. She stared back at him and sneered.

Four days after the Mozell-Johnson funeral, Leonard ordered Ben Daniel, Royal, Francis and Douglas to come to his guest quarters in Ben Daniel's home, to discuss what could be salvaged from the fiasco of the funeral. The pope was in a foul mood as he paced the floor.

"I want to stop the talk and settle this matter once and for all," he fumed. He turned to Ben Daniel. "You realize that you executed them at midnight and then they pulled off this stunt right after noon exactly three and half days later?"

"From December 5 till . . . " Ben Daniel began, but he stopped in confusion."Er, Your Holiness, you haven't made it clear to us about the new calendar. It would be so much simpler if we could just wait until the new year begins."

"'You miss the point. Three and half days from death till . . . till their scene in the temple. Don't you see the significance?"

"It's like the death and resurrection of Jesus," Douglas volunteered.

"Precisely." The pope glared around the room at his cohorts. "Is Douglas the only one who can see what's going on? Can't the rest of you look one inch below the surface? The stakes here reach beyond the natural realm." The blazing green eyes flashed, and Douglas shuddered at the venom they held. He could see arising, like a small cloud on the horizon, the certainty that he would soon have to face that malice and stand against it.

The pope turned from Douglas and glared at Royal. "You were there. What was your reaction?"

Royal shifted in his chair and spoke cautiously. "Well, I was late. By the time I got there, you had already started speaking, so I just stood in the back. I couldn't see very well. It seemed hazy for some reason, but I could see the crowd and they were wild. A surprising number of them were willing to accept it all without question."

"What else could they do?" Ben Daniel asked.

"Well, it seems likely to me that at least a few would suspect it had been staged; that maybe some of their followers stole the bodies, replaced them with living men who resembled the dead ones, to prove some kind of point," Royal said.

"That isn't possible," Ben Daniel said firmly. "Those bodies were guarded every minute. We had a hunch somebody might try something like that, so we made sure it couldn't happen."

"I wouldn't advertise the fact," Royal said, and Ben Daniel nodded in agreement.

"They were mine and they were taken from me," the pope hissed. "Snatched out of my hand!"

"They weren't really yours," Douglas said softly. "They belonged to the other side." As he offered this consolation, he hoped it would placate the pope's anger. He discovered that it had the opposite effect.

"You sound like one of THEM!" Leonard howled. "They rave about who they belong to, and brag about their protection."

"Sounds like they were right, at least this time," Douglas responded. He was frightened by his boldness, but something clean and bright and strong was filling him, and he felt like a crusader. Francis was staring at him in astonishment, and Douglas realized his actions were out of character. He smiled at Francis.

"You fool," Leonard shouted at Douglas furiously. "I killed them; have you forgotten that? Do you call that being protected?"

"Where are they now?" Douglas asked quietly. "Didn't you just say they got snatched away?"

The room was utterly still as Leonard stared in sudden awareness at Douglas. He spoke softly. "Well, well, well. What have we here? Do you have something to tell me, Douglas?"

Douglas shrank back in his chair, feeling the crisis of the moment. There was probably still a chance to retreat, to scramble back into a position of safety. The pope's large body loomed over him, mouth agape, eyes bulging, claw-like hands extended threateningly. Douglas felt his skin crawl. How had he ever accepted the popular fiction that this man was good-looking? He was actually almost a parody of humanity.

Suddenly, Douglas realized there were many things more important than safety. Now it was somehow more important to be right, to be faithful to his new beliefs, than it was to be merely safe. He had always been frightened of any clear-cut statement, of any cast-the-die, cross-the-Rubicon action, but he knew he was facing his final moment of truth. He knew in his heart that this was his last opportunity to make such a statement, or perform such an action, and if he failed now, he would be forever lost.

He was trembling with fear, and he prayed silently. " I can't handle this. Take over for me, please." And suddenly he felt a glorious relaxation, and he spoke with perfect aplomb. "I'm just sorry they're gone. I think they were doing good work, saving souls."

The pope towered over him. "Do you realize all the trouble they caused me? How can you be so disloyal?"

"I didn't really think of it that way," Douglas said. "I just know they brought joy and peace to the people they touched, and that can't be wrong."

"Douglas," the pope's voice was steely and deadly. "I warn you. I have no patience left. It won't be like the last time we disagreed with laughter and forgiveness. There is none of that now."

Suddenly Douglas knew he was hearing the absolute truth. There was nothing left of forgiveness, patience, laughter; nothing virtuous whatsoever remained in this being who stood over him radiating hatred. Douglas was facing incarnate evil and his mind reeled.

"You poor, feeble, mortal thing. Do you think you can fight against me?" The large body was inches from his own. And the glorious voice, a honed and sharpened instrument upon which Leonard had played his false and deadly tune, was now a whisper of diabolical hatred. "Don't you know I was created with powers and privileges you can't even comprehend? And you dare to challenge ME? You wouldn't last one hour under the torture. You're not the stuff of which martyrs are made."

As the waves of Leonard's fury washed over Douglas, he gulped, fought down his panic, and stared back at the pope. "Help me," he prayed. And the answer came. He said, simply, "All you can do is kill my body. I've given my spirit to Jesus."

The pope whirled around and snarled at Ben Daniel. "Have the guards take him away!"

As Ben Daniel walked to the door, Royal and Francis stared at Douglas, their faces twin masks of unbelieving horror.

"Don't you know what they'll do to you?" Royal asked.

"Kill me," Douglas answered calmly. "But there really isn't much left on earth I want to hang around for."

"What's gotten into you?" Francis demanded. "Have you gone crazy?"

"I guess I've just been converted. Saved, born again—whatever you want to call it. I talked to Mozell and Johnson, and it started then."

Ben Daniel, who had returned to the room with two armed security men, heard Douglas' last statement. "You say you talked to those men? When? I haven't had a report of this."

"A week or so ago. It was quite an experience." Douglas found an unbelievable change was happening inside of him. Part of him was screaming in fear at the thought of torture and death, but another part of him was gloriously happy. He had made it finally. He felt like the Good Thief; he had stolen heaven.

Ben Daniel turned to one of the security guards and spoke harshly. "You've had an order to watch Mozell and Johnson for the past three years. How did you miss seeing this man with them? Who's responsible? I want our security nailed down right now."

A thought came to Douglas. "My Security was nailed down—on a Cross," he said quietly.

The pope whirled to face Douglas again. "You are so sure, aren't you? You think it is all mapped out, that you can't lose. Well, you are wrong. There are factors you don't know about. The outcome is *not* predestined. Is that clear?" Leonard was breathing erratically.

"Crap," Douglas replied.

Leonard's face was now purple, his chest heaving, his claw-like hands twitching. "You will die slowly. Very slowly. Then you'll recant. You will beg me to allow you to reject your God."

Douglas turned his back on the pope and spoke to his two

friends who were watching the scene in unbelieving horror. "There's still time for you, Francis. Read the Bible. Give yourself a chance to believe."

He then addressed Royal, whom Douglas had always thought of as brilliant, suave, strong. Now through new eyes, he saw him as an aging, trivial man, his power and personality gone.

"I hope you stay 'lucky,'" Douglas said to him, "and join the winning side." Royal turned his head away, embarrassed or disgusted, Douglas couldn't tell which.

Douglas walked over to the two guards who had been waiting, faces expressionless. They led him to the door where Douglas stopped and turned around. "I wish I could think of some final brilliant word," he said. "I've had a shabby little life. Now I pray I can make up for it a little by dying a good death." He turned and left the room. There was no sound from behind him except a strangled cry from Francis.

Then Douglas heard, within his own heart, the words that sustained him through the long, ghastly three hours it took for him to die: "This day you shall be with Me in Paradise."

# IV

Martha threw down her dishcloth and sank into a chair at the kitchen table, sobbing. Jason and Scott, who were sitting and talking quietly as they finished their tea, looked up in dismay.

"What's the matter?" Jason asked sympathetically.

"I get so sick and tired of it all!" Martha sniffed and wiped at her eyes. "I was trying to wash the dishes. This place is getting just filthy, and the bugs are taking over, and I try my best to keep it clean. We didn't have any soap, but I was at least getting the food off the dishes, then the water quit again. It was too much."

"It could be worse, you know, Martha," Scott pointed out. "If you heard everything I hear, you wouldn't complain about the small inconveniences."

Martha fixed herself a cup of tea and sipped slowly. She looked at Scott with suspicious reddened eyes. "Like what?" she asked.

"Well, there was this family in Orlando that had been storing up food for hard times. Some of their hungry neighbors knew about it and one day they banded together and attacked. They found the food all right, but it was full of weevils and rats and was completely inedible. This made the neighbors so mad they killed the whole family. Then they finished off with a little cannibalism. You can be glad you didn't have any big supply of food to attract hungry mobs."

"That's disgusting," Martha said with a shudder.

"But true," Scott maintained.

"And sad," Jason added. "The Bible says that gold and silver won't save you, and not to lay up treasures on earth."

Scott ignored this aside and continued. "A trainload of prisoners was traveling up the east coast south of Jacksonville. The cars were pulled over on a siding to let another train pass and then somehow were forgotten. The crew took off somewhere and the prisoners couldn't get out of the boarded up freight cars. They all died. I could go on and on." Scott sat back with an air of authority.

"Is this supposed to make me feel better?" Martha asked.

Scott nodded. "Things could be worse. Did you hear about what happened in Rome? There were thousands of people in the catacombs, hiding from the police. Food has been so scarce in Italy that the police saw a way to get rid of many hungry mouths. So they gassed them. Used something pretty powerful, pumped it into the caves, killed them all. We don't have it that bad."

"Not yet at any rate," Jason said quietly.

Martha was watching Scott in silence. "Our whole world is just falling apart, isn't it?" she asked finally.

"We still have a roof over our heads," Scott answered cheerfully. "And we manage to eat."

Jason left to repair his fishnets which were stretched out on the garage floor. Scott went with him. "You like this work, don't you?"

"Mending fishnets isn't work," Jason replied. "I enjoy it."

"Do you realize you all are getting a reputation?" Scott sat on his heels in the garage doorway and squinted against the glare of the sun. "Nobody else catches many fish in the bay, or the Gulf either. But you all do. How come?"

Jason smiled. "There've been some marine biologists from FML asking us about that. I don't know what to tell them. Maybe it's because we know some fishermen."

Scott looked blank and Jason explained. "Many of the apostles were fishermen."

"Oh," said Scott. He looked at Jason in bewilderment for a moment before speaking out. "Maybe you can answer a question that has been puzzling me."

"I can try."

"What do you think about those goings on in Jerusalem? We've heard some of the wildest stories you could imagine down at the newsroom. They say the pope had been dead for ten hours when he suddenly started living again. And that funeral. I heard from a guy who was there that those two men—Johnson and Mozell—not only got up out of their coffins, they seemed to go up into a cloud. He said the official report is a lot of hogwash. I was wondering what you thought."

Jason looked at him quizzically. "Why me, Scott?" he asked. "I never go anywhere and I don't see many people. What makes you think I know anything?"

"Because you're always reading the Bible. Bibles seem to be in great demand today. In Jerusalem I hear they're being smuggled in like contraband. People are paying huge sums to get them. Ben Daniel stopped the sales of the New Testament a long time ago, but that just seems to make everybody want one."

"I think I know what's happening all right, Scott, but you could get in trouble for listening to what I have to say. Does that bother you?"

"No," Scott smiled. "I'm just curious, that's all. Not eager for your religion."

"Come on inside." Jason started toward his bedroom area, Scott trailing behind. The nets were left, forgotten.


The pope went on worldwide television to explain the great new boon to mankind—a giant computer which would bring on the cashless society. It was housed in Rome in three immense grey buildings which soared high, windowless and impenetrable over the Holy City.

"We now have a master computer which will control much of the world's economics," Leonard said grandly. "It will be fed by microwave towers all over the world. The age of man has finally arrived in all its glory. Man has harnessed the marvels of electronics not only to control his economy, but to free him from the tedious burdens of money transactions."

Leonard did not explain that the big computer would also bank and store the important data about each citizen's life wherever the system was used. Not only would his income be credited to his numbered account, and his expenditures electronically debited, but his number would serve for everything from his birth certificate to burial permit. The pope called it a modern miracle and gave the credit to his good friend Naphtali Seth Ben Daniel who had formulated and tested a similar plan in Israel soon after the earthquake. By early 1992, the system was to spread throughout much of the world.

The deadline for all Florida citizens to be marked was set for Thursday, January 30, 1992. The medical profession had developed a chemical to implant the digits upon skin without pain or danger to health. The mark was not visible except under special lights. Bureaucrats in the Tampa area worked day and night compiling a list of all residents and setting up centers to number the citizens.

Those who objected openly to the plan were invited to the FML headquarters to talk things over. When it was pointed out that food rations would be given only to those with a number, most protesters quickly capitulated.


Molly was looking crossly at a pile of laundry on the kitchen table when Craig entered.

"You've never told me how Madame Celeste explained the Mozell-Johnson disappearance," he said pleasantly. She looked at him sharply. There was only a mild interest in his voice and no sarcasm.

"Well, you might not understand, Craig. You know so little about her work."

"Try me," he said. His face was attentive.

"She thinks that sorcerers, hired by the followers of Johnson and Mozell, stole the bodies and took their places in the coffins. They stood up at the most dramatic moment and then used sorcery to disappear."

"That's a good trick, Molly. How'd they do that?"

"I knew you wouldn't understand. Celeste said that the sorcerers were actually astral bodies, Doppelgangers, if that means anything to you."

"Not too much. I gather that they had the power to create a second body and project it into the funeral room, then make it vanish."

"Something like that," Molly nodded.

Craig smiled. "Now what I want to know is this: if you can swallow a thing like that, why do you have trouble believing that Jesus Christ is who He said He was?"

Molly finished folding laundry and began to melt down old candle stubs; the wax would be made into new candles which were used throughout the house when the electricity was cut off. She measured out string for the wicks.

"Craig, I could say the same thing to you, only in reverse. If you can believe in things like the resurrection and the rapture, why can't you accept psychic phenomena? Anybody who really believes that Stubby talked to an angel should accept Celeste's explanation of the funeral."

Craig smiled at Molly. "I guess we're at a stalemate."

Molly smiled back. "I suppose so. I can't swallow your story and you don't believe in mine."

"Wait a minute. I most definitely do believe in sorcery, in psychic phenomena and all that other stuff. I even know a little about Doppelgangers. I think sorcerers who have studied and perfected their arts could probably do just what you said. I just don't happen to think they did with Mozell and Johnson, no matter what Celeste says they did."

Molly looked startled. "You believe in the occult and ESP? I thought it was against your religion."

"I believe they exist. I believe they can even work, if that's the right word to use. But I don't think any of those things are beneficial, safe, or right for us. I think any time you put your faith in powers outside of God, you're in trouble."

Molly's face clouded. "Here we go again. If we keep on talking this way, we'll both end up upset. Let's just visit awhile and talk about other things, okay?" Her firm mouth relaxed and the face beneath the wavy red hair looked suddenly very young.

"Sure, Molly. What shall we talk about? You have any other news from that radio?" He helped himself to a handful of raisins from a bowl on the counter and sat down at the table.

"I was going to ask you," she answered. "You get out more than I do. You know," she stopped for a moment, her eyes dreamy, "I remember when I used to go out five or six nights a week. Now if I see anybody but members of the family, it's unusual. How things have changed!"

"I know," he agreed. "Here I am, a high school dropout and a cop. I never did want to be a cop. I wanted to raise bees, or be a farmer."

Molly arranged the candlemold carefully and began tying the strings to a long stick resting across the top. She did it expertly. Craig looked at her with approval. "You're good with your hands."

Molly's eyes glowed. "I like doing this. But not cleaning fish." Her nose crinkled. "Stubby and Jason better not catch so many more fish than everybody else. It makes them noticed." It was always bad nowadays to be noticed.

Molly had threaded the strings through each of the inverted molds, and she now closed the bottom end of each mold with a piece of old potato to stop the wax from leaking out. Then she began the tedious job of pouring the hot wax into the molds.

"Are these for us, or to trade?" Craig asked.

"I don't know," Molly answered. "Probably for trade. Your mother wants to get some more tomato plants. I think we should try to find some bicycle tires. We're almost out of patching stuff."

"Not many people have tires at all now," Craig said mildly.

"I know. I suppose we're very lucky. We have a bicycle and chickens and all the fish we can eat, and nobody is sick, and the animals no longer bother the garden," Molly conceded. "Things could get worse."

"I'm afraid things will get worse, Molly."

"Craig, don't make me nervous," she said with irritation. "I miss the old life too much to accept this one. So I don't need your gloom about the future."

"Okay, Molly. But I want to tell you one thing. If it ever gets too rough for you and you think you can't handle it alone, remember this: In a sense we're building an ark out there in the garage. It's something like Noah's ark; it only has one door. But it will take us to safety if the elements blow up." Craig patted her shoulder awkwardly.

Molly beamed. "What a charming idea. An ark to take us safely through the storm. I'll remember that. Thank you, Craig."

As Craig walked out the kitchen door, Molly moved the candle-mold to the end of the counter to harden. Then she wiped the table and tidied up the kitchen as her mind replayed Craig's last statement. He was teasing her again but with an intriguing thought. An ark of safety. How lovely.


"Lucky! Darling! And Francis. It's so good to have you back!" Celeste beamed with pleasure. Royal grinned. It was surprising how normal she could seem at times.

"I missed you both dreadfully. New York was dismal without you." She led them into her living room and settled herself in her usual chair. "What's the matter, Francis? Didn't you enjoy the Holy Land? You look like you lost your best friend."

"Celeste, did you have to say that?" Royal grimaced.

"What happened?"

"Douglas is dead," Francis said bleakly. "He was executed by Uriah Leonard for insubordination."

"That surprises me," Celeste said. "He liked Douglas; I heard him say so many times."

"To that man, people are like flies you swat. Douglas was a good friend and deserved better," Francis said mournfully.

Royal spoke soothingly. "Don't brood about it. Just be glad we're home." He turned to Celeste. "We've had a wild time."

"I want to hear all about it," Celeste said. "There have been a lot of reports, but I'd like to know the truth." Francis and his grief were quickly forgotten.

Royal related the events while Francis went to the bar and fixed his usual pink squirrel. Then he slumped in his chair as he listened to Royal wind up his account with a description of Douglas' amazing defiance of the pope.

"Remember—I did warn everybody about Douglas," Celeste pointed out. "I knew from the beginning he didn't belong with us."

Francis glowered at his hostess while Royal shrugged. "What's done is done. Tell us how New York received the news of what happened in Jerusalem."

"It's the top story everywhere you go," she said. "Nothing like it has ever happened before."

Francis spoke up suddenly. "If Douglas were here, he'd tell you that something like that did happen before. Someone did come back from death."

Royal and Celeste exchanged a glance. Royal cleared his throat uneasily. "Don't get carried away, Francis. Things are going well."

Madame Celeste changed the subject. "The ratings for my radio programs have gone so high that we're planning a move to television."

"Better check it out with me before you sign a contract," said Royal. "There are some interesting gimmicks you should know about. Leonard is using one."

"What's that?" Celeste asked.

"Flashing a message on the screen so quickly that the audience isn't aware of it—except at the subconscious level. It's called subliminal advertising."

"I've heard of it," Celeste said.

"The pope has insisted it be used for him," continued Royal. "I think we could work out something similar for you."

"What's his message?"

"Just one word: Worship."

The three sat silently for a moment. "Douglas said the pope is on the losing side," Francis blurted suddenly. He looked from Celeste to Royal in concern. "What if we're wrong and Douglas was right and he's in heaven now playing a harp or something. Then we've been damned fools, haven't we?"

Royal and Celeste looked uncomfortable. "I'm sure he was wrong," Royal replied. He spoke very firmly.


Each member of the family had staked out an area which he or she considered private territory or a place of security. The boys still congregated in the garage, with Hank and Scott occasional visitors. Martha's domain was the kitchen; Susie preferred the backyard. Molly had always chosen the front porch where she often sat with Ragtime, staring out across the bay.

This night after dinner Molly strode angrily to the front porch after a raging argument with Martha who had called her haughty and lazy. She sat on the porch couch, sulking as the door opened and Scott and Craig joined her.

"You're going to have to help out more, Molly," Scott began.

"Why should I have to do housework, Scott? I own this house," she snapped.

"So do I," he countered, "and I bring home a pay check."

"But I have been doing all kinds of jobs about the place." Molly turned to Craig for support.

"Molly's a good worker when she wants to be," Craig admitted.

"Martha is always on my back. She's never satisfied," Molly added.

"Martha's in charge of the kitchen," Scott continued evenly. "She works hard all day long. If she didn't, we wouldn't eat. But she needs more help from you."

"Molly, I think a lot of the problem is your attitude," said Craig gently. "Things haven't been working out right for you, but there is an answer—there really is."

"The last thing I need now from you, Craig, is a lecture," Molly warned. She pulled Ragtime on her lap as Scott patted her on the shoulder and walked off to the garage.

Craig also turned to leave. "Sorry to upset you," he said.

"Don't worry about it," she replied tiredly.

"Let me know if you want to talk about it sometime."

As Craig took a step, she reached over and placed her hand on his wrist. "I'm sorry to be so bitchy. I don't want to be this way. I'm just torn up inside."

Craig sat down beside her, took her hand and held it. "I understand and I want to help."

"Maybe—just maybe you can." Molly took a deep breath. "I don't buy your philosophy, Craig, but I do dig you as a person. I know we've fought a lot. I called you a kid once—I don't think of you that way any more."

Craig's pulse jumped. He looked into Molly's eyes and saw confirmation of her words. Her eyes were smoky. Her fingers had tightened on his. Her lips had softened and parted slightly.

He leaned down and kissed her gently on the lips. She pulled him fiercely toward her. Sky rockets shot through Craig.

"I fell for you the first time I saw you in that tennis outfit," he said a few moments later.

Molly moved closer to him. "Then why have you been so mean to me?"

"I don't know. You were tearing me down and I couldn't let you get away with it."

"Well, that's in the past." She stroked his smooth cheek. "Your face was so messed up then."

"You don't have to remind me." Craig kissed her again and found himself trembling.

Molly drew a deep breath. "Let's go up to my bedroom."

Craig's blood pressure soared. The trembling in his hands increased. He sat very still for a moment, then looked deeply into her eyes.

"I'd like to Molly, I really would. But I wonder—"

Molly shook off his hesitation. "No one will know. I'll see to it."

"It's not that." Craig's eyes had clouded.

Molly stiffened. "Do you want to or don't you?"

Craig took her hand and looked into her eyes. "Molly, I care for you very much—too much perhaps to rush into something I can't handle. Every male hormone I've got is yelling for me to take you upstairs right now. But I can't do it."

"Nonsense!" The softness was gone from Molly's eyes. "You're not man enough to accept me as a woman."

The accusation shot through Craig like a knife wound. He had a wild urge to take her right then on the front porch to prove her wrong. Hot blood pounded his temples. Shakily he stood on his feet. "I'm sorry, Molly."

Her eyes were now blazing. "I thought you were a man. Sorry, my mistake. You're still a boy. Go back to your playmates in the garage."

Craig looked at her sadly, then walked away. Ragtime jumped down and trotted after him as Molly seethed. "Even the blasted cat follows him," she muttered.

# V

"I have application blanks for everybody," Hank said. He sat at the table and began to eat the soup Martha served. The entire family was present for the evening meal.

"Let me see one," Scott asked. Hank handed him a five-by-nine card with questions on both sides. "Is that all there is to it?" he asked. "This is very simple."

Craig picked up a card and looked at it. "Yeah, Scott, very simple and very deadly."

Hank turned to Craig angrily. "I don't want to hear any more of your foolishness, do you hear? You've already split this family in two, and there's no reason for your resistance to this. It isn't like some club you either join or don't join. There isn't any choice about this. We all sign up." He rubbed a nervous hand over his bald head.

"I'm sorry, but I don't agree," Craig said. "There is always a choice and I do not intend to have this mark."

"Mark, mark, mark. You make it sound like something horrible. It doesn't even show." Hank held out his right arm suddenly. There was absolute silence in the room as Martha moved forward to look at her husband's arm.

"I don't see anything, Hank," she said, puzzled. "Where is it?"

"There," he pointed to the back of his hand. They stared at it intently. His hand appeared unchanged. "It only shows up when you shine a special light on it. All the stores and banks will have these lights. And the police."

"You must have been one of the first ones numbered in this area," Martha said.

"They started with the people in FML," Hank replied.

"What's your number, Daddy?" Susie asked. He reeled it off, eighteen digits, then turned again to Craig, his voice resentful. "If you listened, you heard only one 'six' in the whole string of numbers."

"They aren't fools," Craig said mildly. "They're not about to be so obvious as to put three sixes in a row. But they do have three rows of six digits each."

"Well, if you want to see three sixes in a row," Scott said, "I can tell you where to look. The pope's signature. He writes 'Sixtus' real fast with the last three letters just one long scrawl so that it looks like six. Then comes his Roman numeral six. And finally he adds that symbol of his, the number six with a small arrow at the end. That gives you three sixes in a row."

"You're being as silly as Craig and Stubby," Hank said scornfully.

Martha spoke up. "Some of the license plates in Jerusalem have the prefix 666."

"How in the world did you know that?" Molly asked.

"I know more than you think," Martha said sharply.

Stubby spoke up for the first time. "Did anybody get the mark on their forehead?"

"Nobody that I know, Stubby," Hank answered. He turned to his son again. "Craig, I just hope you know what you're doing," Hank said, trying to control himself. "Life here will be almost impossible without a number. For one thing, only those with numbers get a ration card. Had you thought about that?"

"We'll have to leave then, Dad," Craig said.

Hank threw up his hands in horror. "Where would you go? If your own family can't take care of you, who do you think can?"

"While you're yelling at Craig, better include me, Daddy," Susie spoke up quietly. "I've accepted Jesus, too, and I won't wear Satan's mark."

The announcement stunned the group into momentary silence.

"I forbid it, do you hear me? I absolutely forbid it. You're still a child," Hank glared with fury at Craig.

"Dad, please listen," Craig pleaded. "She really is making the right choice. I agree that it will be difficult, but the end result will be . . . "

"Shut up!" Hank stormed. "I won't listen to another word."

"May I say something?" Jason asked politely. "This decision has been coming on a long time. Thirty years ago society's morals and Christian morals were much the same—don't lie, don't steal, don't live unclean lives, love your country and your fellow man. Then society went downhill morally. Being a Christian more and more meant being different. As the world got meaner and more evil, Christians had to separate themselves. It's like the Bible says, the good got better and the evil got more evil. Now the two groups are so far apart it's almost impossible for them to live together."

Jason's eyes glowed softly. "Do you see, Mr. McKenzie? We're coming to the end. The final break. In order to follow Christ you can't be a part of this world at all. Your children are giving up the world, but praise the Lord, they'll gain eternal life." Jason's shining smile lit the room.

Hank spoke again, more softly. "Jason, I respect your views. If you want to risk starvation, that's up to you, but these are my kids." He was pleading now. "I can't just stand by and watch them ruin their lives." His eyes suddenly became moist behind his thick glasses.

Jason nodded. "I know. It's completely beyond your understanding."

Hank sat with his head bowed. Martha turned to Susie and asked calmly, "Do you have all you want to eat?"

Susie shook her head.

"Well, think about this," Martha continued. "We've had ration cards for everybody here. Still we never have enough food. Can't you see how unfair it will be for the rest of us in the future if four of you do not have ration cards?"

Susie's body sagged with sudden guilt.

Hank turned to Scott. "What about you?"

"I'll have to get a number," Scott said calmly. "Jason is very persuasive, but we can't all be fanatics."

"What about you, Molly?" asked Hank.

"I'm no fanatic," she replied coldly, staring at Craig.

Hank nodded, then turned again to his son. "I've heard rumors that an underground movement has started for people who are resisting this numbering system. Is that true?"

Craig hesitated. "I think there may be, Dad," he answered. "I've heard the same rumors myself. Why?"

"I was wondering if there was somewhere you could go if it gets too rough. You obviously can't keep your job." Tears suddenly came to his eyes. "I want you to be safe."

"We are, Dad. Wherever we are, we're safe. Honest," Craig said reassuringly.

The anger was gone. The room was quiet and sad. Hank was defeated. Scott and Molly appeared uncomfortable, while Craig, Susie, Jason and Stubby seemed remorseful but determined. Martha slowly began clearing the table.

Francis was alone again in his apartment. He walked over to his small desk, opened the bottom drawer and took out a black leather-bound book from under a mass of papers and folders. Then he sat down in his favorite turquoise chair.

Carefully he drew out a white envelope from the pages of the book and stared at it. It was addressed to Molly Redmond, Bayshore Boulevard, Tampa, Florida, U.S.A. Once again he opened the envelope, took out the letter and read it slowly.

He sat there for a long time staring into space. Then he picked up the black book and began reading.

"How are we doing, Craig?" Stubby asked hopefully. He was sitting cross-legged on his bed watching as Craig checked the list of articles they were collecting to take to the stadium.

"Not too well, I'm afraid."

"There is no way it will be enough, Stubby. Just accept that," Jason said earnestly. "Even if we get everything on the list, it still isn't enough."

"One good thing. We won't be eating so much fish." Craig smiled.

Jason dropped a handful of safety pins on the bed. "Here's my offering, Craig."

"Great! You always manage to come up with stuff like this. How do you do it? Do you have secret credit cards or something?"

Who would have guessed it would come to this, Craig thought. They sat around the garage like this often now, discussing ways to get supplies, whether to run away or go underground. It was a bit like dying: they knew it would happen someday but they did not want to accept it. Would the four of them, plus Hastings, who like Susie had recently become a Christian, end up living in the towering piles of broken concrete at the old stadium, fugitives from society, hunted and hated? Or would they be arrested, sentenced without trial to an institution of horror? It was all completely unreal.

"Here's something that should be helpful." Jason pulled out a slender, paperbacked book and leafed through it. "This tells how to live off the land, what you can eat, how to start fires without matches, all kinds of things. If we decide to make a run for it, I suggest we go east. Christian underground groups are springing up all over that area."

"I've heard of some too," Craig agreed. "But we're not ready for that yet."

"I'm beginning to get the word for me," said Stubby. "It's Israel."

Craig stared at his Jewish friend. "That's a big thought."

"I wonder if FML will persecute the others because of us?" Stubby asked, worriedly.

"I don't know," Craig answered. "We're all under a cloud because of the judge."

Stubby was checking the list again. "I added scissors, Craig, and how about salt?"

"Both good."

"Eggs will keep sixty days on ice and thirty days off ice," Jason read in his manual. Craig looked at him doubtfully.

"I don't believe it. I think a month-old egg would taste awful," he said.

"You may have an opportunity to find out," Jason said drily. "That's one of the few things we have in abundance. Too bad we never learned how to powder them."

"We were going to smoke fish, too. Probably too late now." Craig completed his list and put it in his pocket. "We have two big sacks ready. I'll take them there as soon as I can."

"I'll be glad to take one," Stubby suggested. "I know the way."

"Too risky. If you got picked up, you wouldn't have a chance."

"If you get caught, neither would you," Stubby pointed out.

Craig shook his head. "As long as I'm driving the patrol car, nobody will stop me. It's not dangerous for me." No one believed that statement, not even Craig.


"He's gone mad! Absolutely mad!" Celeste paced the floor of her living room, twisting her hands.

"Calm down. I think he knows what he's doing." Royal was fixing drinks, watching her in some amusement. Francis was sitting glumly in a chair.

"He's losing his credibility completely. People are talking; they're wondering if the blow to his head damaged his mind." Celeste stopped to accept her drink, then begin again. "It's not going to work."

"Okay, tell me about it." Royal led her to the sofa and sat next to her. "What won't work?"

She took a gulp from her drink. "Leonard told me to cancel my program at the end of this year and to terminate our seances and meetings. He says he is planning to stop *all* worship, except worship of himself. How can he last if he acts like that? It's crazy."

Royal looked startled. "You're right. Stopping worship is not the normal way for a pope to act."

"He's no real pope. We all know that. But I hate to see him appear stupid to the public. It's positively medieval, wanting to be worshiped. People will laugh him out of power."

Madame Celeste drained her glass. "It's a big mistake. I get new believers for us every week. I don't expect any appreciation, but I think he ought to realize we're all on the same team. I'm not going to stop the meetings."

Francis suddenly chuckled. Since his return from Jerusalem, he had become despondent, drinking constantly, and sounding ominous warnings. "You think it matters to him what you think or how you feel? You fools! He *hates* us. Don't you see that? He has a very special destruction prepared for us, just as he did for Douglas." His voice trailed away.

Celeste turned back to Royal. "Lucky, can't you make Leonard listen?"

"Maybe you can put something about him into your next program, Celeste, and he'll let you keep it going," Royal suggested.

Celeste shook her head. "I don't think that will help. I'm afraid that people will think he's crazy and won't follow him any more."

"I wouldn't worry about that, Celeste," Francis spoke again from his corner. "Hitler was insane; so were Caligula and Ivan the Terrible. Many dictators have been crazy but the people still followed them. Leonard is a wild-eyed fanatic who not only wants total obedience but worship. Few will challenge him. They'll give him what he demands. Even Ben Daniel won't dare buck him now."

As Celeste glared at Francis, Royal searched his mind for a way to calm her down. "Would you like to have a worship service, Celeste? Do you think that might help?" He still shrank from these strange sessions, but he wanted Celeste for himself later that night and was willing to make a sacrifice to satisfy his desires.


Christmas 1991 was a quiet occasion at the Redmond-McKenzie household. Gifts by prearrangement were handmade items: a knitted kerchief, a remade skirt, a renovated flashlight, a game of jackstraws. A morning service was held in the living room. Hank and Scott were asked to give the Christmas message; both declined. Craig, Susie, Jason and Stubby divided up responsibilities, with Craig reading Scripture, Jason giving the prayer and Stubby preaching "the good news about the most wonderful birthday of all time."

The most memorable part of the service occurred during the singing of Christmas songs. Susie sang "Oh Holy Night" as a solo and did it with such sweetness that it brought a rare moment of holiness to the whole gathering. It was not because Susie had a beautiful voice. She did not. Several notes were off key and she stumbled over several words. It was the freshness of her spirit that poured through. Love and joy shone from her eyes. The teen-age sulk was gone; she had suddenly become a radiant woman.

Martha wept. Hank blew his nose several times afterwards. Scott stared at her with an enigmatic look. Craig, Stubby and Jason glowed. Only Molly remained expressionless.

For Christmas dinner there was no special dispensation of a frozen turkey this year. Almost all the Yuletime dinner came from items out of their garden. Since the subjects of religion and computer numbering were declared taboo, the mealtime conversation was pleasant and innocuous.

As the New Year approached, Madame Celeste offered a list of resolutions to her followers. Martha wrote in for a free copy, suitable for framing, and had it hung above the sink in the kitchen:

1. Every day I will commune with my own inner self, in peace and quiet, to free the wellsprings of power locked within me.
2. I will reverence all living things, seeing in them the harmony and oneness of nature.
3. I will acknowledge and respect the sanctity of other people, their beliefs and their gods.
4. In every way, by my words and my actions, I will attempt to prove there is no evil on earth, only unfulfilled good.
5. I will grow each day in openness to the world of spirit and willingness to serve mankind.

Martha could not understand exactly what was meant by these wordy resolutions, but they sounded nice. Craig had snorted the first time he read it, and Jason had shaken his head sadly, but neither used it as a springboard for another wrangle over ideologies.

So 1992 began, and most people still called it 1992. The pope's change of dates to the *First Year of Man* went into effect, but there was great confusion as to how to record it on documents and in the new giant all-purpose computer. The transition from one system to another, plus the numbering program for all citizens, created massive problems for the bureaucrats.

The Redmond-McKenzie household was acutely aware that the deadline of January 30th for each citizen to receive his number was but weeks away. If four of their number refused to comply, their way of life would be greatly threatened. As each day passed the tension grew.

Molly began the new year in a state of quiet desperation. Nothing was going right for her. The domestic routine forced upon her was demeaning. She yearned for her old country club life of sports and parties, but it no longer existed. The club had long since been taken over by FML as a recreation area for its officials. Her old friends had either died in the earthquake, left the area or dropped out of circulation.

Molly felt that people were forever letting her down. First, Douglas left her for a homosexual relationship. Then her grandfather lost his life because he had become a religious fanatic. Scott's selfish life seemed to exclude her and Craig's rejection was an especially sharp blow to her pride. When everyone exclaimed over Susie's sweet song at Christmas, it made Molly feel old at 24 and out of it.

On the second morning of the new year she discovered that she was alone in the house. Jason and Stubby were fishing, Scott, Hank and Craig were at work, while Susie and Martha had gone to visit a neighbor. Molly hated to be by herself; she found solitude almost unbearable because she did not like to think.

She tried to read a novel, settled in her upstairs room. She was just beginning to get into the story when a noise startled her. She froze, listening. The sound was a scuttle of tiny animal feet at the end of the upstairs hall. Goose bumps rose on her arms.

Where was Ragtime? Then she remembered—he was outside. Suddenly the noise was outside her door and she gasped in horror. The door had been slightly ajar—now it was slowly opening!

A rat slithered into the room and stopped, looking at her boldly. He was as large as a standard-sized cat, over a foot long, dingy brown and furrier than rats she had seen pictured. His eyes were dull, and his whiskers and nose twitched. He seemed to be looking right at her.

"Please, don't let him come any farther," she whispered, frozen to her chair. They stared at each other for a long moment, then the rat began to move; there was no darting motion like that of a mouse, just a deliberate, slow, steady stalk toward her.

The rat was now less than six feet from her and moving directly toward her feet. She screamed once and exploded from her chair, around him and down the hall to Susie's room. Inside, she slammed the door, slipped the bolt and clambered up onto the bed. She listened intently but could hear nothing over her own raspy breathing. Her teeth chattered and she was sobbing. "Why is he after me?" she whimpered.

Molly calmed her breathing. This was silly; the rat could not go through a locked door. If only Ragtime was with her. Then her terror returned. A scratching sound began on the other side of the door. The rat was trying to claw his way through the bottom of the wooden door!

This was crazy; was he possessed? No normal rat would behave this way. In utter panic Molly grabbed the closest thing to a weapon she could find—Susie's mirror. She ran to the door and banged the mirror at the spot at the bottom of the door where the rat was clawing.

The noise stopped. She heard a rustle. Then the scratching began again.

Whack! Molly hit the door so hard the glass shattered on the floor.

Silence. There was a scurrying noise which faded away from the door. The rat was gone.


Following Molly's encounter with the cat-sized rat, the men of the house banded together to mount an attack against these bold creatures who had infested the neighborhood. Stronger poisons were spread about; a series of traps were set around the house and garage. Jason moved his bed upstairs. Craig kept his gun on a chair beside his bed.

A week passed. The poison remained uneaten; none of the traps was sprung. The rats seemed to have faded away. Jason shook his head. "Rats with almost human intelligence. Who would have thought it?"

Several nights later Craig met with Jason, Stubby and Susie in the rooms over the garage. January 30th was only two weeks away. They had been praying for ten days for an answer.

"I think I know what God wants me to do," Craig began. "I'm to resign my job with the police and move to the stadium."

"Can we go with you?" asked Susie.

Craig shook his head. "Somebody has to stay here and bring in the fish. This is now our main food supply."

"Craig is right," said Jason. "Someone has to mind the nets. Stubby and Susie can do it. I feel I'm supposed to go east and find one of the Christian communities we've heard about."

Stubby was unshakable on one point. "I'm convinced I'm to go to Israel and be with my people as soon as possible."

Craig nodded. "I'd like to join you."

"Why not?" replied Stubby. "All we've got against us is the whole world system."

"Let's see what happens," Craig replied. He picked up a container of food and slung it over his shoulder. "I'm off to the stadium to deliver some rations."

"Can I go with you?" Susie asked.

Craig shook his head, then kissed his sister. She was so eager, so alive, and so filled with joy, it brought a lump to his throat. The way God's Spirit changed people was a never-ending miracle to him. He thought wistfully of Molly. Some nights his physical desire for her was so strong, he yearned to go to her room. Yet when this ache was almost more than he could bear, God somehow gently reminded him that it would bring only unhappiness. The one word always seemed to be: "Wait."

A two-hours' walk brought Craig to the stadium. Though it was dangerous to go out at night, Craig knew a shortcut that kept him off the main roads. Going there in the day time was much too risky.

The stadium had been built within easy approach of several main highways. At the time of the earthquake the land to the east and south had sunk, becoming a large lake. The area to the northwest had been torn up by a powerful tremor. The destruction of the highways that led into the stadium area had sealed its doom. There was no reason to repair roads leading to a deserted, partially submerged section of land. Tampa's huge airport, a few miles to the west, had been repaired, but it could still be approached from other directions. Thus the scene of so many sporting events had become an abandoned, unusable area of desolation, with vegetation soon covering huge piles of rubble.

Craig edged his way through some thick shrubs until he reached the stadium. He gave a soft whistle, and waited until one of the lookouts met him. Together, they walked down a dimly lit incline which led to a series of well ventilated but crudely furnished rooms. Candles and a few kerosene lamps provided the only light.

Craig delivered his container to a young couple working in a makeshift kitchen, then joined a group of seven newcomers who were sitting on slabs of rock, listening to an orientation lecture.

"My alias is Stephan. We don't use our real names," the soft-spoken leader explained. "Since no one can be forced to tell what he doesn't know, we take this one small precaution in case anyone of us is captured. We have several other safety regulations you need to be aware of."

He explained the warning system, three lookouts at all times from three different observation posts commanding a view of the surrounding area. "If you hear the signal, freeze where you are. Don't move until the all clear." Then he explained the procedures about lighting, food, clothing, sleeping, personal hygiene, trips outside. It was frugal, uncomfortable living: the only beds were mats or sleeping bags. Cooking on a wood-burning stove could only be done at night for fear someone would detect the smoke. The dwellers comforted themselves that they probably had it better than the early Christians who lived in cold dank caves outside of Rome.

The leader finished his talk and asked for questions. Craig quickly became involved in the sharing period and prayer time that followed. He left reluctantly, not looking forward to the long walk home to Bayshore Boulevard. Outside the stadium he gazed one last time at the small mountain of vine-covered concrete. It would be his home before long. Somehow the thought was not reassuring.

Craig resigned his job on January 29th. He was not surprised that Hastings did too. The big man moved to a large communal farm east of Tampa near Brandon, where Christians were accepted who did not want to be numbered but were willing to work hard in the fields.

The second part of Craig's plan did not work out. The dwellers at the stadium asked Craig not to move in, but continue to be their liaison with the outside world. Craig agreed reluctantly. Not only must he face the embarrassment of living at home without a ration card, but he was expected somehow to find food to bring to his Christian brothers.

January 30th, the deadline for numbering arrived and passed. Craig, Susie, Jason and Stubby had not been numbered. In the beginning nothing seemed to change. FML workers were overwhelmed with paperwork and organizational problems. A month of grace was offered without penalty to those who had not received the mark. After February 28th all those who had not been numbered would face a fine and imprisonment.

The weather was warm for February and Craig used his free time to expand the garden. Fish continued to be their main food staple. As time went on, however, problems arose. Shoes, for instance. Without a ration card, there was no way to buy shoes and Craig's were falling apart. Stubby lost a filling from a tooth, and without a number, he could not receive dental care. Martha, their resident expert on medical matters, stonily suggested he pray for a miraculous cure.

February 28th passed by. FML offered another grace period of a month, which Craig, Susie, Jason and Stubby ignored despite further pleas from the others. Spring came unnoticed in the balmy weather and the garden grew under Craig's dedicated touch. Then Hank and Scott brought home alarming news: arrests had begun, persecutions increased. People were filled with dread at the sight of a uniform as the American government became more and more influenced by the United States of Europe, and its true power Pope Sixtus VI.

It was early Friday evening. The fish stew had been eaten, and while nobody was especially hungry, nobody was truly satisfied either. This staple of their diet was an affront to the palate after so many years, but it was better than starving.

Martha was playing solitaire at the kitchen table by the light of candles, while Molly and Susie cleaned up. Craig had gone to bed early with a heavy cold. Jason and Stubby, with Hank along for company, walked down to the bay for the weekly cleaning and repair of the traps. Before long, darkness forced them to stop.

They were walking back along the road when they heard the pounding of feet. Jason, in the lead, was suddenly almost toppled over by the weight of a hurtling body colliding with his.

"Whoa, brother! Slow down." Jason held the shuddering man at arm's length, trying to see his face in the dim light.

The man was scrawny and short, a young black of maybe twenty-five. He was breathing in long, ragged gasps. "Let me go . . . They're after me . . . Please. Don't hold me . . ."

"Who's after you? The General Corps?" Hank asked. No mere gang of hoodlums could inspire such panic.

"I didn't do nothing. Honest." The young man was twisting in Jason's grasp, turning to stare behind him at the broad expanse of Bayshore Boulevard.

"Well, you won't find anywhere to hide out this way. Just a few houses and then the water."

"What about the garage?" Stubby asked. "Can't we hide him, Jason?

Hank shook his head. "They'll go through every chicken coop and doghouse if they know he headed this way. We get caught harboring a fugitive, they'll take us all in—Martha, Susie, everyone."

The man said nothing, and Jason relaxed his grip. "What do they want you for?" he asked.

"I stole some fruit." The man had gained his breath. "I was hungry. They picked me up and had me for almost a week. I never dreamed human beings could get like that. I won't go back there. I'll kill myself first." He was losing control again, and Jason braced him with a supporting arm.

"How'd you get away? I didn't know anybody ever escaped."

"They were moving some of us. It's so crowded at the Institute you can't even sit down. They have prisoners jammed in like sardines, and then they forget them. Leave them for days without food or water. The living and the dead are together, and oh, God! you wouldn't believe the things that happen!" The young man was sobbing, and Jason shook him gently.

"We can't stand out here and make this kind of noise. Hush now."

Jason's words seemed to remind the young man of his pursuers, and he moved nervously. "I have to go. They've got dogs." He seemed torn between his fear of capture and the comfort of human contact.

"We have to help him," Stubby said pleadingly. "If he took the rowboat, maybe the dogs couldn't follow him."

The fugitive turned to him eagerly, grasping this ray of hope. "You have a boat? You'd let me take it? In that prison I almost forgot people can be decent and—" He stopped abruptly as a chorus of barks broke into the night, close at hand. The four men froze at the sound of running feet and car engines slowly approaching.

"Oh, God, no! Oh, save me, Lord!" the stranger whimpered in terror.

Suddenly Jason spoke, his voice imperative and urgent. "Get off the road, all of you! Behind the hedge. Quick!"

No one moved and Stubby spoke in a horrified whisper, "You can't do that, Jason! Don't! You'll be killed!"

"Just do as I say, Stubby. I'm ready to go and he's not. A Christian's always ready."

"Jason, it won't work!" Hank pleaded. "The first thing they'll do is check his number, and when you don't have one they'll know they got the wrong man."

"They won't check his number if he's dead," Jason said quietly. "They bury people first and fill out the report later, before any inquiries can be made."

The three stared at him.

"You mean—" Stubby began. "You mean you'd deliberately *try* to get shot?"

"Certainly. You heard him ask God to save him."

"Then let God! Don't you try to do it," Stubby sobbed.

"Stubby, God *is* doing it. This is how He works, you know, through His people. You wouldn't ask me to disobey, would you? Now hide!"

Headlights were visible in the road. Stubby stood in agony, torn between his love of God and his love of Jason. Then he groaned with pain and turned away from his friend. Taking the hunted man firmly by the arm, he pulled him behind the oleander hedge which ran along the side boundary of the yard. Hank joined them in the protective shadows.

"He's giving up his life for you, do you know that?" Hank

said, his voice hoarse with emotion. "You're a stranger, and he's dying for you."

A slowly moving patrol car pulled into sight, its headlights fanning the road. Men with dogs on leashes were running beside it. "Check that yard there, Jennings. Get your spotlight up around those bushes. Tony, did you check that rowboat? He could be lying down inside it." The sounds echoed in the still night; the three men hidden behind the wispy foliage were breathless with fear.

Jason moved into the beam of the car's headlights, his hands high in a gesture of surrender. "Don't shoot! Here I am." His voice had changed. Gone was the confident serenity. He spoke with whimpering servility, the image of a hunted man, and the men closed in on him like sharks surrounding their prey.

The hidden men could not see exactly what happened as Jason was shoved toward the car. But suddenly there were shouts and what sounded like a fistfight. One of the policemen dropped heavily to the ground and then Jason was sprinting away from them down the road. Strangely and illogically he ran in a straight line right in the beam of the car's headlights. They shot him repeatedly in the back. He fell headlong into the street.

A moment later they had dragged his body into the car and driven off.

Stubby rose to his feet on legs that trembled. "It happened so fast . . . and now he's gone. Jason's gone."

Hank made no attempt now to keep back the tears. "He was the best man I ever knew. Nothing will be the same without him here."

The fugitive was apparently still stunned by the series of events that had taken place so quickly. "I didn't ask him to do that. I didn't ask him to get killed for me."

"Of course you didn't," Stubby said gently. "Jason was listening to a far more urgent voice than yours."

"Yeah . . . well, I better keep moving. I want to get so far from Tampa they never heard the name."

Stubby looked at him in concern. If Jason had died for this man, surely there should be more than just this whispered farewell in the night. He should be told of the faith and devotion that had made Jason sacrifice himself. But there was no time and no way Stubby could reach a man motivated by the urgency of flight. He shook his head and said just two sentences, "Remember, Jesus loves you even more than Jason did. He died for you, too."

Then the man was gone, and Stubby and Hank walked slowly toward the house, weighted with the news they were bringing. By unspoken agreement they entered by the seldom-used front door. Neither wanted yet to walk past the garage that had been Jason's home for four years, where with a cot and a broken lawn chair the gentle black man had created a haven of content.

# VI

Molly was alone in the house one morning in late March when she heard the doorbell ring. She took a deep, steadying breath and fearfully answered the door.

The man was a tall civilian, well dressed for the times with a polite formal manner. He flashed his identification before her eyes as he said, "I'm Oscar Hummel from the General Corps. May I talk with you a few minutes?"

Molly stepped back silently and let him in. He followed her to the living room, and she offered a chair. For the first time in months she was conscious of her frayed clothing, the soiled rug and chipped furniture.

"We have a big problem, Miss Redmond," Mr. Hummel began. "It's all these fugitives, the people who weren't numbered. Now some of our people felt it's useless talking to you, but I said, 'Let's give her the benefit of the doubt.' Perhaps your grandfather got in with some bad company. He wasn't really antisocial himself. You think that might be right?"

Molly nodded, her mouth dry and her breath short. The man, for all his friendliness, terrified her.

"So I decided to come here and talk to you to see if you'd be willing to help us." He looked at her searchingly.

"What do you want?" she asked in a strangled voice.

He watched her with interest, then spoke abruptly. "There's Craig McKenzie, for one. He's a problem to us. You people here have been shielding him."

"No, I haven't," Molly said earnestly.

"We've been suspicious of McKenzie for some time. When he didn't get his number, that confirmed it. He's involved with those fanatics. We believe there must be some big hiding area—some main place these fugitives go. And McKenzie knows where it is. These people are a threat to our way of life, Miss Redmond; they have broken the law and we intend to arrest them. We want you to keep an eye on McKenzie and let us know when it looks like he's ready to go to his friends. Then we will follow him. How's that sound?"

Molly sat in silent panic, watching the FML agent. Her mind was racing. Before she could answer, he spoke again.

"Let me make the choice easier for you, Miss Redmond. If you agree to help us by watching McKenzie, all the black marks against you will be erased. If you refuse, I'll take you downtown now and we'll pick up McKenzie too. It's that simple." Hummel sat back and lit a cigarette.

Molly was frightened and confused. She was also trapped. What alternative did she have? "All right," she finally said. "But I can't promise anything. I can try, that's all."

"We understand that," the agent continued smoothly. "That's a wise decision, Miss Redmond. With your grandfather's record, you've been in a shaky position. But that's all past, and now you're one of my people." Then he outlined her new duties as an informer for the police. She listened in a daze.

"You'll need a communicator." He reached into his inner pocket and withdrew a small call radio the size of a pack of cigarettes. "You can reach me any time just by beeping me. It's much simpler than trying to get your phone hooked up again." He chuckled. "How would you ever explain having a phone that worked properly?"

As Hummel explained the functions of the little communicator, she felt like a character in a science fiction novel. When he handed it to her, her sense of unreality heightened.

"That ought to cover it." The agent crushed out his cigarette, stood up and started toward the door. "Remember what I told you to look for—food disappearing, requests for old clothes, that kind of thing." He paused a moment and his voice hardened: "I'll be patient, but if I hear nothing from you in ten days or so I'll be back. And you know what that means."

"I wouldn't want Craig hurt," Molly said with a sudden pang.

"We don't want to hurt him," Hummel said coolly, "We'll take him into custody and put him through a re-education program."

"Oh, that's better," Molly answered. She followed him in a daze as he walked toward the front door and made his polite farewells. As he drove away, she stood by the door looking with wonder and fear at the little radio device in her hand.

What had she done? She would have to spy on Craig, report his movements to the police and help them trap him. If I don't do it, they'll get Craig anyway, she thought helplessly.

She went upstairs to hide her little radio before Martha came home.


It was becoming increasingly difficult to acquire supplies for the stadium refugees since most of those who had been helping were the ones now without ration cards. Craig, Susie and Stubby had put aside a few items, but as they laid them out on a small table in the garage after lunch one day, they added up to a pathetically small package.

"Maybe I ought to go tonight no matter how little we have," concluded Craig.

Stubby agreed. "We know they're really suffering."

"It's too dangerous," Susie protested. "I don't think Craig ought to risk a trip for that little bit of stuff."

"It's not that much of a risk," replied her brother. "Compared to Jason's sacrifice, this is pretty small." The death of Jason continued to weigh heavily on their spirits.

"I suppose you ought to go," Stubby said. "But like Susie, I'm beginning to get nervous about the whole business."

Craig felt uneasy, too, but he was not willing to admit it. He went to the kitchen and opened the cabinet which housed their small store of sweets. If I take them some candy, he thought, maybe they'll overlook how little real food there is.

He found a few old and soggy pieces of cellophane-wrapped hard candy brought home by Scott from the television station, a gift to the employees by someone looking for preferential treatment. Craig took the candy without qualms. He knew it would be missed by his mother, but he was not concerned with her wrath. He only hoped to bring a bright spot to those in hiding.

Molly walked up the back steps just as Craig shut the cabinet. She could see his actions through the back screen door. As he left by the hall, she entered the kitchen quietly, looked in the cabinet and was not surprised to see that the little candy canister was now empty.

Molly knew Craig very well after almost four years. It was totally out of character for him to steal candy for himself. It had to be for his friends who had gone underground. She faced an agony of indecision. Should she use the call radio? She would hate to call the agent on a false alarm.

She was also terrified at the thought that Craig might be arrested by other FML agents and Hummel would find out. If this happened, she might go to jail for failing to inform. Oh, Craig, she thought, if I could only be sure you'd get away with it. But she did not think he would. She was now sure he would be caught one way or another. It would be better for her and Scott and the others if she turned him in.

She slipped up to her room and took the little radio out of its hiding place in her bottom drawer. She turned it over in her hand several times, hesitating, then took a deep breath and plunged in the call button. That was all there was to it. No sound came forth. No voice answered her. But the agent would be notified of her contact, and he would make the next move. She hoped he would do nothing to expose her to the family.

She rehid the radio, then walked to the window and stared out at the broad sweep of front lawn. Even after years of doing without, she found herself suddenly craving a drink. She stood instead, watching the bay as it shimmered through the leaves and branches of the trees outside her windows. To her astonishment she felt the tears trickling down her cheeks, rare for one who prided herself on not being a weepy woman. Her vision blurred. Then for a moment she imagined she was seeing the outdoors as it used to be, with the trees whole and green, the lawn trimmed and even, the double lanes of Bayshore Boulevard full of fast-flowing traffic, and the bay a cool, bright blue.

Her vision cleared. The yard and grounds were pocked with brown, the foliage was scraggly and untrimmed, many of the trees broken. In a sharp moment of self awareness Molly realized that she was broken and scarred too. The upheaval of the last few years had sharply changed her from the well-groomed, poised person she had been. She recognized the core of hardness inside her now.

She moved to her bed and lay down on top of the spread. She thought of Craig, his youth, his good nature, his responsibility and kindness. Then she could see his dark good looks marred by blood and wounds and his strength and faith broken under pain. "Life is a bitch," she whispered. "A real bitch."


Craig waited several hours after dinner, then started out. The walk to the stadium was long and exhausting. He had not realized the extent to which he had been suffering from lack of nourishment. He stopped for a moment in a clearing several hundred yards back from the stadium, the small sack of food held limply in his hand.

"That's no sanctuary," he said to himself, looking at the ruins. "It's just a bunch of broken up concrete and steel. I'll bet they get cold and wet in there." The night was dark and overcast. He moved closer, gave the usual whistle and two men stepped out to greet him.

Suddenly there was a glare of blinding blue-white lights all about them. "You are surrounded," came a deep voice from a bull horn. "Remain where you are. Anyone trying to leave will be shot."

The thundering tones of this voice rolled over the ruined stadium and echoed through Craig's brain. He had been followed. He had brought disaster on his friends. His fear over their plight and his responsibility for it almost drove out the terror of being caught. He backed up against the bushes.

"Come with me," a new voice whispered behind him.

The two men who had greeted Craig were walking toward the lights, their hands held up high in what at another time might have been an attitude of praise.

The voice spoke behind him again, "Drop to your knees and crawl straight back." The voice was calm and strengthening.

Craig dropped to the ground and scuttled rapidly backward until he reached darkness. There he paused, trembling. He could feel the presence of the man beside him, and he listened to the thudding of his own heart while they hunched in the darkness. The voices of the other men drifted in.

"No, we were the only ones here." It was the voice of the man Craig knew as Barnabas.

"We're giving ourselves up, officer." That one was Andrew.

Craig listened as the armed men of the General Corps answered skeptically. It was now clear to him why Andrew and Barnabas had walked unprotestingly toward the lights and certain capture: they hoped the police would arrest them and leave without making a more careful search. It was a futile hope, especially since Craig had disappeared from their sight. They were not about to leave without him. It was clear; he would have to surrender himself to protect the others.

"Don't do anything foolish. The others are now warned and will be scattering in every direction." The voice from behind had answered his unspoken thoughts and now a steady hand grasped his arm. Craig rose on trembling limbs and crept along with his companion toward the bowels of the wrecked stadium.


Stubby paced the floor of the garage, praying silently. He felt a sick certainty that Craig was in trouble. Scott and Susie entered and a look at their faces confirmed his fears.

"Susie tells me that Craig has gone to meet a bunch of fugitives. Is this true? I mean a big hideout full of them?" Scott's voice was full of concern.

"Yes, he has," Stubby replied. "He had a little food for them. Why, Scott? You know something?"

"Oh, Lord, yes. The rumor was all over the studio this afternoon." Scott was pacing between the door and the cot. "There was a tip-off to an agent. They were hoping to round up a bunch of fugitives. I wonder if Craig was the one they were planning to follow?"

"It couldn't be Craig," Stubby protested. "Nobody knew anything about it but him and Susie and me. There wasn't any way for the General Corps to find out."

"They have ways you wouldn't dream about, Stubby." Scott spoke knowingly. "One person out of six is on their payroll as an informer, except they don't pay informers any more. They just threaten them, force them into it."

"Where do you get all this information?" Susie asked.

"We have our news sources. Even if we can't broadcast it, we know what's going on." Scott was pacing again.

Susie was sitting in stunned silence. "What can you find out, Scott? Is there anything we can do?"

"I'll go back to the news room," Scott said. "They'll be getting reports when anything happens."

"Won't that look suspicious? You don't usually go back at night," Stubby said.

"And you'll be breaking curfew," Susie pointed out.

"Don't worry. I'll tell them I had a heavy date and bribe my way through. I've done it before." Scott shot a glance at Stubby. "Did Craig take the bicycle?"

"No. He said it's easier and safer to walk."

"Okay, I'll take the bike then," Scott said. Susie was crying softly as he wheeled the bicycle toward the door.

"We will pray for you, Scott," Stubby said quietly. "The Lord can protect you and blind your enemies. It's not safe out there."

"I don't need any help from God," Scott laughed. "I can take care of myself."

"That's a dangerous thing to say," Stubby replied gently as he watched Scott pedal down the driveway.


Craig crawled for what seemed like hours in and out of the cavernous concrete ruins of the stadium, following his companion without questions. All about them they heard shouts and running feet; twice a volley of shots rang out.

At last the man in front of him stopped. He leaned back toward

Craig and putting his mouth against Craig's ear, he whispered, "Be extra careful from here on. Don't tear the vines, please. They are my friends."

Craig nodded and moved with caution through an opening in the rubble. He found himself standing on a small ledge at one of the uppermost levels of the ruins.

"It's my fifty-yard line seat," the other man said quietly. "The view is usually great." He edged toward the lip of the ledge and looked downward.

Craig followed him warily. They were the equivalent of four or five stories high and the view below was panoramic. Six patrol cars had managed to maneuver through the marshy land around the ruins and were parked now at the base of the stadium. Dozens of uniformed men were running about with lights, bull horns, guns, tear-gas canisters and several dogs on leashes. One man in plain clothes was controlling the action from the dropped tail gate of a station wagon where a communications system was set up. A small cluster of prisoners was huddled together against a big rock, two guards with machine guns watching them. Craig was sick at heart over the sight.

"Most of our people will escape," Craig's companion spoke with assurance. "There are dozens of escape trails worked out."

Craig sat beside him, numbed by the developments. "Who are you?" he asked his companion. "I knew a lot of the people here, but I don't remember you."

"Just call me John." In the faint light from below Craig could see the proffered hand and he shook it warmly.

"Thanks for saving me," he said.

"We're not safe yet," John said. "What do you have in that sack?"

Craig glanced down at the little container of food he had clutched in his left hand. Several times during the wild dash for safety, he had considered discarding it. Some instinct told him to hang onto it.

"A few apples, some hard-boiled eggs, three pieces of corn bread and several pieces of hard candy."

"Candy? Really?" John's voice was wistful. "I haven't had any candy in years. May I have a piece?"

"Sure." Craig rummaged in the sack and took out several

cellophane-wrapped balls. He handed one to John who tore off the wrapper and popped the candy into his mouth.

"Umm. Grape. I'd forgotten how good it was." John slurped happily a moment then added. "Have one yourself."

"No, I wouldn't feel right about it," Craig said. "They're for the others."

"The others will be all over southern Florida by morning. Take one. You're exhausted and the sugar may help you."

Craig slipped a piece in his mouth and sucked on it slowly. It did refresh him.

"They won't start a thorough search until daylight," John said. "Let's make a run for it now."

"I'm ready."

"Good. I want to keep away from those dogs." John rose to a crouch and crawled back to the lip of their little plateau. "I think the back side isn't so well guarded. Let's try it."

John straightened up and moved quickly down toward the rear of the ruined stadium. Craig followed, still carrying his sack. He could now see the vague outline of the horizon above the ruins. On either side of them there were men's voices and the erratic play of lights, but there seemed to be no one directly ahead.

John listened for a moment, then he put his mouth to Craig's ear again. "We're heading toward the lake—that's why no one is in front of us. They don't think it's crossable on foot."

Craig shivered despite the humidity. "We're going to walk across that swamp. It's full of—"

John grabbed his arm warningly. "Don't talk, just follow me." He fell to the ground and began to slither on his stomach to the edge of the water.

Craig felt a torrent of fear wash through him. The idea of crossing the new lake was terrifying. Formed by the earthquake and continually fed from some underground source, it was far different from the bright blue lakes that dotted the area. Instead of herons, ducks and tropical fish, this lake housed snakes, leeches, and alligators. The water was hot too; a nasty, viscous liquid that felt unclean to the touch. The dense tropical vegetation that lined its shores also seemed particularly hostile. The thought of walking into the slimy, foul water, especially at night, made him want to retch.

After several moments of agony, Craig dropped to his stomach and began to wiggle through the weeds and sand toward the edge of the water.

"Slip into the water as quietly as you can." John's voice was so low it was almost inaudible. Craig rose to a crouch, stuffed his food sack into his shirt, and cautiously crept out into the lake. The hot water was revolting and he turned his mind firmly away from thoughts of the slimy creatures who lived there. He reached John's side and wordlessly they began a strange and frightening trip toward the other side.

The water was waist-deep during most of the journey, only once rising to their armpits. Craig moved ahead in a dream-like exhaustion. Soon each step forward in the oozing muddy bottom required a tremendous effort of mind and body. Twice they heard loud splashings as animals of considerable size moved away from them in fright. Small tickling mouths occasionally investigated their legs. Craig's body soon felt so heavy that he wondered if he should stop and remove his shoes and jeans. When he stepped on a wriggling snake, he dismissed that thought.

Once a large reptile glided toward them. John and Craig both froze. An alligator! Two beady eyes stared at them for an endless moment. The gator then moved away.

After an hour or so, John signaled a stop. "We'll turn here and head west; we've gone far enough south. If we can cross the Dale Mabry Highway, I think we'll be safer."

"You know of a safe place to go?" Craig asked.

"I know a Christian lady; she'll give us a meal and a place to rest. It's fairly close." John was moving sluggishly toward the shore, his eyes searching all around for signs of danger.

Soon they both stood on the shore, dripping and reeking of the foul water. The night air was chilly in contrast to the hot lake and Craig shivered.

"Let's go," John said and they began walking faster. Craig had lost all sense of direction; he merely followed John. They moved steadily through high grass now. Craig felt a nip on his shoe. "Not rats," he groaned. Swarming with rodents, this terrain soon became as much an enemy to conquer as the lake had been. Both began trotting to scare the rats. Craig fought down panic at the thought of what might happen if one of them fell.

Finally, the high grass thinned out. They had come to a residential area. Now they could get their bearings. It was almost dawn, the eastern sky a pearly grey to their backs, when John at last gave a grunt of satisfaction. He was reading a decrepit street sign. "This is Cypress. Now I know where I am." They walked faster now, restored by the thought of a safe destination.

The house they were searching for was a small grey ranch-type dwelling, set toward the back of an untended lot. John moved stealthily to the back door and knocked softly. In spite of the early hour and the hesitancy of his knock, the door was opened within a few seconds by a large maternal-looking woman in a faded blue robe. John's face reassured her and she opened the door wide in a gesture of invitation. They crept inside like whipped dogs and sank into kitchen chairs utterly exhausted.

"I know you're tired, but tell me where you came from and what sort of trouble you're in." She directed her questions at John, so Craig leaned his head back against the wall and silently thanked God for momentary safety.

John spoke quietly to the woman about their dilemma. She listened without comment. When he had finished she nodded. "I'll give you a bite to eat, then you must sleep for awhile."

She rose from the table and bustled around the stove, heating some stew. Craig ate in a daze, struggling to stay awake. He followed the woman to a darkened room. When she left, he stripped off his foul clothes and sank into one of the twin beds. He was asleep in seconds.


It was almost five in the morning before Scott returned to the anxious twosome waiting for him in the garage. "What did you learn, Scott?" Stubby asked.

Scott sat at the foot of his cot. "They hit the stadium ruins. I guess the place was crawling with fugitives. The police are still out there."

"That was the place," Stubby said in anguish. "That's where Craig went."

"It was a good hiding place," Scott said. "The General Corps hadn't thought of it." He glanced cautiously at Susie. "They hit it like a commando raid. It doesn't look good for Craig."

Susie nodded, her eyes stricken. "I ought to tell my parents," she said.

310 to September, 1992

"Wait till morning," Scott said. "Let them have a good night's sleep."

"If you think so," Susie agreed.

They sat there until dawn while Scott described his trip to and from the WTBA Studios. He was just finishing his story when they heard a car in the driveway.

"Police," Stubby said in hushed tones.

"Oh, no," Susie moaned. She peeped out the garage door. A two-toned patrol car was pulling up beside the front porch. Two uniformed men sat in front. As Susie watched, one jumped out to open the rear door for a tall civilian. Together these two walked toward the front porch while the driver waited.

Susie heard a gentle murmur behind her and turned to see Stubby on his knees beside the cot, praying softly. Scott had come up behind her; together they watched the house as the uniformed man knocked loudly on the door.

"What do they want?" Susie asked in hushed tones.

"Your guess is as good as mine," Scott answered.

Hank walked outside onto the porch and had a brief conversation with the plain-clothes man. Then the two men entered the house.

"I'm going to join them," Scott said. "I want to find out what's going on."

"How will you explain being dressed at this time of morning?" Susie asked. "You don't want them wondering if you've been out breaking the curfew."

"I'll sneak in the back door," said Scott.

Scott slipped out of the garage and walked quietly toward the back door. Susie watched him enter the house, then she turned back to the kneeling figure by the cot.

"I'm scared to death," she moaned softly.

Stubby smiled at her. "Don't be ashamed of being afraid. I am, too."

The two knelt together as the rays of the morning sun filtered into the garage.


Hank, Martha, Molly and Scott were sitting in a silent semi-circle, facing the smooth-talking FML agent. The room was damp and dismal in the grey light.

"Mr. McKenzie, I'm Oscar Hummel of the General Corps. Where is your son?" The voice was cold, chilling.

"I don't know. He sleeps in the garage apartment." Hank gestured with his hand.

Scott spoke casually. "What's the problem?"

The agent surveyed Scott distastefully, then turned to Martha. "You realize that your son is a subversive. He refused to be numbered and is a fugitive from justice."

Scott's heart jumped. They hadn't caught Craig! He was alive and free. Susie and Stubby would be wild with joy when they heard.

Martha was stammering in her confusion. "I'm sure he's out in the garage asleep right now."

The agent answered Martha angrily. "We know he's not here. We got a tip-off about McKenzie and followed him last night. We saw him reach his destination. But he got away from our police. We know he didn't come back here because we've been watching this place since nine o'clock last night. Now do you understand?"

The room was absolutely silent as the meaning of these words sank home. Martha was the only one who didn't understand what lay behind his words. But Hank and Scott knew what had happened: somebody in their own household had informed. Without hesitation, Hank and Scott stared at Molly whose face had turned ashen.

"You bitch," Hank hissed.

Scott glared at his sister in disgust.

"Why are you so mad at Molly?" Martha asked in confusion.

Molly's face was contorted. "They made me do it. They knew all about Craig anyway . . . "

The agent interrupted. "That's enough, Miss Redmond. You did nothing wrong. You helped society. If we had more like you, our job would be a lot easier."

Hank turned from Molly and stared at the FML investigator in hatred. "You'll get no help from me," he said.

"Mr. Redmond?" The agent turned to Scott inquiringly.

"I have no idea where he is."

The agent looked back at Martha again. "All right, Mrs. Mc-Kenzie. You and your husband come with us. We'll see what you can remember."

"I need to get dressed," Martha whimpered.

"All right. But don't try anything foolish. The house is surrounded."

Molly huddled in her chair, dry-eyed, overwhelmed by what she had done. The tall inspector spoke to her, a bit of warmth in his voice for the first time. "They'll get over it. People always do."

"Maybe so," Molly answered dully.

The agent turned to Scott. "We'll be leaving a couple of men here to watch things, Mr. Redmond, in case McKenzie shows up. Just remember you're obliged to report it if you hear from McKenzie. You give him aid and comfort and you're as guilty as he is."

"I understand," Scott replied. He watched as the investigator called his men out from various observation points around the grounds. Two were left to stand guard. "They really did have the place under surveillance," he thought to himself. Had he eluded them on his trip to and from the studio? Or did the guards have orders to let him come and go? Scott was puzzled and uneasy.

It was late afternoon before Craig was awakened, thoroughly refreshed. During a light meal, he discussed the future with John and the woman who had befriended them.

"I have a friend who joined a farm commune near Brandon, about fifteen miles from here," Craig began. "He said they accept people who aren't numbered. There is a good chance I can stay with him and work." Craig recounted all of Hastings' enthusiasm for his new situation and asked John to join him.

"No thanks. It sounds good, but I'll head south. I have friends who will help me," John replied.

Craig was sorry to leave this new friend who had so dramatically saved his life, yet he did not know enough about the Brandon farm to be very persuasive. He thanked his benefactress, hugged John with real affection and left as soon as darkness fell.

The trip east on Highway 60 was much easier than the one the night before. He had eaten and was well rested; he had fully recovered from the terror of a narrow escape. As he strode along briskly in the dark, he had no difficulty avoiding the lights of police patrols. It was near dawn when he approached the town of Brandon. Just outside the town he saw the lights of a vehicle coming down the road behind him.

Craig scrambled off to the side and stooped down behind a palmetto bush. Just as the vehicle moved into view, the sun edged up over the horizon and the landscape was flooded with a pale yellow light. It was a pickup truck. As it approached, Craig saw the driver and jubilantly recognized Hastings' broad body and bearded face.

He leaped from his hiding place and shouted, "Hastings! Stop! It's Craig!"

The truck swerved as Hastings hit the brakes hard and skidded to a halt about seventy-five feet down the road.

"That's really neat work, Lord," Craig said joyfully as he dashed toward the truck. "I knew You could do it."

The door of the cab burst open, and Hastings clambered down from the driver's seat. They embraced and Craig felt his eyes misting.

"It's a real miracle, Hastings. I've been praying all night I'd find you."

"Well, you sure hit me head on." Hastings was just the same: oversized, unkempt, hearty, but a bulwark of strength to Craig who quickly explained his situation.

Hastings' delight was obvious. "Man, it's good to have you here. You're sure skinny, though. But, we'll fatten you up. Let's get outa here. We're both breaking curfew." They climbed into the truck.

"What are you doing? Something illegal?" Craig asked.

"It shouldn't be since it's a freedom guaranteed in the Constitution. I was at church." He started the ancient truck and drove off rapidly.

"At dawn? Can't you ever be normal, Hastings?"

"Communion service—very quiet, very select group of people who meet together and then go to work early."

Craig shook his head in wonder. "You amaze me."

"It's all your fault, you know," Hastings chuckled. He turned off on a side road and they pulled up in front of a long, low building surrounded by big trees. It was well tended, prosperous looking. Hastings climbed out and beckoned to Craig. "Come on in and I'll introduce you to the elders. We need their okay."

Craig stood beside him uncertainly. "You think it's going to be all right?"

"Has to be. I was praying for you at church." Hastings led him up the steps toward the front door. He walked inside, toward food and shelter and a warm welcome.

Scott stared across the room at Oscar Hummel and licked a trickle of blood from the corner of his mouth. He was frightened and his body ached from the brutality of his arrest, but his primary reaction was one of embarrassment that he had been caught. He thought he had been on top of the situation.

The room was dingy and bare, windowless and featureless. Scott had no idea where they were; he had been arrested on his way home from work, then drugged. He had awakened on the floor of this room.

"Did you honestly think you'd fooled us?" the tall agent asked in scorn. "Nobody gets away with that stuff."

Scott wanted to point out that Craig had escaped from their trap, but he said nothing. Hummel was looking at him with contempt, his eyes narrowed and glittering. Scott wanted to respond with wit and boldness, but he needed first to assess the situation.

"We saw you leave and followed you that night. You went to the television studio. We could have taken you any time, but we didn't bother." Hummel took a package of cigarettes from his pocket, and Scott was amazed to see genuine, commercially produced cigarettes. For some reason this frightened him more than anything that had happened. If this FML official were in a position to obtain real, pre-earthquake cigarettes, he must have tremendous power. Scott swallowed a lump of fear.

"At this point, you are only accused of breaking curfew. That's fairly minor. If you can give me information about McKenzie, I can probably get the charges dropped. If you can't—" Hummel did not finish the sentence.

"I don't know anything. I was never in on their talk or the plans they made. I'm not one of them." Scott heard a pleading note in his voice.

"We know of your relationship with his sister. Can you deny being close to her?"

"That was just a convenience. I mean, she was right there in the house. Would you have turned that down? But her brother is something else. A real fanatic."

"Yes, I know. A Christian." The agent's face hardened and the smooth, placid features changed and took on a darkness which astonished Scott. "They have challenged our authority and hindered our plans long enough. We'll get every one of them eventually. The stupid fanatics!"

"I wish I could help you," Scott said hesitantly, and the angry investigator looked at him as though he had forgotten his presence.

"Do you really? Are you choosing your side, or are you merely trying to save your own skin? What can you do to help us?"

Scott felt panic rising. Not only had Hummel's face changed; his voice was different, too. "I'll keep you posted on the McKenzie girl and that other Christian, Stubby Kraft."

Hummel looked at him scornfully. "They're just kids."

"But they may be in touch with Craig McKenzie."

The inspector seemed not to hear him. "You always try to play both sides, don't you, Redmond? Well your time is up. Come with me." The polished demeanor was gone. Eyes glittering, the agent opened the door and shoved his prisoner out before him.

They moved down a dim corridor and Scott heard his captor muttering under his breath. "He's crazy," Scott thought wildly. "Completely flipped out!" As they passed out from the building into a large, dark, untended backyard, Scott felt hope rising. Maybe he could escape. There were only the two of them, no armed men or guard dogs now. He felt the effects of the drugs wearing off. He gathered his wits, ready to seize any opportunity.

"Back through here." They had traversed the yard and were now entering a grove of straggly citrus trees. The night was moonlit, and Scott could see fairly well. Ahead of them were bobbing lights and several moving figures. If he were going to escape, he must make his move quickly. He looked from side to side, judging his chances. Suddenly he remembered his cocksure voice saying "I can take care of myself." He felt much less sure now, but still he dismissed the idea of calling upon outside help. He would make it on his own, or not at all.

He had no idea of his location, no hint of which direction to run. The grove extended all around them and there was no indication of a road. They were climbing to higher ground toward the scene of some kind of activity. He was about to plunge into the trees in a dash for safety when the agent spoke. "Forget it. You wouldn't get ten feet." Scott felt goose bumps rising on his arms. Could this insane man read his mind?

"We have abilities you never dreamed of," the answer came and a triumphant laugh followed. "And you are totally helpless before us." The man's hand gripped Scott's shoulder and darts of pain shot down his arm. They marched together into a small clearing.

A number of men and women were standing silent around a long, low table. As they caught sight of Hummel and his prisoner approaching, there was a sudden murmur of excitement. Scott faced them with as much courage as he could muster. He was now thoroughly frightened, and his arm and hand were totally numb. It was an unearthly and terrifying situation.

"I have brought you something to offer as a sacrifice," the agent announced. "Lay him on the table."

Scott fought madly with his one good arm as the people overwhelmed him and threw him to the ground. He lay panting heavily, his mind reeling. What horrors did they plan for him? He looked about desperately. Surely this was a nightmare.

His captor stood there tall and powerful, towering over his fallen body; the other men and women leered at him. Even the trees in the background were almost animate in their positions of menace. He squinted his eyes; there appeared to be figures carved into the tree trunks, faces and replicas of birds and animals, but the light was dim and he could not be sure.

"Up here," the agent barked, and the others lifted Scott's body effortlessly. Suddenly Scott wanted desperately to live. He would have traded his soul for another week, day, even hour of life. Then the terrifying reality struck him. It was too late. Too late to believe, too late to accept God. A totally new experience awaited him and he had nothing with which to face it. He whimpered. He trembled.

His body was stripped roughly and placed supine on the table. Now he was shivering and pleading, reaching out in supplication with his one good hand. He could hear his own voice, blurred by tears and fright. He was speaking gibberish.

His tall captor stood by the table, viewing Scott with disgust. "You are a weakling. You wouldn't join us and you wouldn't join them. You are a nothing. As you lived, so shall you die. Death won't release you."

His eyes glittering in the moonlight, he suddenly raised both hands and Scott saw to his horror that he held a long, heavy knife in a double-handed grip. Then the knife slashed down.

In his last second of consciousness, Scott noticed his captor's hands, and wondered how the deformity could have escaped his attention before. It was the last thing Scott saw or knew. On each hand Hummel had six fingers.

# VII

Craig settled down to farm life and found it satisfying. There were about thirty people in residence, and they worked tirelessly to develop the land, growing a wide variety of fruits and vegetables. The owners of the farm had been numbered or the property would have been confiscated. The members who had refused to be marked, mostly refugees, were simply not listed in any farm reports. The isolation of the farm, the low profile of the workers and their prayers as a group had protected them so far from FML authorities.

Craig ate to the point of embarrassment the first few weeks, restoring his weakened body to sound health. The jeans which had hung loosely from his bony hips during the flight from Tampa began to fit more snugly. It was a quiet, peaceful life, fairly safe even for runaways, and Craig would have been content if he could have reassured his family that he was safe. A quick trip home would be risky without a travel permit, even if done at night. And there was always the possibility that the Redmond house was under FML surveillance. Troubled, he sought Hastings.

"I'll have no peace of mind as long as my family wonders if I am dead or alive," he said.

"I'd go tell them myself," Hastings said, "but it's too dangerous. Your house is bound to be watched."

Craig accepted that and sought comfort in his prayers. "Lord, let them know I'm all right."

Almost immediately there was a feeling of the Lord's presence and reassurance. He was to adjust to his new life, build up his body for the new adventure that was soon to come.


Royal and Francis continued to meet with Celeste even though all three had suffered sharp reverses the first half of 1992. Royal Enterprises had gone through a poor year in 1991 and was doing even worse in 1992. After being replaced as chairman of the worldwide television network, Royal found it more and more difficult to concentrate on his affairs. He saw Leonard less and less as the pope seemed to lose interest in his political and economic powers in his strange obsession to seek the worship of the people.

Madame Celeste had begun to deteriorate sharply after her radio program had been terminated. The death blow had come from Leonard who had also been responsible for displacing Royal from worldwide television. Celeste had turned to the spirits for help and ate and slept so irregularly that she seemed to age ten years.

Francis drank almost constantly. He blamed Leonard for their decline in fortunes and his dazed mind was full of resentment for what had happened to Douglas.

In spite of a mutual distrust and boredom with life, these three met frequently. They sat one night in Celeste's apartment and drank mechanically as the candles flickered and danced in the semi-darkness. Francis spoke with anguish. "I dream of Douglas now and then. He always seems bathed in light. I wonder where he is."

"You sleep too much," Royal complained. He turned to Celeste. "He can't stay awake at work."

"How do you know?" Francis retorted. "You haven't been to the office in weeks."

"That's a lie," Royal said angrily. "You think the office can't run without you. Well, I don't need a drunk to tell me what to do."

"I'm not a drunk," replied Francis. "You used to say the same thing about Douglas, remember? Well, maybe he did drink too much, but that's because there's plenty to drink about around here." He giggled at his play on words.

"Is it necessary for you to keep on bringing up Douglas?" Celeste asked.

"I'll talk about him if I want to," Francis said testily. "You didn't like Douglas because his faith made you uncomfortable."

"He made me sick, that's what he made me," Celeste said. "I can tolerate a bad man, or I can respect a good one. But he was a mealy-mouthed weakling."

Royal nodded. "He really was disgusting, Francis. We're better off without him."

"That's not true." Francis sat up with sudden intensity. "He kept us normal, don't you see? He brought something decent and wholesome into this group. At the end he showed us real courage. And since he's gone, we've been different."

"It isn't us," Royal said. "It's the times."

"But you do admit things are different?" Francis asked.

"Will you shut up, Francis?" Celeste rose and walked toward the bar for another drink.

"Why don't I just leave then?" Francis jumped up.

There was no reaction from Celeste or Royal. Francis stood there uncertain for a moment, filled with self-loathing and self-pity. At that moment he made a decision. He would go to Florida and deliver a letter.

If it had not been for Stubby, Molly would have become an outcast in her own home and a candidate for suicide. Added to the guilt over her betrayal of Craig was the jolting news of Scott's death. The cold impersonal letter from FML had arrived several days after Scott had been taken into custody. His death was attributed to resisting an officer.

Molly had read it dry-eyed. This was just another of the horrors that had left her almost mute from inner grief. It was as if the succession of shocks had dried up all her tears. At this point the thought of self-destruction entered Molly's mind. What did she have to live for? Hank and Martha hated her. Both had gone through a mind-numbing experience during interrogation at police headquarters. When they were returned home by the arresting officers neither could talk to anyone about what they had been through.

Meals had become short, almost silent occasions. Short because there was so little to eat. Silent except for Stubby and Susie who tried to bring normality back to the household. During one evening meal Stubby spoke out. "I don't want to be disrespectful to you two," he said looking at Hank and Martha, "but Molly has suffered enough. She has lost her grandfather and brother, not to mention her parents when she was little. We're the only family she has left. I think we need to try and forget our wounds and accept each other and work together."

"I think Stubby is right," said Susie.

Hank sat there stonily for a long moment, then nodded. "Molly, what you did was wrong, but I guess fear can make us all do things we regret. I'll try to forget."

Martha was silent for a long moment. "I'll go along with my husband," she said half-heartedly.

Molly flashed a grateful look at Stubby, but was too frozen to do more than nod her head.


Francis Chapman stared somberly at the big white house and wondered for the hundredth time what had motivated him to make this involved and expensive trip. A fool's errand, his mind told him, but here he was, the Florida sun warming his body as he climbed from the back of the limousine. He still had some influence with FML officials or he would never have attempted it. Travel was difficult and expensive in these days, and few people could have made the journey even had they wanted to.

"Wait here, driver," he ordered.

He recognized Molly as soon as she opened the door. She was a striking woman, he admitted reluctantly to himself, as he noted her red hair, trim figure, shapely legs. She stared at him now through the screen door, sullen and suspicious. "What do you want?" she asked.

"I'm Francis Chapman. Does my name mean anything to you?"

Molly's face blanched. She stared at him in a dazed silence, and he could read emotions playing across her face one after another; bewilderment, recognition, hurt, shock, anger. "You're . . . you're the man who . . . "

"Yes, I'm Douglas' friend."

The color in Molly's face turned from white to red. "You've got gall to come here," she sputtered. "I don't want to see you."

"Do you want to hear about Douglas?"

She eyed him coldly for a long moment. Then with a shrug of distaste, Molly opened the screen door and led the way to the living room; Molly sat on the edge of the sofa, Francis in a wing-backed chair. "What's happened to Douglas?" she asked.

Now that he was face to face with Molly, Francis found himself acutely uncomfortable. "When did you last hear from him?" he began.

"When he took up with you."

Francis drew a deep breath. "Douglas is dead."

He watched as her face twisted in pain. Then she put on her mask of indifference. "How did it happen?"

Francis reached into his pocket and pulled out a letter. "Douglas wrote this to you when he was in Israel last winter. He died not long afterwards." Molly accepted the letter, turned it over in her hands and stared at it numbly. It was rumpled and stained, creased from much handling. With trembling fingers she opened it; Francis watched her as she read the words he now knew by heart.

Dear Molly—

*I need to write this letter. God is asking me to even if I don't know whether it will ever reach you. But if He wants it written, He will get it delivered.*

*First, I need your forgiveness, even though what I did to you was unforgivable. At the time I thought I would find a way to explain, to make it up to you, but I got trapped into a situation I couldn't escape. I see now that I was weak, selfish and greedy.*

*I put my ambition and desire to succeed ahead of everything else. The relationship I entered with Francis Chapman was wrong, and I did it to feather my nest. Instead, I fouled it.*

*I have asked the Lord to forgive me for all this and He has. I've discovered that He is a loving and forgiving God. I pray now that you will forgive me too.*

*You may wonder why all this talk about God? I was certainly not a religious man when you knew me. And the only religion I got from my group in New York—Francis, Lawrence Royal, Madame Celeste and Uriah Leonard, the former bishop and now Pope Sixtus—was from the pit of hell. Don't be fooled by the pope's flowery speeches. His allegiance is to Satan not God.*

*Everything changed for me when I met two Israeli Christians here in Jerusalem recently. Their names—Amos Mozell and Elias Johnson. Before I met them I was a fallen-away Roman Catholic and a materialist. When I left them that day I had taken the biggest step of my life. I had renounced my weak, aimless, self-centered existence and committed myself to Jesus Christ. I have never been so filled with joy. And for the first time I know what it is to love. I love the Lord with all my heart and want only to live for Him from now on. I've been given a Bible and I read it every chance I get.*

*This experience may cost me my life. As I write this, I am on a collision course with the pope. He has had many others executed for their Christian beliefs, and it could happen to me, too. Strangely, I am not afraid. For the first time I can remember, I feel the boldness and faith to take a stand for the Lord Jesus. The change in me is incredible. My heart sings praises, my soul rejoices. Me! Can you believe it?*

*Now back to you, Molly. Be thankful you were spared from marrying me. I would have been a terrible husband. We would have been miserable together.*

*Finally, I urge you to be open to the Lord. He makes the difference. He takes away the fear, the hurt, the self-hatred, and fills us with His joy, His love, His power.*

*If I'm to die, I do it joyfully for Him.*

*Again, I'm sorry, Molly, for hurting you.*

Douglas

Molly appeared to struggle with her emotions for a long minute, then folded the letter and looked up at Francis. "I don't understand," she said. "He became a Christian? Why? He had it made with you all."

"I can't explain it, Molly. But it was a total change. He spoke up to the pope—even rebuked him. That took guts. Then he admitted he had become a Christian through Mozell and Johnson, knowing it would mean his death. It did. The pope had him executed."

"How can the pope get away with something like that?"

"It happens all the time. These Christian believers cause trouble."

Molly sat in silence, thoughtful. "Why are you here?" she asked finally. "How'd you get the letter? This whole thing doesn't make any sense."

Francis shifted about uneasily in his chair. "Douglas knew better than to try and mail your letter. It would have been intercepted by the Israeli security people and turned over to the pope. So Douglas stuck it in his Bible. After he died, I was going through his things and I found the Bible. The letter dropped out. I read it. I don't ordinarily read someone else's mail, but I did this time. Then I couldn't get it out of my mind. I kept reading it and re-reading it. I was trying to figure out why Douglas was so willing to die. It was so out of character. Let's face it, he was a pretty weak guy before."

Molly nodded. Francis continued. "The more I read it, the stronger the urge to deliver it to you. I don't feel guilty for taking Douglas away from you, but I felt I owed him something. He was —well, important to me. I hope the letter helps you somehow."

Molly stared at him stonily. "Very big of you. You show up here after all these years and tell me Douglas is dead—'sorry, lady, but it's all okay, because he's in some rosy heaven now'."

Molly's anger irritated Francis. "I could have just torn the letter up. Or I could have mailed it, in which case you might be in a real mess with that crack about the pope in it. I was trying to do the decent thing. Douglas wanted you to get that letter and I made it possible. I did it at great expense and inconvenience. I don't expect any gratitude, but you don't have to be nasty."

Molly shrugged, "Okay, I'm sorry. I have hated you above everyone else in the world for years. Now you come right in my living room and it's natural for me to want to hurt you like you hurt me."

"I'm sorry about your pain," Francis answered, "but the world is full of pain now. We have to get used to it."

"I guess so." Molly had become thoughtful. "Douglas said that God wanted him to write this letter and He would get it to me. You think it was God that brought you down here?"

"No. I don't believe in that kind of thing."

"Why not? You said it was a hard trip and you didn't have to do it. I've been hearing lately how God manages to get His way about a lot of things whether we want Him to or not."

Francis was uncomfortable again. There had been no answers here, only questions he could not answer. "My car is waiting; I need to get back to the airport." He stood up. They looked at each other in silence for a long moment, two people with nothing in common except their physical love for Douglas and their mutual grief at his death. Molly held the letter tightly. Her eyes were now bright with unshed tears and her lips were trembling. Francis nodded one last time. "Good-bye, Molly," he said.

As she watched Francis Chapman walk down the steps to his waiting limousine, Molly's mind was awhirl. Douglas, too, a Christian. Was there no end to their influence? Douglas was gone now forever. But no—Craig would say he was in heaven.

She clutched the letter as her eyes filled with tears. Molly who almost never cried felt the flood gates of her emotions loosen as the tears trickled down her face. Some hard and frozen part within her melted. Deep racking sobs began breaking down the defenses that had built up over many years since the death of her parents. She sat down on the sofa and wept—for them, for her beloved grandfather, for Jason, for her brother, for Craig, for Douglas. Grief, pain, remorse flooded her soul as the washing, cleansing, healing tears streamed down her cheeks.


Francis Chapman was in turmoil as his chauffeured limousine traversed Tampa's pock-marked streets en route to the airport. He was disturbed and just a little angry with himself. Such an effort and expense, and for what? There had been no answers, only more questions. A fool's errand, he told himself again.

*A fool has said in his heart there is no God.*

Francis sat bolt upright and looked around. The phrase was from Scripture, he knew. He had spent many hours in studying the Bible he had found among Douglas' belongings, but never before had its words appeared, suddenly and sovereignly, in his head. The application to his thoughts was remarkable, too, he admitted. Were they true also? Had he said, "There is no God"?

No, he decided. His interest in the subject had been so superficial he had never formed an opinion at all. It was not so much that he did not believe in God; he did not care. Even if God existed, he decided, it would have no effect on Francis Chapman.

*Be not deceived, God is not mocked.*

The words were so clear and loud this time that Francis looked with suspicion at the driver, but the man drove in seeming indifference to Francis and his inner voice. No, it was no human agent who responded to his whirling thoughts. This was something else altogether, and Francis noticed his hands were shaking.

Suddenly, unbidden, there rose in his mind a picture from the past. He saw himself, a plump and pretty child, kneeling next to his mother in a chilly gothic church, and he heard her fervent words, "Lord, there's no one but You now. You have to be the husband and father in this family." He shook his head in disbelief. How could he possibly remember such a scene? He had been hardly more than a baby when his father left. Could the power of that prayer have followed him all these years?

"I sure can do without this," he thought. With the business depleted, the pope no longer in his corner and matters falling apart everywhere, he certainly did not need an emotional upheaval like this. He had enough problems.

*Come to Me all ye that labor and are heavy-laden and I will give you rest.*

"Leave me alone!" his mind shouted. "Who are you, anyhow?

*I am the Good Shepherd and My sheep know My voice.*

Francis rested his forehead against the car's window and stared at the passing scenery without seeing it. His mind was a turmoil of darting thoughts and feelings. He was excited and frightened by this encounter with the supernatural, annoyed at the presumption of the voice, but strangely touched by its concern. Underneath it all, like a simmering cauldron ready to boil over, was an enormous load of remorse. He was shocked at its presence. He wondered how many years he had carried it without awareness and how long he had mourned his lost innocence.

Another picture arose in his mind: the only time he had ever tried to kiss a girl, a very long time ago now. She was a small and dainty blonde, and he had approached her with awe and adoration. Her mouth had grown cruel as she shrieked out her rejection, "Francis is a sissy! Fransissy! FranSISSY! FranSISSY!" The pain rocked him afresh, and his eyes misted at the memory.

Another scene played itself before Francis' mind: his seduction at the age of twelve by the choral director of his junior high school and the feeling of abnormality and self-loathing it had brought. Then had come the teen years, the pain, the feelings of being an outcast, then learning to enjoy those feelings. The scholastic successes had compensated for his other deficiencies. Then Lucky Royal extending his hand, and saying, "I can use a man like you in my organization." More successes, more compensations. Then he saw Douglas Rymer, tall, handsome and infinitely lovable. Not just the sex object, but the true love. Truly loved, for his own sake and without reservation. Douglas had never known that; it would have made Francis too vulnerable. Better to keep up the shield, not open up for more hurts.

*I love you.*

And suddenly the cauldron boiled over, exploded with grief, sorrow and shame, and Francis found himself kneeling on the floor of the limousine, head buried in his arms on the back seat, sobbing out the years of personal failure which had never stopped hurting in spite of worldly success.

*I stand at the door and knock.*

What am I supposed to do? Francis stared into the emptiness of his own heart and life and longed to reach out and grasp the joy and power and peace Douglas had found. But he had no idea how to proceed. Tentatively, he approached the Voice, and thought: "You show me what to do. If You're not just tormenting me, show me how."

The Voice replied and Francis nodded, his lips moving softly. A few minutes later Francis was back on the seat, looking out the window. He noticed they were taking a different route. The limousine seemed to be heading toward downtown Tampa. "Driver, is this the way to the airport?" he asked.

"No, sir. I have orders to take you to the FML office."

Francis was startled. "Whose orders?"

The driver pointed to his two-way radio. "The boss himself, Oscar Hummel."

A moment of panic shot through Francis. Then he shook himself. Something was different. Whether he lived or died he had nothing to fear now.


For a long time after the tears stopped, Molly sat in the living room reading and re-reading Douglas' letter. Finally, she arose and went into the kitchen. Martha and Susie were both gone, helping Stubby with the fish. A pang shot through Molly. How selfish she had been so many times about helping out the others in the kitchen.

Her thoughts suddenly focused on Craig. Where was he now? How she missed him! Then she put her head in her hands and sobbed again. How could she have ratted on him? How could she have been so cowardly?

Molly picked at some dry cereal and turned her mind resolutely from Craig. If she thought about him, she would start to cry again. A loud meow came from outside and she opened the door to admit Ragtime, her last link to Craig.

"Ragtime. You hungry, boy?" He rubbed against her ankles, purring loudly as she opened the cabinets looking for something he could eat. When he moved between her and the places she was searching, she fussed at him gently. "There's nothing to eat in here. Come on, let's go up to my room."

She carried him tenderly up the stairs, murmuring against his neck. Inside her room, she plopped him on her bed and lay down beside him. She was rubbing his thick orange fur when he raised his head alertly and turned away from her to look toward the hall. A low, grumbling snarl came from his throat as the cat raised his body into a crouch.

"What is it, boy? You hear somebody?" Molly sat up and looked toward the outside hall. She saw nothing, but felt her skin crawl at the cat's actions. She knew his senses were sharper than hers. She crept to the door and opened it wider and Ragtime joined her, his ears flattened and his growl continuing as they stared down the hall.

Then over the rumblings of the cat she heard that terrifying scuttling noise again. "Not another one!" she whimpered. But there he was—a long gray rodent, almost as large as Ragtime, advancing boldly down the hall, long menacing nose pointed toward them.

The cat snarled once and sprang toward the rat. He threw his body onto the rat's back, claws extended and ears flattened. Molly watched in horrified fascination as the two bodies, gray and orange, almost the same size, merged into a whirling mass. Rat squeals mingled with Ragtime's hisses. Molly, frozen in her tracks, heard her voice crying, "Get him, boy! Kill him! Come on, Ragtime!"

The two animals suddenly separated and stared at each other from crouched positions. Neither appeared to have been hurt as they stood looking at each other without a sound. Molly waited breathlessly for the cat to spring again.

But before Molly's incredulous eyes, the cat turned around and began a slow, awkward, lumbering crawl in her direction. Gone was the confident, regal stride of the tomcat; he moved as though he were disjointed, his greenish eyes glazed. The rat followed, mimicking the movements of the cat. As the animals crept steadily toward her, Molly found herself too terrified to scream. Only small whimpers escaped her lips. She knew she was menaced by something other than two small mammals. No mere animal could hate so strongly.

With the two animals within a few feet of her, all that came out of her was a hoarse plea, "For Christ's sake, leave me alone!"

As she heard herself say the word, "Christ," Molly remembered the story of Jason's victory at the fish booth and what Craig had said about the power of this Name and the right of Christians to use it. "Lord, hear me, please," she whispered. "I don't have any right to ask you this. I've rejected you and laughed at you and even hated you. I'm sorry for that. I want you now, Lord. I want to be like Craig and the others."

Then with more desperation than faith, she cried loudly at the two animals, "In the name of Jesus Christ, I command you— *go away!*"

As she spoke these words, the unbelievable happened again. The rat shook himself briefly, turned and darted down the hall in a gray flash. The cat blinked once, his body jerked violently, then with a grace and precision beautiful to see, he turned and sped after the rat. Ragtime's claws slashed into the rodent's body, trailing long streaks of blood, and open jaws closed on the rat's neck.

The fight was brief this time. The rat lay dead within seconds, and the cat crouched over its body, teeth still sunk into its neck, while Molly stood watching with a mixture of emotions.

Craig and Jason and Stubby had been right, she thought to herself, and I've been a fool. She began to cry softly. A gentle peace settled over her. She walked down the hall, avoiding Ragtime and his grisly meal. "Jesus, let Craig know, somehow; let him know about me," she whispered.

# VIII

A law requiring citizens to be numbered was never passed in America. It was not necessary. A directive from the FML organization was tantamount to law in 1992. If caught without marks, violators were forced to comply or were imprisoned, but enforcement during the early part of 1992 was capricious. Some offenders were ruthlessly tracked down and imprisoned. Others were ignored.

Susie and Stubby wondered why they were not arrested.

Reasons for the overall lack of enforcement emerged: food was scarce. The jails were overflowing. The fewer people numbered, the fewer supplies needed by the local authorities.

Meanwhile at the Redmonds' compound, three ration cards, plus the fish, kept five bodies at a low subsistence level. Hank and

Martha settled down to a frugal monotonous routine. Martha didn't have to work nearly as hard as before because there were fewer to feed. And her help was now vastly improved. Susie had grown from a willful girl into a lovely thoughtful young woman, but the biggest transformation was in Molly.

Suddenly she took on the hardest and dirtiest jobs. The first up in the morning, she had the water heated and the table set before Martha appeared. She cooked, she washed dishes, she sewed torn clothes and linens, finding tasks to be done before being asked. Martha and Hank assumed this came from a contrite attitude over her role as informer. Stubby and Susie recognized what really lay behind the change in her heart and welcomed her into the fellowship.

Spring passed and summer came with little variety in their routine. They continued to mourn for Jason and all yearned for news about Craig, clinging to the hope he was hiding out somewhere. Although Stubby became more and more restless to get to Israel, he enjoyed his role as spiritual mentor to two young and very attractive new Christians. The threesome met nightly to study Scripture and pray.

One stormy night in mid-July there were lightning and high winds, but Stubby, Molly and Susie were cozy in the candle-lit garage. The two girls sat in silence as Stubby's deep voice read about the Hebrews' deliverance from bondage in Egypt, words which took them back almost 3300 years to a people as oppressed as the present day Christians and to a time almost as harsh.

As Stubby concluded the Song of Moses, they heard over the sounds of the storm a familiar and beloved voice. "Hey, let me in! It's wet out here!" They rushed to admit a damp, bedraggled but very joyful Hastings. For the next few minutes there were hugs, tears, laughter and a rapid-fire exchange of news. Hastings told briefly of Craig's welfare, listened in sorrow to the news of Scott's death, was thrilled at the story of Molly's salvation. Then he cut short the conversation.

"Look, I didn't just come to visit, you know. Things are getting tight. We know from several different sources that mass arrests will begin soon; it's just not safe for you here. I came to take you to Brandon."

"You're pretty sure of your information?" Stubby asked.

"Yeah," Hastings nodded. "We have some contacts through the underground church. We learned that FML stopped their surveillance here. We also had a word from the Lord at our prayer meeting last week: it is time to get you out of here."

"How'd you manage to get through safely?" Stubby asked. "Even with a truck, you don't have a citizen's number or a travel permit or gasoline."

"We get gas once in a while," Hastings said. "Our generator runs on gasoline and we have a little allotment. With the gas gauge broken in the truck we can't be sure, but it seems like we get about a hundred miles to the gallon. As for not getting caught, I have a special pass for night truck travel, thanks to a man from our farm who works in the police department. God provided the storm. It's raining so hard you can hardly see the road in front of you. I had no problems driving here and we'll make it home too." He grinned.

"What about Mama and Daddy?" Susie asked in a weak voice as Molly put a consoling arm around her shoulder.

"They have numbers," Stubby pointed out. "As a matter of fact, they may be safer with us gone. We're the ones who are bucking the system."

Susie nodded. "Can I at least say good-bye? Tell them Craig is safe?"

"Sure," Hastings said gently. "We won't say where he is, just that he's okay and that we're all going to be together."

They made plans swiftly since Hastings was in a hurry to leave; he hoped to continue using the storm as their cover. Each packed only essentials, then met one last time in the kitchen of the big house to say good-bye to Hank and Martha.

It was a sorrowful parting. The older McKenzies would be alone now, the only ones left from a bustling household of nine. The absent members were felt if not mentioned: the judge, dead. Jason, dead. Scott, dead. Craig, a fugitive. The big yellow kitchen was dismal as the pounding rain and human tears fell unabated. Susie hugged her parents with fierce devotion.

Molly left the room briefly and returned with Ragtime held firmly in her arms. Hastings shook his head emphatically. "You can't take that cat, Molly. This is not a picnic we're going to, you know."

"I can't leave him." Molly tightened her grip on Ragtime and he let out a rumble of protest. "Craig gave him to me." Something of the old Molly was present in the firm chin and Hastings shrugged his shoulders. "I just hope we're not stopped."

Hank and Martha looked desolate as Hastings stationed Susie, Molly and Stubby and their luggage on the floor of the pick-up truck. He then covered them up with plants, shrubs, and light bales of leafy vegetables. It would be a wet and uncomfortable trip.

The precautions paid off. The rain stopped before Hastings drove out of Tampa. He had been on the road but a half hour when the flashing blue lights of a police car signaled him to stop. The officer looked at Hastings' pass, then stared at the load of plants and vegetable bales. The three fugitives held their breath. Ragtime squirmed in Molly's arms and the plants rustled.

The policeman turned back to Hastings. "You got any animals in that load?"

"Don't believe so," replied Hastings. "Rats probably. Some of those big ones gave me trouble."

The policeman grunted. "They can be vicious. Okay. Drive on."

Hastings turned back onto the highway while the three fugitives relaxed. "That Hastings thinks quick," said Stubby. "Rats yet. Just great."

But Molly was shaking. "Are there rats in here?" she cried. "If so, let's take authority over them right now."

Stubby chuckled. "I don't think so, but we can sure pray."


Hastings shook Craig. "We're back."

Craig was out of bed like a cat. "Safe?"

Hastings grinned. "Not only safe, but two more than we thought."

Craig's heart zinged. "Molly?"

"Yes, and Ragtime."

It was a wild and jubilant reunion as they crowded into the dining room for talk and a snack. Craig first grabbed Susie around the waist, then hugged Stubby, next seized Ragtime and finally welcomed Molly warmly. He could not take his eyes off her as they compared experiences. She was excited, glowing, radiant. The anger was gone from her eyes, the cynicism from her mouth. Underneath it all was an inner serenity. Only one experience could have caused this.

Not until after a good night's sleep and a hearty breakfast was Craig able to draw Molly aside. They walked to a bench beneath a large oak tree and sat down side by side. Craig smiled down at Molly, searching her face carefully.

"Now," he said gently. "Tell me about it."

She was nervous and shy, the years of hostility remembered and regretted. "I'm new at this, Craig," she began. The story tumbled out.

"It was a terribly weak prayer," Molly concluded. "But God answered it. Now I'm trying to make up for lost time. I'm sorry I was such a mess, Craig. And for betraying you to the police. I was jealous of you and angry over your turning me down. You always seemed right and I was—well obnoxious. I don't ever want to fight with you again."

Craig took her hand and smiled. "With that red hair of yours, I wouldn't bet on it."

Molly's eyes sparked for a moment, then she laughed. "One way or another you know how to get under my skin."

"I love you, you know," he said more seriously. "I have for years. I kept telling myself to stay away. You were so nasty at times, but I never could get you out of my mind."

"I wanted to get you out of my mind that first time I saw you. You were a fresh kid—with a bad complexion. What a difference a few years makes." Molly laughed softly, then caressed his cheek. "I love you, Craig. So very much. Is it because I love the Lord, too?"

"That's part of it. His Spirit fills us and we then have a lot more love to give."

Molly snuggled up to him contentedly. "Will you teach me all about it?"

"We'll make the most of these weeks," Craig said. "It'll be a lot harder now for me to go to Israel with Stubby."

"You're not serious about going, are you?" Molly's face clouded. "You're a fugitive. They'll pick you up for sure."

Craig shook his head. "If it's what I'm supposed to do, then I'll be protected."

But Molly was not convinced. "We're all together for the first time in months and you talk of leaving. It's wrong, Craig."

Craig kissed her lightly on the lips and Molly's eyes softened. "That fire inside you ignites quickly, doesn't it? I'll have to be ready for these flare-ups."

"Just stay with me," Molly replied. "I'm a very needy person in every way."

"There's a lot we can learn together . . . about growing things and having our own grapevine and our own fig tree . . . " Craig's voice trailed away because it was difficult to kiss and talk at the same time.

Ragtime joined them and rubbed against their ankles.


After Susie, Stubby and Molly had slipped away to the Brandon farm, the big Redmond house became very quiet. Hank and Martha discovered that they had little to say to each other. Hank's job had become more and more a dull routine. Martha fixed food, cleaned house and sought pleasure from the scanty fare on radio and television. Madame Celeste's going off the air had been a sharp disappointment to her. Was everything she enjoyed being discontinued?

One morning Martha awoke early. She started to go back to sleep when she noticed that Hank was lying there with his eyes open. She had never seen him look so sad and defeated. She sighed heavily.

"What's the matter, dear?" Hank asked quietly.

She sat up in bed and began crying. Hank was startled. He could not know that the tears came because she was touched by one of his rare expressions of affection. She knew how prominent the grey was in her hair, how limp the strands and how unattractive she had become. When he patted her gently on the shoulder, she moved toward him.

"They're all gone now," she said woefully. "It seems like nothing is left."

"I'm still left," he replied with an attempt at humor and she brightened. "Maybe we can help each other."

She moved still closer to him. "You know the children seemed so happy. They have something we don't have."

Hank nodded, his eyes staring out the window, his mind far away.

"Is it too late for us to find it, Hank?"

Her husband did not answer.

*Book Five*

# Cure

*January 1, 1995*
*to*
*June 5, 1995*

# I

Stubby rose from his uncomfortable cross-legged position on the ground and stood on the stony ledge behind Craig. They looked toward the west—toward Jerusalem, unseen but felt.

"It won't be long, you know," he said softly. Not only the calendar, but also the worldwide preparations for war convinced all of them that the end was approaching. "This is January, old time, and according to prophecy that means only about four more months."

"I'd feel better if I knew what we're supposed to be doing," Craig muttered. "Are we supposed to fight? Defend Israel? I can't see joining Ben Daniel's army, but—maybe some kind of guerrilla group?"

"I think just waiting is our assignment for now. Unless you want to study something."

Craig laughed. "Trust a bunch of Jews to bring books when they go into hiding. You may forget food or clothes, but never books."

Stubby chuckled in agreement. When they had joined the Hebrew Christians here in the Judean wilderness, he had been delighted to find books of Scripture, Hebrew grammars and histories. He studied every minute of his spare time.

"We're like the Maccabees," Stubby said. "Like when they took to the hills to defend the faith against Antiochus. And I bet they weren't far from where we are now." He took a book from his knapsack.

Craig was more of an activist and Stubby constantly had to preach patience to him: "We are as well off here as anywhere. We have food; we are free to worship as we choose; we have comradeship. Learn to relax."

Stubby found the place in his book. "Look, did I tell you? 'Naphtali' means 'trickery' in Hebrew. Naphtali Seth Ben Daniel. I wonder how old Jacob knew? Back in Genesis he prophesied that the tribe of Dan would bring a serpent."

"You know, every time I think about Ben Daniel and Uriah Leonard I wish I could go back to America and talk to my mother for a while," Craig said. "I'd like to see how she reacted to Leonard putting her beloved guru, Madame Celeste, off the air. Mama always resented anything we said against him; I just wonder how she likes it now that he's gone mad, saying that he's God and that people should worship him. My mother isn't dumb, but she has a way of explaining things to herself that makes a good substitute for being dumb."

"Yeah," Stubby agreed. "People thought for a while he was really bringing in an age of peace. Now the world is on the brink of the biggest war of all time."

They turned suddenly as excited voices reached them from below where people were emerging from cave mouths all over the hillside. "It's Abram," they were saying. "Abram is back!"

Craig and Stubby scrambled down the rocky terrain to join the throng. Climbing wearily toward them was a tall bearded man who had been on a scouting expedition to Jerusalem and was returning now with eyewitness reports of the situation there. The news they received by radio was unreliable, censored and manipulated.

The man arrived panting and accepted long draughts of water from a leather-covered canteen, while his audience waited in growing impatience. He grinned at them, wiped a trickle of water from his chin, and then spoke rapidly in Hebrew for about twenty minutes.

When he finally stopped Craig turned to Stubby in frustration. "How much of that could you follow?"

"He said over a third of Jerusalem is Christian now," Stubby translated. "The men in Ben Daniel's security police are deserting by the hundreds. The city is tense. Oh yes. He said one man who had escaped from prison told him he had been interrogated by mentalists—people with ESP."

"What did he say about the war?"

"According to him, they're preparing for it against all the

African nations and Iraq, Syria, Jordan, Lebanon, Saudi Arabia—
I don't remember all of them. Ben Daniel's running around to
meetings trying to calm things down. He waves his treaty with
U.S.E. in front of their faces and scares them off for a while, but
peace can't last. There's too much wealth in Israel now and too
much hate against her."

Craig's face was sober. "There'll be a war all right. Both human
reasoning and Bible prophecy predict it."

"He said some more about the other coalitions," continued
Stubby, "but I couldn't follow it all. It doesn't matter too much
anyhow."

Stubby looked out over the dun-colored wilderness around
them, the sparse vegetation, the stony outcroppings and the cave-
riddled limestone hills almost unchanged since the days when
John the Baptist and Jesus retreated into this same wilderness to
seek solitude. It had been home to Stubby and Craig for over
two years now.

Both had prayed for a miracle to provide the transportation
from the Brandon Farm to Israel, and like every other man in the
camp, each had a story of divine protection and deliverance.

Just when he needed them, Craig had found contacts open to
the underground church, the body of believers who had been
raised up to cooperate worldwide to help bring the Jews back to
their homeland despite border guards, government regulations
and the computer's mark. And quietly, step by step, his needs
were met through brothers and sisters around the world.

It began with a fake travel permit, provided by a friend of another member of the farm community. Then another believer
smuggled Craig through the guards and immigration officials at
the Tampa Airport and hustled him aboard one of the few international flights still operating from Tampa. As dangers and problems melted before him, he was not surprised when the flight
steward proved to be Christian also, and the Israeli passport and
the expertly tailored clothing which he provided seemed in-
evitable. The routine check of computer numbers passed while
Craig waited in the plane's tiny rest room. When they touched
down in Tel Aviv, Craig left the big plane in the clothing of an
airline attendant, and by-passed customs again by the simple
expedient of using the employees' entrance. His transportation

to the Judean hills was as simple and providential as the rest of his provisions had been; he walked in Arab dress at the head of a flock of fat-tailed sheep, unable to communicate with the Arabic Christian who shepherded them, but feeling a kinship nevertheless.

Stubby also discovered the existence of the underground network of caring which linked little communities like the Brandon Farm one to the other. But Stubby moved in a different realm. He knew of God's provisions for the children of Israel: Jonah had been carried in the belly of a whale, Elijah had been lifted up in a fiery chariot, and Philip the Evangelist had been transported by the power of God when the need arose. Stubby's faith had been exercised for years, and was now fully strong enough to believe for a miracle of this calibre. God honored his faith and moved him miraculously from Florida to Israel.

Their existence in the Judean hills had become a daily prayer walk. They asked for provision and for safety and it was granted. Craig learned that there were similar groups all over Israel. Now that January 1995, old time, had arrived Stubby estimated that the 144,000 "sealed Jews" were almost all there. The time was growing shorter. The eagerness and the tension of the thousands upon thousands of fugitives was increasing. It was in all the faces.

"They gave us a handbook on atomic radiation and fallout shelters today," said Hank as he came into the kitchen.

Martha served Hank the usual eggs and added a small square of dried beef. He smiled his pleasure. Even if it were almost totally synthetic, it had a nice flavor, and they delighted in such small treats on the rare occasions when they were available. He ate slowly, reading the pamphlet as he ate.

"If you're not too close to the blast, you may have as much as twenty minutes to get to shelter," he reported. "It takes that long for the fallout to get back to earth. You can protect yourself by getting behind two inches of lead or three feet of dirt." He read on in silence a minute, then spoke again. "Four feet of stacked newspapers may protect you. I wonder how long it's been since anybody had four feet of newspapers?"

"What does it say about the fire storm?" Martha asked. "I heard something about that on the radio. It's the fire which causes the high winds."

"Sure," Hank explained. "The heat of the fire causes air to rise, so there's a vacuum created and more air rushes in. You can get real gales—hurricane force."

By February of 1995, the whole world was expecting war, but in the little backwater of Tampa few specifics were known. The merger of the Arabian, North African and Black African nations the year before, and the mobilization of their armies, were only vague rumors and hardly anyone knew the truth of events in Russia and the Orient.

Supper over, Hank rose to take his usual walk around the property. Then they would settle down for the night, their hours of waking and sleeping determined by the sunlight, as had been the custom for most of mankind's existence. Martha decided to go with him and the two started toward the front of the house, walking in companionable silence.

"I really ought to do something about this yard," Hank said. He felt depressed each time he saw the lawn knee-high in weeds, and he felt an obligation to take some sort of action. He did not seem to have the time, however, and never any spare energy.

Martha patted his hand consolingly. "Don't worry about it. It doesn't bother me." He looked at her in surprise that she could, after all these years and disasters, still think he was motivated by a desire to please her.

They reached the bay and Martha spoke hesitantly, looking away from him as though embarrassed. "Do you really think there will be a war, Hank?"

"I don't know. I guess so."

"Well, I was just thinking. If there is, then that really will be the end, won't it? I know we keep saying that. After every new catastrophe we think that it's the last straw, but war really will be." She paused and glanced at Hank's face, seeking some signal of how he was reacting. He just nodded.

She went on, "I guess what I want to say is that I honestly don't care any more. If we have a war and atomic bombs and all, I'd rather just die than have to start all over again with even less."

"A lot of people feel that way, Martha. It's not just you."

Darkness came early this time of year. They stood watching the bay, its phosphorescence an eerie glow in the dimming light. Hank thought suddenly of the children, of their fishing venture that had seemed so inexplicably successful. His throat grew tight as he remembered their joyful, loving companionship, their happy assurance that even in a world gone mad, all things were ultimately under control. He turned back to Martha and was surprised to see tears running down her cheeks.

"Sorry," she muttered. "I was just thinking about the boys and about Susie and Scott. I miss them. Even Molly."

Hank said nothing. They turned back toward the house, a vague white hulk in the dying light.

Craig was shocked when Stubby announced that they were leaving the security of the mountains to gather with other Christians in Jerusalem. "Right in Jerusalem, Stubby? Isn't that dangerous?"

"Not when it's where God wants us." Stubby was twenty-two now, fully a man, and more knowledgeable in many ways than Craig at twenty-five, but his innocent face was still boyish.

The preparations for the trip to Jerusalem were brief. Craig had one spare shirt, a change of socks and underwear. That, with his eating utensils, his comb and a straight razor which he loved and valued, comprised all he owned. He thought back to the past when his possessions filled a room and still failed to satisfy him. As time progressed, he owned less and less. Within a very short time, a matter of a few weeks he guessed, his life would be changed beyond recognition, and he doubted he would need a stereo, a surfboard or an AM/FM radio. He had been cutting out the nonessentials for years, stripping himself down to basics, ready to face whatever God had planned for him.

They began their long trek toward the capital on February 17 —Stubby and Craig along with about five hundred others— starting out in the early morning with the rising sun warming their backs as they marched. The terrain was rough, and even though all were in excellent physical condition, they were exhausted by the time Jerusalem's golden skyline appeared ahead of them and the sun shone directly in their faces.

Although he had been in Israel for over two years, Craig had never before dared approach a congested area where he might be accosted by the police. Now groups of refugees were converging from hiding places in the barren hills all around Jerusalem, coming together in a monumental, prearranged celebration, to praise God and to usher in the last stages of His plan. Some of these men had taken refuge in the hills right after the deaths of Mozell and Johnson three and a half years before.

As they stopped to rest, Craig looked at his comrades. The men were poorly dressed, almost all bearded, tanned and roughened by their long siege of outdoor life. Yet they shared a common expression of joy and excitement. Most ranged in age from late teens to late twenties, and exuded a power that was thrilling. Craig was not the only non-Jew among them, but he was in a very small minority. Yet he felt honored to be there with these stalwart, consecrated men.

"Come on," Craig urged. "I want to see the city before it gets dark."

"You were the one who was so afraid," Stubby laughed. "Here we are coming right into Ben Daniel's spider web like stupid flies and now you want to take a sightseeing tour."

Craig looked around at the men and boys who were resting in the grass along the roadside. There was no way this invasion of people could be ignored. There were too many of them, and they were too vibrant, too joyous, to pass as ordinary country people coming to the big city.

"How much farther?" he asked. Stubby shook his head and Craig asked the man on his other side.

"We have to circle the Old City," the other man explained. "Mount Zion is at the southwest corner. We don't have any recent maps, and things have changed a lot because of the earthquakes, but we can find our way all right."

All around them men were stirring and they started off again, walking unhurriedly but steadily. They entered the city at its northeast border and moved south toward the Old City. Since their ranks spread out over several city blocks, they attracted stares from the few natives scuttling about. There were surprisingly few people on the streets. It was after business hours and before the onset of what night life existed in these perilous times, but it was still an astonishment that they met no police patrols at all. Jerusalem was the richest city in the world now, center of the country which owned an unthinkable wealth of oil, yet it appeared to Craig almost a ghost town. The nervousness of the citizens they met and the feeling that eyes were peering at them from behind closed shutters, all contributed to the strangeness of the scene.

"It's beautiful, isn't it?" Stubby said. They were busy looking on all sides, entranced at their first taste of civilization in more than two years. "I never saw so many church buildings. I wonder how they found uses for them all."

Craig nodded. For the past three years, all religious institutions in Israel except the temple had been converted to secular use: museums, social halls, child care centers, government offices.

The throng of men entered the Old City by way of the Damascus Gate, uncannily preserved through the earthquakes of the past seven years. It rose majestically as it had since the 16th century, and each man slowed a little to drink in the history and wonder of its construction. Then they moved as quickly as possible toward the south, wondering at the absence of people. The shops and bazaars were silent, closed and bolted. It looked like a movie set after the day's shooting was done. Even the towering new temple seemed devoid of life.

They left the Old City by the Zion Gate and stared at their destination, Mount Zion. The slopes of this gentle hill were crowded with churches and shrines. The traditional site of the Last Supper, the Coenaculum, hallowed to Christians for twenty centuries and now a center for the fine arts, stood before them.

As they started the climb toward the summit of the hill, each man wore an expression of fulfillment. Craig found himself sharing their joy; the almost unendurable happiness they felt at the anticipation of the future. Once again they had been vindicated in their faith; they had walked unchallenged through the streets of Jerusalem to their holy mountain.

The men found places to sit and eat their evening meal. They were solemn now, sensing their role as men of destiny. Seven o'clock arrived and with it Jerusalem's curfew. This was the most open city in the world; too many rich and powerful men lived here to make regimentation perfect, but these believers were not part of the elect few who could escape the curfew. If noticed, they would be arrested. And they were so very noticeable. For hours they had been streaming into the city, heading straight as an arrow for Mount Zion. As the night passed, more and more men joined the early arrivals, until thousands were congregated together. It would certainly take miraculous protection to save them from arrest.

It was a chilly but sparkling clear night; an almost festive atmosphere prevented sleep. Shortly before dawn, Craig and Stubby found a grassy spot and fell asleep, pillowing their heads on their backpacks. In spite of their short rest they awakened fresh and eager as dawn came to the east. Tea was brewed in pots all over the hillside. One group had taken responsibility for feeding them all; these men came by with bread, cheese and fruit. Craig wondered if they had started with only a little and had prayed that it be multiplied, or if they had somehow managed to find enough food by more conventional methods. Either way would be a miracle.

After breakfast the singing began—if it could be called singing, Craig thought. He was not surprised that he did not know the words, he had made little progress so far with his Hebrew, but the melody was strange to him too. Not only unfamiliar, but ungraspable. Try as he might he could not catch the harmonies that the others were pouring out with such obvious bliss.

He knew that what was taking place here this morning was the fulfillment of a prophecy. He knew this meeting must take place, these special men on this holy mountain, to work out in the natural what was happening in the spiritual realm. Still, his reaction was one of disappointment. It seemed so . . . normal. He wanted to see thrones and angels and heavenly beings. He had expected to hear harps and voices of thunder. He was fretful and frustrated when the "music" ceased at last.

"Wasn't it glorious!" Stubby exulted.

"To be honest, I thought it was a big fizzle. It seemed like a lot of noise to me. A lot of trouble for nothing." Craig was determined not to give a phony reaction.

"You're reacting to what you could see and hear—us humans, and that's wrong," Stubby reproached him. "Just because something isn't visible to us doesn't mean it doesn't exist."

Craig blinked as the words hit him. Of course. He had assumed that the drama was played for the human audience. But that was wrong; humans might be the very smallest part of the congregation at Mount Zion today. There were undoubtedly participants in the ceremony just completed that would have overwhelmed the humans present if they had been aware of them.

Stubby spoke, "The war will start in a day or so. Jerusalem will be surrounded on all sides. We'd better head for the hills."

With the others they started down the hill, retracing their steps through the city and out toward the mountains beyond. The climax of history was at hand.

With Christians all over the world being persecuted, imprisoned, tortured and killed, it was incredible that the little farm community in Brandon survived the years from 1992 through 1994. The members had not only managed to live through the bad times, they had even flourished in a modest way. They cultivated more land, their dwellings were improved, and they owned animals now—chickens, a cow and pigs. It was a small bright spot in the generally dismal picture of life in the 1990's.

Molly found the years at the farm the happiest of her life. She worked harder than she would have dreamed possible, long days in the out-of-doors that brought glowing good health. She had close friends, satisfying work, and her plans for the future with Craig. Above all, she had a close daily relationship with the Lord. It was a quiet, simple, virtuous life that would have seemed impossibly dull to her a few years earlier, but now was completely fulfilling.

Molly was one of the first ones to realize her right hand was sore. It started as an irritation in the area that had been marked with her citizen's number. She realized what was happening, and she was resigned to the pain. After all, she had asked for it.

As the days passed, others who had been given the mark began to show the same symptoms, a burning in their right hands followed by oozing, purulent wounds. This community was fortunate because many of the fugitives, like Susie and Hastings, had refused to be marked, and they could now aid the stricken ones and carry on the work of the farm.

No one made the trip into Brandon to attend the Citizens'

Clinic. It would have been useless if they had. There was nothing that helped these sores. The doctors had decided the cause was a long-delayed reaction between the dye used to implant the marks and atmospheric pollution. Nothing they tried was of any benefit, and they tried everything: antiallergens, antihistamines, anti-inflammatory agents, and the full range of steroids.

On the evening of February 22nd, 1995, Molly's first day out of bed, she and Susie sat on the porch of the farmhouse, talking quietly.

"Everyone says the war will start in Israel," began Molly. "I hope Craig isn't in it."

"If only he could get a letter through to us," said Susie. "I miss Stubby too."

"Craig and I have plans," Molly continued. "If there is a holocaust and we die, then we'll be together in the next world. If not, we'll get married in this one and we'll go into the millennial kingdom together."

Susie nodded. "I like that. It seems, well, submitted and yet full of faith. I get so tense at times wondering what's best to do. If the end is near, you wonder, why bother to plant a garden or knit a sweater."

"That bothers me some too. Should we go about our business as usual, doing what we always do?" Molly asked. "It doesn't seem like that's good enough for the last days."

"If what you're doing is God's will, then I suppose that what's good enough for any day is good enough for the last day," Susie reflected. "They say we're not to worry or run around looking for extraordinary things to do. These have all been done for us."

They fell silent, watching the sky grow darker and the first stars of evening appear. Like expectant Christians elsewhere they continued doing the difficult: they waited.

# II

On February 23, 1995 (by the old Gregorian calendar), the United Arab and African Coalition attacked Israel, coming in solid waves of men and mechanized equipment across the Sinai Desert from Egypt. Simultaneously Afghanistan, Pakistan, Iraq and Iran poured through Jordan and Syria across the eastern borders of the tiny country devastating the land along both sides of the Jordan River. Saudi Arabia attacked from the south and moved from the Gulf of Aqaba up the Negev Desert toward the populous central portions, while the Lebanese moved down from the north. Israel found herself fighting fiercely on three sides and casting anxious eyes toward her western coastline along the Mediterranean.

For six days the armies fought without letup. The superiority of men and material were all on the side of the invaders, but Israel fought back with great courage. Then, on March 1, a second blow hit.

The combined armies of Russia, Mongolia, Turkey and the Iron Curtain satellites (East Germany, Yugoslavia, Austria, Czechoslovakia, Poland, Rumania, Bulgaria, Hungary, Lithuania, Finland and Denmark) swarmed across the Bosphorus, through Turkey, and down the land-bridge to invade the beleaguered little nation. They also hit the Mediterranean coastline in wave after wave of amphibious landings. The land of Israel was covered by invaders, and it seemed she must surely capitulate.

Then the unpredictable happened. Russia and her satellites suddenly turned on the Arabic-African Coalition. A three-way war was now being waged. The Russians severely damaged the fighting potential of the Arabic-African armies, giving temporary respite to Israel. Then, with a wild thirst for conquest, Russia moved south through the Sinai, crossed the Suez, and defeated Egypt and the North African countries. This action continued from March 7 through March 13, when the Russian troops turned back toward Israel.

On March 14th, the Russian forces were spread out across the Sinai when another series of earthquakes hit that area. The Russians withdrew into Egypt and waited, regrouping for battle.

The earthquake accomplished more than forcing a retreat by the Russians. The tremors moved northwestward through the Negev, through Jordan and Syria, until they reached the headwaters of the Euphrates River in central Turkey. There the earthquake accomplished the next necessary step in the long-determined schedule for this last of all wars. It dried up the Euphrates River. In Peking this news started another massive movement of troops and equipment.

An incredible 200,000,000-man citizens' army began moving out toward the west to join the war. No longer were political motivations or hopes for gain the cause of actions. Hatred and the unreasoning urge to destroy were the dominant human emotions. In long-range troop transport vehicles equipped for defense with both head and tail guns, the armies of China and its satellites (Vietnam, Cambodia, Laos and Thailand) poured onto the highway through the Himalayas and India begun back in 1974.

Meanwhile, seeing his nation the focal point of unprecedented hostility, Prime Minister Ben Daniel sent plea after plea for help to the United States of Europe, using as his diplomatic channel the office of Pope Sixtus, the instigator of the original treaty between Israel and the west. This treaty had resulted from the initial clandestine meeting between Ben Daniel and the then Bishop Leonard in June of 1988. Since it was still a valid treaty of mutual protection, Ben Daniel called loudly for support.

These two world leaders also called on the dark powers for support. "Help us, Lord Satan," they cried, "lest we be destroyed by the armies that encircle us."

And help came. Contrary to logic or self-interest, the few nations not committed at this point poured assistance into the meager defenses of the United States of Europe. America was one. With a ruinous economy, with its dreams of world power far in the past, and with nothing whatsoever to gain of profit or glory, America conscripted men, taxed its miserable citizens and supported the U.S.E. in its defense of Israel.

When the Russians heard that reinforcements were coming to Ben Daniel's aid, and of the enormous eastern army en route across Asia, they rushed their preparations for the re-invasion of Israel. By April 2 they considered themselves ready, and once again they moved northward across the bloody sands of the Sinai Desert. They hit swiftly and with devastation.

Several days later the first U.S.E. troops were airlifted to the battlefront. They landed in the midst of unbelievable chaos, and savage fighting took place.

It was the U.S.E. which first employed nuclear weapons. They hit the Russian homeland with annihilating effect on April 17 and 18 and thus started a chain reaction of atomic bombing. The Chinese, although they had not been hit by atomic weapons, launched thermonuclear bombs against the North American continent and against western Europe. By the 22nd of April, a third of the world's population was dead. The atmosphere was polluted, water unpotable in most places. The fear of so many seemed at last realized: the earth had been abused beyond her ability to recover. The protective atmospheric blanket was torn and ragged, and the heat and light of solar radiation blasted through in killing amounts. The only relief came with the swirling clouds of contaminated pollutants from the bombings, large black clouds of radioactive particles that came between the earth and the sun blocking its rays, bringing a darkness that was not restful.

Through the rest of April and the first three weeks of May, the world groaned under almost untenable conditions. On May 26, the army of the eastern powers crossed the Euphrates and headed toward Israel. The trip had cost them staggering numbers of dead, many from exhaustion, and since the expedition was poorly supplied, many starved. The rarefied heights of the Himalayas had taken their toll as had the radioactive fallout, but it was still the largest army ever fielded. Those who viewed the masses of men and women spreading like an evil tide across the Syrian Desert were awe-struck.

It took eight more days for this unwieldy organism of war to reach the point of its destination—the ancient Valley of Jezreel, the Plain of Esdraelon—Armageddon. They invaded Israel just south of the Sea of Galilee, moving southwest to meet the other armies encamped there—the army of western Europe and the remnants of the depleted armies of the Arabic-African Coalition. There they spread out in unthinkably vast ranks of men, ready for the last whimper of human folly.

Other men were massed along the Jordanian border south of the Dead Sea, and around the City of Jerusalem. Even at this moment a few among them must have wondered why they were fighting. Then the battle began; every nation attacking in one last, gigantic expression of man's ability to hate.

During the 4th and 5th of June, the battle raged on. As more thermonuclear warheads were used, the earth recoiled and struck back at humanity with her own forces—lightning, thunder, hail of awesome size. And as man persisted in his madness, nature struck again with an earthquake that leveled cities and islands, mountains and forests, and threatened to shift the planet from its axis.

The world economic system was destroyed. Commerce and industry, manufacturing and transportation, all the vast intricacies of man's organizations were devastated. Gone was the world of beauty and sustenance; gone was the society of man; gone was all that which enabled man to live by his own devices. And without Divine intervention, all life would have been destroyed.


"Is it radiation, do you think?" Royal asked, peering into a hand mirror. Since the announcement of Francis' death through an "accident" in Florida, just he and Celeste now met. The remnant of Royal's business had folded. They had no other human contacts.

Royal was lying stretched out on Celeste's couch, one bent arm protecting his eyes from the light. His face was a mass of sores, both the original sore where Royal had received his citizen's number (on his forehead as a sign of his importance to the organization) and more recent ones which had appeared after fallout had blanketed New York.

Celeste was in a chair near Royal's head. "It's anemia. We have bone marrow depression and can't replace the blood cells when . . ."

"Shut up about that. I can't stand to hear that medical jargon." Royal looked away from the mirror and scowled at Celeste.

She looked at him without expression.

"Is there anything to eat?" he asked. "I don't think we've eaten since the bombing. When was that?" Royal tried to focus his mind. It had been in late April. Or early May? What was today? He thought hard. There was no way to keep track of the days, no newspapers any more, no television or radio. He could not ask Celeste. She was not using the old calendar. It must be June now. Over a month, and he felt sure they had not eaten at all. The two of them were still alive in the stricken building, exposed to the killing radiation for over a month. He could not accept that figure. There must be something wrong with his calculations.

Back some time ago, back when they had first realized their minds were going, Celeste had explained that man was composed of three parts: spirit, soul and body. They had long ago given up their spirits to Satan by a voluntary act. Now they were losing their minds, too, to the dark powers; very little of reason or intellect was left them. Before long their bodies also would be taken from them. Royal had a vague memory of all this and he whimpered. "I think I'm hungry," he said. "Is there any food?"

"Go see for yourself," Celeste answered. She shifted in her chair and waves of odor drifted from her body. She no longer had the energy to walk to the bathroom, and she nested without awareness in her own filth.

Royal walked with concentration toward the kitchen. It occurred to him briefly that he might ask Celeste if she wanted anything. But he ignored this impulse. This one charitable inclination, this last, fleeting vestige of humanity was too much effort. He walked on toward the kitchen with no thought for another's comfort, and that flickering urge was the last spark of light within him.

And for that reason, when the Light came, Royal did not respond to it. Even when he realized the Light was Christ, he did not receive it. Royal saw and somehow knew, but there was nothing left within him to be enlightened by this glorious and holy Light. Just before he slipped into eternal darkness, his last thought as a rational human being was,

"I guess I'm not hungry after all."


The night of June 4 was terrifying, even in Florida. The epicenter of the first earthquake was in the Middle East, but the shock waves encircled the globe just as they had seven years before.

The little group of Christians who lived together on the farm in Brandon had spent most of their time the past three months in prayer. They knew that the world was dying around them. Devastation both natural and man-made mounted on all sides. The fallen cities entombed millions. The oceans were rotting red pools, sustaining no life. Only the most fragmentary reports of the battle in Israel reached the inhabitants of the farm, but they knew life on earth was being destroyed. So they turned all the more trustingly to God, casting themselves on His mercy.

Tonight had brought an incredible storm combining the destructive power of a hurricane with hail of tremendous proportions. Lightning flashed continually; the earth shook with the fury of the elements. Into the midst of all this tumult walked three people.

"I want to go outside," Susie had said. Instead of telling her how foolish such a venture would be, Hastings and Molly had decided to go along. It was wisdom, actually, for nothing so fragile as a man-made shelter could protect against this storm. And so they walked outside—out into the storm and the lightning, treading the quivering earth to stand facing the east and a gradual increase of light as dawn came.

"This reminds me of the big earthquake in '88," Hastings said. "I was scared then and this is worse. Now it doesn't matter if I get killed or not. That's what makes the difference."

"This is the end, isn't it?" Susie asked in a hushed voice.

"I think so, Susie. Man, look at that!" Hastings pointed as a hailstone weighing at least a hundred pounds landed on the wellhouse, obliterating it in one blow.

They stood in breathless excitement as the sky grew lighter and the storm grew more fierce. The light was strange. An impossible kind of light for the time of day and the stormy weather. They could see each other perfectly, as though in full daylight, but there were no shadows. The soft, pearl-grey light seemed to be diffused from the whole sky. It grew ever brighter and brighter.

"What is it?" Susie asked awed.

"Don't be afraid," Molly answered. "I believe it means we won't need the sun any more."

"I'm not afraid. I'm honestly not. But I can't breathe," Susie's voice was jittery, and she clung to Molly's hand as to the last touch with the commonplace and normal.

The light grew brighter—so bright it seemed impossible to endure it without photophobic pain, but it was gentle, too, in spite of its brilliance.

"He's coming now!" Hastings said suddenly. "He's coming now!"

"Don't be frightened," Molly said. "We were made for Him. Surely He won't scare us."

Molly's words calmed them as they stood together, facing the east, waiting. They stood in humility without groveling, without fear. In their total humanity they awaited the totality of God.

The time had passed for all the doubts and speculations about this God-King who would save the world and reign in splendor and glory for a thousand years. The prophecies about the King who came to save were completed now. The believers who waited in anticipation found it not an incredible miracle. It suddenly seemed the most natural thing in the world.

And they saw before them the sign of the Son of Man—the eternal Being who had been a Baby in Bethlehem, a Man in Jerusalem and God on Golgotha. He came now "like lightning from the east to the west." As they saw Him arriving in the clouds with all His power and glory, they fell to their knees in adoration. And all the types of love ever known to mankind were mere shadows of the love that now encompassed them and filled them.

They knelt in awe and adoration, totally absorbed in their love, as they heard in a stupendous triumph of joy, "Come, Blessed of my Father, take possession of the kingdom prepared for you from the foundation of the world."


They slept very little, especially after the hail started. Martha sat in a frightened stupor at the kitchen table as Hank ran throughout the downstairs, checking the damage. The upstairs was already ruined, she knew, but maybe the downstairs would be safe for awhile.

He walked into the kitchen, shaking his head. "It's simply unbelievable. The hail is huge, some of it as big as the oven." Martha turned to look at the microwave unit, then shot him a disbelieving glance.

"If you don't believe me, come look," Hank cried, angered by her skepticism. But before Martha could reply, the wind struck again with renewed force, causing the room to shudder under its lash.

"Is the house going to hold up?" Martha asked in fear. "I never heard such a wind."

"It isn't just wind," Hank said. "There's lightning like I've never seen, and I think there's been an earthquake."

"Not another earthquake!" Martha glared at Hank as though by denying it he could prevent the additional tragedy.

"It's like nature wants to finish destroying the world. Whatever was left after the bombings is being flattened now." Hank moved away from the window and sat at the table with his wife.

"I wish we had some coffee," Martha said suddenly. It had been years since they had had real coffee, but Martha could suddenly taste its acid, pungent bite in her mouth.

"It's spooky, isn't it?" Hank asked. "I've been in storms before, in hurricanes and electrical storms and the big earthquake, and I never saw anything like this. It's like the storm is alive and trying to get us."

"Don't talk that way," Martha snapped in irritation. "It's bad enough without you imagining things."

"No, think about it." Hank leaned forward, intense. "It's like the end of the world. The end of everything. I remember Jason talking about there being hydrogen bombs before the end and then another earthquake."

"So just because Jason said it, you have to believe it."

"Your children believed it," Hank countered.

A barrage of the enormous hailstones against the side of the house cut short the argument. "If only we still had the radio," Martha moaned. "It's awful not to know what's going on. It does seem like they'd have left one station broadcasting, doesn't it?"

"People lived through storms for thousands of years without having the radio to tell them how bad it was," Hank said. He sat up suddenly, alert. "Look," he said. "It's getting light. The storm must be passing."

They listened briefly to the still raging storm. There was no sign of its abating, but Hank was right. The room was noticeably lighter. It was almost bright, in fact. Martha looked at her husband in amazement. This was certainly not the sunrise. It was altogether different. They watched as it grew even brighter.

"What is it?" Hank asked in hushed tones. He shrank back in his chair, terrified of the unknown which approached them in this splendid light.

For Martha the growing brightness brought a deluge of guilt. She stood exposed before her own eyes in inescapable truth, fully revealed in all her weakness and self-indulgence. She gasped in astonishment. She saw parading before her all the old sins: the child-Martha manipulating her father with tears and sulks, the woman-Martha blaming her husband, her children, a vague and impersonal "them," whenever things went wrong—anything but face her own accountability. She understood that this woman had so few friends because only her own small family's welfare was of any concern to her. She had failed her fellowman; she had failed the God who created her. She had failed in every possible way. And now it was too late to do anything about it.

She slumped across the kitchen table, sobbing in despair. For almost all her life, over fifty years now, she had ignored the God whom angels and demons feared by putting herself on the throne.

In the sounds of the storm and the radiance from the light, two people sat, saw their sin and hated it. And then, the Sinless One entered their lives in reality for the first time, silently, quickly, fully, in all of His abundant reality. And He judged them with infinite mercy and justice.


Jerusalem was in pandemonium, but there was no panic within the temple area. The control exerted by Pope Sixtus and Ben Daniel over the men who served them was so strong that not even the chaos of this hour could shake discipline.

The two men sat now in the room which had been used by the General Staff of the Russian army until its demise in the middle of April. The command post of the European army was still housed within the temple area even though the majority of troops had been moved northward toward Megiddo the week before. But Ben Daniel and Pope Sixtus sat in privacy.

"Do you plan to go to Armageddon?" Ben Daniel asked.

"I don't think so," Leonard answered. "We will be kept informed."

"Do you feel any fear? Any doubts?" Ben Daniel was standing, his back to the wall.

Leonard was sitting in regal splendor in a huge armchair, his feet propped on a low stool. "I have spent too many years, too many centuries of effort to be stricken now with doubts. I must do what it is my nature to do."

"Do you think we might win?" Ben Daniel moved closer to Leonard as though drawing strength from the other's presence.

"I have already won much," Leonard answered. "I have altered the history of their race, changed the whole nature of these creatures. This world was given to me by Adam, and there was never any doubt that I ruled here. I have won many souls; many are mine that might not have been. Oh, yes, my old friend. We will count many victories before we are done. Trust me. I know what I am doing." Leonard rose ponderously and walked toward the door. He opened it and spoke to the sentry outside, "Is there any water? Anything at all to drink?"

"I'll find out, sir." The sentry saluted smartly and moved down the hall.

Leonard sat down again and Ben Daniel walked slowly back and forth across the room. "I have so many disquieting thoughts," he said. "Sometimes it seems as though the whole thing has been useless. Just a lot of effort to end up exactly where they wanted us. You understand? Almost as though the whole thing had been planned, and we were both being used."

"Don't be foolish."

"But isn't there a chance," Ben Daniel persisted, "that we have been doing just what—" he drew a shuddering breath, "what *He* wanted us to do all along, or, at least, what He allowed?"

As Ben Daniel asked the question the earthquake struck Jerusalem. And with it came the supreme encounter.

On one side was Pope Sixtus, the Antichrist, who had sat in the temple of God, claiming for himself all the attributes of God. The proud being who had said "I will" was now facing the humble Son who had said, "Thy will."

This was not their first confrontation. They had faced each other before, not far from this same site. In the Judean wilderness the Evil One had urged, "Make bread of stones, worship me, test God and see if He is able to protect you. Doubt Him, listen to me; do anything but submit your will," and three times the perfect answer had thundered back, "It is written . . . it is written . . . it is written."

Three years later they met again in a garden on the outskirts of the city, this time with a kiss of betrayal, before the poor human tool had been discarded. Then, three mortal blows had been hammered out against the Evil One; first on Calvary, then at the empty tomb on Easter morning, and later in the Upper Room, as the Spirit of God descended on one hundred and twenty weak and frightened sinners and transformed them into vessels of indescribable power.

The penultimate meeting now occurred. The room was suddenly full of light as the Son, the flesh and bone man who sits at the right hand of the Father, descended and redeemed and restored the region lost by Adam. Evil could not exist in His glorified presence. The Word came forth and with the brightness of His coming, they were destroyed.

The sentry had been knocked flat by the earthquake. He regained his feet, requisitioned the precious glass of water from the temple reserve, returned and knocked twice before opening the door. He peeped in hesitantly and saw to his astonishment that both the pope and the prime minister were sprawled dead on the terrazzo floor. They had died in some terrible agony if their expressions were an indication. He stared in awe for a moment, then moved swiftly to inform his superiors. Suddenly he stopped and looked around him suspiciously. Seeing that he was in truth alone, he quickly drank the glass of water he held. Cool, pure water was almost nonexistent on earth now, and the young soldier was terribly thirsty. These two powerful world figures were beyond the need of water now, he thought. Wherever their spirits had gone, they were not thirsty.


"The Bible says He is coming like a thief in the night," Craig said, "But I think I know when He is coming."

"You probably do," Stubby agreed. "I'm convinced that all those references about 'no man knowing the day or the hour' and about 'coming like a thief in the night' were referring to the Rapture. Once the seven years begin, you'd have to be pretty stupid not to follow the predictions."

They were sitting in a small oasis of quiet on the Mount of Olives amid the raging noise of war. They had traveled a great deal the past few months, avoiding the wars and armies that swept back and forth through Israel, but they had not returned to Jerusalem until today, their first visit to the Holy City since their pilgrimage to Mount Zion. Many of its spires, domes and steeples had been destroyed in the ravages of war, but it was still a lovely sight in the murky light, with the jagged tower of David's tomb to their left and the glorious new temple before them. They were too far away to be affected by the dead and dying that littered the ancient streets or to see the destruction that the fighting had wrought.

"What time is it?" Stubby asked.

"Close to two, I guess," Craig answered. "I know it's after lunchtime. I can guarantee you that much."

"Well, I have some bread and an orange. Let's eat." Stubby eased his arms out of the straps of his backpack. He opened the pack and took out a stub of dark bread. "I guess it's kind of dirty. I'm sorry."

"Who cares about a little dirt?" Craig asked. He accepted half the bread from Stubby and after saying grace they sat munching contentedly. Suddenly he pointed toward the floor of the Valley of Kidron which spread between them and the city.

"It looks like some kind of procession," Stubby said. "It's not an army. Those aren't uniforms, are they?" The war by now involved the armies of over forty nations, and even those fighting sometimes found it hard to separate friends from enemies.

"They're civilians," Craig agreed. The long lines of slowly-marching people came out of the Golden Gate and the eastern border of the enclosed Old City. They wound slowly down into the Valley of Kidron, following in reverse the steps taken by Jesus on Palm Sunday as He entered the City through this same gate, sealed in the 16th century by the Turks.

"Do you think they might know something we don't?" Craig asked. "They seem, well, purposeful or something."

Stubby was looking upward, squinting his eyes against the glare of the polluted sky. As the sounds of jets were heard, Craig hunched his shoulders in subconscious reaction against more bombings, more radioactive death poured out on the pitiful remains of humanity.

"Are they Israeli?" Craig asked.

"Look, Craig," Stubby said in awe. "Look at that."

By some freak of wind, the sky had cleared suddenly, and for the first time in weeks, they could see the deep blue of the heavens. Against this startling color appeared two long strips of white—contrails from two jets which flew high above the hovering overcast. One headed north, racing toward the battle raging at Armageddon. The second plane was heading eastward, winging in from the Mediterranean and heading toward Jordan. The planes passed overhead, and their trailing jet streams formed an enormous white cross in the suddenly clear sky above.

"That's got to mean something," Craig breathed in excitement. "It's just too pat for it to be a coincidence."

"They think so," said Stubby pointing to the masses of people below who were in a state of wild excitement at the sign overhead.

"How beautiful!" Craig exclaimed. "It could be jet streams to unbelievers, but the Sign of the Son of Man to people with faith." He thought a minute. "Maybe it's always like that. If you have the faith, you see things as being from God. If you're a pagan, you see it as natural phenomena."

As Craig sat ruminating about his own insight, slowly as though scales were being peeled from his eyes, he began to understand much that he had either ignored or misinterpreted. His life had not been a series of random happenings; each step, each event had been lovingly designed by a loving Father to bring him to salvation. His whole life, and particularly the last seven years, had been engineered in order that he might know the stupendous joy that had been awaiting him forever. In every way, he had been held safe in the palm of God's hand.

They were both standing now. Craig was racked by more and more revelations. Knowledge, wisdom and understanding crashed into his consciousness as he stood, head bowed and waiting. He suddenly saw the invisible world his Father had created for him. The world of atoms, electrons, of fantastic intricacy and energy, obedient to the laws of God as was the higher creation. And he saw the whole realm of the microbe, of minute life, ordered and created as he was. Then his mind was filled with visions of the heavens—of endless reaches of empty space, full only of God and His creativity. He saw unimaginable creations spinning in their own tracts, mind-numbing realities of size, distance, number and strangeness. But he saw too, that none of this was as beloved as was the man whose mind could only dimly comprehend these fantastic creations. He saw, for the first time, an intimation of how very beloved he was, and he was humbled before this amazing love.

The crowd was almost upon them now and their voices could be heard. There were chants, songs and shouts: "Blessed is He Who comes in the name of the Lord!" Craig realized suddenly he was understanding Hebrew without difficulty and it seemed perfectly natural to him. The curse of Babel was reversed now. The crowd milled around, singing and shouting joyously, their faces transfigured by their delight.

Craig was crying. He dwelt lovingly on the thought of eternal sorrows, eternally consoled, and he knew with a glorious certainty that he would never hunger or thirst, never suffer again for he would be guided to the waters of life and God would wipe every tear from his eyes.

Healing flowed down from on high and the lame, the blind, the deaf were made whole. The memories of pain and sorrow were healed and within his own soul, Craig saw the desert blossoming, the wilderness of his spirit being filled with pools, and the dry lands of his life springing up with unquenchable waters. He opened the gates of his own temple, that tabernacle of God on earth which is the heart of every believer, and the King of Glory came in.

The crowd of people was chanting now, a spontaneous agreement on the proper thing to say at this time, "Thy kingdom come," and Craig was suddenly as happy as they, full of utter conviction that the kingdom was coming, and that he would be a part of it.

The redeemed of the Lord had come with singing unto Zion and everlasting joy was theirs. They awaited the pleasures which would be theirs forevermore at the right hand of God. Every promise was now fulfilled; death had been swallowed up in victory, a victory which was eternal.

Craig heard the resounding words, "Behold, thy Salvation cometh. Behold, His reward is with Him." And with awe he witnessed the fulfillment of the prophecy: every knee was bowed and every tongue confessed the Lordship of Jesus Christ.

He looked again at Stubby, ready once more to share these

experiences with another human, and he drew back instinctively as he saw his friend. Stubby had been glorified almost beyond recognition, his face a shining light, and his form transfigured into an undreamed of beauty. He was still recognizably Stubby, but a glorious, holy and beautiful Stubby. Stubby looked toward Craig, and Craig could see his own emotions mirrored in Stubby's face. They moved together in fraternal charity and stood side by side as the end came.

That which is perfect was coming and that which was in part was done away. They knew as they were known, perfectly. Joy overwhelmed them.

Craig was conscious of sounds, of music of all sorts surrounding them. What had previously been mere noise was now music; the wind, the voices of nature sang out as all creation witnessed the manifestation of the sons of God. The heavens resounded with angelic psalms; the great host of winged messengers who had spoken of God to mankind from the beginning chorused their bliss. The lower creation, animals, plants, even the stones, cried out in joy and praise. Everything extant strained upward to meet the Creator. All things were made by Him for His pleasure, and each thing surged forward and upward now to bring this pleasure, and to receive in return above measure.

Without effort, order was restored, and mankind regained dominion over this earth. What Adam had forfeited was now redeemed in fact, and Craig was quietly filled with knowledge of nature, of its systems and rhythms and patterns. He understood the animals and insects and their ways. He could grasp the rationale behind their naming, understanding the function and position of each. And the beauty of each, the perfection of the created universe, made him weak. All the ages of animosity between his species and the others were gone. The fear, the strangeness vanished. He felt a tremendous respect and love for each individual life, and a responsibility for its existence.

The heavens were alive with color, rainbows and ribbons of light which flowed and twined and changed. The beauty of sight captured his attention, but he still heard the music. His consciousness seemed to expand to include all his senses, and the increase in stimuli increased his ability to respond.

His other senses were filled, odors and tastes of indescribable delights, and he basked in it; glorious sensation with no hint of the forbidden, no trace of guilt.

The mountain beneath their feet heaved once, and began a ponderous movement, splitting open to divide itself, one half moving northward, the other southward. Unbidden, there rose in Craig's mind the words, "The mountains skipped like rams, the little hills like lambs." Here was faith to move a mountain, to cleave a rock to allow the free flow of crystal-clear water, toward the Mediterranean and toward the Dead Sea, water which bubbled up as from a spring. They stood steady, unshaken by the movement of ground beneath their feet, founded and grounded on a Rock, so that they could not be shaken.

Seven times the New Testament predicted He would come with clouds, a great cloud of witnesses who had been perfected to rule and reign with Him for one thousand years. And the heavens opened and the armies of saints descended, and the multitude on the mount knelt in homage to the splendid One on the white horse.

And for the third time since the dawn of creation, the words rang out: *Consummatum est!* As God had said following the creation of the universe, as Christ had said on Calvary as He gave up the Ghost, so now a Voice rang out for all the earth to hear: "It is finished! I am the Beginning and the End. To him who thirsts, I will give of the fountain of the water of life freely. He who overcomes shall possess these things, and I will be his God, and he shall be My son."

The One who testifies of these things says, "Surely I come quickly." Amen. Even so, come, Lord Jesus.

# Appendix

# Appendix

## Scriptural Prophecies for the Tribulation Period

1. Knowledge is increased and abounds and travel increases.
   Dan. 12:4
2. Jews are gathered from their dispersal and restored to the
   Holy Land.
   Isa. 11:11–12, Isa. 66:8, Jer. 23:3, 31:8–11, 46:27–28, Ezek.
   28:25–26, 34:13, 37:21–25
3. There is an increase in occurrences of and interest in supernatural happenings.
   Isa. 59:19, Isa. 66:15–17, Nah. 3:4–5, Zech. 10:1–3, Mark
   13:22, 2 Thess. 2:8–12, Rev. 9:20–21
4. Wars, threats of war and conflict between nations increase.
   Matt. 24:6–7, Mark 13:7–8, Luke 21:9–10, Rev. 6:4
5. Strife and discord within family increase; the "generation
   gap" is increased to the point of real hatred between genera-
   tions.
   Ezek. 38:21, Mic. 7:6, Matt. 10:36, Mark 13:12, Luke 21:16
6. Civil rioting, violence and crime are increased.
   Isa. 59:4–8, Jer. 30:4–7, Ezek. 7:23–27, Dan. 12:1
7. Economic upheavals increase, with inflation and no financial
   security. Gold fluctuates in price and wealth proves inef-
   fective against disaster.
   Ezek. 7:19, Zeph. 1:18, Hag. 1:6, James 5:1–3, Rev. 6:6
8. Famine spreads, with humans starving and animals killing
   people for food.
   Jer. 15:2–3, Ezek. 5:16–17, 14:13, Joel 1:15–16, Matt. 24:7,
   Mark 13:8, Luke 21:11, Rev. 6:5–8
9. Apostasy rises in the institutional church.
   Matt. 24:12, 2 Thess. 2:3, 2 Tim. 3:1–5 and 4:2–4
10. Pestilence and epidemics spread due to uncontrollable patho-

gens increasing and the effectiveness of pest control decreasing.

Ezek. 7:14–15 and 14:19, Amos 4:10, Matt. 24:7, Luke 21:11

11. Heresy is rampant, with materialism and the social gospel replacing a true faith.

Jer. 23:16–22, Matt. 24:12, 2 Thess. 2:3, 1 Tim. 4:1–2, 2 Tim. 4:2–4

12. False messiahs rise; Oriental mystics infiltrate the church and self-appointed saviors preach on street corners.

Matt. 24:11 and 24:24, Rev. 13:11–12

13. False religions gain strength.

Jer. 23:20–21, Matt. 24:11, Mark 13:5–6, 1 John 2:18

14. Occultism, astrology and Satanism gain adherents and their influence becomes more open.

Isa. 2:17–21, Isa. 8:19–20, Jer. 10:1–6, Mic. 5:10–15, Nah. 3:4–5, 1 Tim. 4:1–2

15. Drug abuse rises.

Rev. 9:21

16. Christians are persecuted more and more, though not necessarily the institutional church.

Matt. 24:9 and 24:24, Mark 13:9, Mark 13:13, Luke 21:12

17. Martyrdom is increased.

Dan. 7:21, Dan. 8:23–25, Mark 13:12–13, Luke 21:16, John 16:2, Rev. 6:9–11, Rev. 14:12–13

18. The Holy Spirit is poured out on all who desire Him; the charismatic renewal continues and becomes more divided from the institutional church.

Isa. 44:3, Joel 2:28–29, Acts 2:17–18

19. The gospel is preached to all nations.

Matt. 24:14, Mark 13:10, Rev. 14:6

20. Ecumenism increases within the institutional church, leading to a one-world religion.

2 Thess. 2:9–12, Rev. 13:4 and 13:15, Rev. 17

21. Sincere believers increase in devotion and faith.

Dan. 12:3, Mark 13:13, Rom. 13:12–13, 1 Tim. 6:13–15

22. Non-believers become hardened in faithlessness and worse in conduct.

Ezek. 16:49–50, Luke 17:26–30, Matt. 24:12, 2 Pet. 3:3–14, Rev. 22:11

23. Sin increases.
    Isa. 5:20–23, Ezek. 7:8–11 and 16:49–50, Hos. 4:1–5, 2 Tim. 3:1–5, Rev. 9:20–21 and 12:12
24. Homosexuality, sexual immorality and pornography are increased.
    Luke 17:28, Rom. 1:26–32, Jude 17–19
25. Idleness and indolence increase, and people scoff at religion as they lead self-indulgent lives.
    Amos 6:1–6, Zeph. 1:12, 2 Tim. 3:1–5, 2 Pet. 2:10–22, 2 Pet. 3:3, Jude 17–19
26. Unusual weather is increased with violent storms, snow, hail, floods, etc.
    Job 38:22–30, Isa. 29:6 and 30:30, Jer. 3:3, Amos 4:7–8, Zeph. 1:14–18
27. Destructive wind, hurricanes, typhoons, cyclones and tornadoes become more prevalent and more damaging.
    Isa. 42:15, Jer. 23:19–20, and 24:30–33, Nah. 1:2–6
28. Earthquakes become more frequent and more intense.
    Isa. 24:17–23, Ezek. 38:19–23, Matt. 24:7, Mark 13:8, Luke 21:11, Rev. 6:12
29. Unusual discoveries continue in the sky, i.e., black holes, quasars, pulsars, white dwarfs, cosmic storms, etc.
    Joel 2:30–31, Luke 21:11 and 21:25–26, Acts 2:19–20, Rev. 6: 12–14
30. Humans continue to destroy the atmosphere and ionosphere, admitting more solar radiation affecting health, agriculture, environment and ecology.
    Ps. 102:25–26, Isa. 24:3–6, Isa. 51:6, Heb. 1:10–12
31. Antichrist rises in power, a traditional parody of Christ.
    Dan. 7:8 and 7:21–26, Dan. 8:9–12 and 8:23–25, Zech. 11: 15–17, John 10:10–13, 2 Thess. 2:1–12, 1 John 2:18, Rev. 13
32. Antichrist signs a treaty with Israel.
    Dan. 9:27
33. A vast earthquake hits.
    Rev. 6:12
34. The sun darkens and the moon turns red.
    Isa. 13:10–11, Joel 2:1–2 and 2:30–31, Matt. 24:29, Mark 13:24, Acts 2:20, Rev. 6:12

35. The stars appear to fall from the sky, and the sky seems to disappear.
    Matt. 24:29, Mark 13:25, Acts 2:19–20, Rev. 6:13
36. Mountains and islands shake.
    Rev. 6:14
37. The winds cease, and everything is still for a time.
    Rev. 7:1
38. The believers are taken out of the earth—the Rapture.
    Dan. 12:1–3, 1 Cor. 15:51–55, 2 Cor. 4:14, 1 Thess. 4:13–18, 2 Pet. 2:9, Rev. 3:10, Rev. 7:14
39. 144,000 Jews are chosen and sealed.
    Rom. 11:25–26, Rev. 7:3–8, Dan. 9:24–27
40. Another great earthquake hits, with fire, hail and blood coming upon the earth.
    Zeph. 1:14–18, Rev. 8:5
41. A third of the earth burns, destroying a third of the trees and all the grass.
    Rev. 8:7
42. A burning mountain falls into the sea, destroying a third of the ships, turning a third of the sea red as blood and killing a third of the fish.
    Rev. 8:8–9
43. Israel becomes wealthy.
    Isa. 60:5–17, Isa. 61:6
44. A third of the earth's water is poisoned.
    Rev. 8:11
45. The sun and moon are darkened by a third.
    Rev. 8:10 and 9:2
46. A coalition is formed of ten European nations, and this group is controlled by Antichrist.
    Dan. 2 and 7, Dan. 9:26, Rev. 17:10–13
47. Two great Christian prophets begin a ministry with supernatural powers over nature, weather and fire and plagues.
    Zech. 4:11–14, Matt. 16:28 and 17:9, Luke 9:27–36, Mal. 4:5, Rev. 11
48. The bottomless pit is opened and smoke pours out. Locusts come out of the smoke, and they live for five months, stinging all except the sealed 144,000 Jews, killing no one however.
    Rev. 9:1–11

49. People long to die but are unable to; suicide is impossible.
    Isa. 13:6–9, Hosea 10:8, Rev. 9:6

50. The Jewish temple is rebuilt in Jerusalem.
    Dan. 9:27, Matt. 24:15, 2 Thess. 2:4, Rev. 11:1–2

51. Ancient Jewish rite of blood sacrifice is re-instituted.
    Dan. 9:27

52. Angels bound at the Euphrates River are loosed.
    Gen. 3:23–24, Rev. 9:14

53. An army of Oriental nations is mustered.
    Ezek. 38, Rev. 9:16

54. Satan is loosed on earth, and his activities become much more open.
    Isa. 14:12–15, Obad. 3–4, Luke 10:18, Rev. 12:7–13

55. Antichrist tramples the host in the sanctuary and destroys the daily sacrifice.
    Dan. 8:9–25 and 9:27 and 11:31 and 12:11, Matt. 24:15

56. A one-world religion is growing as religions merge and each faith becomes broader.
    Rev. 17

57. Antichrist stops the blood sacrifice in the Jerusalem temple; desecrates the temple.
    Dan. 9:27 and 11:31 and 12:11, Matt. 24:15

58. Antichrist receives a mortal head wound, lives and is possessed by the Dragon—Satan.
    Rev. 13:3 and 13:12–14

59. The two prophets are killed by the Antichrist.
    Rev. 11:7

60. The prophets lie unburied for three and a half days, and the world celebrates their death.
    Rev. 11:8–10

61. False Prophet creates an image of Antichrist, and the image speaks and forces people to worship it.
    Rev. 13:14–15

62. The prophets live again and rise to heaven.
    Rev. 11:11–13

63. An earthquake hits Jerusalem, destroying a tenth of the city, killing 7,000 and converting others.
    Rev. 11:13

64. Antichrist has power over God's people, to kill or to arrest them.
    Dan. 7:19–22 and 8:23–25, Rev. 13:1–7
65. Antichrist changes dates, festivals and feast days.
    Dan. 7:25
66. The mark of the beast is required for all, the mark (and the beast's name) somehow related to the number "666."
    Rev. 13:16–18
67. 144,000 Jews go to Mount Zion in Jerusalem and celebrate the victory.
    Rev. 14:1
68. Russia and her satellites start for the middle east, merged and armed for war.
    Ezek. 38:8–23, Dan. 11:40
69. Babylon, the occult religion, falls.
    Isa. 13:19–22, Ezek. 16:35–43, Rev. 14:8
70. Egypt and the North African and Black African nations attack Israel.
    Dan. 11:40
71. Russia and her satellites invade Israel, headquarters are on Mt. Moriah, site of the Jewish Temple.
    Dan. 11:40–45
72. War particularly vicious and meaningless with small children dashed to the ground and killed and pregnant women disemboweled.
    Hos. 13:16, Zech. 14:1–3, Dan. 12:1
73. Russia goes into Egypt and attacks; starts back to Israel and is stopped.
    Dan. 11:42
74. False Prophet, Antichrist and Satan use miraculous means to get military help for Battle of Armageddon.
    Rev. 16:13–14
75. Russia hears rumors from the east, of the Oriental army approaching, and launches a premature attack on Israel from its base in Egypt.
    Dan. 11:44
76. Sores appear on the people who received the mark of the beast and worshipped the beast.
    Rev. 16:2

77. Fire and brimstone fall on Russia, Europe and North America.
Isa. 24:19–23, Ezek. 38:22 and 39:5–8, Nah. 1:5–6, Zeph. 3:8

78. Oceans become as blood, and all life in them dies.
Rev. 16:3

79. Rivers and springs become as blood.
Rev. 16:4

80. The sun's rays penetrate strongly, and the sun scorches the earth (probably due to atmospheric damage).
Mal. 4:1, Rev. 16:8

81. Pollution and fallout contaminate the atmosphere so that there are periods of utter darkness.
Isa. 8:22 and 13:9–11 and 24:1–3, Ezek. 32:7–8, Joel 2:30–31 and 3:15, Rev. 16:10

82. The eastern army of 200,000,000 crosses the Euphrates River which has been dried up.
Rev. 16:12

83. All cities are destroyed, and man's governments, commerce and industry are ruined.
Nah. 1:3–6, Hag. 2:21–22, Rev. 18

84. Any remnants of any organization which is manmade, including religions, are destroyed.
Isa. 13:19–22 and 47:8–15, Hag. 2:21–22, Rev. 18

85. Islands vanish, mountains are destroyed and there are terrible natural disasters, lightning, thunder, hail, earthquakes, etc.
Isa. 13:3–13 and 24:17–23 and 34:1–4, Joel 2:10–11 and 3:16, Nah. 1:5–6, Hag. 2:6, Matt. 24:29, Luke 21:26–33, 2 Pet. 3:10–14, Rev. 16:20–21

86. The battle of Armageddon is fought in the Plain of Jezreel, north of Jerusalem.
Isa. 34:1–4, Joel 3:9–16, Zech. 12:9–11 and 14:1–3, Rev. 16:16

87. The sign of "The Son of Man" (Christ) appears in the Heavens.
Zech. 12:10, Matt. 24:30

88. There is an abnormal light; daylight and dark are altered.
Isa. 60:19–20, Zech. 14:6–7

89. Christ returns to earth in power and glory.
Matt. 24:27, 30, Mark 13:26, Luke 21:27, Acts 1:11, Col. 3:4, 1 Thess. 3:13, Jude 14, Rev. 19:11–16

90. The earth splits from the Mount of Olives to the Mediterranean Sea.
    Zech. 14:4
91. The False Prophet and the Antichrist are thrown into the lake of fire.
    Rev. 19:20
92. Satan is chained for 1,000 years.
    Jude 6, Rev. 20:1–2
93. The Millennium.
    Isa. 2:2–4 and 11:1–9, Mic. 4:1–4, 1 Cor. 15:24–26, Rev. 20:4–5, and Rev. 21
94. Final Judgment.
    1 Cor. 6:2–3, 2 Cor. 5:10–11, 2 Tim. 4:1, Heb. 9:27, 1 Pet. 5:4, Rev. 20:11–15

Carol Balizet